MODEL LIFE

ANDREW O'CONNOR

POOLBEG

Published 2005
by Poolbeg Press Ltd
123 Grange Hill, Baldoyle
Dublin 13, Ireland
E-mail: poolbeg@poolbeg.com

© Andrew O'Connor 2005

1 3 5 7 9 10 8 6 4 2

A catalogue record for this book is available from the British Library.

ISBN 1-84223-197-9

Typeset by Patricia Hope in Palatino
Printed by Nørhaven Paperback A/S, Viborg,
Denmark

www.poolbeg.com

About the Author

Andrew O'Connor studied English and History at NUI Maynooth, before completing postgraduates at Central London College and Trinity College Dublin. He worked in Marketing and Public Relations for several years and now works in Property Development. He lives in Dublin and Meath.

Acknowledgements

I would like to express my gratitude to all the team at Poolbeg for their diligence and expertise: Emma in PR, Claire in Production, Aoife, Lynda, and Kieran. A special thanks to Paula Campbell who advised and nurtured this project from the beginning.

And thanks to my editor Gaye Shortland, whose ability is matched by her sense of humour. I would also like to thank Janice Scanlon, Deirdre Heavey of Mediavest and Orla McCarthy of Trinity College Dublin for her technical advice. And thank you to Adrienne Dunne.

For Phyllis, Pat & Monica.

CHAPTER 1

The photo shoot Audrey Driver had been on that morning had run two hours late, throwing her day's schedule into chaos. She tossed back her long chestnut-coloured hair impatiently as she opened the front door of her apartment. Hearing a phone ring, she groped in her handbag for her mobile.

"Yes?" she snapped as she kicked the door shut behind her.

"Audrey, the final casting for the shampoo contract is tomorrow," said the harsh voice of her agent, Hazel Harte.

"That's fine," Audrey said, quickly tapping the code into her burglar alarm which was bleeping loudly and threatening to start screaming any second.

"What's the story with that gig anyway?" She threw her shopping bags on the sofa.

"Looking good, actually. They love your look. Modern with attitude is how they described you, which is the image they want."

"I could do with this break," Audrey admitted.

"They even said you were a pleasure to work with."

1

Hazel allowed herself an uncharacteristic giggle "Wait till they get to know the real you!"

"Very funny. Any idea when I will know for sure?"

"The shampoo's PR is flying back into Dublin tomorrow, so we should know in a matter of days. You know, Audrey, if you get this contract, you'll be made for life – the face of a brand across America – TV, magazine commercials and posters."

"It would certainly take me into a different league from the Irish modelling circuit. I'd better dash. I'm running very late for the rehearsal for the Childwatch Fashion Show."

"No doubt a shopping trip delayed you. Catch you later!" Hazel hung up.

Audrey rushed into the bathroom and gazed in the mirror, brown eyes anxiously viewing her appearance. Her skin colour was naturally sallow, but she decided she could do with a session on the sunbed.

She had been told some press would be at that afternoon's rehearsal and wanted to look her best. She was twenty-nine years old but still could pass for twenty-one.

She looked after herself and exercised regularly, mainly by jogging on the nearby beach. She always made sure to catch up on her sleep if her social life kept her out too late some nights. She rarely drank, as it didn't agree with her. Experience had warned her that alcohol either made her cringingly emotional or inflamed her temper. But she loved her food as much as the next person, and made no apologies for it. Lettuce diets were not for her.

"Twenty-nine," she said aloud. About to enter a new decade. She had been one of Ireland's top models for a long time and the work still flowed in. But she had never got the big break internationally. And time was running out for her. When the American cosmetics firm came searching for an Irish model to be the face of their new shampoo, it sounded like it could be the breakthrough she was looking for.

The ringing of her phone cut into her thoughts and she raced to answer it, expecting it to be her partner, Aran.

"Audrey Driver speaking."

"Audrey, it's Peter." The voice on the other end of the phone sounded unhappy. "You should be here at rehearsal! What the hell are you doing at home?"

Audrey cursed herself for having given Peter Reynolds her home phone number. "The traffic was terrible. I'm on my way now."

Peter became even more irritated. "It will take you at least an hour to get here. You'll be going into rush hour. It's not good enough –"

"Won't be long!" And she hung up.

CHAPTER 2

The Berkeley Court Hotel was awash with models, stagehands and organisers rushing about. Peter Reynolds angrily walked through them all, wishing he had never bothered with Audrey Driver. He loosened his tie and ran a hand through his dark hair.

He should have known, from previous modelling assignments, that she had no sense of timekeeping. She often screwed up whole jobs by arriving late. However, his client, the charity Childwatch, had insisted on employing her. And he could understand why. Audrey was one of the country's most high-profile models. She was constantly in the papers about something or other, either through her work or in the gossip columns. The latest story circulating about her was that she was about to win a big contract as the face of the American shampoo, Silk. Peter hoped she got the contract soon, as the media would pay extra attention to Audrey and he could use this to further publicise the fashion show. Two journalists, one from a tabloid and one from a broadsheet, were waiting impatiently in the foyer to interview her. And because he had been the one who had organised the interviews, he was now being blamed by both journalists for Audrey's lateness.

Stuck in traffic, Audrey was tempted not to answer her mobile when it rang, fearing it would be Peter again. As the phone refused to stop ringing, she took a deep breath and answered. "Hello".

"Simon Lawless here, Audrey. What's this I hear about you endorsing some shampoo stateside?"

She groaned inwardly. Smarmy Simon was PR for a cosmetic company she was contracted to. "It's only hearsay, Simon. There's nothing concrete."

"I'd like to remind you that you can't endorse other cosmetics because of your contract with us."

"That's crap, Simon. Shampoo isn't make-up."

"I'm going to take this up with Hazel at Boom. We wouldn't hesitate to sue you."

"Sue me! For what?" Tears stung her eyes as she glanced at her watch and realised how late she would be for the rehearsal. She felt she was being dragged in so many directions at once.

"For breaking your contract with us. Speaking of which, we need you at an opening on Saturday."

"But I've something on then," she objected.

"It's part of your agreement with us. So you had better be there!"

She was sure he was about to launch into a torrent of abuse, but he obviously thought better of it.

"Where are you off to now?" he said, softening his tone.

"Not that's it's any of your business, I'm going to a fitting for the Childwatch Show."

"Myself and my wife are going to that with some friends. We can all have a drink together."

"Sure," she said, realising he would use her to impress some clients. It was always the same – just because she was contracted to companies, they believed they owned her.

Having parked in The Berkeley Court's carpark, she raced into the hotel, and saw Peter Reynolds straight away. He looked half in control and half hassled as different people approached him asking questions.

Audrey never knew where she stood with Peter. She knew he had the ability to be an absolute bastard when under pressure. However, he could also be thoroughly nice. Today, he looked in absolute bastard mood.

He marched over to her. "What the hell kept you?"

"You said yourself, I was heading into rush hour –"

"I'm not interested. Go into the dressing-room for them to take measurements."

Audrey decided it was safer to say nothing and did as he asked.

As she walked into the dressing-room she saw her friend Leslie Taylor seated in front of a huge mirror as a hairdresser combed through her hair.

"Where have you been? He's been going mad looking for you," said Leslie. "This morning's job ran late."

Audrey raised her eyes to heaven as she was descended upon by two dressers with tape measures.

Leslie was also with the Boom Agency and, unlike a lot of the other girls, Audrey knew she was not two-faced and could be relied upon.

They were good friends.

Peter rang Hazel at the Boom Model Agency.

"You've got to do something about Audrey," he complained.

"What wrong with her?"

"What's ever wrong with her?"

"Late again?"

"Of course she was. When isn't she? I will personally kill her if she pulls any stunt like this the night of the fashion show."

"I'll have a serious talk with her, Peter," she promised, pushing back her black bobbed hair and trying to think of any way she could appease him.

Hazel was in her late forties. By adhering to a strict policy of undercutting the competition she had established Boom as Ireland's premier agency. Oddly for the business she was in, she paid little attention to her own appearance.

"You heard Audrey's about to become the face of Silk Shampoo?" questioned Hazel, hoping to impress him.

"I heard a rumour. Which reminds me –" he covered the mouthpiece with a hand and roared, *"Audrey!"*

Audrey stuck her head from around the dressing-room door.

"There's a couple of journalists in the foyer and they want to have a word with you, urgently."

"I'll be out to them in a couple of minutes."

"Now, Audrey!" he roared before turning his attention back to Hazel.

"Don't worry," Hazel assured him. "She'll be on time for the show, if I have to drag her there myself."

Kitty Mulcahy had worked for *The Independent* for five years. After graduating with a degree in journalism, she had envisaged herself covering hard-hitting and groundbreaking stories. Contrary to her plan, her career had so far entailed writing fashion reviews, and occasionally filling in for the social columnist. Kitty hated models. Her editor had forced her to the Berkeley Court that afternoon to interview Audrey, who Kitty imagined to be the embodiment of the worst of this breed. Her editor was convinced Audrey was about to become "the next big thing". The other journalist, who had also been waiting to interview the former beauty queen, had become bored waiting for her to appear and had gone back to his office.

As Kitty observed the tall, undeniably beautiful young woman stride towards her, she remembered Audrey's reputation for being difficult. She was always in the tabloids over some misdemeanour or another. Kitty sharpened her pen in anticipation of writing a hatchet job.

"Kitty?" asked Audrey, smiling broadly and sitting down opposite her. "So sorry I'm late. Traffic was desperate. And I know how busy you are."

Kitty's frown softened and she cut to the chase. "So I hear you are about to become a supermodel?"

"Hardly a supermodel. But an American company have met me about working in New York. Nothing's definite, though."

"That would mean lots of travel back and forth?"

"Probably. I'd love that. I don't want to leave Ireland permanently."

"Where are you living now?" Kitty scribbled away in shorthand as she spoke.

"I have an apartment by the sea in Sandymount. I'm also buying another property as an investment."

"You must be raking in the big bucks to be able to afford another property in today's market. Where is it?"

"Ballsbridge." Audrey decided some self-deprecation was in order in case she came across as boastful. "Well, it's actually in Ringsend, but Ballsbridge sounds a better address, doesn't it?"

Kitty raised an eyebrow. "I see. So tell me about your glamorous life in the modelling world."

"I can truly say I love it. I meet lots of great people. But the work is hard."

"Is it? All that posing?" Kitty raised an eyebrow.

"It's not just about how you look. It's also about what's happening up here." Audrey tapped her index finger against her temple. "It's a business like any other. And I have to live in the commercial world."

"Explain?"

"Well, marketing people know that I enjoy a high profile, so they hire me knowing that, firstly, they'll get their products into the press and, secondly, they are associating those products with my image – a glamorous image. I have to exploit that "

"Interesting . . . hmm, how's the love life?" Kitty moved in for the kill.

"I'm very happy, thank you."

"You're still seeing the guy from the big solicitor family?"

"Myself and Aran Murphy are very happy together, thank you." Audrey was coy, realising Aran's family hated any kind of publicity.

"And your thoughts on the Childwatch Fashion Show?" said Kitty, remembering she'd better mention the show or else Peter would go mad, and not feed her any stories in the future.

"I'm delighted to be involved. Anything that benefits children is good."

Kitty exaggerated a smile. "For sure. How long have you been modelling anyway?"

"Too long to admit," laughed Audrey.

"And it's just been one big piece of apple-pie ever since, I suppose?"

"It might look like that from the outside, but nothing is ever plain sailing. My career certainly hasn't been."

Peter recognised his wife Lynn's number on the screen of his mobile as it rang.

"Hiya," he answered. "Are you all set for tonight?"

"No, I am not." Her clipped well-spoken accent was cold. "You have been no help at all."

Lynn managed an art gallery in Temple Bar. She was due to launch an exhibition that evening for the artist Rory Ryan.

"Darling, you know I've been up to my eyes with this fashion show."

"Always too busy with your precious work. Never a thought for mine."

"That's not true –"

"Journalists I've been speaking to have said I'll get no coverage unless I get some big names here tonight. You're the PR genius, Peter. I need big names!"

She hung up.

Peter ran his hands through his hair in frustration. He grabbed Audrey as she walked by. "I know it's short notice, but my wife's having an exhibition at her Gallery tonight and –"

"Your wife?" Audrey had never imagined that Peter was married. She wasn't sure why. He had a lot going for him, being extroverted with a good sense of humour, when he chose to show it. But she supposed she had always thought of him as married to the job.

"It's going to be a high profile event," he continued. "Lots of press will be there. Would you come . . . as a favour to me?" He smiled at her, and leaned his tall frame a little closer.

She studied his typical Irish colouring – the pale skin set against the black slightly curled hair and blue eyes. Even though she had rarely given Peter a second thought in the past, his burst of temper earlier had intrigued her and now she was curious to meet his wife.

"Sure. What time and where?"

"Eight," he said and handed her one of Lynn's cards.

"See you then! " She flashed a smile at him as she walked off.

"I'm off, Peter." Kitty tapped his shoulder. "I'll need a photo of Audrey."

"I'll get Boom to email you one. How did you find her?"

"Total fizz-brain, but sure what could you expect?"

He handed Lynn's business card to Kitty. "My wife's having a launch tonight. Could you make it?"

"I have to go to a function," she saw the disappointment in his face, "but I'll try to drop by."

CHAPTER 3

Arriving home at eight, Peter quickly stripped off his Armani suit and changed into more casual clothes. Home was a three-bedroom apartment in Christchurch with excellent views across the city. Unlike many of Dublin's new apartments, theirs had an impressive balcony. Lynn had excellent taste and the interior was beautifully furbished. At a not-so-beautiful price, Peter thought, remembering the bills they were still paying off. Opening the fridge he grabbed a pre-made sandwich and began eating it as he left the apartment and tore down the corridor towards the lift. Why was he always running late these days, he questioned himself as he hurried down Dame Street. He was nearly as bad as Audrey Driver.

The Gallery was fairly crowded when he arrived. Taking a glass from a passing trolley dolly, he spotted Lynn. Tall and elegant, at thirty-three she was a year younger than him. She was engaged in a conversation with a group of people which involved much laughter. When she saw Peter, her eyes froze. Excusing herself from her small audience she approached him. She went to kiss his cheek, but purposefully missed and hissed into his ear, "Why are you late? And where are all the big names you promised me?"

Lynn looked like she had spent quite a while being groomed, Peter reckoned. Her soft fair hair was expertly tied up in a bun, her smooth skin made up to perfection, and she was decked out in Chanel.

"You've a good crowd here."

"No thanks to you!"

He looked around and gratefully spotted Audrey talking to a tall man. "There's Audrey Driver."

"I owe you so much!" she spat. "That tuppenny model would go to the opening of an envelope! Is that all you could muster?"

He felt his temper rise. "Last week you said you didn't want any help."

"I don't want to talk about this now." She turned and rejoined her group, leaving him alone and feeling awkward.

As he wandered around, everyone seemed deep in chat and he knew there was nothing worse than somebody butting clumsily into a conversation.

"Sorry about being late today," said a voice behind him.

Swinging around he was glad to see Audrey. " Oh hi, thanks for coming this evening!"

"It's a good turnout." She looked around the gallery. "Come on and I'll introduce you to my boyfriend." She beckoned and he followed her over to the man he had seen her chatting to earlier.

"Aran, this is Peter Reynolds. He's with Blast PR and he's organising the Childwatch Show."

"What do you do yourself?" Peter asked as he shook Aran's hand. He smirked to himself as he remembered reading somewhere that this is the question PRs ask first in any conversation.

"I'm a solicitor," Aran stated.

Peter decided Aran had the real rich-boy rugby-player look: blondish hair, big frame, handsome, and aware of it.

"Your wife's very pretty," said Audrey. "I didn't realise you were married. You always looked too busy to have a wife."

"I'll fetch more drinks." Aran went off to search for a waitress.

"So the romance with the footballer is off?" questioned Peter when they were alone.

Audrey shot a cautious look. "That was never serious anyway. The Press blew it up out of all proportion."

"But you and Aran are serious?"

"Yeah, very."

"What firm does he work for?"

"His father's, Murphy Hennessy."

Peter blew a long low whistle. "Planning to marry into money?"

Laughing lightly she said, "Isn't that what all models want to do – marry a millionaire?"

Chloe Gallagher pushed open the smoked-glass doors of The Gallery and stepped inside. Surveying the crowd, she realised she knew half the people there. She was greeted enthusiastically by various people as she made a beeline for the star of the night, the artist Rory Ryan. She cut a glamorous figure, her thick blonde hair perfectly groomed, and her slim figure dressed in Dior.

"Well, Chloe, what do you think?" Rory asked, kissing Chloe's cheek, and waving expansively at his paintings at the same time.

She linked his arm. "Brilliant!" She smiled at the several people gathered around them. "Of course, I give myself

14

credit for, if not discovering you, then for patronising your early career."

"Chloe gave me work as a photographer when nobody else would," Rory acknowledged to the others listening. "Chloe, this is Lynn Reynolds who runs The Gallery."

Chloe's smile hovered slightly and then returned full blast. "Great turnout. I should get you to organise some of our launches"

"Chloe is a Director with Macken Communications," Rory explained to Lynn.

"My husband is in PR as well," said Lynn.

"He's at Blast PR, isn't he?"

"Yes, do you know each other?"

"Not really."

"That's him over there talking to Audrey Driver. You know Audrey?"

"Doesn't everybody?" Chloe laughed.

"If I get this shampoo contract, it'll catapult me into a different league. Move over, Kate Moss!" laughed Audrey.

"Fingers crossed then," said Peter.

Audrey felt somebody tap her shoulder and she spun around to see Chloe Gallagher there.

"I didn't realise you were coming here." Audrey kissed Chloe's cheek.

"Last-minute decision," explained Chloe. The two women had met through work years previously and struck up a social friendship. 'Social friendship' was the best term to describe it, Audrey thought. They would meet for lunch every so often or have long chats when they met at functions. However, Audrey wouldn't think of discussing anything intimate with Chloe. Which was just as well because she had realised over time that Chloe kept her cards very close to her chest. Chloe Gallagher was a serious player in Dublin and Audrey knew she was only one of many social friendships Chloe enjoyed.

"Do you know each other?" Audrey asked.

Chloe and Peter looked at each other blankly. "No, we haven't met."

"Peter Reynolds from Blast who's organising the Childwatch event – Chloe Gallagher from Macken."

"I hear you are doing good work with that show," Chloe complimented.

"Well, my therapist, Valium and copious amounts of alcohol are playing their part too!" said Peter.

"Just popping to the loo," said Audrey.

"I'd like to get tickets for that Show. Any left?" said Chloe.

Peter frowned. "Very few. Call my office tomorrow, and I'll see what I can do"

"I'd appreciate that."

Peter had heard all about Chloe Gallagher. Macken Communications had been established in the 70's by Brendan Macken and the company had risen to become one of the three biggest Public Relations firms in Ireland. Of course, back then they had a clear run. Until ten years ago competition had been thin on the ground. However, since then an explosion of PR companies throughout the capital had been riding high on the back of the Celtic Tiger. Blast PR was one of the most successful of these. Macken was still the big name but was losing ground and accounts to the competition. Recently, they had lost one of their best clients, Celtic Vodka, to Blast.

Chloe had joined Macken straight from college. Having worked her way up the corporate ladder she was now Brendan Macken's right-hand woman.

Just then, Lynn approached them. Having spotted her

husband talking to Chloe and, seeing her as a significant contact for his career, she had decided to join them.

Audrey returned to find the three of them deep in conversation about work. "I just spent the last ten minutes explaining to two women in the loo what I am looking for in my ideal man!" interrupted Audrey with a laugh.

Lynn looked Audrey up and down glacially. "Really?" she said. "How long does it take to say the word 'money'?"

The night had wound down by midnight. All the guests had drifted happily off to nightclubs, parties or home.

"Nice meeting you," Chloe said to Peter before leaving.

"You too. Give my office a call about the tickets."

"I'll make sure to do that."

Lynn gave the waitresses permission to go home, and Peter waited for her as she switched off the lights and locked up.

Walking home to Christchurch she didn't say a word and ignored his occasional compliment about the launch. They entered their apartment, and she maintained her frosty silence as he turned on the television and she put on the kettle.

She walked silently to the patio doors and gazed at the lights shimmering across the city.

"Everything OK?" he ventured.

She turned around with her eyes blazing. "No, it is not! You knew how much tonight meant to me and you didn't give a fuck. You didn't lift one finger to help me –"

"You said you –"

"I turn up to all your fucking work do's and smile and act like the perfect wife. You, on the other hand arrive late and can only deliver that idiot, Audrey Driver."

"You told me I was being patronising when I offered to help."

"I did not!"

"Then you ring me the last minute and expect me to deliver results. It doesn't work like that, baby!"

"Don't 'baby' me!" She stormed into their bedroom and slammed the door behind her.

He sank back into the couch, riffling his hands through his hair.

She suddenly re-emerged. "If you could see how professional Chloe Gallagher came across tonight, you'd understand why she is where she is and why you are going around in circles at Blast!" And again she stormed back into the bedroom.

Peter was left staring at the closed door, trying to figure his wife out. If she had given him a little notice, he'd have helped as much as he could.

CHAPTER 4

Audrey sat at her kitchen table, reading Kitty Mulcahy's interview in the newspaper. Aran had just come out of the bedroom in his dressing-gown and taken a cup of coffee which he was drinking while looking out at the sea view.

"That bitch, Kitty Mulcahy!" she screamed suddenly, giving him a fright.

"Huh?"

"That journalist who interviewed me yesterday. Just listen to this crap!" Audrey began to read from the article: *"'Gorgeous as she is, Audrey Driver also fits that other stereotype of models insofar as a high IQ doesn't feature on her agenda. Audrey told me her impending contract with an American shampoo company would enable her to travel (which she would love!). But readers may rest assured she has no plans to leave these shores permanently. She is also modelling in the forthcoming Childwatch Fashion Show because "anything to do with children must be good". Audrey is at pains to point out she lives in the real commercial world. She informs me that modelling is all about selling yourself so people will buy you. Where I come from, we call that something else. She is also buying a second property (business must be good!) in Ringsend, which she asked me to say was in*

Ballsbridge. Image means everything to our favourite ex-beauty queen, model and girl-about-town. Yes, indeed, Audrey lives in the business world and she told me "Modelling is a lot to do with what's happening up here," as she tapped her manicured finger against her very pretty but empty head.'"

Audrey crumpled up the paper and flung it across the room. "And I was so nice to her!"

"My mother reads that paper. You should be more careful with what you say if you insist on giving interviews," Aran said unhappily.

"Is that all you can say?" Audrey's temper rose. "No sympathy at all, only what your mother may think!"

Aran hurried over to her and took her hand, hoping to calm her down. "Of course I feel sorry for you."

"I've just about had enough of people's sarcasm recently. That Lynn Reynolds, whoever she thinks she is, was very unpleasant to me last night at her stupid launch and kept looking at me as if I wasn't welcome. I was doing her damned husband a favour by going!"

"They're just jealous," Aran soothed, mindful that his parents' dinner party was on in a couple of days and he didn't want Audrey in a bad mood for it.

Peter chuckled as he read Kitty Mulcahy's interview in his office at Blast Public Relations. Especially when Kitty mentioned Audrey had tried to relocate her property to a posher address. He gathered some papers from his desk and walked out to Reception.

He saw Michael Cassidy's door open. Michael was Managing Director and sole owner of Blast PR. To Peter's surprise Michael came out of his office followed by Chloe Gallagher, dressed in a mini-skirted white business suit, and another man.

"Ah, Peter! This is Brendan Macken," Michael introduced, indicating the neat middle-aged man, "and this is Chloe Gallagher."

"We've met," said Chloe smiling.

Peter hid his surprise and quickly smiled. "Yeah. Hope you enjoyed last night."

"Last night?" asked Brendan Macken.

"Peter's wife runs a small gallery near the quays. I was at a launch there yesterday evening," explained Chloe before turning her attention back to Michael. "So, if we get those contracts over to you today, take a look through them and send them back to us tomorrow."

"Will do." Michael opened the front door for them and said goodbye.

Ignoring Peter's quizzical stare he headed back towards his office.

"What contracts are these, Michael?"

Michael pretended not to hear Peter as he reached his office door.

"Michael, is there something you want to tell me?" Peter pursued, alarmed.

"Later, Peter, later," Michael smiled and closed his door.

That evening Chloe, Brendan Macken and the third Director at Macken Communications, Vincent Boyer had a board meeting.

Chloe handed both men a folder. "I compiled these files on all the personnel at Blast."

"What are we dealing with here?" asked Vincent. He had been a friend of Brendan's since college. Now he headed Personnel at Macken, and ruled that department with a rod of iron.

"In terms of employees, Blast is a small company. Michael himself, three Account Managers, and four admin staff."

"The admin can simply be absorbed into Macken," said Brendan, "What about the Account Managers?"

"Only time will tell if their faces will fit in here. It depends how we plan to operate Blast after the takeover. If, as we have agreed, we initially want it to look as though Blast is maintaining its own separate identity, albeit under Macken's guardianship, then we need the core of the Account Managers to stay."

Brendan became irritated. "That's only short term. Make it look like business as usual and then when the time is right we simply absorb the company and their accounts into Macken."

"We don't want Blast to flourish," Vincent backed up. "We want to destroy it and take their accounts, most of which were ours in the first place."

Chloe nodded in agreement. "A simple case of wiping out the competition."

Brendan glanced through the files. "Anyone of interest?"

"Trixi Carroll seems respected enough. Before Blast, she did things like PR for English County Councils," she pulled an unimpressed face, "which probably entailed answering phones to irate pensioners."

"Would she be any good at political lobbying?" asked Brendan.

"Highly unlikely. She lacks any real contacts or the backbone needed."

"Anyone else?"

"The guy we met in Reception today: Peter Reynolds. After graduating from UCD, he worked for the marketing departments for banks and semi-state companies before specialising in PR. He's been with Blast for a long time."

"Any good?"

"He was instrumental in getting a lot of Blast's clients, including some of our former ones. He's good. Tough but charming. I believe he likes things his own way."

"Then his face definitely won't fit in here," Vincent stated. He hated any strong characters who might confront his authority.

"Who are his family?" asked Brendan.

"They run a stud farm in County Dublin. Successful enough in that horsey way. Not particularly wealthy when you scrape beneath the husky coats and Wellingtons."

"Married?" asked Vincent.

"His wife, Lynn, runs an influential gallery in Temple Bar – The Gallery."

"Not just a little gallery by the quays then, eh?" Brendan smiled knowingly at Chloe, having remembered her earlier comment.

"No. But we don't want to give them big heads, do we?"

Peter was aware that Michael had been avoiding him all day.

By six, there were only the two of them left in the building.

Michael popped his head around Peter's office door. "I'm off. See ya tomorrow."

"Fancy a quick pint?" Peter suggested.

"Nah, not tonight. Promised Caoimhe I'd be home in time for dinner."

"But I need to talk to you about the Fashion Show."

"Can't it wait till the morning?"

"No. Michael – I've tried to talk to you all day, but you've been avoiding me. What's going on?"

Sighing, Michael walked slowly into the office and sat opposite Peter.

"I've been made an offer to sell Blast by Macken Communications."

Peter's mouth dropped. "Sell Blast!"

"Sold Blast. It's a done deal. Before you start – nothing changes. Everyone's job is safe. I stay on as MD."

Peter became angry. "You sold out! After starting from scratch and building this place up from nothing – with a lot of my help, may I add!"

"It's business as usual. Nothing changes –"

"That's shit! And you know it. You never even discussed it with me. I thought we were mates as well as colleagues!"

Michael squirmed uncomfortably. "It's a cut-throat business and everything could go bang overnight. A PR business is different from having a pub or a hotel. You don't own assets, only talent. And clients are notoriously fickle."

"You didn't just sell *your* talent, you sold *ours*."

"I can't afford to say no to them. I have to think of Caoimhe and the kids."

"As you said, it's a cut-throat business," said Peter sardonically.

Something smelt good cooking in the kitchen when Peter arrived home.

Lynn, with her hair tied up and wearing a flowing purple dress, was laying the table. She glanced at him coolly, although there had been something of a thaw since the morning.

After a couple of minutes she asked, "Did you see the papers?"

"Yeah. Well done, you got great reviews."

"No thanks to you," she got her dig in.

Wearily he sat down at the table and took off his blazer and tie.

Lynn served the carbonara.

Eating in silence, he looked around their luxury apartment. They were heavily mortgaged in order to afford it. And he was the main breadwinner. At the end of the day, Lynn's job was high profile but low pay. When they were buying this place, he expressed concerns that they were going in over their heads. Lynn had insisted they proceed with the purchase, saying they needed the apartment to elevate their image and to enhance their careers.

"Michael sold Blast," he said eventually. "We're being taken over by Macken Communications."

Lynn put down her fork. "Taken over!"

"Seemingly there will be no changes."

"Well, then, that's fantastic news!" Standing up, she began to pace the room. "Why the worried look?"

"Because it's going to be a vulnerable time for us."

"Macken is the big time. Peter, this is an amazing opportunity for you to show your talent to a prestigious big company. You saw the power and influence Chloe Gallagher has," She saw his frown deepen. "Wipe away these doubts. It's you who built Blast. When Brendan Macken realises how good you are, you'll be up there with Chloe!"

CHAPTER 5

Chloe sat opposite Michael in his office as he signed the contracts.

"Congratulations!"she said. "You're a rich man."

"Mm. It makes me feel nervous."

"Just enjoy your wealth."

"I'm concerned about my staff."

"Have you told them yet?"

"Just Peter."

"How did he take it?"

"I suppose . . . surprised."

"As I said before, there will be no interference in the accounts. Brendan and myself will probably have a 'get to know you' chat with the Account Managers."

"They'd appreciate that."

"Maybe we can offer assistance with their work. I'm going to draft a Press Release about the takeover, and after I get yours and Brendan's approval, I'll issue it to the media."

"Cool."

"Perhaps we could hold a Press Reception to announce the news. Bring all our clients and managers together. How do you feel about that?"

"Great idea."

"Make everyone feel included," she smiled.

"Sounds cool." Michael felt at ease with their attitude.

"Do you know what? We could kill two birds with the one stone and announce the takeover the night of Peter's Press Reception for the Fashion Show. What do you say to that?"

Michael thought of Peter's reaction "Er . . . I'm not so sure . . ."

"We would get double the mileage by combining both stories."

"Er . . ," Michael looked down at the contract and thought of the money. "Great idea!" he smiled.

"There is no way I'm letting Chloe Gallagher steal my Press Reception!" Peter shouted.

"I think it's a great idea," Michael tried to calm him down. "An opportunity to show there are no changes at Blast."

"Are you blind? It would show the opposite. It would show everyone that Macken are in charge here. Starting with the fashion show."

"C'mon, Peter. Give it a chance."

"And Macken will get lots of free press."

"Look, to show how interested the guys at Macken are in helping Blast, they want to meet everyone here. Starting with you."

Peter stopped in his tracks. "When?"

"Today at three. Don't look so worried. You're the spin-doctor. Show them how good you are."

Peter shifted uncomfortably in the Reception room at Macken Communications. The building was far too warm.

He looked around the large elegant room and the gigantic chandelier twinkling from the centre of the ceiling.

Why did he feel he was going to a job interview? He quickly buried that thought and concentrated on the positive things Lynn had said. He was a respected and established Account Manager. One who would now be playing a central role in one of Ireland' s leading PR firms.

He nervously jumped when the receptionist came in.

"Mr Macken will see you now, Mr Reynolds," she said.

What was with the Mr? he wondered. He was struck by the formality of it all.

He followed the girl down a long corridor. She knocked on a door, opened it, indicated he should go in and closed the door behind him.

Peter found himself in the boardroom with Brendan and Chloe sitting at the far end of the board table.

He hovered nervously, not sure where to sit.

"Hi, Peter. Why don't you join us up at this side of the room," said Chloe as if reading his mind.

He returned her smile, then confidently walked to them and shook both their hands before sitting down.

"How's your wife?" asked Chloe.

"Er, fine thanks. Busy, of course."

"Of course," responded Chloe still smiling.

Peter was alarmed to see Brendan was opening his Personnel file from Blast.

"We'll start by running through your CV," said Brendan. Now he definitely felt he was at a job interview. The temperature of this room was even warmer than the last. But neither Brendan or Chloe, in her sleeked groomed manner, seemed to notice.

"You graduated from UCD in 1992," began Brendan. "Isn't that the year you graduated from there, Chloe?"

"Indeed it was. In fact Peter and I were in the same English classes for a while,"

Peter was startled by this revelation. Studying her face, his memory drew a blank. He was sure he would remember somebody as attractive as Chloe.

"Were you?" he tried to keep the surprise out of his voice "I can't really remember."

"I'd be surprised if you did." She turned to Brendan. "Peter was one of those cool kids who were always going to parties and surrounded by girls."

Remembering Brendan's stern religious reputation, Peter decided this was not a flattering reference.

Brendan looked disapprovingly at Peter.

"Unlike me," continued Chloe. "The quiet shy type, stuck in the library all the time."

Looking at Chloe's cool confidence, Peter was sure this couldn't be a true description of herself.

"Then you became a marketing junior in a bank." Brendan raised an eyebrow.

"It was a good opportunity for me to get experience and meet lots of contacts. I managed to establish myself quite well with that job."

Brendan peered through the CV. "After some more adventures, mainly with public bodies, you joined Blast. An interesting, if not conventional route into Public Relations consultancy, don't you think?"

"I think it gave me a more rounded view than if I just went straight to work for a PR company out of college."

Brendan and Chloe stared at him while remaining expressionless.

"At Blast I believe you played a key role in getting important clients."

"Including some of ours," added Chloe.

Again, Peter sensed Chloe wasn't doing him any favours. He was becoming tired of this charade.

"Look, let's face it, PR is a highly competitive business. And if Blast wasn't a competitive company, you wouldn't have bothered buying it."

Again Brendan and Chloe stared at him without expression.

Finally Chloe spoke. "We don't want any changes at Blast, whatsoever. We want the company to continue functioning as it always has. Except now it will be a subsidiary of Macken. I will play a part in the day-to-day running of Blast, but that's as far as it goes."

Peter nodded.

"We want to reassure Blast's clients they are in the same safe hands as before. We want projects to continue without disruption, especially the Childwatch Fashion Show."

"I agree that a sense of continuity is important for clients," nodded Peter.

"Just one small change I do recommend. The forthcoming Press launch for the fashion show. I do think we should use this opportunity to announce the takeover."

Peter decided it was a small price to pay for the reassurance they had given him. "If it's OK with the client, it's OK with me."

Chloe strode into the reception area at Blast. She had a word with the receptionist and then entered the boardroom. Five minutes later, John Power, a junior accounts executive, followed her in.

"Take a seat, John."

The young man did as Chloe asked and sat down nervously.

"John, we were impressed with you yesterday," continued Chloe. "We feel that Michael and Peter have been overlooking your obvious talents."

John's nervous expression suddenly switched to a bright grin.

"There a couple of accounts I'd like you to get involved in. How do you feel about that?"

"I'd love to."

"Good. You'll still be working from here, but spending more time at the Macken building, head office." She paused and drew nearer to him. "I'd also like you to keep me informed of any irregularities here."

"Irregularities?" He looked concerned.

"Just keep an eye on things for me. I think we understand each other. A pay rise will reflect your new role."

The grin jumped back on his face. "I'm really grateful."

"You'll also be taking full responsibility for the Smithford Property Account."

John was confused. "But that's Trixi's client . . ."

From his office, Peter saw John emerge from the boardroom smiling. Five minutes later he saw Trixi go in.

"But there weren't supposed to be any changes at Blast!" objected Trixi.

Chloe hadn't liked Trixi from the beginning. She found her bland and uninteresting.

"Don't take it personally, Trixi. We've paid a great deal of money for Blast. Money we now need to start making back. We now have to save money where we can, which includes your salary."

"Michael won't let you do this!"

"Michael no longer has a say in the hiring and firing.

That's down to me. And I say you go. A word of advice, Trixi: I don't think PR is for you. Maybe you should take a look at other things more suited to your talents," Chloe paused as she saw Trixi was becoming upset and then continued." Look at it this way – leaving PR is a bit like dying. Nobody knows exactly where you've gone, but they hope it's to a better place."

"I don't believe it." Peter was sitting in the pub with Trixi.

"Believe it. The bitch sat there, cool as a cucumber, fired me and then told me I was crap at PR!"

"I'm calling Michael to sort this out." He reached for his mobile.

"Don't bother. Michael's on holidays."

"Holidays?" Peter nearly shouted.

"Reception told me he left for Spain last night. His mobile is out of coverage. The bastard knew what was coming and ran for cover."

"What are they playing at?"

"Be careful, Peter. They can't be trusted."

"Well, she would say that." Lynn was unsympathetic. "Perhaps Trixi – I always thought it a ridiculous name – was pathetic at her job."

"No, she was good!" defended Peter.

"As good as you?"

"She had a different style."

"Yes, a crap style! It's called business, Peter. I won't exhibit an artist's work just because he's nice. They can't afford to keep Trixi on."

"It's just so unfair!"

"Think about yourself, Peter. Show Brendan how crucial you are to Blast's future."

"And what if he doesn't want Blast to have a future?"

Lynn's cheeks burned red. "Are you completely losing it? You don't pay a fortune for a company if you don't want it to have a future!"

CHAPTER 6

Boom Model Agency was situated on one floor of a gleaming glass office block in the city centre. Hazel's office was situated at the back of the building. Her office walls were a glass partition, allowing her to keep a watchful eye on the rest of the activity in the office. She could observe the bookers busy making deals on the phones. She could spy on the models as they continuously drifted in and out to collect cheques, enquire about castings or to just kill time, depending on how successful they were.

As usual Hazel was smoking a cigarette as she sat behind her desk.

"The cheques I received for the last three photo calls were only about half of what they should have been," stated Audrey, who was seated opposite Hazel.

"That's right. I deducted half your wages, as a fine for arriving late for three jobs."

"But, Hazel!"

"But Hazel nothing! Your constant lateness can't continue. Peter Reynolds was only saying to me the other day how unreliable you are."

"Peter Reynolds!" Audrey was horrified. "He said that? Who cares what he says? He bores me!"

"He may bore you. But his company has just become part of Macken Communications and they could send a lot of work your way. So shape up."

"If they don't want me, then I don't want them." Audrey tried not to sound too petulant.

"Oh, grow up!" Hazel's voice, always harsh, seemed to rise an octave. "You've been in this game long enough to know how it works."

Thank you, Hazel. Get the dig in, thought Audrey.

Hazel dragged on her cigarette. "You piss people off, then they don't give you work. Simple as that. When you don't earn money then I don't earn money and that pisses me off."

"I don't piss people off."

"At the end of the day, I don't give a fuck what you do. But when you are late you're tarnishing my agency's reputation. And that's a no-no."

Audrey stopped herself from delivering a torrent of abuse. The one person she couldn't afford to fall out with was her agent. And she had always been one of Hazel's favourites. In a funny kind of way, Hazel had always admired Audrey's temper and spirit. She had said she always knew where she stood with Audrey.

She knew it was time to back down. "Sure, I'll make a real effort to be on time in future."

Audrey thundered down Grafton Street, seething. To add insult to injury when she had left her meeting at Boom, she had been greeted by a parking fine, her third in a week. Her phone rang and, seeing Aran's number coming up on the caller ID, she looked forward to some sympathy.

"What time will I collect you tonight for the dinner party at my parents?" he asked straight away.

She had totally forgotten about the dinner party. The last thing she needed or wanted was an evening with the Murphy clan. "Darling, I've had a bad day. Had a big flare-up with Hazel. I think I'll just skip tonight, if you don't mind."

"The hell you are! My parents have gone to so much trouble!"

"I'd be crap company. Better off without me."

"You're coming tonight," he insisted.

Her voice became stern. "I said I'm not!"

"You're so selfish, Audrey. You don't give a damn about messing up people's arrangements!"

"If I'm selfish, then you're a bully!" She was shouting now and people were looking at her as she continued to walk down the street. "And you never even asked me how I am!"

"You can tell me tonight . . . . over dinner. I'll collect you at eight!" He hung up.

She threw her mobile into her handbag. There was nothing for it but to go to Brown Thomas for some retail therapy.

Two hours and a large credit-card bill later, her anger still hadn't subsided. Carrying five shopping bags, she was about to leave the store when she spotted, of all people, Peter Reynolds in the men's department.

She marched straight over to him and hissed, "You're a bastard!"

He looked up from the shirts he was studying and said, "Sorry?"

"You should be. You rang up Hazel and complained about me."

He was taken off guard but still felt the need to defend himself "If you're paid to be somewhere, you should be there on time."

"And after I attended your wife's crummy exhibition!"

He felt a stab of guilt as he remembered that favour. "I, er, I'd spoken to Hazel before you came to that." He knew it sounded lame.

"You're still a bastard," and as she turned to walk off he noticed tears had welled up in her eyes.

Audrey and Aran sat in silence as he drove them to his parents' Howth mansion. As the car swept up the driveway she was surprised to see an array of expensive cars already parked there.

"I thought this was supposed to be a small affair," she said.

"Tonight is a good chance for you to meet some powerful people."

She sighed. "But I told you I wasn't feeling well. I don't want to make small talk with lots of people."

"You don't appreciate anything! I'd have thought you'd be delighted to meet my parents' friends. No, not our Audrey, everyone owes you something."

She sighed and got out of the car, following him as he opened the front door and they walked into the marble hallway.

In the drawing room, cocktails were being served to twelve people.

Aran's mother Muriel and father Reginald immediately came over to them.

"How are you, my dear?" Muriel said, as both she and Reginald greeted their son's girlfriend with a kiss on the cheek.

"Busy," Audrey smiled.

"Come with me," Muriel took a firm grip of Audrey's arm, "and I'll introduce you to everybody."

Like her husband, Muriel was a qualified solicitor. However, she had given up working when Aran, their only child, was born. Muriel was always careful to be nice to Audrey, even though she had no time for her. The last thing she wanted for a daughter-in-law was a flashy model, of average background, who was prone to temper tantrums. She knew a gold-digger when she saw one.

It maddened Muriel that no matter how many eligible young professional women she introduced to her son, he only had eyes for Audrey.

"This is Audrey, everybody." Muriel announced. "Aran's friend."

"I saw you recently at the Brown Thomas Fashion Show," said a matronly lady-who-lunches type. "Great frocks!"

Audrey sensed they were looking at her with a curious mix of awe and contempt.

"Audrey, this is Brendan Macken," said Muriel. Remembering Hazel's comment about how Macken had taken over Blast, Audrey shook his hand and smiled brightly.

Conveniently, Audrey found herself seated beside Brendan at dinner.

"Have you known the Murphys for long?" she enquired.

"Myself and Reginald are old friends. We do some work for his firm. Political lobbying."

"I'm taking part in the Childwatch Show. That's been run by one of your companies, isn't it?"

"You're working with Peter Reynolds on that?"

"Ah yes," her voice dripped sarcasm, "the lovely Peter."

"You don't like him?" Brendan was concerned.

"To be honest with you, he's very rude and a bully."

After dinner, Audrey escaped to the bathroom upstairs. She opened the window and breathed in the fresh air.

She couldn't resist taking a look through some of the rooms upstairs.

Even though Aran still lived there, she was only in the house for formal occasions. He spent most time at her apartment anyway. She was dazzled by the antiques and the obvious trappings of wealth everywhere.

She allowed herself to imagine being Mrs Aran Murphy, and living in that house. Being part of one of the top solicitor families in the country. Then she could tell them all to go take a hike.

"Making yourself at home?" Audrey was startled to hear Muriel's voice as she was examining a side table. She was even more uncomfortable to see the hard cold expression on Muriel's face.

"Just admiring your lovely house," answered Audrey.

"I'm sure you were." Muriel crossed the hall and ran a finger across the side table. "This is from my side of the family. Nearly two hundred years old. The portraits," she waved her hand to indicate the hanging paintings, "are from Reginald's side. The silver has been in my family for generations. That's what attracted Reginald and me to each other. We come from the same place. Same class. We understand each other. That's so important." She started to smile. "We must have your family to tea. How far away do they live, did you say?"

That night Peter worked at home on the press release for the launch of the Childwatch Show. The launch, which was to be in The San Juan Club, was only two days away and the release would have to be dispatched the next morning. He was finding it difficult to incorporate the news of the takeover. Finally, he decided to give it a small mention in the second paragraph.

The phone rang and looking at his watch he realised it was after midnight.

Lynn was out for the night and he knew it would be her.

"Peter, I'm at Lillies with Rory and a few others!" She was shouting to be heard above the music.

"Do you want me to collect you?"

"No, no. I'll just grab a cab. Don't wait up." The phone went dead.

One of the reasons why their marriage was so successful was because they didn't put undue pressure on each other, Peter thought. Each realised the other had a demanding career which did entail some late nights.

Thinking of his own parents, he knew one of them wouldn't dream of going out without the other. But he and Lynn lived in a different era and world. The last thing either of them needed or wanted was a nagging, possessive, insecure spouse. Trust and loyalty played a major part.

As he put down the press release he thought of his confrontation with Audrey that day. She was spoilt and pampered, he told himself. Why then did he feel guilty? And that was a feeling he was uneasy with.

It was late when Aran dropped Audrey off at her apartment. She was exhausted and all she wanted to do was go to bed. She threw her keys on the table and bolted the door, then cursed when the phone rang.

"Hello," she snapped.

"You don't sound in a good mood, love?"

It was Kathleen, her mother.

"Oh, hi, Mum. Just had a hectic day. And then I was over at Aran's parents for dinner."

"Wasn't that lovely of them to invite you!"

Yeah, really lovely, thought Audrey. She thought of her mother and father and younger brother Jack Junior living life contentedly and easily in Ballyabbey, the little seaside town in the west where she grew up. They were such normal people, good and honest, and so proud of her. They had nothing in common with the Murphys.

"How's it going with Aran? Are things still going well?"

"Yeah. We're getting along great."

"That's good. I'm glad you finished with that politician. I never liked him."

Audrey smiled at her mother's judgement. She had never met the man, but formed her opinions from what she read in the papers.

"When are you coming home next?"

"I'll get down soon. After the Childwatch Show, I'll take a few days off."

"Great. You know Shaun? Himself and his wife had a baby."

Audrey became irritated. Why did her mother insist on telling her news about a boyfriend from eight years ago? After all the powerful and high-profile men she had gone out with, what did she care about Shaun? The local petrol-station owner's son, who was content never to leave Ballyabbey. "You sound exhausted, I'll let you get to bed," said Kathleen.

"I'll call you tomorrow and we'll have a proper chat," promised Audrey. "Give my love to Dad and Jack"

"Of course. We love you, Audrey."

The tears that had been threatening to come all day spilled over as Audrey hung up the phone.

CHAPTER 7

Peter faxed the press release to Macken for approval. Thirty minutes later Chloe rapped on his door.

"I read your release. Perfect. Very concise English. Always your strong point in college."

It bugged Peter that he couldn't remember her at all. It gave her the upper hand. Lynn had been in the same year in college as well, and it had been where they had met. He had asked her if she could remember Chloe, but she drew a blank as well.

"I've made a couple of adjustments," she said handing him the release.

His heading, which had previously focused on the Fashion Show now read:

"Macken Communications Announces Takeover of Blast at Childwatch Fashion Show Launch."

With alarm he read on. "But this isn't acceptable . . . you've changed everything!" he objected. "Childwatch will hit the roof."

Chloe looked alarmed. "I hope not. I've already faxed it through to them."

43

"You had no right!" He grabbed the phone and phoned Jack Houlihan, Chief Executive of Childwatch.

"Jack, I'm sorry about the release –" Peter stopped as Jack interrupted him. "I see, Jack, OK . . . in that case, we'll send it out today right away." Peter hung up and stared at Chloe, feeling confused. "He said it was fine."

"Oh, I'm so glad!" Chloe sighed with relief. "You had me worried for a second. Was that Jack Houlihan? I didn't realise you were dealing with him. He's a good friend of mine."

"I'll send out the release to the media now." Peter tried to regain control of the situation.

"Oh, I already told Reception to start faxing it out." Smiling, she was about to leave but then paused and took her seat again. "Peter, could I have a private chat? Strictly between the two of us."

"Certainly." He was still dazed.

"We've heard you haven't been very nice to Aran Murphy's girlfriend, Audrey. His family are personal friends of Brendan's. They are also one of our clients." She allowed herself to smile again as Peter looked at her wide-eyed. "I can't express to you how important it is to stay on the right side of our clients."

Damn Audrey Driver! Damn Brendan Macken! But most of all, damn Chloe Gallagher! Peter spent his lunch-time walking around Stephen's Green trying to work off steam. A short while ago he barely knew who Chloe was. Now, he couldn't make a move without her knowing it. As for Michael Cassidy, well, it was obvious he had been completely removed from the picture already. Chloe was in full control. He was consumed with a desire to quit. Just leave them in the lurch before the fashion show. This, however, was impossible. It would cast him in a very unprofessional light walking out at such a late stage of the event. And then there was the mortgage. Most of all, there was Lynn.

On the evening of the Press Reception, Peter left the office at five o'clock, heading straight for The San Juan Club. He had spent the day tending to last-minute details. This entailed everything from sending late press releases out, to responding to enquiries. As always there were last-minute requests for invitations, that had to be sent out by courier. The invitation's stated arrival time was eight. Chloe arrived at seven.

"How's everything going?" she asked him, but didn't wait for an answer as she swept over to the owner of The San Juan, Noel Flynn, and engaged him in a flirtatious conversation.

Not that Peter cared. He was too busy plaguing himself with the usual questions. What if no guests turned up? Or no photographers? Or VIPs?

The takeover had added an extra dimension of pressure. Brendan or Chloe would not be supportive if the night turned into a disaster, he reckoned.

Guests began to trickle in at eight, and Peter checked that a Promotions girl was posted by the signing-in book at the door. By nine, the place was jam-packed.

Lynn arrived and was suitably impressed. Kissing his cheek, she said, "It won't be long till Brendan Macken is offering you a promotion."

He kissed her back, grateful for her support.

"You'd better introduce me to him," said Lynn.

Although Peter knew it was the correct etiquette, he dreaded the request. But he took her hand and walked over to Brendan who was deep in conversation with Chloe.

"Brendan, I'd like you to meet my wife, Lynn."

"Very nice to meet you," he said, shaking her hand. Brendan was always careful to be civil and polite to his employees' spouses. Then when they went home from work and called him a bastard, he could rely on an occasional ally.

While Peter was making sure the photographers got their shots of the models and VIPs, he came face to face with Audrey.

"I guess you decided to pay me back," he said coldly.

"One good turn deserves another." She walked off.

Peter was used to public speaking, but the presence of his new bosses unsettled him.

He stepped up to the microphone. "Ladies and gentlemen, just a few words to remind you of what tonight and the forthcoming fashion show are all about."

The crowd hushed and he tried to ignore Brendan's and Chloe's fixed stares.

"It's always heartbreaking to see children suffer, but in today's affluent world, it's inexcusable. Since Childwatch was established, the charity has worked tirelessly to help the children who are marginalised in our society. That's the aim of this fashion show: to raise funds for a new centre in Ballymun. So although it's a night for everyone to enjoy themselves, it also has an important goal. Thanks to all of you for coming tonight, for your support, and we hope to see you at the fashion show."

The crowd applauded and he smiled appreciatively. He still managed to smile when he saw Chloe cut through the crowd, sidle up beside him and adjust the microphone to her height.

"Thanks, Peter, for those words," and she shot him a warning look to step out of the way. Confused, he stepped down into the crowd.

"Indeed, a great show for a great cause. This show is coming at a crucial point for Macken Communications. As you are probably aware, we have taken over at Blast. An exciting merger. A young company joining forces with an older and more experienced one. What more could a client want from Public Relations professionals? We like to see this fashion show as a showcase for our new stronger, brighter firm."

As Chloe continued to highjack his – and indeed Childwatch's – evening, all Peter could do was look on in amazement.

Peter was knocking back glass after glass of champagne.

Lynn was handing out her business cards, while Chloe thanked people for coming.

"Can I get you some champagne?" Chloe asked Audrey and Aran, noticing Audrey was sipping Ballygowan.

"No, thanks. This is fine," said Audrey.

"Do you mind if I take your photo?" a pressman asked Audrey. She handed Aran her glass and followed him to a corner where she posed.

"You know, at all the receptions I've seen Audrey at, I've never seen her drink," Chloe said to Aran.

"She never drinks."

"Oh?"

Aran gave a little laugh. "To be honest, she can't handle her drink."

Chloe was intrigued. "What do you mean?"

"She'd kill me if she knew I was saying this, but she goes a little nuts when she drinks. Either starts shouting the odds or goes hyper. I suppose she just never built up a resistance to it over the years, like the rest of us did."

"What are you two gossiping about?" Audrey rejoined them.

"Nothing," said Chloe. "Are you around for lunch this week?"

"You let Chloe take over." Lynn was furious in the back of the taxi.

"Well, that's what she does best, take over – events, parties, companies."

"Shut up, Peter. This is no time for your silly jokes."

"You saw her. What the fuck could I have done?"

"Talked about the merger in your speech, leaving her nothing to say. But no, you were too busy talking about saving the planet! Even after the speeches you should have mixed more. You should have been in control."

"I was in control."

"No," she snapped, "you weren't. You jumped into a champagne bottle and stayed there."

They sat in silence before he reached over for her hand, but she pulled away.

"For a talented guy, you can be such an idiot."

CHAPTER 8

Despite his tiredness, Peter couldn't fall asleep. He weighed up his options in the dark, as Lynn slept beside him. He was only too aware how much he needed Macken. But if he left the fashion show at this stage, it would also be a disaster for them. They needed him as much as he needed them. That night at the Press Reception, he had been pushed too far. If he failed to stand up for himself now, they would walk all over him in the future. He would make it clear he would not tolerate any more interference from Chloe. Whatever the consequences were.

As instructed, the receptionist informed Peter as soon as Chloe arrived into Blast the next morning. Steadying himself, he knocked on the door of the boardroom, which she seemed to have claimed as her own office.

"Congratulations on last night, Peter. Brendan was very happy with how everything worked out."

"Thanks." He sat down. "Unfortunately, I'm unhappy."

"What's the matter?"

"The whole event was eclipsed by the Macken-Blast merger."

"I didn't hear any objections from Childwatch. Did you?"

"Surprisingly not. But that isn't the point."

"The only point is that the client is happy."

"No, Chloe, my job is to make sure that next week's show is a success and as profitable as possible. Your press release and your speech hindered my work."

"I can't see how."

"By obscuring the promotion of the show and making attention drift away to the takeover," He paused. "If the Show isn't a success, the buck stops here."

Chloe waited before speaking "I understand your concerns. From now on I'll keep out of your way."

Filled with relief, he managed to smile "Thanks, I don't mean to . . . it's just that . . . "

"No need to explain further. As you said, the buck stops with you."

Peter was elated for the rest of the day. He arranged for flowers to be delivered to The Gallery. Lynn was delighted and rang him to say so.

They arranged to meet in O'Neill's after work for some drinks and ended up getting drunk. The romance that seemed to have been missing from their marriage for a while crept back in.

They agreed to go down to stay at Peter's parents for the weekend. In spite of how busy work was, Peter made sure to leave the office early on the Friday and they drove to his parents' stud. Peter's parents fussed over them and even though his mobile was constantly ringing, he managed to relax. He went horse-riding while Lynn, usually not one for the country, enjoyed country walks.

On the Saturday night, while Lynn and Peter relaxed in front of a roaring fire drinking brandies, Chloe was opening the front door of Blast.

She flicked on the switch and was followed in by two men.

"How long will it take?" she asked.

"About an hour," answered one of them as they went to work on opening all the phones. "This system is better than the one we fitted in the Macken building. With this system you can listen into the conversation as it's happening. You don't have to wait till it is taped and then replay it."

"But it will still record the phone calls?" asked Chloe.

"Of course."

CHAPTER 9

Audrey regretted she had agreed to model in the fashion show. There now existed a very bad atmosphere between herself and Peter, very evident during rehearsals. They barely acknowledged each other's existence, and kept a cold distance from each other. She didn't regret complaining to Brendan Macken. It had been Peter who had started it, and she had shown him that she could finish it.

"You heard the latest?" Leslie Taylor sat down beside her in the hotel bar during a break, the day before the show.

"What?"

"Peter's only gone and banned any alcohol backstage the night of the show."

It was irrelevant to Audrey because she wouldn't be drinking anyway. "I'm not surprised," she said. "He's a very mean-spirited man."

"You two still not speaking?"

"Only when we have to."

As always Audrey marvelled at Leslie's beauty. She

was twenty-three and her look was pure Bond girl. She had a sultry innocence.

Although she did well as a model, Leslie was not established as much as Audrey, though she deserved to be. Audrey put this down to the fact that Leslie refused to play the game and lick up to the right people to get ahead. And because of this, Hazel didn't give much of her time to promote her. Basically, Audrey felt Leslie was too nice for this business.

Luckily for Audrey, Hazel always pushed her career. Hazel had phoned her that morning to tell her she had reached the final shortlist for Silk Shampoo. It had been narrowed down to her and just one other girl. Such huge success being tantalisingly dangled in front of her was beginning to make Audrey feel very nervous indeed.

"Going out tonight?" asked Audrey.

"Just to dinner with Jimmy."

Audrey knew Jimmy was a down-to-earth insurance salesman who had been going out with Leslie long before she entered modelling.

"Doesn't Jimmy ever get jealous of the people you mix with?" Audrey was curious. "Isn't he frightened you'll be swept off your feet by some big shot?"

"No, he knows he's stuck with me now!" Leslie laughed. "I'll leave the millionaires to you!"

It hadn't always been the case, and Audrey thought of Shaun, now married in Ballyabbey with a young baby. Audrey felt herself becoming envious of Leslie and the normality of her relationship with Jimmy. She had to laugh at herself. She was totally happy with Aran – he was everything she wanted and more.

In the distance, they could hear Peter shouting for everyone to come back to rehearsals.

"Better get back," said Leslie.

"I can't wait for tomorrow night to be over."

Audrey stood on stage with five other models listening to Peter issue directions loudly.

Peter always had a habit of interfering with the choreographer's work when he had an idea. Audrey found his interference irritating.

"Audrey, you're walking too quickly down that ramp – why don't you try it again?" Peter suggested.

Audrey walked across the stage as instructed and repeated this action.

"You're doing it too quickly," Peter snapped.

She tried it again and, to his annoyance, she still didn't get it right.

"You're fucking it up," he said.

Audrey saw red. "And who the fuck are you to tell me about modelling? This is the choreographer's job, not the PR's!"

Peter erupted in an equal bout of anger. "I'm paying you so you'll do as I damned well tell you to! You can just lose your big ego around here!"

"There's no room for egos here because yours is so fucking inflated!" She paused before playing her trump card: "And I thought it was Brendan Macken paying our wages, not you!"

The choreographer, Jessie, jumped up on stage. "C'mon, c'mon, everyone calm down."

"Let's take a break." Peter stormed off.

As he paced through the foyer to the exit to get some fresh air, he was stopped by a woman from Banqueting who showed him the menu for the show for his approval.

"I don't want The Berkeley Court's logo on the top of

these menus – I want the Childwatch logo," he snapped at her. "I'm not paying you to advertise yourselves."

That night, Peter found himself still in his office at eleven. When he started in PR, he never dreamed so much time would be taken up with small details.

He needed a holiday badly. He would take Lynn away as soon as the dust had settled after the show. Thinking of the last few days, he thanked God they were getting on much better, almost like the beginning when they had met.

On-off was a good description for their relationship. Sometimes they were romantic; sometimes they acted like enemies. Often they were supportive of each other; often they acted like rivals. They could love each other passionately and the next day feel something bordering on hatred. They blew hot and cold.

When his phone rang, he expected it to be Lynn.

"Hi, just finishing up now, will be home shortly . . . Lynn?"

He called hello a couple of times but nobody spoke and so he hung up. The phone rang twice more with the same charade. Becoming irritated, he left the ringing phone and went home.

CHAPTER 10

The next morning, Peter shaved, showered and dressed in casual clothes. He pulled his tuxedo out of his wardrobe and grabbed a bottle of aftershave. He wouldn't have time to come home to change that evening, so he needed to take everything with him for the night. He drove out of the underground carpark and began to negotiate the Dublin rush-hour traffic. His first port of call was a warehouse on the outskirts of the city where he had to collect some stock for the show. They were one-off creations, and the designer had insisted he came out personally to collect them.

Finding the warehouse easily enough, he laid the gowns out in his backseat and headed to The Berkeley Court Hotel.

Then, as he motored along the dual carriageway, steam began to erupt from his engine. Swearing loudly, he pulled over to the side of the road. As he opened the bonnet of his car he was engulfed in a cloud of smoke. He kicked the car and phoned AA, who informed him it would be an hour and a half until they could get to him.

"Not today of all days!" he shouted out loud as he sat down on the kerb and began ringing taxi firms.

Chloe was driving along the dual carriageway when she spotted the broken-down car.

She did a double take as she saw Peter Reynolds sitting beside it, mobile in hand.

She quickly pulled over and pressed the button to unwind her window.

"Everything under control for tonight?" she asked.

Looking up and seeing Chloe, Peter was overcome with embarrassment. However, this was quickly followed by relief.

"Of all days to bloody break down!" he said, standing up.

"Want a lift?" she offered.

Without answering, he raced to his car and got the garments out of the back.

"I really appreciate this," he said, putting the clothes into her back seat and jumping into the front. "I had to collect these for tonight and I need to get them to The Berkeley Court as quickly as possible."

"No problem. I'll drop you in there . . . I just have to go by my house first to collect a document."

"You've saved my life . . . of all days to break down."

"Murphy's Law," she smiled as she indicated and pulled out onto the dual carriageway. "What will you do about your car?"

Peter observed Chloe was a cool and controlled driver. "I'll get it collected. I think I'll have to invest in a new one – unless Macken decide to give me a company car?"

Glancing at him, she saw he was smiling cheekily. "Even I don't get a company car."

He pretended to be shocked. "Not even you! Oh, my God!"

"However, I do get a company jet," she said sarcastically.

Was he seeing a lighter side of Chloe, he wondered.

"We're near my home. You don't mind me dropping in to grab some papers?"

"Of course not. Really appreciate you giving me the lift."

She drove down an exclusive street in Killiney. Pressing a remote control, an electric gate opened and she drove into the short driveway. Her house was very modern and on one level. It was set in beautiful mature gardens that sloped down to the edge of a cliff, which had a sheer drop to the sea.

"Obviously, Macken pay their senior executives a hell of a lot more than Blast does," said Peter, admiring the house as he followed her inside.

"I was lucky because I bought this property before prices went through the roof." She closed the door behind them. "Fix yourself a drink." She walked off down the corridor.

"Do you want one?" he called as he went down the steps into the large sitting-room and admired the sea through the patio doors.

"No, I'm fine!"

He tried to detect if she lived alone. But there were no personal items on display, such as photographs – not even of herself. Curiosity got the better of him. "Anyone special in your life?"

"Not at the moment, not enough time," she replied from a room down the corridor.

"Yeah, PR is hard on relationships."

Chloe came into the sitting-room holding a file. "How does Lynn feel about your long hours at work?"

"She understands. Her work can be unsociable as well."

"I remember Lynn at college. I thought her very

ambitious. I imagined her ending up married into aristocracy or something."

He laughed. "Maybe she saw herself like that too. But you can't help who you fall in love with, can you?"

"Very true."

Chloe pulled her Mercedes up near the kerb outside The Berkeley Court Hotel.

"Listen, thanks again," Peter said, getting out of the car and gathering the garments from the back seat.

"No problem. I'd better head back to the office." She drove off.

Peter walked up to the hotel entrance and was surprised to see an distraught-looking Audrey, standing looking at her car, near the front door.

"Audrey, is everything okay?" he said, approaching her.

"I banged my damned car into a postbox on my way in here!"

He looked down and saw a medium-sized dent on the side of her driver's door. He had no doubt the accident was caused by Audrey's bad driving which was legendary.

"You know, this damned show has caused me nothing but hassle since I signed up for it!" He sighed to himself, hoping Audrey wouldn't use this as an excuse not to focus on what was important – making the night a big success.

"Well, it doesn't look too bad to me. It should be easily fixed."

She looked at him with annoyance. "Easily known I wouldn't get any sympathy from you!" she said, pushing past him and walking into the hotel.

The lead-up to the night was always pressure and adrenaline mixing as one. Two hours later and Peter's temper was at boiling point. Not only was he mortified at having been caught in such a ridiculous position by Chloe earlier that day, but on top of the mounting pressure, Audrey was choosing to make a song and dance about her accident with the postbox.

She was sitting on the side of the stage, with four of the other models sitting around her listening to her moans about the dent on the side of her car.

"I'm not even fully insured," Audrey wailed. "I'll have to pay for the dent to be fixed myself! Everything I earn tonight will have to go on mending it – and more!"

"That's a real pain," remarked Leslie.

"And I got such an awful shock when I hit the postbox! It was such a loud bang, that was the worse part of it."

Peter couldn't contain himself any more and he marched over. "I'm sorry, but what the hell is going on here? We are just a few hours from the biggest show of the year and you're all in group therapy over a small accident?"

Five sets of beautiful eyes turned to him in surprise.

Audrey's were furious. "Small accident! That's easy for you to say, you heartless bugger! I'm still shaking from it."

"Oh, please!" he rolled his eyes to heaven. "Nobody was hurt, were they? Nobody needed to go to hospital or see a doctor, did they? Get over it, Audrey!"

The models all started to get to their feet.

"I've never met such a rude and uncaring man as you," Audrey fumed.

"Ah, go and complain to Brendan Macken, if you want. You're distracting everyone with your tales of woe, and there's a lot of work to be done."

Audrey's voice rose. "I'll tell you something: I will never work with you again! I don't care what the job is or how much it pays, I never want to see you again after this!"

Peter's voice raised too. "That suits me just fine. Let's just hope the next few hours pass quickly and we never have to set eyes on each other again!"

"I can't stand you!" Audrey spat, before storming off to the dressing-room.

The Berkeley Court was buzzing with excitement by the time Chloe came back in the late afternoon. She had just dropped by to take a look at the stage, before going home to change for the night. As she made her way across the foyer, she was stopped by Jessie, the choreographer.

"I hate to go over Peter's head," Jessie said, "but he's still not allowing any drink backstage for the girls."

"It sounds unreasonable to me, too. But I can't get involved. Maybe Peter will change his mind," said Chloe.

"Peter Reynolds change his mind? That'll be the day."

A little while later, Chloe found Peter in a temporary office he had set up in the Banqueting Department.

"I was just down in the function room – the stage looks amazing," she said, smiling.

Seeing he looked less than happy to see her, she held up her hands. " Just making sure you're all right – not about to interfere!"

He relaxed. "Everything's under control."

"Audrey is not too unnerved, is she? One of the models was telling me about her car-crash."

"Car-crash? More like car-scratch – I saw the damage done, it's only a dent. She's been exaggerating it all day for attention. As it was caused by her colliding with a postbox, and since postboxes are stationary, I think we can safely say whose fault it was."

"I see," Chloe smirked. "But you know how petulant

models can be. Well, if there's nothing else, I'll see you tonight."

"OK – and thanks, Chloe."

"And how do you feel now?" asked Hazel over the phone, after hearing Audrey's description of her run-in with a postbox.

"OK, I guess."

"Well, I've got some news which might cheer you up . . ." Hazel drew in her breath. "You got the shampoo contract!"

"You're joking!"

"Ricky Nash, the PR guy for Silk just phoned me to confirm they want you."

"I can't believe it!" Audrey hollered.

"Believe it. He's coming tonight to the show as my guest. Make sure you charm him."

Audrey could hardly contain herself. "I'll show him he's made the right choice!"

In the dressing-room, Leslie hugged Audrey warmly. "Congratulations! A big American contract!"

The other models also wished her luck, but Audrey felt they weren't as genuine in their congratulations as Leslie was. In fact, some barely concealed their resentment.

"I'm just going out to the foyer to ring Aran to tell him the news," she said.

"Audrey, don't be long!" Jessie, the choreographer, shouted after her. "Peter said nobody was to leave this area till the show starts!"

"Thanks, Aran, I'll see you tonight . . . where are you and your parents sitting? Where? That's near the stage . . . . good . . . see you then." Audrey turned off her phone. She looked around the foyer, still not believing the news. Her life was going to change dramatically. She had finally made it. She tried to imagine Muriel's and Reginald's reaction. Aran seemed genuinely happy, although he complained she would be spending time in New York.

"Well, you look like a happy girl," said Chloe as she walked up to her in the foyer.

"Oh, Chloe, I've just been signed up as the face of Silk in the States."

"I'm delighted for you," Chloe kissed her cheek. "Let's go for a celebratory drink in the bar!"

"Oh, no, Peter will go mad."

"I'll handle Peter."

"OK, then." Audrey giggled and linked Chloe's arm.

"You're made for life now, Audrey," said Chloe. "A gin and tonic please," she said to the barman. "What are you drinking, Audrey?"

"Just a Diet Coke, please."

"You deserve a proper drink, after the day you've had."

"But I never drink."

"One won't harm you. You've just been told you're going to be famous in America, for God's sake! Now I insist you have a drink."

Audrey's head was spinning from the news. "I guess a gin and tonic too."

An hour and a half later and Audrey had consumed four gins to Chloe's one.

"I'd better get back before Peter kills me," Audrey rose to her feet. "Thanks for the drinks."

"No problem. And, again, well done on the contract! Best of luck for tonight!"

Chloe saw Audrey stumble slightly as she walked out of the bar.

Once Chloe was in her car she dialled the Banqueting Department at the Berkeley on her mobile.

"Hi, it's Peter Reynolds' secretary here at Blast PR. He asked me to order wine for the models backstage, red and white, for tonight's show. I'll just give you the company credit-card details . . ."

Peter looked at his watch. It was seven o'clock and he was running late. It took him exactly five minutes to change into his tuxedo in the toilets on the first floor. He threw some aftershave on and went downstairs.

The foyer was filling up with guests. Everyone was dressed extravagantly in evening wear.

Most people were having a drink from the bar first or from the waiters circulating with free cocktails. Security was ensuring nobody was getting into the ballroom without a ticket. A quartet was playing classical music.

Peter spotted Lynn in the crowd, looking stunning.

"How do you feel?" she asked, taking his arm.

"Nervous."

"Don't be. I've already spotted Lisa Stansfield and Andrea Corr here." She took two glasses of champagne from a passing waiter and handed him one.

"I don't want any."

"You deserve to enjoy the night after all your hard work." She pushed the glass into his hand.

Hazel waved at them and came over. "Hi, you two." she kissed them both, "This is Ricky Nash from New York, PR for Silk Shampoo. You heard Audrey got the contract?"

"Yeah, good choice," Peter shook Ricky's hand and gave Hazel a knowing look. "Audrey's always a pleasure to work with."

"Would you mind if we go backstage to say hello to her?" asked Hazel.

"Fire ahead. Tell Jessie I said it was cool."

Hazel allowed Ricky to walk ahead and then turned to Peter and whispered, "Thanks for the endorsement. I know Audrey has been a bit difficult the last couple of weeks."

"A little difficult?" Peter laughed. "I just feel sorry for that guy when he experiences the full force of Audrey's personality."

"Well, she's a strong woman," defended Hazel.

"That's one description for her."

"A strong woman," Hazel sighed, "with a weak heart."

Jessie had been delighted to see the bottles of alcohol delivered backstage.

Peter must have changed his mind after all, she thought. She looked around the dressing-room and everything seemed to be under control. The models were having their make-up done. Audrey had a glazed expression on her face.

Jessie put it down to the news she had received earlier about the contract, combined with the earlier accident.

Her make-up done, Audrey went and positioned herself beside the wine. She knew she shouldn't but she started to knock back a couple of glasses. The earlier drink had given her a taste for it. Anyway, all the other girls were drinking, so why shouldn't she?

"Audrey!" Hazel's voice boomed across the room.

Audrey got up and hurried over to her, giving both her and Ricky Nash a hug.

"Thank you so much for choosing me! And thank you, Hazel, for getting me this far!"

"We're delighted to have you," said Ricky, "and looking forward to seeing you in the show tonight."

Chloe moved through the crowd with ease, as the bell rang indicating people should go through to the ballroom and take their seats, as the meal was about to be served.

The top table was reserved for Chloe, Brendan, Peter, Lynn, Jack Houlihan and the rest of the board at Childwatch, and the main sponsors of the night.

Chloe took her seat beside Peter, noticing everyone was in great form as the wine continued to flow.

Backstage, the dressing-room began to sway in front of Audrey as she downed another glass.

Aran and his parents arrived late. He was irritated with his mother. He had expected Muriel to be delighted with the news of Audrey's American contract.

However, all she did was speak about his girlfriend more derisively. All three were hardly speaking to each other when they took their seats.

Brendan was impressed with how Peter and Lynn effortlessly charmed the sponsors throughout dinner. He had also heard excellent reports on Peter's organisation of the show.

As desserts were being finished, the lights throughout the ballroom darkened and the audience quietened. Maeve Kelly walked onto the stage to great applause and positioned herself in front of the microphone. Maeve was a daytime presenter on RTE. In her early fifties, she had managed to preserve her looks and figure. Her image was that of the happy mother and wife who also happened to be a television star. She was the epitome of middle-class respectability.

"Lord Mayor, ladies and gentlemen, on behalf of

Childwatch I welcome you to tonight's Fashion Gala. I ask you to sit back and enjoy tonight's outstanding collection from the world of Irish fashion. First, though, I would like to tell you where tonight's raised funds will go . . ." Maeve continued to read from the script.

Backstage, Jessie shouted, *"We're about to start, everybody! Everyone into sequence. Let's go!"*

Audrey finished off the last of a bottle of wine.

"The first part of our show is called Serenity," said Maeve as the lighting on stage became a deep blue and the first of the models emerged and began to sashay down the catwalk. "Leslie is wearing a gown by Orla Hurley, available at Brown Thomas. The gown is a shimmering gold, with clusters of diamonds sewn into the bodice . . . each single diamond-cluster is valued at a thousand euros . . ."

A gasp of appreciation rippled through the audience.

"Audrey!" hissed Jessie. "You're next! Get a move on!"

Audrey jumped to her feet and stumbled up to the steps. Steadying herself, she walked onstage and set off down the catwalk.

"This next outfit is designed by Donegal-based Grainne Fashion. This company has come a long way in ten years. This creation is available at Brown Thomas and Harvey Nichols."

Audrey desperately tried to concentrate and keep her balance, but the ballroom was spinning in front of her.

"The off-black gown clings to the figure all the way to the knee, but then gathers into a train at the back . . . And, of course, our model on stage is lovely Audrey Driver."

As Audrey made the turn at the end of the catwalk, she tripped over the long train of the gown and staggered, nearly falling. The audience gasped as she managed to save herself. She continued along the catwalk but her legs felt as though they were about to give way under her and she stumbled again as she walked offstage.

Brendan Macken, seated at the top table, had been treated to a close-up view. "What's the problem with Audrey Driver?"

"Probably the high heels. Can't imagine how anyone can walk in them," Peter said, prompting laughter from the sponsors.

At the Murphys' table, Aran's parents were frowning.

"I have to say, she seems a little unstable on her feet," said Muriel.

Aran ignored her.

Backstage, Jessie snapped at Audrey, "What happened to you out there?"

"I tripped over the train and –"

"You knew you were supposed to watch out for it! And what happened the second time?"

"I just lost my balance."

"Pull yourself together and get changed for your next appearance."

Audrey hurried over to a dresser, grabbing a glass of wine en route.

Once changed into her next dress, she waited in the wings to go on.

"Now we welcome Audrey back on stage," said Maeve Kelly.

Out front, Peter and Chloe shot each other concerned expressions as there was no sign of Audrey on stage.

Jessie, who had been distracted, suddenly realised what was going on and ran over to Audrey. "Get out there!" she hissed, propelling Audrey on stage.

A murmur of giggles circulated as the audience saw Audrey literally flung onstage.

Maeve continued, ignoring the disturbance, as Audrey very shakily walked down the catwalk.

"This silver-grey gown plunges to the waist at the back, which I'm sure you'll agree is very elegant –"

As which point Audrey lost all co-ordination and collapsed in an inelegant heap on stage. There was an outburst of gasps and the ballroom erupted into talk. Two security men jumped on stage and tried to help Audrey up.

"What the hell is wrong with her?" demanded Brendan Macken.

"She's drunk," said Chloe.

"Get your hands off me!" Audrey shouted at the security men. "I said leave me alone!" She struggled to her feet and pulled free of the men, then slapped one of them hard across the face.

The two men backed off as the spectators' voices were raised in shock.

"What's wrong with you all?" shouted Audrey as she went to the side of the catwalk and clambered down.

Muriel look at Aran, horrified. "I can't believe you've been seeing this tramp! Let's go, Reginald. She's made a public fool of herself and us. Aran, we are leaving."

Aran remained stationary. All he could do was stare at Audrey as she continued to make a spectacle of herself.

"Aran, I'm not telling you again. Let's go," said Muriel.

He looked up at his parents and murmured, "I can't."

They stormed out.

Audrey was going from table to table, over-complimenting some people and insulting others.

"It's the drink," Hazel told Ricky Nash. "She can't handle her drink, never could. She's a delight to work with usually. You just have to keep her away from drink . . ." Hazel was giving damage limitation her best shot.

"There's no way that woman is going to represent our shampoo," Ricky Nash said firmly.

"But you confirmed –"

"Silk Shampoo is wholesome. Girl next door. Not that woman over there."

Audrey reached the head table and stood in front of Peter. "As for you. You're a bully! I'm surprised nobody has tried to kill you yet."

"Audrey, let's go outside and calm down," urged Peter.

"Forget it. I wouldn't go anywhere with you. Patronising bastard!" She turned her attention to Lynn. "And as for you and that tacky little shop that you sell tat in and try to pass it off as art. I came to your party as a favour and you didn't even thank me. Just looked down your nose and made sarcastic comments."

Brendan, who hated any kind of public scenes, hissed, "Get her out of here!"

"Audrey, let's go for a walk." Peter put his arm around her.

"Get off me," she pushed him away. "I'm outta here!" She marched out of the ballroom.

Aran Murphy stared after her, unable to move.

"Ladies and gentlemen, please, please, take your seats," Maeve urged frantically from the stage. However, the night was over as a large section of the audience lost all interest in the show and were making their way to the bar, gossiping madly about the spectacle they had just witnessed.

"How did that happen?" Brendan was furious.

"Who allowed drink backstage?" demanded Chloe. "It's common knowledge Audrey has a drink problem."

All eyes at the head table fell on Peter accusingly.

"The night is ruined," wailed Jack Houlihan. "It'll be in all the papers tomorrow."

"I'll prepare a press release distancing the show from Audrey's behaviour," said Chloe.

"I'll go see what happened backstage," said Peter.

"No," Chloe took control of the situation. "I'll go and see. You track down Audrey and make sure she stays out of any more trouble."

Peter sensed everyone was blaming him.

Lynn stayed out of the conversation, feeling embarrassed and humiliated by Audrey's insults. She, too, hated public scenes.

"Are you all right?" Peter put an arm around his wife.

"I'm going home." She stood up.

"I'll get you a taxi."

"Leave it, Peter." She couldn't look him in the eye. She wanted to be a million miles away from him and this whole horrible night.

"What happened?" Chloe shouted at Jessie backstage.

"She was drunk."

"That was obvious. I thought there wasn't supposed to be any drink backstage."

"Peter changed his mind, and sent some bottles through."

"*I want everyone's attention!*" Chloe shouted. "One of your colleagues seems to have self-combusted on stage. There isn't much of an audience left, but I want you to continue with the show as though nothing happened."

Audrey was nowhere to be found in the hotel.

Finally, the concierge told Peter he saw her heading out to the carpark. He set off into the night air to find her.

Audrey's sports car screeched to a halt beside him.

"Get out of the car. You're not fit to drive," he ordered.

"I'll be the judge of that."

He shook his head. "You fucked up the whole show."

"Who cares? I'm going to paint this town red!"

"You're too drunk to drive!"

"Watch me!" She began revving up the car.

Before she tore off, he managed to open the passenger door and jump in.

Lynn was horrified when she saw the length of the queue at the taxi rank. Many people had had enough entertainment for the night and were waiting to go home. She contemplated ringing Peter, but felt too angry to speak to him. He had handled the whole situation so badly.

Nothing was ever smooth with Peter. Nothing went according to plan, no matter how much support she gave him.

She dialled Rory Ryan's number. "Hi, Rory. I've had a tragic night. Could you collect me?"

Chloe sat in whispered conversation with Brendan. The show was over and they had spent an hour trying to pacify an hysterical Jack Houlihan, with little success.

"There's nothing more we can do tonight," said Brendan. "We'll meet first thing in the morning to discuss our options."

"Fine, see you then." Chloe grabbed her handbag and was walking through the ballroom when she saw Aran Murphy sitting alone at a table.

"Are you OK, Aran?"

He slammed his mobile on the table. "Her phone is off. I've been trying to get through for ages."

"I checked with Reception – she left almost immediately after – the incident."

"I'm worried about her. She's in a vulnerable state," said Aran.

Chloe stopped herself from saying something sarcastic. One thing Audrey could never be was vulnerable.

"That up there tonight," said Aran, "that's not her. You see, she can't take drink. She never could. Why did she drink? Probably the shock of the accident and the excitement of the contract."

"Probably." Chloe nodded in sympathy.

"People judge her, you know. They don't know her like I know her. She can be the sweetest and most giving girl in the world."

"Really?" Chloe was finding it hard to keep her voice even.

"She's just a bit insecure."

"Well, don't worry about her – Peter will look after her."

"Peter?" Aran was confused.

"The concierge told me Peter Reynolds left with her in her car."

Aran stared into the distance with a troubled look .

"Best thing for you to do now is go home. I'll give you a lift," Chloe offered.

Realising there was no reason for him to stay, he stood up and grabbed his jacket.

"And Aran, I know this is a difficult thing for you. If you need someone to talk to," Chloe put her hand on his arm, "just give me a call."

CHAPTER 11

Audrey drove the short distance to Stephen's Green, and then Peter managed to persuade her to park the car there. Then she insisted they visit all the pubs and clubs around Grafton Street. He felt like her bodyguard shadowing her, as she partied from one spot to the next, both of them attracting too much attention because of how they were dressed. She danced and flirted outrageously with men she met on the way.

At six o'clock in the morning, Peter found himself in a smoky basement wine bar sitting beside Audrey who was drinking red wine. All the time the repercussions of the night flitting through his mind.

"Do you think I look better in black or white?" she asked him seriously.

"Huh?" He was exhausted and wished he could persuade her to go home.

"Black or white? I think I prefer black. However sometimes white contrasts better with my colouring. What do you think?"

"Does it matter?" he asked wearily.

"Actually, yes, it does. These things are important for

my career." She was still slurring her words, but not as badly as before.

"I don't think you have a career any more. Nor do I, for that matter."

"What do you mean?"

"Your antics tonight. Running wild around the place. Remember?"

"Haven't a clue what you're talking about. I'm feeling tired now, and want to go home."

At last, he thought.

He drove her car through the deserted Dublin streets to the address she'd given him. Audrey was asleep in the passenger seat. He found it hard to believe that someone so peaceful could cause so much trouble. He found the Academy Apartments in Sandymount and pulled into the carpark. It was a small Victorian apartment block. Very elegant and tasteful.

"Come on, Audrey." He pulled her out of the car and, putting his arm around her shoulder led her, half sleeping, to the building. Opening the main door with her key, he led her up the stairs to her apartment on the first floor. He positioned her against the wall as he took her handbag and desperately searched through it for her apartment key. Not being able to find it, he tried to shake her awake.

"We're locked out. Where's the key?"

He couldn't get any sense from her and she slid down the wall onto the floor. There was a window open at the end of the corridor. He went to it and saw that a ledge led to an open window in Audrey's apartment.

It wasn't that high up, and after one glance at Audrey, a crumpled wreck on the floor, he was out the window and carefully shuffling along trying not to look down. It seemed to take forever, but he finally reached the open window.

Pulling wide the window, he started to climb in. He already had one foot inside on the window sill, and was carefully raising the other when suddenly the window slammed back, knocking him off balance. He felt himself flying through the air.

Audrey awoke to the sound of a loud roar. She looked around, her head throbbing, and wondered what she was doing in the corridor. She managed to get up and wandered over to the open window. Looking down, she saw Peter Reynolds stretched out on top of a skip full of rubbish bags.

"What are you doing down there?" she called. He didn't answer.

She quickly made her way downstairs and, standing by the skip, she looked in at him and asked, "What are you doing in the rubbish?"

"I fell from the ledge outside your apartment." He was dazed and sore but the rubbish had given him a relatively soft landing.

"Let's get you out of there." She gave him her hand.

He was shaken and now it was her turn to let him rest his arm around her as she led him back into the block. She rang the caretaker's apartment.

"What all the fuss about?" he asked as he opened his door and saw Audrey propping up a dishevelled man.

"I need the spare key," she said.

"Do you know the time?" he snarled.

"Just the key, please," she said dismissively.

He gave her a disapproving look and went to find it.

They traipsed across the landing, while a neighbour's daughter stood at an open door staring at them in amazement.

As Audrey opened the door of her apartment she asked Peter, "Do you need to see a doctor?"

"I'm fine. Just need some sleep." He winced as he stretched out on the couch. Then, sinking into the mattress, he fell asleep immediately.

Audrey went into the kitchen, drank a glass of water and ran her fingers through her hair

Coming back into the living area she looked down at Peter sleeping. She could remember little episodes. Episodes that filled her with revulsion and fear. She got a duvet from the airing cupboard and put it over Peter and wearily headed to her bedroom.

CHAPTER 12

Audrey's head throbbed when she woke up the next day. She looked at her clock and saw it was ten. As she lay in bed staring at the ceiling, there was a strange unreality about her memories of the previous night, as if it had all been a dream. The episodes she could remember started linking together, providing a horrible sequence of events. She closed her eyes tightly, wishing the images away.

Remembering Peter, she pulled her dressing-gown around her and went to check on him. Maybe her memory was exaggerating everything. Maybe it wasn't as bad as she thought. Peter would be the key to unlock the chain of events.

"Peter!" She gently nudged him awake.

He got a shock and sat up quickly, forgetting his injury from the fall, and shouted in pain. "I'll grab you a painkiller." She walked into the kitchen, rubbing her temples to try and ease her own pain from her hangover. In the kitchen she dropped some tablets into a glass of water.

"I'll call you a doctor," she said, handing him the glass of fizzing liquid.

"No, I'm fine," he insisted. "The rubbish skip broke the fall, thank God"

She wanted to ask him about the night, to seek reassurance that it wasn't as bad as she remembered.

"I can't remember much," she said eventually, looking down at the floor.

He wasn't sure which emotion he felt most towards her, hate or pity. "Probably just as well."

"That bad? I'd better ring Hazel."

"I'd give it a while. Prepare yourself first."

"Why do I always ruin things for myself?" She ran her fingers through her hair again. "A few hours ago everything was brilliant. Now I've probably ruined my career –"

"Our careers," he corrected.

"What's my behaviour got to do with you?"

"Because it was my show. And it was a disaster." He remembered his words to Chloe: 'The buck stops here.'

"But they can't blame you for my mistake." Audrey was consumed with guilt.

"A lot was resting on last night. And I have enemies who were looking for an excuse to finish me off."

Audrey was visibly upset. "I'm sorry, so sorry. I'll write them a letter and tell them it was all my fault. That it would be unfair to take it out on you."

Her unexpected innocence about dealing with a situation like this touched him.

"Yeah, we'll work something out." He sat up.

There was something in the way Peter spoke that Audrey found reassuring. That told her everything would be all right. That they could salvage something from this mess.

"I'd better go." He stood up and pulled on his shirt.

"I'll call you a cab."

"It's OK. I'll find one outside."

As he moved to the door, she felt a strange sense of loss. She knew he had looked after her all night. She didn't want to lose that protection. She knew it was just the fear of the situation she was in , but she felt if he walked out the door she would be left to deal with reality and her world would fall apart.

"Peter," she called, "thanks for watching out for me! Thanks for making sure I got home all right."

He nodded and opened the door.

"I'll give you a call later," she said.

He smiled sadly. "Don't take it personally, Audrey, but please don't."

He walked back in to the direction of town. He cut a strange figure walking along in a tuxedo at that time in the morning.

A couple of women joggers ran by.

"Are you just coming from your Debs?" called one after him, and she laughed.

He couldn't put it off. He would have to face the music, starting with Lynn.

Gently, he eased the key into their front door. But Lynn wasn't there. He had a hot shower and changed into casual clothes. He cooked and ate breakfast and then headed in to The Gallery.

He found Lynn sitting at her desk looking through a brochure.

"I was about to call the guards." Her voice was angry more than concerned.

"I had to look after Audrey. She was a mess."

"I think the whole country knows that!"

"I didn't get out of her apartment till this morning."

"Nice to know where your priorities lie."

"Don't try to twist it around. You said you didn't want me near you last night."

"I didn't mean for the whole night." She got up abruptly and lit herself a cigarette. Lynn only smoked during times of extreme stress.

"I have to say you surpassed yourself," she dragged on the cigarette, "and that takes some doing"

"She went nuts on alcohol. What could I do?"

"It was the most disastrous night I've ever been at. The public humilation that bitch threw at me!"

"If it makes you feel better, she feels terrible this morning."

"I couldn't give a shit! It's always the same with you."

"What are you talking about?"

"No matter what you do, it's guaranteed to end up pear-shaped in the end. No matter what support I give, you fuck up in the end. Even our wedding day!"

Peter had a flashback to the beautiful marquee erected at his family home, and how it had started to collapse during the speeches. He banished the thought.

"You should have been more in control last night! *As always!*" Her voice had risen to a shout. There was silence for a minute while Lynn smoked away. "Your problem is and always has been the fact you don't believe in yourself. You have the ability. You have the talent. You have the brains. But you don't believe you have and that's why everything you do gets fucked up at the last minute. You're scared of success. Scared to allow yourself to succeed. That's why Michael Cassidy is sitting on a beach in Portugal with a wad of money that you made for him. And I am tired of pushing you and supporting you only to get results like last night."

He sat down. "If my own wife thinks that, what can I expect from Macken Communications?"

"This won't affect your standing with them."

"Of course it will. Chloe Gallagher wants the old Blast staff out. She was out for my blood anyway, and she has it now."

Lynn's anger was replaced by fear. "You're not suggesting . . . they couldn't . . ."

"Fire me?" he said the words for her. "Yes, they could. That's a PR's lot. If an event is successful you get pushed to the background while everyone else takes the credit. If it's disastrous the PR gets all the blame."

"We aren't in a financially stable enough position for you to lose your job – the mortgage!"

"I know."

"So why are you here and not in your office trying to sort it out?"

"Nobody goes into the office first thing after a big night like last night."

"They do if it ended up like your show did!"

"Will you shut up and let me deal with this my way?" His voice was raised. "The dust needs to settle for a few hours. I need to gather my thoughts so I know what to say."

Lynn stubbed out her cigarette. "Peter, I don't want this insecurity in my life. I don't want to worry about mortgage repayments and bills. I want a life where I'm somebody. Where I have social standing and no money hassles."

"Why didn't you marry a millionaire then?"

"I saw the potential in you. You have the ability to get to the top. If you could only see it in yourself."

"And did being in love feature in your reasons for marrying me at all?"

82

Lynn became exasperated and sat behind her desk. "Of course, it did. If you are going to sit there talking rubbish, instead of talking about the practicalities of solving this situation, then we're wasting time."

"What do you expect me to do?"

"Just sort it out, Peter."

CHAPTER 13

It was just after lunch when Peter walked into the Reception at Blast. The receptionist gave him a sympathetic smile.

"I guess you heard?"

She nodded. "Every last detail. Sorry."

"Has Macken been on looking for me?"

"No. They summoned everyone else over to their office this morning and they haven't come back yet."

"But they didn't ask for me?" He was surprised. He should have been the first person they wanted to see after the debacle last night. "Could you get Jack Houlihan from Childwatch on the phone for me?"

Why hadn't they rung looking for him? Why were they meeting everyone else?

As Peter sat down at his desk, questions kept spinning through his mind.

Reception rang and he picked up his phone.

"Peter, Jack Houlihan's secretary said he was at a meeting and wasn't expected back today," the receptionist informed him.

"I see. Thanks."

"I have this morning's papers if you want to take a look through them."

The receptionist had thoughtfully marked the pages where the fashion show had been reviewed. As expected, it was bad. The only thing that had saved the situation from being worse was the fact that it had been late when Audrey erupted and the papers were going to press, so the journalists couldn't go into too much analysis. However, he could look forward to the Sunday papers to finish off the job and really go in for the kill. Audrey was disliked enough for the vultures to be ready to pounce.

He read one of the articles:

"What was supposed to be one of the social highlights of the year turned into farce last night with an unexpected turn. Top model and socialite Audrey Driver, who was modelling in the Childwatch Fashion Show, acted in a bizarre fashion. After much stumbling on stage, she collapsed. When two security guards went to assist her, she assaulted one of them. As shocked guests looked on, Ms Driver proceeded to attack members of the audience verbally. As she had just been named as the new face of Silk Shampoo in America there was much speculation. Witnesses said she was drunk and some suggested drugs. However, her agent, Hazel Harte from the Boom Agency, insists otherwise. 'Audrey has been under intense pressure recently,' said Ms Harte. 'With her contractual obligations as well as taking on her new role in the States she's been working very hard, and I guess reached breaking point.'

Meanwhile there was no comment either from Childwatch or Blast PR, the organisers of the event. However Chloe Gallagher of Macken Communications, parent company of Blast, was quick to distance the company from Audrey's behaviour saying, "The event has been a success in that we reached our target for raising funds. Although we cannot control the behaviour of an individual, we are carrying out an investigation into what happened."

Reading quickly through the other papers, Peter realised they were all much the same. Staring at the phone, he waited for it to ring. Waited for the dreaded call from Chloe summoning him to the Macken Offices.

He scribbled on notepaper his best lines of defence. But it was useless until he heard what they had to say. Blast remained eerily quiet for the rest of the day as none of the Account Managers returned. By six o'clock nobody had rung for him. The waiting had been much worse than the call that never came could have been.

Feeling exhausted, and with his back still hurting him from the fall, he grabbed his jacket and stood up.

The receptionist was putting on her coat too.

"Nobody rang for me today at all?" He was incredulous.

She looked embarrassed. "Chloe told me all calls for you were to be immediately forwarded to herself."

"You mean she's been taking my calls?"

"'Fraid so. Go home and sleep, Peter. You look exhausted."

Little chance of that, he thought, with Lynn waiting for him with a million questions.

Audrey had turned off her mobile, plugged out the main-line phone, taken to her bed and ignored the world for the whole day. At seven in the evening she forced herself to get up, wrapped herself in a silk dressing-gown and studied herself in the mirror. She looked a mess. She felt alone and scared. She imagined what everyone would be saying about her and it hurt. It hurt most because it had been all so unnecessary. Her golden rule was never to drink.

Why had she broken it? Why had she pressed the self-destruct button? She had been swept away with the euphoria of the contract. What must be going through Aran's mind? He must have been trying to phone her all day. She cringed as she remembered that his parents had witnessed the whole scene. She couldn't bear to think about it any more and headed back to bed. I'll deal with it tomorrow, she thought.

"They didn't call you? Then why didn't you call them?" demanded Lynn.

Peter poured himself a brandy. "They're the bosses. They see me when they want to. And they'll ring me when they want to."

"So what did you do all day? Sit waiting for the phone to ring?"

"In a word, yes."

"What was I saying today about taking control of situations?"

"Lynn, I'm shattered from last night. My back is still sore from the fall –"

"Fall?" She looked concerned.

"Long story. Can we just leave it till tomorrow?"

CHAPTER 14

Audrey jumped out of bed at eight, fixed herself a healthy breakfast and ran a hot steaming bath. She soaked in the scented water for a full hour, before selecting a "Knock 'em dead" outfit from her wardrobe. She applied her make-up meticulously, and brushed her hair, leaving it flowing and luxuriant.

She checked her appearance one last time and strode out to face the world.

Peter felt much better after a few hours' sleep. Lynn had left the apartment early, probably to avoid further confrontation. As he showered he felt he could face whatever they threw at him. Whatever they said, he would be ready.

Having found a convenient parking space, Audrey walked confidently the short distance to Boom. It was only when she got to the steps leading up to the Agency, that she felt sick in her stomach.

"C'mon, it'll be fine," she whispered to herself and climbed the steps.

As Audrey opened the front door, the whole agency became silent. She stood still, taking in their expressions. Some were startled, some sympathetic, others smug. She ignored them all and went to Hazel's door. Seeing Hazel was occupied on the phone, she gently opened her office door and stepped in. As she closed the door behind her, the agency erupted in talk.

Hazel was winding up her call. "Sure, sure, I'll get those pics over to you today and let me know what you think. I think she's the girl you're looking for." She hung up and looked at Audrey. "Well, well, she has decided to grace us with her presence!" Hazel sat back in her swivel-chair and lit a cigarette, "I tried phoning you all day yesterday."

"I was in bed."

"I'm not surprised." She gestured to a chair opposite her. "Sit."

Audrey did as commanded.

"There isn't any point in having a post-mortem on what you did. I think you know how bad it was. I kept yesterday's papers for you, if you need reminding. Let's just deal with the consequences. Firstly you've lost the Silk contract. I suppose you guessed that."

Audrey's heart sank. She had guessed it, but it didn't make hearing the confirmation any better.

"I did try my best to salvage it," continued Hazel. "But Ricky Nash wasn't having any of it."

"I'm sorry you lost your commission. I'm sorry about everything."

"Let's keep sentimentality out of this and be pragmatic. All existing contracts you're in have been cancelled. I've threatened to sue them; they've told me you've broken the contracts by your reputation being in disrepute. I'm not prepared to spend money investigating this legally when I can just have you replaced by another model and keep my commission." She softened her tone when she saw the hurt look on Audrey's face. "Business is business, and I can't afford to be sentimental. This is nothing to do with me or Boom. The fact is, Audrey, nobody is going to want to hire you after what happened."

"I could try other agencies."

"Fire ahead. But to save you time, I can tell you that you've become unemployable as a model."

Audrey breathed in deeply.

"What does Aran say about it all?" Hazel asked.

"I haven't spoken to him yet."

"Why don't you take some time out? Go back to your family in the country. Give yourself some time and space from all this."

Audrey became angry and her voice rose. "That's what everyone wants, me to just go away quietly! Well, I'm not going to slip away. I've come too far to do that."

"No. You *had* come a long way. It's in the past now. Nobody will hire you."

"All I can do is model. I can't do anything else."

"Get it through your head, for your own sake. That world is over for you. Being high profile is over for you." Hazel looked at the despair on Audrey's face and softened her voice again. "The only thing you can do is join the commercial sector doing promotional work and going to castings."

"Start at the bottom again?" Audrey was horrified. "At my age? I can't lower myself to do that."

"It's all I can offer."

Peter's initial upbeat mood wavered as the day progressed

and still no call came from Macken. He felt isolated as none of the Account Executives arrived to work at Blast. When he questioned the receptionist, she told him all she knew was that they were out with clients.

He sat swivelling in his chair, looking out the window. When the phone finally rang at five thirty he jumped into the air.

"Mr. Reynolds?"

"Yeah."

"This is Mr Macken's PA. Could you please be at the Macken building at six-fifteen this evening precisely." Her tone was clipped upper-class. The phone went dead after she finished speaking. She hadn't even waited for a response.

As instructed, he rang the doorbell at Macken at exactly six-fifteen.

"This way, Mr Reynolds," a receptionist said and led him to the boardroom. The building seemed more hushed than usual and he assumed most people had gone home.

The receptionist knocked on the boardroom door, opened it, and gestured for him to enter.

Brendan Macken sat at the top of the board table, with Vincent to his left, and Chloe to his right. All three faces were stern and expressionless.

"Take a seat," instructed Vincent.

Peter tried to ignore his nerves and sat down.

"The show," Brendan Macken stated simply.

"Needless to say the night was a disaster which has badly damaged Blast's reputation and tarnished Macken's as well," said Vincent

"And destroyed your own reputation," finished Chloe.

"We feel the responsibility for the fiasco must lie squarely with the Account Manager in charge," said Brendan.

"The buck stops with you," Chloe reminded him of his own expression.

"The night was grossly mismanaged and you rejected any advice offered along the way," said Vincent. "Most worrying of all, you allowed alcohol backstage when you are aware there is a strict anti-drink ethos in this company."

At last Peter had an accusation he could fight back on. "I didn't allow alcohol backstage."

"Banqueting at The Berkeley informed us alcohol was ordered for the models by you," said Chloe.

"I forbid drink backstage! Anyone can tell you that! There's some kind of mix-up. I don't know, perhaps one of the models ordered it."

"That's not possible," said Chloe. "The Blast credit-card details were handed to the hotel's Banqueting Department, and the order was registered as coming from you."

"I can't explain how that happened," said Peter.

"It's certainly a mystery," said Brendan. "We've put a lot of manpower into damage limitation. Childwatch are understandably furious. We've had to come to a costly financial arrangement with them to avoid being sued."

Peter prepared himself for the next line where he expected to be fired.

"It's apparent to us you lack the ability to run an event of this size. We feel you don't act professionally under pressure," said Chloe. "We want you to leave Blast –" Peter's heart sank, "and come to work here at Macken," she concluded.

His heart rose. "Here?"

"I've drawn up a new contract for you to sign," said Vincent. "You'll no longer be an Account Executive. Your strengths, if I can use that word after the show, lie in copywriting and devising PR plans."

"You'll have no further contact with the Press or clients," continued Chloe. "You'll be working solely on drafting press releases and ideas. This –" Chloe paused before saying the dreaded word, "demotion – will be reflected in a decrease in your salary."

Vincent indicated a paper on the table before him. "I have also drawn up this written warning for you to sign. It indicates you are guilty of mismanagement. You must sign it before we offer you this new contract." He pushed the warning across the table. "Please sign it now. We want to wrap this up quickly."

Peter sat in shock, not knowing what to say or do. This was humiliation on a grand scale. All eyes stared at him, warning him not to waste time. He took stock quickly. His career was in tatters. What other PR firm would touch him now? The mortgage needed paying and Lynn would never understand or forgive him if he walked out. He took the sheet of paper and read quickly through it.

It was full of legal jargon. He grabbed a pen and scribbled his signature on it. Chloe passed him his new contract and he gulped when he saw the reduction in salary. Again he scribbled his signature.

"Please report to me at nine-thirty in the morning and I'll show you to your new office," instructed Chloe.

Peter stood up, said "Thank you." and left.

The three waited until he had closed the door before speaking.

"I still think we should've just fired him," said Vincent.

"We made the right decision. We have him exactly where we want him. We can take advantage of his excellent skills and ideas for future projects without him being actually involved," said Brendan.

"And if we let him go, there's always the chance he'd

find another job and we'd risk risk losing that talent," agreed Chloe.

Vincent was unconvinced. "He wouldn't find a job that easily now after that show. We're giving him a chance to rehabilitate himself with Macken."

"Look, we're burying him in copywriting, where nobody will even know where he is after a while. Besides," Chloe smiled, "by the time I've finished with him, his confidence will be so low, he won't even stand up without first asking permission."

Audrey sat in her apartment that evening in a state of depression. She'd contacted all the other agencies that afternoon but none was interested in meeting her after her spate of bad publicity. She should be preparing to go to New York – instead her life was in tatters. Switching her thoughts from her career to Aran, she was surprised he hadn't phoned that day. She had gone to dial his number many times but had drawn back, too embarrassed, not knowing what to say. Not knowing how to explain her behaviour. She'd wait until he contacted her and she was sure he would come by the apartment that night. His parents would be putting him under huge pressure to dump her. Within the tight monied circle his family mixed in, she had embarrassed him by her actions. So many thoughts rushed through her head. She knew he loved her. She knew she cared deeply about him. The pragmatic side of her realised Aran could rescue her from the mess she was in. She could be rescued from her disastrous career by marrying him. He'd hinted at marriage before. But as much as she liked him, she also knew he wanted to control her and he had informed her if their relationship was to have a future she would have to give up her career. And now with her career over, she would have no independence from him. The problem with Aran had always been his insane jealousy. He hated her talking to other people, or doing anything with anyone other than himself.

Sometimes she had felt smothered in the relationship and reacted by trying to get her own space back. This used to drive him crazy and he used to accuse her of treating him badly. Now that her career was effectively over, he would have complete control over her.

By midnight, the doorbell still hadn't rung.

Peter was very surprised to see the change in mood in Lynn when he arrived home. She sat at the table, nervously smoking and looking scared. Her usual confidence had vanished. Her earlier anger was now gone. He realised how desperately worried she was about his job.

"Well?" she asked.

"Well, I still have a job."

The tension evaporated from her face as she was swept by relief.

"Before you get overexcited, it's not great news. They've brought me over to work at Macken in a new position with a lower salary."

"But they didn't fire you?"

"No. But the knife has been pushed in a long way." He handed her the new contract.

She gasped when she saw his new salary. "Can we live on this?"

"We won't have the same lifestyle, but we will be able to afford the mortgage – just."

"The bastards!" she spat. "But we've bought some time. After you've worked on some new projects with

Macken the show will be long forgotten. Then they can either give you a promotion or you can move on."

His heart went out to Lynn, listening to her trying to rescue the situation in her mind. She wanted that comfortable life with no worries so much. He chose not to tell her his career would be given no opportunity to resurface at Macken.

He sat down and hugged her tightly. "Yeah, of course. Everything's going to be OK."

CHAPTER 15

Audrey got up early the next morning, as she had a lot to do. She rang Boom first thing. "Hazel, it's Audrey here. I've been doing a lot of thinking and, if you'll have me, I'd like to join the commercial section." She could almost hear Hazel drag on her cigarette.

"You're sure about that? You know how big a back step it is?"

"I'm sure."

"Fine, come in and see Ben Egan."

Then she rang the estate agent and cancelled the purchase of the second property she was negotiating. Then she popped into her Bank Manager to see how she was fixed financially. She had managed to earn quite a bit over the years. Luckily she had bought her apartment in cheaper times and ploughed a lot of her earnings into paying off the mortgage quickly. So although she wasn't cash rich, she was secure in her home. There was no need to panic.

She was devastated Aran hadn't phoned. Having said that, she reasoned, she hadn't picked up the phone to him either. He could be equally as devastated.

And looking at the situation logically, it had been she

who had acted appallingly in public and she should be the one to ring first. She had arranged to go into the commercial section at Boom at two and, just before that, she sat in her car, breathed deeply and rang Aran's mobile. Nervously, she waited for him to answer. But after ringing for a minute it went into his message minder. She then rang his office only to be told he was at a meeting.

"I can't promise you anything straight away," Ben Egan, who headed the commercial section, told her honestly. "You're a well-known face, and lots of Marketing Managers prefer unknown faces to advertise their products. That's because they don't want their cans of soup or whatever overshadowed."

She nodded, understanding that what he said made sense.

"Also, you're a bit too striking for what Commercial usually wants."

"I never thought such a compliment could make me feel so down," she smirked.

Luckily, she had always got on well with Ben. Even though she didn't know him that well, they had never had a run-in. She knew if it was one of the other bookers they would be delighted to gloat over her downfall as they sent her out to badly paid unglamorous jobs. Ben, however, had greeted her with a sympathetic smile, and made no reference to her now notorious behaviour.

"Did you think about changing your look?" he questioned.

"In what way?"

"Play down your looks. Cut the hair, different make-up. Dress down. Changing your image may make you more employable."

She panicked with each word coming from his mouth.

She glanced over to two models whispering and giving her smug looks. She couldn't even contemplate doing it.

"No, I'm happy with the way I look. I'm not going to mess around and give them all another reason to bitch about me."

Ben nodded. "Well, I suppose then, we'll just start sending you to castings and see what happens. I think I can get you promotional work without too much hassle, handing out leaflets at events, that kind of thing."

She forced the tears not to fall, as she thought of how the mighty had fallen.

Peter was kept waiting by Chloe for a full hour in reception.

"Ms Gallagher will see you now, Peter," said the receptionist finally. He had always thought it sounded stuffy and old-fashioned when staff at Macken had called him Mr Reynolds in the past. The irony wasn't lost on him that the newly found first-name familiarity reflected his new lowly status. He followed the receptionist upstairs, down a corridor and to a door that she knocked on before opening.

As he expected it was a large grand office. Chloe sat behind an ornate desk and she seemed busy signing documents.

"Take a seat," she instructed without looking up from her work, which she took her time to finish. Finally she sat back and took off her reading glasses which he had never seen her wear before.

"Peter, these are press releases I want you to work on." She handed him a large pile of papers. "The writing is poor in them as it stands, certainly not eye-catching. This –" she handed him another bundle of paper, "is information about a computer firm, one of our clients, who are compiling a brochure. I want you to condense this info, taking out the important parts. And this –" more paper came his way, "is all about another client's new product. I want you to devise me a full PR plan, full of innovative ideas. All your work must be handed directly back to me, nobody else. And company policy dictates that you must not discuss your work with co-workers."

He got the picture. He would do all the work, and she would get the credit.

She placed her reading glasses on the desk. "I suppose I should tell you that Macken operates very differently from most PR companies, certainly from what you're used to at Blast. We don't believe a loud jovial atmosphere contributes to good work. We're the top end of the market dealing with blue-chip companies and giving serious PR. Our work ethic is what has us at the top for so long." She searched his face for a reaction and finding none continued. "I know at Blast everyone tended to go out for drinks together after work etc. We frown upon that here. Obviously our Account Executives have to socialise at events for clients, but that won't apply to your role. What I'm saying, Peter, is keep your head down and get on with your work. Any questions?"

He wanted to throw all the paper at her and shout, stand up and storm out.

"No, I understand," he answered.

"Good. Then I'll show you to your office."

Following her up the winding staircase to the third and the fourth floor, he wondered if they were putting him on the roof. It might as well have been as she stopped at a door and opened it. His office was a small attic, with just a skylight, and a bare desk apart from a computer.

He sat down and looked around.

"If you need anything, let me know," she said.

He switched on the computer. "Thanks, Chloe."

Her face froze and she approached his desk "There's a kind of rule here, a code. Junior staff don't address senior staff by first name. Now because we started working originally on a more even keel I don't mind you calling me Chloe. But in front of others, it's Ms Gallagher, OK?"

Leaving Boom, Audrey bumped straight into Leslie.

"Hi, I left loads of messages on your phone? How are you feeling now?" enquired Leslie.

"A bit better, I suppose. Do you want to grab a coffee?"

They went and found a little pub around the corner and ordered two cappuccinos.

"So I've joined the Commercial section," Audrey explained. "What else could I do? Modelling is all I know . . . I guess a lot of the girls are delighted."

"You know what they're like. Delighted at somebody else's downfall."

"Let's face it, I didn't go out of my way to enamour myself to everyone over the years. I made a lot of enemies what with my temper and when I let my head get too big."

"You made a lot of friends too." Leslie put a comforting hand on Audrey's.

"Thanks, Leslie."

"What does Aran say about it all?"

"I haven't even spoken to him yet."

"No?"

"I rang him today, so I guess we'll meet up later. Really not looking forward to it. I showed him up as much as myself."

"He'll support you no matter what."

Aran didn't know what to do. Sitting in his office he looked at his mobile which showed a missed call from Audrey. He deliberately hadn't answered it. Since the show he'd had nothing but blazing rows with his parents. And that had stopped him even having time to sort out his own thoughts on the whole issue.

They had shouted and insisted he finish with Audrey immediately.

"I don't care who you see, as long as it's not her," wailed Muriel.

He had retorted that he was in his early thirties, and old enough to decide himself who he wanted to go out with. Then both his mother and father had said they would have nothing more to do with Audrey. They also pointed out he was jeopardising his future and reputation by being associated with her.

And in the middle of all the rowing, he realised Audrey hadn't phoned him once. Not once in two days. Not to check how he was. Not to tell him she was OK. Nothing. Now he was very confused. Did she just expect that he wouldn't dream of abandoning her and was she taking him for granted? Then there was the subtle rumour circulating that she had spent the night with Peter Reynolds. They had been seen trawling through Dublin's nightspots. He loved her, but he had always been uncertain how much she loved him. Her not contacting him till that afternoon left him feeling hurt and unsure.

Aran's secretary rang in to him. "Chloe Gallagher from Macken Communications on the line."

"Put her through." He remembered her kindness the night of the show.

"Hi, how are you?" Her voice was cheery.

"Fine, thanks."

"I was just checking to see how Audrey was."

He hesitated before speaking. He didn't know Chloe that well and didn't want to give her too much information. Especially as she had already seen him vulnerable the night of the show.

"She must be upset she lost the contract in the States?" Chloe sounded sympathetic and she also seemed to know more about what was happening to Audrey than he did. So, thought, Aran, there had been a big price to pay for Audrey's behaviour. He felt bad for her, as he knew how much that contract had meant to her.

"It's been a disaster trying to sort out the fallout from the show. Childwatch were furious," continued Chloe.

"I can understand why."

"Not that I'm blaming Audrey or anything. I feel responsible for letting somebody incompetent in charge."

"Peter Reynolds?"

"Although to be fair to him he did look after Audrey for the night."

So what Aran's friends had told him was correct.

"Aran, as I said before, if you need to talk, I'm here."

Maybe that's what he needed. To talk to somebody removed from the situation. His family and friends were too biased against Audrey. Also, Chloe seemed to have a lot of information about what happened.

"Are you around after work for a drink?" he asked.

"Just let me check the diary. Meeting at six, but I should be finished by seven."

"Cool. I'll meet you in Café en Seine."

CHAPTER 16

"Well, you can always come home. Your room is always waiting for you," said Audrey's mother, Kathleen.

Audrey was huddled up on the sofa, pouring out her troubles to her mother on the phone. She thought of Ballyabbey, her small beautiful hometown. The drab boring place she had longed to escape from. It wasn't even an option to return. However, her mother's words were reassuring and comforting.

"Thanks, Mum, I know. But I've come too far to give it all up now."

"Drink never suited you. Remember your cousin Laura's wedding when you were eighteen? I had to ring everybody up the next day to apologise."

Audrey raised her eyes to heaven. "Don't start dragging up ancient history, Mum. I know it doesn't suit me. That's why I never touch the stuff, usually. I just got carried away with the contract."

"Could you go abroad? I'm sure London or Paris agencies would sign you up, a beautiful girl like yourself."

"I'm too old."

"For God's sake, you're only twenty-nine!"

"I'm too old in this business to start from scratch abroad. It was different with Silk Shampoo, I was going in as an established model. But when models are starting off, they sign them up at sixteen or seventeen."

"I never heard such rubbish," snapped Kathleen, causing Audrey to smile. She always liked her mother's straight talking.

They said their goodbyes and hung up. Aran hadn't returned her call, leaving her anxious and hurt. In fact a lot of people she had considered friends in Dublin hadn't called her since her downfall. But Aran not calling hurt by far the most.

Café en Seine was nicely full. Aran found a corner table and waited for Chloe.

When she arrived a couple of minutes later it was a welcome change. Audrey sometimes kept him waiting for up to an hour. Chloe was dressed in a black business suit and carried a slim briefcase.

"How's Audrey today?" she asked him, having ordered a gin and tonic.

Maybe this was a mistake, he thought. He wasn't sure what to say.

"Well . . . she lost her contract in the States," he said, repeating what he had heard from Chloe herself earlier.

"I hear their PR was pretty pissed off," said Chloe. "They'd spent a lot of time and money on the selection process and then all this exploded. To be honest, I know everyone is giving out about Audrey, but I feel sorry for her."

"Why?"

"Because she has lost so much. Her career is over. And as I said today, it's as much Peter Reynolds' fault."

"Was he fired?"

"It came close but we decided not to. Peter's a talented guy. But we now know he's more suited to backroom stuff."

"And he did look after Audrey that night." Again Aran probed by giving Chloe back her own information.

"To his credit, yes. God knows what would have happened to her otherwise."

"He brought her home?"

"Mmm," she nodded while taking a sip of her drink. "And stayed the night, it appears. At least, someone saw him making his way home the next morning."

Aran tried to read her expression. He suddenly felt he was becoming a laughing-stock. Not only had Audrey shown him up, and waited two days to call him, but now there was this hint being sniggered around that something had happened between herself and Reynolds. It was too much for him to take. Studying Chloe's sympathetic and good-looking features, he remembered his father's firm had recently employed her company to do some PR for them. He might be seeing a lot of her and he didn't want her thinking he was still seeing Audrey under these circumstances. He didn't want to look like a fool.

"Actually, I'm not seeing Audrey at the moment. We're taking a break."

More sympathy oozed out of her eyes as she lightly placed a hand on his. "I'm sorry to hear that. You made a great couple."

"I'm not saying it's over for good," he covered himself. "We're just not seeing each other at the moment."

Lynn hadn't gone to work that day, but had spent it in bed. When things got bad, she always did this. It was her self-defence mechanism.

Peter leaned against the door after closing it when he came home. What he wanted was sympathy and understanding. He wanted to be able to pour out all the troubles of the day to his wife. What he wanted her to say was that they would manage. That the apartment didn't matter and they could always move to a smaller place. That she would support him no matter what, because what was important at the end of the day was they had each other.

What he got was the sight of Lynn in bed in the exact position she had been that morning. He remembered what Chloe had said about picturing Lynn married into the aristocracy and living in a manor. He could see it too. It was the life she always craved and wanted. To be secure and wealthy with a high profile.

He sat on the bed and touched her. She stirred and looked up at him.

"How was it?"

"Good."

"Really?"

"They've put me to work on some big projects. It's not like at Blast. But you know, I was thinking. In a year's time, having been with Macken, my CV will be brilliant. Macken's the biggest and the best. I'll be able to have my pick of jobs."

"Do you really think so." The light was coming back into her eyes.

"Yep."

She pulled herself up and started running her fingers through her hair.

"Are you going back to work tomorrow?" he asked.

"I'll try."

CHAPTER 17

Chloe had to admit after reading through Peter's work that he was good. She was scheduled for a meeting at Murphy Hennessy, Aran's father's firm, that afternoon concerning the latest political lobbying they wanted Macken to do for them. She had set Peter to work on different ideas that she could propose, and all his suggestions were excellent.

She dialled his number on the internal phone. "Peter, could you come to my office, please?"

Five minutes later he dutifully knocked on her door.

"This work for Murphy Hennessy is fine. But these press releases need more attention. I feel you aren't putting your all into them."

"I can't see how they could be improved," he objected.

"There's always room for improvement." Chloe's face turned sour. "When I ask for something to be done, I don't want back-answers. You understand me? My way or no way".

He wondered if she treated everybody in Macken like this, or if she reserved extra contempt for him. What shocked him most was how nice she had come across when they had first met. He put the paperwork back in his office and then headed to the kitchen and staff rest area on the third floor. There he found people divided into small groups, talking quietly. He noticed the administrative staff and PRs never sat together. He remembered some stupid rule about them not mixing. After pouring himself a cup of coffee, he went and sat by himself.

"Anyone sitting here?" asked a blond man, about the same age as himself.

"No, go ahead."

"I'm Dermot." The man put out his hand and Peter shook it.

"I'm –"

"I know who you are." Dermot smiled and sat down.

"I'm glad somebody does. I thought I was invisible the way everyone looks through me here."

"Don't take it personally. It's company policy. So you're settling in all right?"

"Yeah, sure is a real warm friendly place," said Peter, putting on a Southern States accent.

Dermot smiled at his sarcasm. "We like to make people feel at home."

At last, thought Peter, he had met somebody here who not only seemed human, but was also on his wavelength.

"What do you do?" Peter asked.

"Account Manager."

"Tell me, why does everyone here look so serious?"

"Shhhh . . . keep your voice low!" Dermot was keeping his own voice to a whisper. "The walls have ears. Because it's a serious company offering serious PR. Square-jawed men, dark suits, no frivolity allowed." Dermot suddenly looked nervous. Chloe had entered the staffroom.

She glanced at them as she got a can of Diet Coke out

of the fridge. Without acknowledging anybody, she then left.

"She rarely comes into the staff area. It's too dangerous to talk in here. Meet me for a drink after work."

"All right. I'll see you in Reception."

"Don't be stupid. See you in Neary's at seven."

Chloe shook hands with Reginald Murphy and Larry Hennessy at the offices of Murphy Hennessy, which were situated in Merrion Square. She had decided to take over the running of their account personally.

"I'm very pleased you will be the one handling our account," said Larry. "We didn't expect a Director's full involvement."

"Well, you are an important client to us and we want to accommodate you in any way we can," she smiled. She guessed Larry to be approaching the sixty mark. Like Reginald, he was hugely wealthy and influential. He had never been married, and Chloe understood he had a reputation as a ladies' man.

"We are dealing with very sensitive stuff here," explained Reginald.

"I'm aware of that," she replied.

"To put it in a nutshell, our company, myself and Larry bought a sizeable amount of land here in Dublin in Finglas a number of years back as an investment. We would now like to build a shopping-centre complex on this land. However the Council has earmarked it for housing. This is where you come into the picture. We want you to lobby politicians, councils, media and whoever else you think necessary to ensure that we construct a shopping centre on that land."

"To be honest with you, this will be a very difficult

campaign," she said. "There is so much sensitivity these days concerning planning."

"That is why we want you to handle the lobbying with the utmost sensitivity," said Larry.

Aran knocked on the door and walked in.

He was surprised to see Chloe. "Sorry, I didn't realise you were in a meeting."

"Pull up a chair, Aran," said Reginald. "I want you to sit in on this. You two know each other, don't you?"

"Yes," Chloe smiled at Aran and continued. "And it's because this will be so sensitive, I've taken control of this account myself. It needs somebody at the top to handle it, and we'll all have to work closely. Firstly I'll get my staff to conduct sociological reports on the area showing it is in need of a shopping centre, and listing the spin-off effects, like employment. And I will start lobbying."

"Aran, I want you to help Chloe in any way you can on this one," said Reginald.

After Chloe had left, Larry turned to Reginald "How effective will this lobbying be?"

"We haven't a hope without it. Let's face it, Macken are the best, and Chloe Gallagher is the best they have."

Larry turned to Aran "There's a good catch for you, now you've dumped the mad model! Would you say Muriel would approve of Chloe, Reg?"

Reginald looked at his son seriously. "Muriel would approve of anybody other than Audrey Driver."

CHAPTER 18

That evening Audrey decided to try ringing Aran again. To her surprise he answered.

"Hi . . ." She was lost for words. "Where are you?"

"Still at the office."

"I tried ringing you yesterday."

"I know."

"You're avoiding me?"

"You took your time to phone me, didn't you?"

"There was a lot going through my mind," explained Audrey.

"I can imagine."

"I think we should talk. Can you come over tonight?"

"This is all very cloak and dagger." Peter sat down opposite Dermot in Neary's.

"You have to be in that place." Dermot took a gulp of the Heineken Peter had just got him. He suddenly laughed.

"What's funny?" Peter asked.

"I'm sorry but every time I see you I think of that awful Whitney Houston song 'Didn't We Almost Have It All?'!"

In spite of himself Peter started laughing too. "I certainly screwed up big time."

He realised he hadn't laughed for a long time.

"Don't be too hard on yourself. You didn't have a chance really."

"Huh?"

"First of all you had that maniac Audrey Driver on board. That shampoo in the States should pay you a huge commission from saving them from her. Secondly, the lovely Chloe is out to destroy Blast and you. It's only a matter of time before Blast is no more."

"So what did they get out of buying us?"

"You were becoming a threat. That's what Macken does. They buy up companies and gobble them up. They're ruthless and that's what keeps them at the top. You taking that Celtic Vodka account from under their noses was the final straw. They make a habit of it. Remember Calder Media? They took it over about a year ago for a huge amount of money and slowly took it apart."

"Why is she being particularly vindictive towards me?"

"Believe it or not, you were becoming really well known. I'm hearing that Whitney Houston song again. Chloe does not like being challenged as PR Supreme."

"How did she become so powerful?"

"She's genuinely brilliant at PR. Macken and Boyer, who incidentally are absolute bastards, are eating out of her hand. That's why she's a Director. She's of the same mindset as them. Destroy anything that gets in your way. That included you."

"If I had any choice I'd be out of there, but why do other people work for them?"

"For the experience. A few years with them and you can work anywhere. They also pay well."

Peter grimaced. "They aren't paying me very well."

"Even by Chloe's standards, she's been extra sadistic with you. Word of advice: be careful what you say in there and who you say it to. Never say anything bad on the phone – they're all bugged."

"You're joking."

"Wish I were. It became clear to me when I discovered they knew everything about my private life."

"That doesn't affect me anyway. They haven't even allowed me an outside telephone line."

"Just as well. You'd probably already have hung yourself. Hauled in front of them and tortured for slandering them. Macken is a cold man, pure ice running through his veins. Seen his eyes?"

"Pretty penetrating," agreed Peter.

"Sure are. And he's *sooo* puritanical."

"What's his story?"

"He has a really quiet wife who never attends any functions. And you want to know something strange about Macken? You never see him either arrive or leave work."

"What's Boyer's story?"

"Sadist. He takes great pleasure in humiliating people. There's a rumour he's separated. Of course, for the image of the firm he keeps that well hidden. I certainly wouldn't blame any wife of his from running a mile."

"And Chloe? When I was over at her house I didn't see much evidence of a personal life."

"You were at her house?" It was Dermot's turn to be intrigued. "Nobody ever visits each other's homes at Macken. Her story? She's always been photographed in the society pages with a number of eligible men."

Audrey nervously prepared herself for Aran's arrival.

When her doorbell went, she took a quick look at herself in the mirror and went to answer it. She opened the door and he casually walked in without a word. She couldn't read his mood. He seemed a mixture of angry, hurt and confused. His whole body language told her to keep away from him and so she didn't try to hug or kiss him.

"How could you be so stupid?" He didn't waste any time getting to the point.

"I wish I knew," she sat down and was wringing her hands. "A lapse of judgement."

"You should hear what my parents are saying about you. What everyone is saying about you."

"Do you know how I feel about it?"

"What about how I feel, Audrey? As always, you only care about yourself."

"I'm really sorry I showed you up." There were tears in her eyes.

"What does Hazel say about it all?"

"Well, I lost the American contract."

"I heard."

Audrey was surprised. "Bad news travels fast in this town." She decided not to tell him her career was in tatters. "But my other contracts are safe. So it won't make that much difference to my career."

"That's good."

"I don't care about my career. I care about us. How does all this leave us?"

Aran became upset and sat down. "You didn't even call me for two days."

"You didn't call me either!"

"I did! I tried phoning you all that night and the next morning. But your phone was off. Too busy out playing with Peter Reynolds!"

"What are you on about?" asked Audrey.

"Did he come back here that night?"

"Reynolds? Yeah, he looked after me because I was out of my head. Big deal."

"He spent the night here?" Aran's voice was full of venom.

"You're not suggesting . . ." Her voice trailed off as she laughed bitterly. "Me and Reynolds? Are you serious? He brought me back, very late, and had an accident with his back, so slept on the sofa."

"You wouldn't even remember if you two had been together."

"How dare you! I wouldn't do something like that no matter how pissed I was! Anyway, he behaved extremely kindly to me. It wouldn't even cross his mind. He's happily married!"

"He's finished anyway from what I hear." There was satisfaction in Aran's voice.

"What did you hear?"

"He's been demoted to the backroom. He was lucky he wasn't fired."

"He didn't deserve that. It was my mistake, not his."

"Good enough for him. I never liked him anyway, and neither did you."

"He still didn't deserve to have his career ruined."

"Who gives a shit about him anyway? Our relationship has been severely damaged."

His words were like a knife going into her heart as she realised how much she cared about him. "I can't see how this can affect us. It was a work thing that went wrong for me and has nothing to do with you at the end of the day."

"You're so naive. You know who my family are. Of

116

course your reputation is important. My parents will hit the roof if I keep seeing you."

"Oh, Aran, grow up! You're thirty-two years old. Mummy and Daddy shouldn't be able to dictate your life."

"I can't risk my position because of you. Or would you like me to leave Dad's firm?"

"Of course not!"

"No, because it's their wealth and power that you are attracted to, isn't it?"

"That's a stupid question. We can't change who we are, Aran. If I hadn't been a model, didn't have a profile, maybe you wouldn't have been interested in me."

"You've always looked after yourself first, Audrey. Always put me second and I've had enough of that."

"You want to finish it?"

"I don't know what I want at the moment. I need time to think and rebuild my trust in you. Let's just take it easy for now. We can still meet up, but I don't really want to go out in public too much. Let's see how things go . . ."

She didn't like the sound of this at all. But her confidence and ego were at an all-time low. The only thing keeping her going was Aran in her life, and so she would take what she could.

Lynn was back to her old self when he got home. His talk the previous night, painting a rosy picture of the future was what she had wanted to hear. He marvelled at how Lynn, normally so strong, could go to pieces in a crisis.

"Where were you?" she asked casually.

"Out with a guy from work called Dermot. He's an Account Manager."

She was delighted with this information "So you're making friends already?"

"They're all a nice bunch."

"Keep networking with them, Peter. This is an opportunity in disguise. You'll end up as powerful as Chloe in there."

Yes, he thought, she was definitely back to her old self, with her grasping for social and financial success. If only she knew how far down the ladder he was, she'd take to her bed for a month. But there was no point in being honest with Lynn. The fact she was smoking a cigarette was a full-sure sign she still hadn't recovered from the shock of the past few days. The truth would only spiral her into depression.

CHAPTER 19

Peter opened the file Chloe had handed him, which was entitled Murphy Hennessy.

He immediately remembered this was the family of Audrey Driver's boyfriend. The file concerned land in Finglas owned by the firm. He idly wondered if Audrey and Aran's relationship was still on. His usual sources for information had dried up. Sifting through the documents, he realised there was a bad smell about them. It was obviously an area in desperate need of housing, but he had been given the job of producing data to prove a shopping centre was more needed. Then Chloe's job would be to manipulate the political system.

"Remember, Peter," Chloe had told him during the briefing, "there are lies, there are damned lies and then there are statistics. Use whatever artistic creativity you need to adjust the data to prove this area is crying out for that shopping centre."

Easier said than done when all the data seemed to indicate otherwise, he thought.

His phone rang.

"Peter, this is Reception. Ms Gallagher is having a staff

meeting in the boardroom in thirty minutes. Please attend."

Twelve employees, most he recognised as Account Managers, filed into the boardroom with him. Chloe sat at the top of the table and waited for them to take their seats. There was no banter between the colleagues. Peter noticed they had all brought paperwork and he cursed himself for not doing the same.

Dermot took a seat by Chloe and Peter smiled over to him. Dermot, his face set in a frown, ignored him.

"For those who don't know, the new face amongst you is Peter Reynolds," began Chloe, "who has joined us as a junior."

Peter ignored the description and gave a bright smile to everyone.

"Peter, we have weekly meetings to access how projects are progressing. Because of the size of Macken, you won't always be attending, or when you do it won't necessarily be with the same colleagues. However, it's an opportunity for me to measure progress."

Peter's heart was thumping in this totally uncomfortable setting.

"Dermot, the Department of Health account you've been working on. Tell us how that's going."

Dermot cleared his throat. "I had a meeting with the Minister on Monday who explained that one of the key objectives of her department is to have an anti-smoking campaign directed towards teenagers. She feels this is being neglected, particularly for teenage girls."

"Your proposals are?" asked Chloe.

"The obvious answer is role models. For young girls, I was thinking a poster campaign in schools featuring a beautiful, healthy-looking model saying she doesn't smoke because it's un-cool, ruins her hair, that kind of thing."

Chloe smiled wryly and looked at Peter. "Maybe we could employ Audrey Driver to do it. I hear she's going cheap at the moment."

Peter blushed, but nobody raised an eyebrow at the comment.

"I don't agree with the model idea," said Chloe. "The sight of a stick insect lecturing young girls about smoking is only going to intimidate them. I feel it may even drive them to smoking to try and be as thin as the model."

Everyone around the table began interacting, giving suggestions and comments.

Peter noticed they were all extremely articulate. Which made him realise how good Chloe must have been to rise to the top there.

He was dying to suggest something, but couldn't bring himself to speak. He realised he was totally intimidated.

"I think the best idea is to get a celebrity on the posters," said Chloe. "A singer or TV personality. The girls will be able to identify more closely with this kind of a female role model. They would be more familiar with her because they already know who she is. Also she won't be as drop-dead gorgeous, so the girls won't be intimidated."

Dermot shook his head. "I did think of that, but our budget won't stretch to employing a celebrity."

"Come on, Dermot. We must be able to get somebody to do it for free." There was a sharpness in Chloe's voice.

"Can I make a suggestion?" Peter forced himself to speak and all eyes turned to him. "If the main target is teenage girls, instead of giving them a female role model, why not give them a male one? Hire a male model and have him staring dreamily down from posters, saying he only likes girls who don't smoke. Then you are back to model fees, not celebrity ones, and so it won't cost the earth."

Chloe's eyes bored into him. Everybody's expression told him it was a great idea.

"It could be a little risqué for the Department of Health," said Chloe. "Why don't you suggest it to them, Dermot? That and other ideas you've heard today."

The meeting moved on quickly to discuss other people's projects. At the end of the meeting, Chloe took two press releases out of her file and walked down to Peter.

"Peter, I want to draw your attention to something. You left two spaces between these two words in these releases. I can't stress how important it is that everything must be perfect before it's sent to the media. Macken's name equals excellence, no room for mistakes."

The anger burned up inside him as he made his way up the stairs to his attic office. He heard someone whisper his name and looking around saw it was Dermot beckoning him into his office.

He went inside and the door was quickly closed.

"You pissed her off. You shouldn't have made the suggestion about the male model."

"Why?" Peter looked around the large comfortable office.

"Because it was a better suggestion than hers."

"C'mon, Dermot, why bother inviting me to the fucking meeting if she didn't want any fucking input from me?"

"Shhh! Keep your voice down. She wanted to demonstrate how high and mighty she is."

Peter sat down and buried his face in his hands. "I can't take much more of this, of her games."

"That's why she said that rubbish about the press release, putting you back in your box. She won't be inviting you back to any meetings for a long time."

"Good. As she said herself, from now on, I'm just going to keep my head down and do my work."

"Probably for the best," advised Dermot. "Incidentally, great idea about the male model. The Minister will love it."

CHAPTER 20

Audrey stared at the Nescafé T-shirt in her hands. Ben had got her a promotions job at the RDS. There was an exhibition on and Nescafé had a stand there. Her job for the afternoon was to stand there giving out coupons. She forced herself to take off her Chanel shirt and put on the T-shirt. It was too tight.

The Manager at the stand handed her a bunch of leaflets. "Hand out as many as you can. If they buy a coffee and give in one of these coupons, they get another one free."

As she started giving them out, she prayed nobody she knew would see her.

But she met lots of people she knew. The exhibition was focusing on women in the twenty-first century, with a strong emphasis on fashion. This had attracted many PRs and people from the fashion industry. Some came over and chatted pleasantly, others smirked as they ignored her. Oh, how she'd wished she had the power of a couple of weeks ago when she was in demand.

"Audrey, what are you doing here?" Chloe asked, her features lit up in surprise.

"Handing out leaflets. Take one – if you hand it in you get an extra coffee free."

She smiled sarcastically.

"I'll pass, thanks."

"What has you here?"

"Macken organised this exhibition. I'm just checking how everything is,"

Audrey shifted uncomfortably. "I'd like to apologise for my behaviour at the show. It was inexcusable."

"Yes, it was," said Chloe. There was an awkward silence before she added, "Let's grab a sandwich at the restaurant."

Audrey glanced over to the Nescafé Manager busy pouring coffees. "Sure."

They found a corner table in the RDS restaurant and ordered a light lunch.

"I take it your career has taken a nosedive?" said Chloe.

"Yeah. I try not to think about it too much or I'll go mad."

"What about Aran?"

"We're on very shaky ground. Is it true Peter Reynolds was demoted?"

"It's true. I hold him very responsible for the debacle."

"But, that's not fair, Chloe. He really looked after me that night."

"So maybe he should switch careers and become a nursemaid. As a PR, he stinks."

"I can't see what he could have done to save the night."

"Number one, not order drink backstage. Number two, as soon as you started – acting peculiarly – on stage he should have had security take you out of sight within seconds. I could go on and on . . . Besides, I thought you couldn't stand him."

"I just hate to think of somebody else suffering because of my actions. I'd better get back to work."

"Audrey, I know things are hard for you right now. I just want you to know you have a friend in me."

"Thanks, Chloe"

"Call me, and we'll meet up soon."

Audrey got back to work. "Want a free coffee?" she offered to the passing crowds.

"Thanks, honey," a man said, standing in front of her. It was Simon Lawless, the PR for the cosmetics company who had immediately cancelled her contract after the fashion show. "But I think you've more need of a free coffee than me!" He laughed loudly and walked on.

When Peter got home late into the evening after work, there was a note from Lynn, saying she had gone out to a cocktail party. He smiled and he was glad she seemed to be back to herself.

He had started undressing in the bedroom when he spotted some shopping bags from Brown Thomas and the Irish Design Centre. Rummaging through the bags he saw they all contained new clothes for Lynn and he gasped when he saw the price-tags.

How could she spend so much when they were in a financial crisis? He heard the front door bang and he quickly fixed the bags as if he hadn't touched them.

"So how was the party?" he asked, as she came into the bedroom.

"Fantastic," she threw herself on the bed. "You should have seen their apartment. Absolutely amazing. It's in an old converted warehouse and all on different levels."

"Really?" He tried not to think of the new clothes.

"Straight from the pages of a magazine. An interior designer did it all out for them. It's perfect for entertaining. You know, I think it's time we moved on."

"I was thinking the same myself," Peter said quickly.

"Really?"

"Yeah. We need to be more practical."

"Mmmh . . . there's an apartment for sale in that warehouse. Not as big as the one I was in tonight, but it would be perfect for us."

"The warehouse?" He was incredulous.

"This place is lovely, but I think we need something grander for entertaining."

"Darling, have you completely lost the plot? We can barely afford to stay here, let alone upgrade."

"Oh, Mr Negativity has returned, has he?"

"Mr Practicality."

"You are what the image you project is. How many times have I said that? If we had a place like the one I was in tonight, we'd be giving off the right signals and helping our careers."

"Try telling that to the Bank Manager."

Standing up, Lynn shook her head. "I'm going to bed. And since I don't wish to sleep with one of life's losers, I'm going to use the spare bedroom."

Aran had arrived at Audrey's apartment at seven as had been arranged. She was exhausted from standing on her feet all day, but cooked him a meal and tried her best to humour him. He spent two hours informing her the latest names his parents had been calling her and other people's equally ego-destroying comments.

After dinner he sat on the couch playing the martyr

and playing games with her mind that she would have never thought possible of him. Finally he went to kiss her and she was delighted that he was still interested in her.

Aran pushed Audrey on to the bed, and started to unbutton her dress as she reached and undid his shirt.

He looked at her with a mixture of desire, anger and hurt and he wanted her to feel the same way about him as he kissed her neck aggressively. Usually Audrey could more than match his passion and energy, but there was something too urgent about him tonight.

"Don't leave any marks," she said.

"Why? It's not like you'll be doing photo-shoots any more." His eyes were mocking as he continued.

"Right, I'll head off now," said Aran putting on his tie.

"So soon?" Audrey was pouring herself a Coke in the kitchen.

"Yeah, I'm late for that party."

"You never said anything about a party. You're going on your own?"

"With friends"

"And I'm not invited?" Her voice had risen.

"Actually, no."

"I can't believe you. You come over here, play the victim. We make love and you're off without so much as a chat."

"Like I said, I've a party to go to." He looked at her coldly.

"Bastard!"

"You know the score. We're taking it slowly. I can't be seen out with you right now."

"But I'm OK for a shag?"

"You're being stupid."

"Yes, I have been stupid. How dare you come over here and treat me like this!"

"You're getting paranoid."

"You forget who you're messing with."

"No, I know exactly who you are. You're yesterday's girl!" He gave a hollow laugh. "So, your little performance at the show didn't affect your career? Then why the hell did you spend the day dressed in a Nescafé T-shirt in the RDS? Hardly the high fashion world you're used to, is it?"

"You're enjoying this, aren't you? Enjoying making me suffer?"

"Well, you made me suffer long enough. If you weren't standing me up, you were flirting with somebody in front of me. Treating me like shit!"

"I told you all the time, Aran, you were too possessive and jealous."

"With you going around like a princess! Well, you aren't any more. So let's see how you enjoy the treatment for a while. The old Aran is gone, sweetheart – I've wised up. I'll call you later." He slammed the door behind him.

Consumed with rage she threw the Coke out of her glass and searched the cupboards for some alcohol. Finding a bottle of whiskey she poured a glassful and downed it in one gulp. She went to pour herself another glass but stopped. She looked at the bottle of whiskey and then put it away.

"I won't let you destroy me," she promised, as she settled onto the couch with a box of chocolates instead.

Ben sat uneasily across the desk from Audrey at Boom. He felt he was treading on eggshells, waiting for her to erupt any time with that famous temper of hers. But she had been very calm and polite since he had become her booker.

"There's a promotion job tonight, if you want it."

"Great. Where?"

"The San Juan Club."

"What doing?"

"It's a drinks promotion for Celtic Vodka. Just mingle with guests with a tray offering free drinks."

She frowned. "Sounds like being a waitress."

"The money's good."

She sighed. "What time do I have to be there?"

As Audrey drove to The San Juan that evening, she couldn't get Aran out of her mind. He hadn't called her all day. He had always been so in awe of her, she couldn't believe he would treat her in this way. When they had argued in the past, he was usually the one to give in first, even when she was in the wrong. She was no saint, she was the first to admit that, but she had always cared a great deal for Aran, and she didn't deserve this from him.

She parked the car and walked along the quays and through the front door of The San Juan. The place was already fairly full.

"You're late!" a voice snapped at her straight away. She turned to see the speaker was Dermot from Macken. She had dealt with him before and knew he didn't like her.

"I'm sorry. The traffic –"

"Old habits die hard, eh?"

She swallowed a smart answer and followed him into a back office. To her horror she realised she knew most of the people there. How could she serve drinks to these people she had considered friends? She knew if Hazel heard she dropped out of a job she would be shown the door at Boom. She would have to swallow her pride.

In the office, Dermot unzipped a bag. "This is your outfit for the night."

He took out the outfit and handed it to her. She examined it in disgust. It was a very skimpy *Playboy*-bunny type outfit.

"I'll leave you to change into it – then come out and you can start serving."

"But I can't wear this," she objected.

"Why not?"

"It looks tarty."

"It's supposed to be."

"I know a lot of people out there and I'm not going to serve them dressed like a cheap tart."

"You have no choice. You're booked to do the job."

"I wouldn't have taken the bloody job if I'd known this outfit was part of the deal!"

"We're running late, and I don't have time for one of your silly little tantrums. Get changed and be out serving within five minutes – with a big smile."

"Sorry, but I'm going home." She went to walk past him, but he grabbed her arm.

"You're not walking out leaving me without a promotion girl!"

"Watch me!"

"If you do this, I'll be on the phone to Boom so fast, they won't touch you again." He tightened his grip on her arm.

Her eyes narrowed and her voice became angry. "Get your hands off me now, before I start screaming this place down and charge you with assault."

Her venom and threat made him let her go immediately.

"But what will I do with the bunny outfit?" Dermot asked.

She picked up the outfit and flung it at him. "Wear it your fucking self!"

Audrey laughed out loud all the way as she drove herself home, thinking of Dermot's expression. It felt good to laugh like that again. It was a release of all the tension. She'd had enough and was proud that she hadn't allowed herself to be intimidated into doing something she didn't want to. She had made a silly mistake, that was all. Why should she be punished for the rest of her life? She was fully aware of the consequences of walking out. Hazel had only reluctantly given her a second chance and now that was blown. But she didn't care any more. She wanted time away from the whole social scene. She needed time out. She needed to sleep on late in the mornings and go for long walks on the beach. She wanted to eat what she liked without worrying about her figure. She needed time away from Aran to think about the strong feelings she had for him, despite his atrocious behaviour towards her.

She needed to decide if she would run back home to Ballyabbey or stay and fight.

She turned off her mobile and went over and plugged the phone out of the socket.

CHAPTER 21

"Audrey Driver walked out and left me high and dry," complained Dermot to Peter. They were in Dermot's office.

Peter couldn't help but laugh. "That sounds like our Audrey all right."

"I held her arm as she tried to leave and she said she was going to start screaming for the guards or something."

"She would have too! They broke the mould when they made Audrey Driver."

"Celtic Vodka were furious because they were left with no promotions girl. Between ourselves they are confused with the takeover of Blast anyway. One minute they leave Macken for Blast, then they find themselves back with Macken. We're going out of our way to please them."

"Don't take it personally, but I hope they give you hell."

"I can't blame your feelings, considering. I made a big complaint to Hazel at Boom and told her Audrey had already ruined one of my colleague's careers and I didn't want her to do the same to me."

Peter was unhappy on hearing he had been drawn into the drama. "What did Hazel say?"

"She told me she was kicking Audrey off Boom's books."

"Well, did you really think a model of Audrey's calibre, despite her recent fall from grace, would serve drinks while scantily clad to leering businessmen?"

Dermot was affronted. "If she's paid to do it, then yes. I didn't want to hire her anyway. I've worked with her before and find her awkward. It was Chloe who insisted I use her for last night."

"Chloe? Why should she go out of her way to give Audrey work?"

"Probably felt sorry for her. I think they are friendly."

"Can't imagine Chloe feeling sorry for anyone." Peter mused before the penny dropped. "I know what she was up to! She enjoyed the thought of Audrey being humiliated in a bunny outfit."

"You are becoming too cynical. As I said, they're friends."

Peter felt bad for snapping at Dermot. He was the only person who had been kind to him at Macken.

"Sorry for being thorny. It's just that the thought of Audrey gets me going."

"No probs. Pint after work?"

CHAPTER 22

Audrey had slept late that morning, and then went for a jog along the beach. One of the reasons she had bought in Blackrock was because it was near the sea. She had grown up beside the sea and couldn't imagine living far from it ever. As she jogged along she thought about the beautiful farmhouse that was her family home in the west of Ireland. However, she knew that Aran's family and her other friends in Dublin would consider her home to be only worthy as a pretty holiday house. She thought of her mother Kathleen, and her father Jack, Ballabbey's town sergeant, and her younger brother Jack Junior. They were a close family and very supportive of each other, and the temptation to go running back was overwhelming. They were very proud of her success so far. As her father said, she was the town's most famous export. But she needed time on her own. Besides, the way she was feeling, if she went home, she might never leave again. And she didn't want to made any decisions without careful consideration.

It was early afternoon by the time she got back to her apartment. She went for a hot shower, wrapped herself in a bathrobe, plugged in the phone and settled down on the couch while she dialled her home number.

"Hello," answered Kathleen.

"Hi, Mum, it's just me."

"This is a nice surprise," said Kathleen. Audrey usually never rang during the afternoon as she would be busy out working. "I'm on my own in the house, and I've just made a cup of tea and so we can have a good chat."

"How is everyone?"

"They're fine. Your dad's out working. And your brother is at college studying hard."

"How are he and that young Clancy girl getting along?"

"It seems serious but you can never tell at that age, can you? We all had you and Shaun off married, and look what happened there . . . You know when I see them they remind of how you and Shaun used to be, all full of hope and innocence . . . I hope you're eating well up there?"

"When do I ever not eat well?"

"We were watching this programme the other night about young models, starving themselves to death for a bit of work. Your father was saying he didn't know what was attractive about looking hungry."

Audrey laughed to herself. Her family were so down to earth, so refreshing compared to all the bullshit she was usually surrounded by.

"So, come on, tell me?" said Kathleen.

"Tell you what?

"Tell me what has you home in the afternoon? And why do you sound like you're going to start bursting out crying any minute."

"Oh, Mum. I've made such a mess of everything!" and suddenly Audrey was pouring out all her sorrows, keeping back some bits she thought too much detail for her mother.

"And how do you feel about Aran now?"

"I don't know. I feel confused. I'm not going to allow anybody to treat me that badly."

"We brought you up to always stand up for yourself, no matter who their family is."

"I know, and it's served me well with people over the years." It's true, she thought, even though a lot of people mistook her confidence for arrogance. Having said that, if Audrey was true to herself, she had to admit that a lot of the compliments lavished on her over the years had made her somewhat arrogant.

"Well, there's nothing keeping you in Dublin now your modelling career is over. You still have your nursery school qualification to fall back on and your friend Josephine could fix you up with a job at the crèche here."

"I don't know what I'm doing right now."

"Well, will you promise me you'll think about it? There's no point being on your own and unhappy up there when you could be here with us."

"I will think about it, and thanks, Mum."

Audrey was sitting entranced by an old black and white movie when she heard a kick at her door.

She looked outside and it was dark. She feared it might be Aran. She went over to the front door, looked through the peep-hole and saw it was Leslie. She undid the locks and opened the door.

"Well, you're still alive anyway!" Leslie declared.

"Just about?" Audrey sighed. "Come on in."

Leslie entered and Audrey closed the door behind her.

"I've left lots of messages on your mobile. I was worried sick."

"I'm sorry, I haven't checked for any messages."

"What are you doing?" Leslie, looked at the box of chocolates half eaten and at Audrey with her usual perfectly groomed hair hardly combed, and dressed in a grey track suit. "Let me guess, staying holed up in here and feeling sorry for yourself?"

"Got it in one." Audrey sighed and sat down on the couch.

Leslie sat beside her. "Audrey, you can't stay in here for ever. You have to come out and face the world?"

"Why? Is there a position still available for me at Boom?"

Leslie smiled sympathetically and shook her head. "No, Hazel hit the roof when she heard what you said to that PR. She actually used that infamous line 'She'll never work in this town again!'."

Audrey tutted. "She's so over the top."

"So what are you going to do?"

Audrey adopted a mock haughty tone. "Consider my options . . . which are rather limited. In fact the only one I really have is to move home to Ballyabbey."

"Would you do that?" Leslie was surprised.

"Well, people love me for who I am there. They loved me long before I entered modelling, and they'll love me long after I've finished leading this life."

"And what would you do there? I "

"Well, I have a nursery school qualification. I could go and do that."

Leslie started to laugh "You have a nursery school qualification?"

"Yeah, I mean I was all set to become a teacher before I entered modelling."

Leslie leaned forward, intrigued. "I never saw you as that type."

"Look, if fate hadn't stepped in, I would be leading a

very different life now. Ballyabbey is just a small town. Though, I must admit, when I was growing up there I was obsessed with fashion. I used to get all the magazines all the time and devour them. I mean I wanted to be a primary school teacher, but my heart was leading me towards modelling."

"Go on," Leslie pushed.

"I was kind of unlucky in love as a teenager. Guys were a bit intimidated by how I looked, so I never got asked out."

"You made up for lost time since," joked Leslie.

"But I had a great time. I'd lots of friends and I was always going to parties and stuff. Then when I was eighteen this guy called Shaun asked me out. He was the local petrol station owner's son. He was really popular and I was mad about him. We started dating very seriously. Around the same time I started doing local fashion shows in hotels around the county. Shaun was totally supportive of me and pushed me all the way. After school, he went and worked in his dad's petrol station and I started training at the local nursery school. And at the weekends I did some modelling. Then one of the promoters of a wedding fair I was doing gave me the number of a Dublin agency and suggested I give them a call. Shaun got the train up with me and they signed me up."

Leslie poured herself a glass of wine. "What happened then?"

"Well, I got some work around the country and I was totally delighted. But I honestly thought my future was going to be in Ballyabbey, married to Shaun, teaching, with a couple of kids. I mean, everyone was waiting for us to announce our engagement. Then Shaun saw an advert in the local paper asking for entrants into the local beauty competition. He sent some photos of me in and I went on to win the county final. Three months later I was at the national contest. I wanted to win it. I really got carried away with the glamour and excitement in the lead-up to the pageant. I started exercising and eating really well and preparing for the final. I was in tip-top condition and came across as full of charm and confidence on the night. When I won the national final, it was like all my dreams come true. The media swirled around me on the stage on the winning night and I thought nothing was going to stop me now."

"And what about Shaun?"

"I fully thought I could have both a successful modelling career and Shaun. But I was suddenly swept away into schedules and photos and interviews. I was so busy in Dublin I didn't get home for a week. I was so excited to see Shaun. But then he told me he didn't want to see me any more."

"What?" Leslie was incredulous.

"We went for a walk on the beach and he said he just wanted a normal life and didn't want to be involved in my new world." Audrey took a sip of her Ballygowan. "My God, I was in tears, and I begged him to come to Dublin with me. He said no. I insisted I would give up modelling and return to Ballyabbey to be with him. He refused. He told me he always knew this day would come and said we were no longer compatible. He said I'd end up hating him if I didn't take the opportunities being offered to me. He was as upset as I was."

"Oh, Audrey!" Leslie was full of sympathy.

"So I moved to Dublin and pursued my dreams. And my life did transform very quickly. I shied away from dating for a long while. Then I went out·with an actor for a year. Then a TV presenter. Both experiences told me that everyone wasn't like Shaun and that I was now operating in sophisticated and treacherous circles. I learned my lessons and became an expert player of the game. High-profile romance followed high-profile romance and then along came Aran. At the beginning I thought it wouldn't last, but he seemed to genuinely care for me. And he put up with my demands and my temper!"

"What's Shaun doing now?"

"Still working in that petrol station, married locally with a kid. I've been wondering a lot of these past days if I made the right decisions and choices back then."

Leslie put her arm around her and hugged her.

"I've always relied on my looks," said Audrey. "It might be time to try something else."

CHAPTER 23

Lynn sat at her desk in The Gallery opposite Rory Ryan. He was due to have a large exhibition in London in two weeks' time. As he stood on the brink of international acclaim, she marvelled at the difference between his good fortune and their bad luck.

She had co-ordinated with the owner of a Bond Street gallery in London to show Rory's work. Rory's success had enhanced her own prestige and contacts considerably.

"I've organised the shipment of those paintings over to London. They should be there Monday. Is there anything else you want to go over?" asked Lynn.

"That about wraps it up. I'm nervous as hell." he admitted.

"No, you're not. You damned well know the critics will rave about you. You'll be rich and famous."

"Thanks to you!" He reached over and gave her hand a rub. "How's Peter doing?"

"Great. He's at Macken now."

"Tell him I said hi."

"Will do."

"What date are you coming over to London?"

"Me?" Lynn's eyes widened.

"You have to be at my London exhibition!"

"I'd no plans to."

"You really should be there, Lynn. You should get some credit for my success. You took a chance on me."

She thought hard. There was no chance of asking the partners at The Gallery to pay for her to go – they were extremely tight. And she imagined Peter's face if she said she was going under the present circumstances. How she hated this existence of watching every penny. But . . .

"OK," she was laughing like a schoolgirl, "I'll go."

"London? But you know we can't afford it," Peter said.

"It's very important for my career to be there. I discovered Rory and I want to share in the limelight."

"Reality doesn't seem to be sinking in, Lynn. We're practically broke."

"Exactly. I need this trip to help recover from this horrible experience."

"I'm putting up with so much crap at work every day and you're swanning around as if nothing has changed."

"Since you were the one who got us in this mess, you can get us out. I'm not prepared to sit around and wallow in self-pity and be poor. So you'd better start thinking of ways of getting us back on the right track!"

"I give up!" Peter snapped and stormed out.

Lynn reached for a cigarette and lit it. She would go to London. Why shouldn't she? She had worked hard and managed to establish herself in Dublin, even if she didn't earn that much. If Peter had managed to fulfil his potential, she would be a socialite by now. She would be leading a life where popping over to London or New York for a shopping trip was the norm.

Chloe was at a meeting at Murphy Hennessy. Reginald and Larry had spent an hour poring over the data that Peter had prepared as Chloe talked them through it.

"It certainly seems to offer a good argument for the shopping centre," said Reginald.

"These are the building bricks we need to push through the planning," said Chloe.

"Apart from the council policy, what other opposition are we up against?" asked Larry.

"The local community have formed a group called 'Mothers For Housing' or some such nonsense," said Chloe.

"Great!" Larry threw his hands in the air.

"They don't have any political clout, but the media tend to give these community groups a voice," said Chloe. "You know the kind of thing – interviews on the Nine O'clock News."

"What's our next stop?" asked Reginald.

"Let the political lobbying begin. I have meetings arranged from tomorrow morning," said Chloe.

Aran sat in his office looking out the window. He had loads of work to do but couldn't motivate himself. Audrey's phone was turned off all the time. He had been out with a group of friends the night before and they had all urged him to forget about her. You've been at her beck and call for far too long, they told him. It was time for him to have some fun. Play the field and find somebody new, they advised him. He had to admit he had felt empowered since he had begun to treat Audrey badly. Or had felt empowered before she stopped answering her phone.

He got up and went out into the corridor where he bumped into Chloe.

"How are you?" she said with a smile.

"Just great."

"You look a lot better," she complimented.

"Thanks."

"Anyway, see you later." She smiled again and began to walk off.

"Er, Chloe . . . just wondering what you're up to tomorrow night?"

"Nothing planned, as yet."

"Would you like to go to dinner with me?"

"I'd love to."

CHAPTER 24

"I'm not going," said Peter.

"Yes, you are," Lynn insisted.

Lynn had been invited to a book launch that week and now Peter refused to go with her.

"I'm sick of those launches."

"You're just embarrassed to show your face."

"You usually don't mind if I accompany you or not. Why not go with one of your friends? Take the gorgeous Rory with you."

"Rory is in London preparing for his exhibition. The sooner you get out in the scene again the better. I refuse to be married to a social retard who stays at home all the time."

Peter had to admit it was time he started to go out socially again. He couldn't hide away forever. He certainly would be forgotten very quickly if he wasn't at least seen around.

"OK, I'll go," he conceded.

"Good. We'll need something special to wear. I'll meet you outside Brown Thomas tomorrow after work for a shopping spree."

"Lynn, we can't afford it!"

"Oh, shut up!"

Audrey slowly felt the strength and fight come back to her. All kinds of possibilities were going through her mind as she thought about her future. If she sold her apartment, she could buy a lovely house in Ballyabbey. Unlike a lot of her model friends, she had not squandered her money but invested it wisely. She could probably now afford to open up a crèche in the town. Or she could explore the possibility of opening a Beauty Salon. The customers would flock to her because of who she was. She would have her family and friends around her and never live her previous stressful life again.

It was a lovely evening as she took a solitary along Sandymount strand. She had been thinking so much about the past in Ballyabbey. About her and Shaun.

A sadness came over her and she didn't know why. She felt jealous of their youth and that they'd had so many decisions ahead of them. Decisions like she had made along the way for herself. Some of them right and some of them wrong. But whatever the case, she had made them. And then she realised she couldn't turn back the clock. And going back to Ballyabbey wasn't going to change that. Besides, she'd been gone too long and had led too much of a different life ever to go back now.

Patrick Guilbaud's was Chloe's favourite restaurant and so she was delighted when Aran suggested it for their rendezvous. She relaxed in a hot bath with a glass of wine before dressing.

A taxi collected her at seven thirty and delivered her exactly at eight to the restaurant.

Aran was already waiting in reception.

"I hope I'm not late," she said.

"No, I was early."

They made their way inside.

"You look lovely," he complimented as they were shown to their table. He wondered if she had taken offence. Audrey always needed reassurance, maybe a woman like Chloe didn't.

"Ah, Ms Gallagher, how are you this evening?" the manager asked, greeting her warmly.

Chloe returned his smile and began a conversation with him in French.

French had always been Aran's worst subject at school, and he couldn't follow what was said.

"The manager's a friend of yours?" asked Aran after he had left.

"An acquaintance," replied Chloe. When the waiter arrived, Chloe gave her order in French.

"You sound as though you are fluent," observed Aran.

"I am," said Chloe before checking herself. She wanted to impress him, but not to intimidate him. "It's just conversational French, really"

Chloe felt Aran was awkward in her company. A sure sign of somebody fresh out of a relationship, who was used to the company of one person and finding dating difficult again. To counteract this, she ensured his glass was constantly refilled. After an hour he began to relax.

"You spend a lot of time at your parents' home?" asked Chloe.

"I do have a couple of properties, but the house in Howth is a very big house and I'm an only child so I have it to myself a lot."

She had seen the house and knew he wasn't lying.

"We all do our own thing, so I can come home after an evening out, and not see anyone at all. Besides, I spent a lot of time at Audrey's."

"Your father is a lovely man."

"You have to say that. He's employing you," he smiled.

"No, I wouldn't say it if I didn't mean it. And I wouldn't flatter him – he's very shrewd."

"He sure is! And you should meet my mother! They both hated Audrey. Couldn't stand her."

"Really?" She filled up his glass. "Do you miss her?"

"Enough about me. What about you?"

"But you know everything about me."

"Not really. I know you are big in PR with a big car and that's about all. Where are you from?"

"I'm a Southsider."

"Big family?"

"Like yourself, I'm an only child."

"What does your father do?"

"He's a bank manager, though he's close to retiring."

"He's probably where you get your business brain from."

"Since my mother is a housewife, that must be true," smiled Chloe.

After the meal, Chloe glanced at her watch to see it was after eleven. "I'd better go. I've a heavy workload tomorrow." She reached over and touched his hand gently. "I've really enjoyed tonight."

They walked out onto the street.

"I need a taxi," she said, looking around.

"I'll probably leave the car and grab a cab myself. I've drunk over the limit." He reached forward and took her hand. "I've really enjoyed tonight too. I'd like to see you again."

"I'd like that." She paused before pulling away. "There's a cab."

A taxi pulled over and the restaurant doorman opened the back door for her. She reached forward and kissed Aran lightly on the lips. "Ring me tomorrow," she said before getting in and being driven off.

The next morning Audrey got up early and jumped into the shower. She at last knew what she wanted from her life, or at least what she didn't want. She had come too far to turn back. Lots of ideas were spinning through her mind. She knew she would have to change direction, but didn't want to throw the baby out with the bathwater. She had a wealth of knowledge about the beauty industry and the celebrity circuit. When she had her act together, she got on very well with people. She needed to utilise her assets to earn herself a living and re-establish herself. But on her terms. She also knew that in spite of her feelings for Aran, she could not allow herself to be treated like a doormat. And, strangely, there was another person spinning around her head: Peter Reynolds. The man she had detested, but who had looked after her. The man whose career she had destroyed. She had worked with many people over the years, but rarely with somebody with as many good ideas and an ability to get things done. And what intrigued her most about him was that he was totally oblivious to his own talent.

Chloe's skills in the kitchen were limited. She always made sure she stuck to a simple but elegant recipe.

"That was delicious," complimented Aran, as he pushed his empty plate away.

"Hardly delicious, but it will do," said Chloe as she

refilled his glass of wine. They had eaten in her kitchen. She always preferred to entertain there rather than the dining-room. "Will we retire into the lounge?" She stood up and walked through with the bottle of wine. The patio doors were open and they could hear the waves crashing against the rocks nearby.

Sitting down on the couch, she gestured for him to join her there.

"I love your house."

"So do I."

"It must have cost you a bomb."

"I believe we can choose how we live our lives. Some people waste their time over things . . . or people, who just aren't worth it. I see what I want and go for it."

"I believe that too," Aran nodded.

"I think you'd like to think of yourself like that, but are you really?"

"What do you mean?"

"Often when people have been born privileged, as you were, they can lose a sense of priority. Go with their heart rather than their head."

"I take it you are referring to Audrey?"

"Somebody like you should never have bothered with somebody like her."

"I guess love is blind."

"And did you love her?"

"I don't know, any more. Listen, that's all in the past. I don't want to talk about her. That's all I ever hear from people – Audrey, Audrey, Audrey!"

"I don't want to talk about Audrey either . . ." Chloe put down her glass of wine and leaned forward to Aran. "All I want to talk about is you."

CHAPTER 25

Audrey had an early night, and then went for an early morning jog along the strand. Then she took out her address book and started jotting down numbers to ring, putting a big X beside the important ones. Her first call was to Noel Flynn, proprietor of The San Juan Club.

"Good God, I thought you were dead!" exclaimed Noel

"That was just everybody's wishful thinking," answered Audrey. Obviously he didn't know about her most recent visit to his club . . . Noel was a very successful entrepreneur. In his early forties, he had asked Audrey out many times. She had always declined.

"Rumour had it you were drying out in a private clinic," Noel informed her.

"That's funny, rumour had it you were joining a monastery."

Noel roared with laughter. His reputation as a womaniser was notorious. "And what do I owe the pleasure of this call to?"

"I'd like to bring you out to lunch," said Audrey.

"You want to bring me out? Times must be hard for you, Audrey."

"The Shelbourne? One thirty?"

"I've appointments all day."

"Well, cancel one! You know how I always love to eat with a handsome man."

Peter was in his office when his mobile rang. "Yeah?"

"Peter, it's Audrey Driver."

Peter sat stunned for a few seconds. "Yeah?"

"Guess you didn't expect to hear from me."

"No, I didn't." He couldn't or wouldn't keep the hostility from his voice.

"First of all, I'd really like to apologise for all the trouble I've caused you."

Silence from Peter.

"There's a few things I'd like to talk to you about. Could we meet for a drink after work?" asked Audrey.

"I don't want to be offensive, but I have no interest whatsoever in meeting you or talking to you about anything."

"I understand how you feel. I don't blame you. But I think what I have to say may interest you."

"Audrey, I never want to see or hear from you again. You've caused me enough hassle. Now, goodbye." He hung up.

Audrey turned heads as she strode into The Shelbourne's restaurant. Noel Flynn gave Audrey a big embrace. He always came across as a jolly, charming man but his jolly image hid a shrewd and sharp mind. He came from an impoverished background, and many rumours connected him with underground figures. He had come up the hard way and didn't mind now buying respectability when it suited him.

"You look smashing," he said, as they sat down.

"As do you." She glanced down at his ever-expanding stomach.

They ordered a light lunch and white wine.

"I was kicking myself for missing that fucking fashion show! I heard you sent the hoi polloi into shock," said Noel.

"I'm like you, Noel. Never had much time for all the bullshit."

"Don't you talk fucking bullshit! You were up the establishment's arse!"

"Maybe," she conceded. "But they never trusted me. I was never the good little girl who did as she was told."

"It's a pity you didn't or you might have been Mrs Aran Murphy by now. What happened between you and lover-boy?"

"Please!" Audrey's body language flirted continuously with Noel. "I'm trying to digest my lunch!"

"Well, to be fair to you, you were always your own woman."

"But I did get too caught up in the crap. That's over now."

"So, as they say, there's no such thing as a free lunch. What do you want?"

Audrey leaned back in her chair. "I'm looking for a job."

"What kind of job?"

"I want to work as a hostess in the San Juan. Just a couple of nights a week."

Noel put out his cigarette "Sorry, babe, no can do."

"Why?"

"Number of reasons. First of all, I have a hostess. Secondly, you have no nightclub experience. Thirdly, I'm

154

not giving you the opportunity to go nuts in my club. And lastly, you are, or were, a top model. It wouldn't look right you now being a hostess."

Audrey shot back at him immediately. "To answer your objections. Firstly, I'm sure even you give your regular hostess a couple of nights off a week. I can just fill in for her. Secondly, I've spent my life talking to people in clubs. Thirdly, I won't be drinking again, so I won't go nuts. And lastly, what do you care if I was a top model – it's great for San Juan's image."

"I really don't think so." He scratched his head.

"I'm not taking no for an answer. I'll just go into the club and pretend I work there every night until I shame you into paying me something."

"You're pretty sure of yourself."

"If I work there people might even start gossiping we're sleeping together – that could be good for your image."

Noel roared with laughter. "What's in it for you? The money for a couple of nights ain't gonna be that impressive."

"It will be getting me started again, getting me seen. I may never model again, but I'll be damned if I'm going to disappear."

Peter didn't stay too long in the office, as he had promised Lynn to attend that book launch. As he left the building and walked to his car a voice called his name. He turned to see Audrey.

"What are you doing here?" he asked.

"As I told you, I need to speak to you."

"Look, just forget about the show. Is that what you want to hear? I forgive you, does that make you feel better? Now, can you just let me get on with my life?" He continued to his car.

She kept pace with him. "Ten minutes, that's all I want and then I'll leave you alone."

"I told you on the phone I've nothing to say to you." He reached his car and unlocked it.

As he opened the driver's door, she pushed it shut and stood in his way.

"Just fuck off!" he roared at her. "Haven't you destroyed enough? Get out of my life!"

She was shocked by his temper. But then she knew he could be as volatile as herself. But only when he was pushed.

She held her ground. "Ten minutes, Peter, and then I'll be gone."

They found a coffee shop. She got them both a Diet Coke and they sat at a corner table.

"What are you going to do now your modelling days are over?" He didn't even try to sound interested.

"I'm starting work at The San Juan Club as a hostess."

"Bit of a comedown, from being a New York supermodel."

"Bit of a comedown from being a senior at Blast to being Chloe Gallagher's dogsbody," she shot back.

"Thanks to you, yeah. Enough of the niceties, what do you want?"

"I've been thinking a lot."

"That's a first."

"I've been thinking about Ireland."

"Oh, are you thinking of running for President? That's a natural progression – model – drunk – President."

She ignored his sarcasm. "About the Irish modelling scene and PR scene. It needs a shake-up."

"I thought you achieved that the night of the show."

"Will you listen!" she raised her voice. "What I'm saying is, there's no young blood coming up. Hazel and the others are only concentrating on their reliables who earn money. I should know – how long have I been on the scene?"

"Too long," he said dryly.

"Look at my friend Leslie. She's fantastic, but Hazel won't put her forward or put in the time and effort needed to make her a top model. The money needs to be improved in modelling here. We need to link up more with London, New York and Paris. Supply these centres with the models and go for the big bucks. Look at the Irish music scene over the past ten years. We have produced so many bands and singers who have conquered the world –"

"I'm glad you're not taking all the credit for it."

"But we haven't really produced any international models."

"I thought you were going to be our first."

"So I fucked up. But the opportunity I got in the States was very much the exception. Why is that?"

"Lack of talent?"

"Nonsense. The potential here is amazing." She took a sip from her drink. "What we need is a shake-up. We need an agency that grooms models and then takes them to the world market. To do the same with the modelling market as has been done with the Irish music scene. But there's more –"

"Indeed, why stop there?"

"That's the long-term ambition –"

"Rome was not built in a day."

Audrey ignored him. "But we shouldn't limit the Agency. We should also be a Celebrity Management Company representing TV people, actors, sports personalities –"

"I'll just give David Beckham a call, will I?"

"We can also organise events like shows."

"As I have seen at first hand, shows were always your speciality."

"Clients can contact us and we organise everything, the show, models etc."

"Wait a minute – what's this 'we'?"

"That's my proposal. What do you think?"

"Proposal! All I heard was Audrey Driver talking crap as usual. You are suggesting you and I open this agency?"

"Yes."

"But we hate each other!"

"Hardly hate –"

"After the trouble you caused me? It's a pretty good description."

"So are you going to go through the rest of your life being Chloe's dogsbody?"

"None of your business."

"Peter, I didn't approach you about this without giving it serious thought. I came to you because you are the best. You are better at PR than anyone I've ever met. I know the beauty and celebrity business inside out. That's an unbeatable combination. You've the ideas, the attention to detail – the business brain. I've got the confidence, the beauty business experience, the charm –"

"Ha!"

"When I want to have. We can make this work, Peter."

"Have you been on the drink again?"

"I've had a quick word with my Bank Manager, and he advised that to set up an office and to start everything rolling would cost twenty thousand. So, it would only cost us ten thousand each."

Peter roared with laughter. "I can hardly repay my mortgage, let alone invest in some crackpot scheme of yours." He stood up. "Good luck, Audrey." He walked away.

"Peter!" she called after him. "You built Blast, everyone knows it was you! Why is that other guy out in Portugal sitting on a fortune? You can do it again, but this time for yourself. For once in your life, take a risk!"

"Sorry, Audrey, you're too much of a risk." And he left the café.

CHAPTER 26

"The cheek of that woman!" said Lynn as she touched up her make-up in the bedroom mirror.

"She's living in cloud-cuckoo-land," said Peter. "Even if the whole agency business needs a kick up the arse, it's not waiting for Audrey Driver to do it. And me in business with her! I'd throw her out the window on the first day."

"She's grasping at straws. I still can't believe what that bitch said to me the night of the show. If I ever see her again, it would be too soon. I'd give her a piece of my mind."

Peter approached her and put his arms around her "No, you wouldn't. You hate any kind of public scene. You'd just give her one of your haughty condescending looks."

She kissed him. "You smell good, and look good." She decided she would wait till after the book launch before she told him about her departure for Rory's exhibition in London.

The book launch was full of the usual crowd. As Peter looked around he realised the same crowd must just go from one gig to another. He never cared about this when he was arranging events; he was just grateful they turned up.

The launch was being held in a bookstore on Dawson Street that had been elaborately decorated for the occasion.

As he walked around, people kept coming up to him asking questions like "Where have you been hiding?". Some remarks were sympathetic, others sarcastic.

"Could have happened to anyone," commiserated an old PR friend from a rival firm. "Most models live on drugs, you know. I'm surprised it doesn't happen more often."

At least he could tell people he now worked for Macken. It sounded impressive, whatever the reality was.

Lynn was in her element mixing with the in-crowd. "Yes, I'm off to London the day after tomorrow for Rory's exhibition," she boasted to a small circle around her as she tossed her hair. "You know, there's been such a demand for his work. I'm sold out at The Gallery. If London's a success for him the sky's the – *owww!*"

Peter had just given her a small pinch on the arm. "London?" he whispered into her ear.

"We'll talk later." She shot him a filthy look.

He was about to launch a barrage of objections when he was distracted by the sight of Chloe walking through the main doors with Aran. He wasn't sure if he was more surprised to see her, or to see her with Aran.

In Chloe's usual confident manner she worked the room. People were so used to seeing Aran with Audrey, they were giving the couple double-takes.

Peter tried to read from their body language if there was anything going on between them. Chloe, ever the professional, was giving nothing away.

"Peter! I didn't have you down as a book lover!" Chloe was equally surprised to see him.

Peter felt like a kid having bumped into a teacher after school.

"Lynn's more the fan." Peter nodded at Aran. "Hi."

Aran took Peter's hand and gave a tight hard handshake. "Good to see you again," he said, without smiling. He was studying Peter intensely.

"Chloe! How are you?" Lynn turned from the people she had been speaking to and bent forward to kiss Chloe's cheek. "And Aran too!" She tried to keep surprise out of her voice.

Lynn began babbling to Chloe about Rory's exhibition in London, leaving Peter standing beside an obviously hostile Aran. Maybe Aran blamed him for the demise of Audrey's career, thought Peter. He embarked on small talk. "Busy at work?"

"Busier than you, by the sound of it."

"What's that supposed to mean?"

"Tell me, in your line of work, have you had much access to models?"

"Why?" asked Peter, puzzled by the question.

"Just wondered how many others you've been with besides Audrey."

"What are you talking about?"

"Yourself and Audrey. And the fact you were together the night of the show," hissed Aran.

"That's crap. Who said that? Did Audrey say that?"

"Hardly. Do you honestly think she'd go around boasting she'd been with you? You're not up to her standard, let's face it."

"Why do you care anyway? I thought you two were history?"

162

Chloe was winding up her chat with Lynn. "Well, wish Rory the best of luck from me," she said.

"I will, of course," said Lynn, who had observed Peter and Aran deep in conversation. Then she whispered, "I take it Audrey is off the scene?"

"Audrey who?" Chloe raised an eyebrow.

"Precisely my thoughts," Lynn nodded. "I'm so glad Peter has moved over to Macken. He's so much more suited to a bigger company."

"Er . . . yes, he is."

"And he's so much happier there than at Blast."

"Is he?"

"Oh, yes. You know what would be lovely – if yourself and Aran came over to dinner soon," Lynn suggested.

"Sure, that would be nice." She turned away. "Aran! There's somebody over there I need to speak to. Peter, I'll see you tomorrow."

She crossed to the other side of the room and, from afar, observed Peter and Lynn mingle and charm. Like the golden couple they had been at university years ago.

"What's wrong, darling?" Chloe asked Aran as they lay in bed.

"Nothing, just a little tired".

There was silence for a few minutes.

"Do you think Peter Reynolds is attractive?" Aran finally asked.

"Not in the least. Why?"

"No reason. But he would be considered conventionally good-looking?"

"I suppose, but it takes more that that to make someone attractive. You're wondering if he really was with Audrey, aren't you?"

"Not at all . . . what's his wife like?"

"The lovely Lynn? Full of her own importance. I was in college with both of them."

Aran sat up, suddenly interested. "What were they like?"

"We didn't really know each other. We hung out in different crowds."

"But what did you know of them?"

"They were small-time people who thought they were great. You know the type. They thought they were going places, but ended up doing nothing. Life has a habit of putting people in their place."

"Where do they live?"

"Some apartment. Look, they aren't even worth talking about. They're not in our league."

"Well, I have to hand it to Chloe Gallagher," said Lynn as she took off her earrings at home. "Can you believe it? Her and Aran Murphy."

"Imagine the children!" said Peter.

"I wouldn't mock them. They are going to be some couple together."

"What are you talking about?" Peter was irritated. "All I can compliment Aran Murphy on is his appalling taste in women. First mad Audrey and now Superbitch herself. And the only reason they are flocking to him is because of who his family is. It's little short of prostitution." He flung his tie in the drawer.

"When did you become so bitter?" asked Lynn. "You'd better start to like them, because I've asked them round to dinner."

"You did *what*?"

"They're people we should be mixing with socially."

"Even if I could stomach their company, Chloe wouldn't dream of coming around here."

"And why not?"

"Because she wouldn't condescend to sink to our level."

"Do you know, I'm just so glad I'm getting away to London for a little bit – to get away from listening to you! You've become so defeatist."

"And what the hell is this about you heading away?"

"I told you a while back. I'm going to Rory's exhibition."

"And I told you we couldn't afford it."

"And I ignored you and went ahead and booked it all on the credit card anyway!"

CHAPTER 27

"Take a seat, Peter," Chloe requested, without looking up.

He sat down and waited for her to finish signing documents .

Finally, she sat back in her chair and peered at him. "Peter, I'd like to talk to you about last night."

"The book launch?" He was confused.

"Yeah, the book launch. I don't want to be put in an embarrassing position like that again. An embarrassing and a compromising position."

"I don't follow you."

"The fact that I met you socially and had to speak to you."

"I really do not understand." He shook his head.

"You know there's a policy here at Macken to limit socialising. We don't permit admin to mix with PRs, or seniors with juniors. And you are very much my junior."

"So, you are suggesting we ignore each other if we bump into each other out socially?" He was astonished.

"That would be childish. I'm saying that you shouldn't

attend these events in the future. I have to attend these functions because of who I am. But it's irrelevant for you now you've left Blast."

"Chloe, my wife has to attend a lot of these events as well. I, naturally, have to accompany her."

"I suggest in future she brings a friend. I'm sure she has plenty."

"But this is outrageous. You can't dictate to me what I do in my free time."

"Yes, I can. When I go to official events like last night, I'm representing Macken. I become the face of Macken. PR is all about image. And I can't risk you tarnishing the image of Macken by people thinking that in some way you are representing us. You are not the image we want, Peter."

"And, if I refuse?"

"I'm not asking you. I'm telling you."

"She can't get away with it," Peter said to Dermot in his office.

"She can."

"You can't tell somebody what to do outside work."

"You can in this place."

"But, Lynn lives to be out socialising at these events and to be seen. I can't not go with her." He began to pace up and down.

"Will you calm down!"

"I've taken a lot, but I'm drawing the line. I'm going to make a complaint."

"To who exactly?"

"Macken himself."

"Are you mad? Make a complaint against Chloe?"

"Just watch me." Peter headed towards the door.

"Don't do it, Peter!" Dermot called after him.

Peter put in a request to see Brendan Macken. He was kept waiting an hour outside his office as a stern-faced PA with a tight hair-bun stared at him.

After receiving a phone call she said coldly, "Mr Macken will see you now."

Peter walked over to the door, knocked and let himself in. Brendan's office was even bigger and grander than Chloe's. Brendan's penetrating eyes bored into him as he took a seat across the desk.

Peter's anger was stronger than his fear. "I'm sorry for disturbing you . . . it's just, I'd like to make a complaint."

Brendan's eyebrow twitched for a second, but apart from that there was no reaction.

"It's Chloe, actually. I, er, obviously respect her a great deal as a professional. She – does a brilliant job. But I had a conversation with her today. She, kind of, banned me from socialising at public events." Peter paused for Brendan to say something, but he didn't. "It's just that my wife, Lynn, runs a gallery, and it's essential for her to attend events, and for me to accompany her."

"And your wife's gallery pays your salary, does it?" asked Brendan.

"No – of course not. It's just I think it unfair for somebody to be told what they can and can't do after work hours. I have a lot of respect for Chloe. But on this point, I think she's wrong."

"I won't go over a Director's head. Whatever she thinks best stands."

Peter felt totally humiliated "I see . . . thank you anyway."

Chloe sat opposite Brendan. Although Brendan never lost

his temper with her or they never even had a disagreement, she could see he was irritated.

"I don't need to be hassled with somebody coming into my office and complaining about their social life," said Brendan.

"Of course not. I can't believe he did that."

"I wasn't even listening to what he was saying. Something about you not allowing him to go to parties, or some such nonsense."

"It's a long story, which I'm not going to bore you with, Brendan. However, I was acting in the company's best interest," Chloe explained.

"Whatever. I don't really care. I don't want to know trivia."

"Of course." Chloe nodded.

"If there is a problem, it's Vincent who should be involved. He is Personnel."

"There's absolutely no need to bother Vincent with this either. I'll take care of it myself."

"Please see that you do," Brendan said sternly.

Chloe marched up through the Macken building. Her cheeks burned brightly. She had never allowed herself to lose her cool before. She couldn't believe what Reynolds had done. She was just grateful he had gone to Brendan rather than Vincent. Although Vincent would never dare go against her, he would take great delight in registering the complaint and exploring every detail of it. He had nothing better to do.

She pushed Peter's door open with such strength it smashed against the wall.

He looked up from his desk, stunned.

"How dare you complain about me!" she shouted. "Who

do you think you are that you went into Brendan's office to talk about me?"

"I had no option."

"They all wanted to fire you. It was me who argued to keep you on."

"For what? To humiliate me?"

"I'm not going to argue with you. But I'm telling you this: *you watch your every step*. I don't want to hear a squeak from you in future. You're on very shaky ground. And if I ever see your sorry face out at an event again without my strict authorisation, you're fired. My way or no way!" With that, she marched out, slamming the door behind her.

CHAPTER 28

Audrey was jittery with nerves. She was starting her hostess job at The San Juan Club that night. Noel had been very kind and brought her around to introduce her to the rest of the staff before starting work. All she had to do was go around and have a few words with the clientele, paying particular attention to VIPs and members – making sure everyone was happy and getting good service. If there was a quiet period, she would just collect glasses or give a wipe to the tables. As the night went on, she laughed off the numerous invitations to dance or to dinner. Some patrons were hard work to talk to, while with others she had a great laugh. By the end of the night, she felt invigorated and alive again.

"Did I pass the test?" she asked Noel as she got somebody's coat from the cloakroom for them.

"Kid, you were great. I'm genuinely surprised. I thought you'd walk out after thirty minutes. thinking you were lowering yourself."

"I'm a changed woman – although this nightclub atmosphere will play havoc with my skin!"

"Glad to see the old Audrey isn't totally gone!"

Peter sat down on the balcony while he polished off a bottle of whiskey.

Lynn was out with friends, a fact he was grateful for.

He felt so low. He had wanted so much to be a big success. To make Lynn proud of him. To be proud of himself. When the bottle was finished he dragged himself off to bed. He was fast asleep when Lynn got in. She grabbed a couple of hours' sleep and then got up at six in the morning. She had organised a taxi to bring her to the airport at seven and she hastily wrote Peter a note:

See you next week – X

When he woke the next morning his head was thumping. After reading the note he crumpled it up and threw it over the balcony. He cooked himself a big fry-up and decided he was going to enjoy the next few days alone. He was going to think out his life.

Muriel had received some calls from friends on the Sunday morning advising her Aran was mentioned in some of the gossip columns. She sent out for *The Sunday Independent*.

The article read: "*Latest power couple around town is eligible bachelor Aran Murphy, scion of the solicitor dynasty, and Chloe Gallagher (pictured), Director at Macken PR. Readers may remember Aran is an ex-squeeze of Audrey Driver. Audrey came to our attention recently when she disrupted the Childwatch Fashion Show. She has since retired from modelling and works as a hostess at trendy San Juan Club. Chloe, one of Dublin's most powerful PR figures, has dated a series of men with immaculate credentials before, but nothing, so far, too serious. Aran and Chloe made a glamorous couple at the book launch . . .*"

Muriel studied the photo of Chloe. She hated it when Aran was in those tacky columns. How could a former relationship be described as "an ex-squeeze"?

The columnist had always taken a subtle interest in him, but really started to go to town when he started seeing Audrey, because of her high profile.

She found Reginald in the drawing-room.

"Do you know this young woman, Chloe Gallagher?"

"She's handling our political lobbying. She's a Director at Macken."

"Seemingly she's dating our son."

"Really? So? I thought you'd be glad that Audrey was out of the picture?"

"Oh, I am. But who is this new one?"

"I told you, a – "

"But who are her family?"

"I don't know. But I do know she's a very talented young lady. Brendan leaves her to run his company, by the look of it."

"I just wish Aran would date somebody whose family we knew. Doesn't Brendan himself have any daughters?"

"I assure you, Aran's doing well with Chloe. In fact, she could be just what we're looking for."

Chloe sat in her dressing-gown on her patio scrutinising the photo of herself in *The Sunday Independent*. She looked good and she was thrilled with the story.

She got up when the doorbell rang. She had been expecting Aran.

"Hi," she said as she opened the door and kissed him.

He followed her out to the patio.

"Wondered if you felt like going out for a drive into the country? Have lunch in a pub somewhere," he suggested.

"Sounds good to me. Did you see the papers?"

"No." He picked up the article and started reading it. "Shit!"

"What's wrong?"

"My parents will hate this."

"Will they?"

"They hate any kind of publicity. They are really protective about their privacy. That was one of the reasons they hated Audrey, because she was so high profile."

Chloe thought fast. "Mmmh. I know how they feel. I've worked too hard and come too far to be the object of tittle-tattle. I'm friends with the editor of this paper. I'll have a word with him tomorrow and try to stop this kind of thing appearing about us again."

"That would be really cool."

"I'll just change. Won't be long." She padded off to her bedroom.

He admired the sea view. He had to admit Chloe was impressive. She seemed to know everyone and had achieved so much. She was in control of her life. In fact, she was the total opposite of Audrey. There was no crap with Chloe. She never played mind games or tried to screw him around. He had gently tried to probe into her past, without sounding too intrusive. But so far he hadn't found out anything, not even a long-term boyfriend. With her looks and charm, she couldn't have been short of suitors. He wondered what it was about him that made her want to go out with him. It was very relaxing to be seeing Chloe after the rollercoaster of arguments and outbursts with Audrey. However, it was sometimes a strain, as he felt he should always be on his best behaviour with her. Almost not be himself.

As Chloe emerged back on the patio looking great, he

told himself he was being stupid. Of course he was being himself with her. Just because they weren't screaming at each other, like he had been with Audrey, didn't mean he wasn't being himself.

"The papers, have you seen the papers?" Leslie gasped down the phone to Audrey.

Audrey was exhausted. The club had stayed open extra long the night before. She had got up two hours previously and had something to eat while glancing through the papers. She had screamed out loud when she had read about Aran and Chloe and had taken to her bed again.

"I've read them – several times," Audrey groaned.

"I thought she was supposed to be a friend of yours."

"She was."

"And as for him, now you know why he hasn't been ringing you." Leslie was furious for her friend.

"We haven't even officially finished!" said Audrey.

"Well, you are now," informed Leslie.

"True."

After a further hour of analysis, Audrey said goodbye and hung up. She lay back into her pillows and closed her eyes.

"*Fuck!*" she shouted as the phone rang again. She grabbed the receiver and snarled, "Yes?"

"Audrey, it's Peter Reynolds. Could we meet up for a talk?"

CHAPTER 29

Dublin's streets were wonderfully empty as Peter drove to Blackrock to meet Audrey. He'd had enough. He felt physically sick at the idea of going back to Macken the next day. He was going to recapture his confidence and drive, before it was lost for good. He would lose his sanity if he spent the rest of his life in a backroom in that place. He might even lose his marriage. He knew what Lynn expected from life, and he wasn't providing it. He was going to explore every avenue to get his life back on track. Including meeting Audrey.

He pulled his car up beside the pub they had arranged for the rendezvous. He was surprised to find Audrey already inside. He had been prepared to wait for up to an hour, with her usual lateness.

"Thanks for meeting me at such short notice," he said, sitting down.

"Glad to get out of the apartment for a while. You read the gossip columns?"

"About Aran and Chloe? Yeah. I saw them together at a book launch last week."

"Did you?" She wanted to quiz him, but fought the inclination. "Well, as far as I'm concerned, they deserve each other. His mother will be delighted – a successful professional woman, just what she wanted for her wonderful son."

"His family disliked you?"

"That's putting it mildly. They think they're the royal family. You know, nobody had even heard of Aran before I went out with him. Even in today's article, they talked about him in relation to me" She stopped herself as she realised she was saying too much. "Anyway, we're not here to talk about my love life. What exactly are we here to talk about?"

"I've been giving your proposal some thought."

She raised an eyebrow. "You were very dismissive before."

"Do you blame me? After the shit you caused?"

"Are we here to talk about ancient history or about my idea?"

They glared at one another.

Peter broke the silence. "A Model and Celebrity Management company, that was the idea, wasn't it?"

She nodded.

"With me and you as partners?"

"Fifty-fifty."

He shook his head slowly. "Such a big step to take."

"If you weren't interested you wouldn't be here."

"Why would I need you as a partner?"

"Because I'm famous."

It was Peter's turn to raise an eyebrow.

"You know what I mean, I'm well known. People know who I am. The press would give us immediate attention. And, as I told you, I know the beauty and the fame game."

"And why do you need me?"

She sighed "I told you, your business brain. Your ideas. You are excellent at PR and promotion."

"I'm glad somebody thinks so."

"You only get one life, Peter. There's no point in fucking it up."

"I've very little finance to be starting up a business. I'm heavily mortgaged."

"Your wife works, doesn't she?"

"Lynn's salary is nothing to write home about."

Audrey smirked. "You wouldn't think it, the way she holds herself."

Peter looked at her cautiously. "That's strictly confidential."

"Of course. I've already spoken to my Bank Manager. I've got shares I can sell and I can raise equity on my apartment."

"Your modelling years seem to have set you up nicely."

"I'm by no means well off, but I didn't squander what I earned."

"I thought you had an extravagant lifestyle. One of the advantages of going out with wealthy men I suppose is that you can save your own money."

Audrey's cheeks burned. "A lot of that is image, as you should know. I've always paid my own way, for your information. Could you ask your family for money?"

"My family have a stud farm and everything's tied up in that. And my brother is taking that over."

"Lynn's family?"

"Her family are connected , but they aren't in any way loaded either. She's away in London at the moment. She'd hit the roof if she knew I was even talking to you."

"Listen, this isn't getting us anywhere. The great thing

about starting up this kind of business is that it doesn't cost a fortune. All you need is an office, fax, phone, email and talent."

"C'mon, this kind of business is all about image!" said Peter. "You need a big plush office straight away."

"OK, but we rent that out. As I said before, if we both put up ten thousand we'd be home and dry."

"We wouldn't be able to draw a salary until the money starts coming in. If the money comes in." said Peter.

"We wouldn't pay ourselves much to start off with," Audrey answered.

"That's easy for you to say – you have a second job at the San Juan, according to the papers."

"That's only a couple of nights a week."

"Or you could just find another rich boyfriend to support you."

Audrey's eyes blazed. "Look, if you are just going to hurl insults, I'll leave." She stood up.

"I'm sorry. Sit down and keep talking. I think we're getting somewhere."

They ordered a lunch, and the hours passed away as they kept talking.

"When we form a company, all the expenses would go immediately through it."

"I can't afford to miss even one month's mortgage repayment," Peter warned.

"Hopefully," she answered, "you won't have to."

"Wouldn't it cost a fortune to have the models photographed and produce model cards?"

"It won't cost us anything. The models can pay for it themselves. We come to an arrangement with a photographer that we send our models to them and we get a commission. If a model is exceptional, and we feel she'll be a big earner, we'll pay for her photos. Because we might lose her to another agency otherwise."

Ten minutes later, she began to talk about deportment classes.

"Deportment classes?" Peter was incredulous.

"They can be big money-spinners. Mothers love sending their daughters on these courses and it would be a lucrative sideline till we establish the business properly."

"We don't want to be in the business of taking money from kids!"

"They are paying for a service. And also it's a great way for talent-spotting. We'll sign up any good girls to the agency."

"And you could give these classes?" asked Peter.

"It's second nature to me."

"When we have all our model cards," said Peter, "we'll send them out to every advertising agency, PR manager and marketing manager in the country."

"When we start the agency it would be essential to have as much PR in the papers as possible so everyone knows who we are. What about a launch party?"

"Too expensive." Peter shook his head. "A photo call could generate us as much publicity at a fraction of the cost."

It was eight in the evening before they were ready to leave.

"So you are genuinely interested?" asked Audrey as they walked to their cars.

"Yes, I am. But there are two major obstacles. Money and Lynn."

"Meet your Bank Manager and see what he says." She thought for a second, "Maybe I could put some extra money in –"

"No!" snapped Peter. "I want to have equal control if it's going to happen." He got into his car. "I'll call you tomorrow."

Peter tossed and turned all night. He was full of excitement after the day's plans. Full of excitement, and dread and worry. Was he mad even to contemplate it?

No, just desperate, he thought. But he also noticed a huge change in Audrey. She seemed much more earnest and down-to-earth. But he still found it hard to consider her as a business partner. But he found it harder to think of continuing to work for Chloe. He heard Lynn's voice in the darkness whispering that he hadn't achieved in the past, because he never believed in himself.

CHAPTER 30

"I'm sorry, but it's just not feasible," the Bank Manager sat sternly opposite Peter. "You are too heavily in debt already with your mortgage. The Bank can't risk lending you any more money. And on a personal note of advice, Mr Reynolds, I'd be very cautious about leaving full-time employment to start your own business, with a mortgage like yours hanging over your head."

Dejected, Peter walked back to the Macken Building.

Audrey rang his mobile. "Any luck?"

"Not a chance."

"For God's sake, it's not like you're asking for a million, just a few thousand!"

"It's a lot when you consider our mortgage."

"Why don't you just move to a more affordable place?" Audrey reasoned.

"Are you kidding? It's Lynn's pride and joy living there. She's even talking about moving up, not down."

"Sounds like a practical kind of woman! Keep thinking anyway. Any assets you can sell off? I'm going looking at some offices this afternoon, see what's out there, suss out rents. Talk later." She hung up.

As he entered the Reception at Macken he passed Chloe who snapped, "My office in five minutes."

"These reports you gave me concerning the shopping-centre project for Murphy Hennessy just aren't good enough. Sure, they tell me the area needs a shopping centre. But I want reports that scream this at me. I want you to up the tempo and word them more enthusiastically."

He was about to say that reports carry more clout if they are presented in a neutral fashion. It made them more believable. But he thought, what the hell, what did he care?

"OK." He took back the data.

She threw some press releases at him. "And check these over."

He looked at her and wanted to say something sarcastic about her photo in the *Sunday Independent*. There would be no stopping her once she got her claws into Aran. As he left her office, Brendan walked in. They exchanged nods.

Brendan waited until the door was closed before speaking. "Is he giving you more trouble?"

"No, I had a serious chat with him about attitude. He's finding it hard to adjust to the fact he isn't a hotshot any more."

"Well, don't take any rubbish from him." Brendan's previous irritation about the matter had evaporated, and his tone was much softer to her.

Then he uncharacteristically smiled, "I didn't realise you were seeing Reginald Murphy's boy."

"Er, Aran, yes. We've known each other for a while." Chloe very uncharacteristically blushed.

"Very good. Very good. I must have a word with you later about how their account is going."

The price of office rents in the capital shocked Audrey. She spent a couple of days touring around and finally found one that interested her. It occupied the first floor of an old Georgian building, not far from Grafton Street. There was a very large room at the front with long Georgian windows that let in plenty of light. There was a reception area at the top of the stairs on the landing and, down a corridor, there were two smaller offices at the back. She got the keys from the estate agent and arranged to meet Peter in the evening there.

"It looks like it hasn't been used in years!" He was horrified by the shabbiness of the place.

"That's why the rent is cheaper. I spoke to the agent who said we could refurbish it to our own taste."

"And at our expense?"

"Yes, but that's why the rent is cheaper than elsewhere," Audrey explained.

"This front room is very big," he said doubtfully.

"We need that. Models look at an agency as their home. They come in sometimes just to hang out, meet other models, their friends, and have a coffee or a cigarette. Modelling can be soul-destroying with all the rejection and they need to know they can come in here and support each other and just chill. The Ford Agency in New York treats its whole business as a family. The Fords live upstairs from the agency, and models regularly stay with them."

Peter realised she knew what she was talking about. "So this room is for them to hang out in?"

"Yes, but also for bookers to work from, when we can

afford them, and for clients to meet the models or view model cards. Kind of the heart of the business."

"But we can also meet them in our own offices in the back," observed Peter.

"Exactly."

"Do Hazel's models treat Boom as a home?"

"To a certain extent. I certainly felt a huge wrench when I left there. But Hazel always kept everyone on edge, so you could never really relax there."

They walked out onto the reception area on the landing.

"This is still an impossible dream," said Peter. "I have no financing, and I haven't even discussed it with Lynn."

"When's she back from London?"

"Tonight. I'm looking at this reception area and realising we can't even afford a receptionist."

"At the beginning, no. We'll do most things ourselves, but models often like to help out, you know. Make their own calls, try their hand at booking even. Some of Hazel's best bookers are failed models."

"That sounds exploitative." Peter frowned.

"I never had you down as being too concerned about using people in the past."

"It's amazing what working for Chloe Gallagher can do for the soul."

CHAPTER 31

"Hello, darling," called Lynn as she bustled through the front door laden down with shopping bags from Harrods and Harvey Nichols. She was followed by a taxi driver carrying her luggage.

Peter had been trying to rework their finances and quickly tidied away his paperwork.

"Thank you, so much," said Lynn to the driver, tipping him generously.

She then took off her new cashmere coat and scarf and went to kiss him. He didn't respond, as he stared at the shopping bags in alarm.

"I tried ringing you all day, but your phone was off," he said. "I was going to collect you at the airport"

"It was no problem. I shared a cab with Rory." She disappeared into the study.

Peter looked through the bags and grew angry when he saw the still-attached price-tags.

He stormed into the study after her. "You just went over there for an excuse to shop, didn't you?"

Lynn kept many paintings stored in the study and she was riffling through them. He was always giving out to her about her "art collection" which he saw as another waste of money that just gathered dust.

"I don't think you realise how bad our situation is. It just can't continue!"

She continued to ignore him as she pulled out painting after painting.

"Things have been happening while you were away and I need to talk to you –"

"Seven – seven in total." She carried the seven paintings out into the sitting-room.

"What are you talking about?" He followed her.

She spread the paintings out on the floor. "Seven Rory Ryans."

"I thought one of him was bad enough!"

"Very funny." She frowned. "Do you realise you haven't even asked me how my trip was?"

He gestured to the shopping bags. "I can see how it was."

"The exhibition was a huge success."

"I'm happy for Rory, but that doesn't change our situation."

"You know what I was getting for a Rory Ryan painting here in Dublin? Four or five hundred euros. He got such good reviews in the UK, that his paintings were fetching two thousand pounds sterling."

Peter dropped to his knees and studied the paintings. "That much?"

"And I met dealers over there who said they would buy any of his paintings I could lay my hands on. But there are very few available. Rory's been very tired lately and not been producing much. The Gallery certainly has none left."

"And you own these ones?"

"I bought them for a song about four or five years ago. In fact, I remember you berating me about wasting money at the time."

"That's fantastic!" he shouted, jumping up and hugging her.

"Are you mad?" Lynn asked.

They had opened a bottle of champagne to celebrate their good fortune. Then Peter began to tell Lynn about his discussions with Audrey.

"I can't believe you met her, let alone entertained thoughts of going into business with her. The girl is nuts –"

"Yes, but full of zest and she's well known –"

"For all the wrong reasons."

"People just love to hate her, that's all."

"*You* hate her!" she reminded him.

"I clashed with her. This would be different."

"And you are expecting me to put my money from the sale of these paintings into this crackpot scheme? I'm not even going to discuss this any further with you. That you would even contemplate leaving a good job at Macken –"

"It's not a good job," Peter snapped. "It's a shit job. And I'm treated like shit there. Last week Chloe Gallagher told me I wasn't allowed to attend any functions with you in future because it was bad for the company's reputation for me to be seen around – in case people thought I was representing Macken."

"*What?* She can't do that. I hope you told her to get lost?"

"She threatened me with the sack." He buried his face into his hands. "You don't know what it's been like. I've been covering up to protect you, but I can't continue like this. I'm in no way in an executive position at Macken. I'm just a dogsbody, and being treated as one all the time . . . that's the other reason she has forbidden me to go to functions – because she would have to demean herself by speaking to me if she met me at one . . . and you're always putting so much pressure on me for us to be a success . . . This could be the last opportunity I get, Lynn."

Lynn had visibly paled. "I – I'm very tired . . . after the flight. I'm going to bed."

She stood up and walked to the bedroom.

"Yeah, you just walk off," he said. She stopped and looked around. "Like whenever the going gets tough or there are setbacks and you can't face reality. Go into one of your depressions. Let me deal with everything and you just retreat into your dreams!"

"I'll see you in the morning." She continued into the bedroom and closed the door.

But Lynn didn't stir from the bed the next morning.

"Are you going in today?" Peter asked.

She didn't answer him.

"Suit yourself."

"Bad news, I'm afraid. She went ballistic," he told Audrey over the phone while he drove to work.

"You kind of expected that."

"Maybe we should just forget about it. It was a nice dream," he sighed.

"Come on, Peter, we have the adrenaline going. I know we can do this."

At the same time Chloe was driving to the Macken building from the other side of the street. She had a tape playing. The tape was an American voice repeating, *"I am a strong and capable person. I can and will achieve this."*

Both of their cars went to turn into the carpark together

but the entrance was only big enough for one vehicle at a time. Chloe gave him a warning look and he backed out of her way. She continued and parked into her director's parking space.

"I just nearly collided with Chloe," Peter said down the phone.

"Give the bitch my love," said Audrey.

CHAPTER 32

Chloe was having lunch at the Burlington Hotel with Ronan Flatley, when she spotted Larry Hennessy across the restaurant dining with a pretty young blonde. He was flirting outrageously with her and rubbing her hand. Chloe kept an eye on them over Ronan's shoulder as she argued her case for the shopping-centre.

Ronan was a very well known and popular Dublin politician. Aged fifty, he held great sway with the media and the public. When he spoke, people tended to listen and he wielded great power. The Murphy Hennessy land was right in the middle of Flatley's political patch and Chloe realised he would be a key ally in getting permission for the shopping-centre planning passed. So she had arranged to meet him.

"I just can't see how this shopping centre would benefit the area as much as housing. I have people ringing my office on a daily basis screaming for housing. We are so behind in supplying it that, at this stage, I don't know what we are going to do. And that land could help solve our problems."

"I understand your concerns, but the owners of that land very much want to develop it as a retail centre."

"At the end of the day, it's doesn't matter what they want. If the council earmarks it for housing, then that's that."

Chloe cringed at this thought. " I don't see it that way at all. I don't need to tell you how depressed that area is. There are few jobs there. A shopping centre will breathe life into the place and provide employment. Putting more housing there without further amenities or jobs will just create a ghetto."

"It's a fair point," Flatley conceded.

"Give these people something more than just housing – give them jobs and a future. That's the way to help them –" She broke off as she saw Larry Hennessey and his guest rise from the table, he helping her put her coat on. She smiled at Ronan. "Could you excuse me one second?" She got up and walked out into the foyer just behind Larry and the girl, hoping that Ronan would assume she was visiting the ladies' room.

"Larry!" she called. "Good afternoon!"

Larry swung around, surprised to see her. "Chloe, what are you doing here?"

"Having lunch with Ronan Flatley. I'm working on your account."

"Excellent . . . er . . . this is Danielle," he introduced his companion and the women smiled at each other. "We must have a meeting about that this week. I'll get my secretary to call you."

"Do that." Chloe turned to Danielle. "Nice meeting you."

Then, she turned away, taking out her mobile as if she were about to make a call. To her surprise, instead of leaving the hotel, Larry collected a key from reception and he and Danielle entered the lift.

As expected, when Peter arrived home, Lynn hadn't moved from the apartment all day. She was sitting on the couch in her dressing-room, pale, and her hair pulled back. Her smoking was the clearest give-away sign of her mood.

"I didn't realise things were so bad at Macken," she said quietly.

He sat beside her. "I wanted to protect you from the truth."

"I had hoped you would have a big future there."

"It's a closed shop," he sighed.

"I . . . I don't mean to pressurise you into being a success."

"I know that. But you expect a lot from life. As do I. And we were well on our way to getting there. But this setback . . ." he trailed off. "I really miss it, you know. I used to complain about my old job and the hassle it gave me. But I miss my phone ringing constantly. I miss all those problems arriving on my doorstep for me to sort out. I miss being pulled in all the directions at the same time, with people needing my attention or decisions."

"And you really think this business idea with this girl is the answer?"

"How many times have you told me to believe in myself and go for it? For once I want to do it," said Peter.

"But she's so unreliable, Peter. Why can't you just set up on your own, if you have to?"

"Many reasons. She's willing to put in half the money. She knows her side of the business very well. I'm the kind of person who needs a partner."

Lynn looked at Rory's paintings stacked against the wall. "It's a lot of money to risk. Not to mention losing your salary at Macken."

His eyes were pleading. "I want this chance."

Lynn put out her cigarette abruptly. "I'll broker a sale for the paintings tomorrow. You can have the money and set up the agency. But Peter, I'm warning you," she narrowed her eyes, "there's no room for failure with this. No room for any classic Peter Reynolds fuck-ups. None of your usual self-doubts or last-minute blunders. You go for success and get it. Because, I can't handle any more catastrophes. I really mean it. I don't think I could stay and watch you mess this up."

He leaned forward and took her in his arms.

"I bumped into Larry today," Chloe told Aran. They had met for a drink in Café en Seine after work. "He was with a very attractive woman."

"He's always in the company of an attractive woman," Aran smirked.

"I wonder why he never married?"

"Larry could never commit to one woman. He's too promiscuous."

"Many people are promiscuous, but still get married."

"Maybe the women don't stick around him too long either. He treats women like dirt. Dad had to help him cover up a few nasty rumours over the years."

"Rumours?"

"Forget I said anything." He took a sip from his drink. "And I mean it. He's a brilliant solicitor and he's been Dad's partner for years."

"I haven't said anything negative about him," Chloe reminded him. "I've always found him charming."

"Even my mother thinks highly of him. Of course she would, with him being from a very old, very rich family. Just what she likes."

Hmmm, thought Chloe, just what I'm not.

"Aran!" Muriel called from the drawing-room, when she heard Aran slam the front door.

Aran threw his eyes to heaven and popped his head around the door to see his parents seated and enjoying cocktails.

"Won't you join us for a drink?" invited Muriel.

"No, thanks. I've an early start."

"Anywhere interesting tonight?"

"Not really." He turned to go.

"I read about your new friend in the Sunday papers." Muriel kept her voice pleasant.

Here we go, he thought.

"I must say we are delighted you have terminated your friendship with Ms Driver."

"Yeah, I thought you might be, all right," he said.

"And when are we going to meet your new friend?"

Aran frowned. "Dad already knows her."

"Only on a professional level. It would be nice to meet her socially," said Reginald.

"So you can pick flaws in her?" Aran regretted his swipe as soon as it was said.

"I've known Chloe for quite a while and have found no flaws in her yet," said Reginald.

"And I haven't met her at all. I was thinking of having her over for dinner." Muriel suggested.

"Oh, whatever," Aran snapped and left the room. Sometimes he wished his parents had ten children so they wouldn't be so stressed checking on his private life all the time. Or he wished his mother had continued to practise law, so she wouldn't have all this time to concentrate on ensuring their great genes were passed correctly on to the next generation.

"Audrey had such a bad effect on him." Muriel shook her head sadly. "He's so defensive now. Never used to be like that."

"Just be grateful she's gone."

"And you really think this new one is good?"

"She's very impressive," confirmed Reginald.

CHAPTER 33

"I don't believe it!" shrieked Audrey.

"I don't think I can either," said Peter. He had called her as he drove to work the next morning.

"Where did you get the money from?"

"We can sell some assets."

"I'm delighted. And Lynn's fine about you going into business with me?"

"Not exactly. I'm not even going to go there. Let's get down to business. Are we happy with those offices we viewed?"

"I'm happy – with the rent and location and the layout."

"I'll meet you there this evening to view them again. And I'll contact a solicitor today about forming a company."

"Not Murphy Hennessy, I hope!"

"Certainly not! And listen, not a word to anyone until we're ready to go. It'll take a couple of weeks to refurbish and get the ball rolling. Money's short, so I'm staying on at Macken till then."

"No probs."

Lynn sat smoking at her desk in The Gallery. She usually wouldn't dream of smoking at work, but today she didn't care. Rory Ryan was sitting on her desk.

"It seems a little rash," he commented.

"What else could I have done? Put my foot down and said no and condemn him to a life of misery at Macken?"

"But he's risking both your futures," said Rory.

"I know. And with Audrey Driver, of all people. The cause of our problems in the first place. Do you remember the state I was in that night, Rory, when you collected me from The Berkeley? I wouldn't mind if she was any good, but she couldn't organise the proverbial piss-up in a brewery. Now, if he said he was going into partnership with someone like Chloe Gallagher, I would say great. But not Audrey!"

"It's not too late to say no."

"You haven't seen him lately, Rory. I suppose I didn't open my eyes to realise everything couldn't have been right at Macken."

"But it's time for Peter to realise he has a wife and he has a duty to look after her!"

"I know. I certainly didn't envisage all this stress when we set off down the matrimonial path." She dragged on her cigarette.

"For richer, for poorer," Rory sighed.

"He told me I put a strain on him by trying to make us into some kind of power couple."

"That's shit. Peter wanted that just as much as you. Now, just because everything has gone pear-shaped he wants to blame you."

"You are actually right." Lynn nodded in agreement. "I've told him this business has to be a success, because I can't take much more."

Audrey was already at the offices when Peter got there that evening. She was dressed in jeans and a T-shirt and she was busily cleaning and scrubbing.

"Now, that's something I never expected to see," he commented.

"If you weren't dressed in your fancy suit, you'd be on your hands and knees helping me. What kind of decor are we going for?"

"Something that catches the eye. Apart from all the models' photos there's nothing that stands out about Boom. It looks like a normal office."

After much deliberation they decided to go for white and red. White walls, with very long red curtains for the Georgian windows that stretched to the ground. Red couches and white carpet. Everything, including phones and desks had to be either of these two colours.

"I've been devising a business plan. Take a look through it and tell me what you think." Peter passed her a folder.

"When did you get time to do all this?"

"Your ex-boyfriend's account has been suffering because of it." He smirked.

"Good! Any ideas for a name?" she flicked through his report.

"Reynolds & Driver?"

"No, that sounds stuffy and old-fashioned. I want something catchy, like the name of your old agency, Blast."

"I came up with that name."

"In that case you can come up with an equally good

name for here." She went out to Reception and came back into the front office with a bottle of champagne and two glasses.

"What's all this about?" he laughed.

"Some champers to celebrate our new company." She cracked open the bottle and filled their glasses. "To our company. That it will be one big money-spinner!"

They clinked glasses.

Peter drank back his glass. "Money-spinner," he repeated. "Spinner. Spin is another word for PR. How about the name Spinner?"

"Brilliant!" She clinked her glass against his. "To Spinner!"

CHAPTER 34

Both of them worked flat out over the next two weeks. As soon as Peter finished at Macken each evening he went straight over to the new offices and got to work. So much had to be done, from arranging furniture to setting up a computer system. Most nights Peter didn't get home until after midnight.

"I still think we should have a launch party," said Audrey as they sat down exhausted after a night's work.

"We just don't have the budget. But we do need a lot of publicity to get us known and we need to get the ball rolling on that. I came up with a plan to kill two birds with one stone."

"I'm listening."

"Your rehabilitation." He drew his chair nearer to hers. "We re-launch you. Set up a series of interviews with the press about your battle with the bottle."

"My battle with the bottle! But I hardly touch the stuff." Audrey was aghast.

"That's not what most people think after the Childwatch Show. We could get you to become a patron of a charity dealing with alcoholics. You can talk about how the pressure of being a top model drove you to drink. And how you have now overcome that battle and are launching your own agency."

Audrey was horrified. "Absolutely not. I don't want to be in the papers being labelled a drunk."

"But that's what they're saying anyway. This way you can put your own spin on the situation and come across as a martyr. And help out a charity's profile into the bargain."

"I want to forget about what happened, not remind everyone."

"It will get the agency untold publicity. Everyone loves the story of someone overcoming an addiction."

Audrey's eyes were fiery as she stood up abruptly. "But it wouldn't be true. Apart from that bloody night, I rarely drink more than one glass of wine, if even that!"

"So what? You'll still be discouraging people from drinking, which can only be a positive thing. And it's all publicity."

"Fuck you, Peter. I'm not going to set myself up as a laughing-stock."

"Look, when they find out you've started Spinner they will try to tear you asunder anyway. This way we have control. We can turn what happened that night to our advantage. Think about it. We'll promote it that you know all the pitfalls in this industry, so you are the perfect head for an agency. Trust me."

"What part of 'no' don't you understand?" shouted Audrey.

"I think we should offer an exclusive first to Kitty Mulcahy . . ." Peter jotted down ideas in his notebook.

"Kitty Mulcahy! That bitch destroyed me in print last time she interviewed me. Said I had a pretty but vacant head, remember?"

Peter chuckled. "Yeah. That's precisely why she should get the exclusive. I know Kitty stereotypes models whom she sees as drama queens, which she mistook you for," he momentarily remembered Audrey's reaction when she hit that postbox, but dismissed the thought, "but give her a sympathetic story about alcohol abuse and she'll have nothing but sympathy."

"Peter, if I agree to this, I'm not going to be portrayed as an alcoholic. Just someone who was under huge pressure and took some drink to alleviate that pressure, OK?"

"Which is nearly the truth. I'll get in touch with some charities in this field and see if they are interested in you becoming a patron."

She felt uncomfortable about the whole idea. But she could see where he was coming from, and that was why she had picked him as her partner.

"Ms Gallagher. I have Mrs Muriel Murphy on the phone for you," said Chloe's secretary.

Chloe paused while she gathered her thoughts.

"Ms Gallagher? Will I say you are in a meeting?" the secretary asked.

"No. No. Put her through . . . Good afternoon, Mrs Murphy."

"Hello, Chloe, forgive me for calling you at work."

"That's no problem, Mrs Murphy."

"Please, call me Muriel. I'll get to the point. I'm having a very small dinner party tomorrow night."

At that moment, Peter knocked on her door and walked in.

Chloe looked up in annoyance. "Could you please just hold on for a second, Muriel." She pressed the mute button on the phone and roared at Peter: *"Get out!"*

Stunned and shaking with fury, Peter quickly retreated back outside where Chloe's secretary gave him a sympathetic smile.

Chloe knocked off the mute button. "I'm sorry, Muriel. A dinner party?"

"Yes, here at the house. Just Reginald and me, Laurence Hennessy, and Aran and yourself."

"That would be lovely, thank you."

"Good. See you then." The phone went dead.

Chloe sat in contemplation for a while and then buzzed her secretary. "Send Peter Reynolds in."

She was surprised to see Peter's red face and angry eyes. "Do you think that was an appropriate way to talk to an employee?" His voice was harsh.

"Don't ever walk into my office without permission again. And your work on the Murphy Hennessy account has been slack to say the least. Buck up your ideas and work with Dermot to come up with some new stuff."

"How dare she shout at me like that!" Peter was in Dermot's office. "She has no respect for anyone."

"Only unless you can do something for her," agreed Dermot.

"Can I trust you with something?"

"Sure." Dermot nodded.

"I'm handing in my notice on Monday."

"I see. Where are you off to?"

"I'm starting an agency with Audrey Driver."

Dermot hooted with laughter. "You are having me on?"

"I'm deadly serious."

"After the trouble she caused you? And she's so unreliable –"

"Save your breath. I've heard it all before. We have some brilliant plans and ideas," said Peter.

"Well, best of luck!"

"Thanks."

"No point in discussing the Murphy Hennessy account, I suppose. Chloe really must have treated you badly for it to come to this."

Peter discovered there was a new support group for alcoholics called Abacus. They were geared towards helping addicts rebuild their lives after they had conquered their addiction. He chose them because they were small and struggling for press attention. Having spoken to them, he found out they were extremely interested in meeting Audrey. After he set up a meeting, he put a call through to Kitty Mulcahy.

"You've been keeping a low profile," she commented.

"Been buried in corporate PR at Macken. I need to speak to you off the record."

"Fire ahead."

"Remember Audrey Driver?"

She sounded bored. "Hmmm."

"You know about how she overdosed on drink at my show?"

"Yeah, I always thought she was a silly cow."

"Yeah, maybe. But she's been doing some really interesting stuff since then."

"What, like working in a nightclub?" she giggled.

"Look, Kitty, I'll offer the story elsewhere if you're not interested."

"Sorry, continue."

"In a nutshell. She was about to crack America.

Pressure turned her to drink. Self-destructed. Retreated to rebuild her life and is now opening Spinner, a Model and Celebrity Management company. And she's about to become a patron at Abacus. I'm offering you an exclusive interview. It's heavy stuff."

There was a pause. "I'll have a word with my editor and call you back."

She called back thirty minutes later, agreeing to interview Audrey the next day.

Audrey was aware of how quickly Peter could work, but even she was surprised by his speed as she went to Abacus for the meeting that afternoon.

"I want to help people to understand how to balance their lives correctly so they don't turn to alcohol abuse," Audrey told the board of Abacus. "Or I'd like to show people who are dependent on alcohol that there's light at the end of the tunnel."

"I'm sure your story would act as an inspiration to many people," said the Chief Executive of Abacus. "I'm just wondering how we could best get your message across."

"Well, I'm going to be doing a series of interviews with the press about my problem. If I'm a patron with Abacus, I could also highlight the good work you are doing here. Also I could do a series of PR stunts for you. For example, run the Dublin Marathon in aid of Abacus."

"That sounds excellent," said the Chief Executive, looking duly impressed.

"They told me they would be honoured to have me as a patron," Audrey informed Peter at the Spinner offices that night. They were putting the final touches to it before the opening on Monday.

"Well, they are getting a well-known face offering to work for free, why wouldn't they be delighted?" Peter reasoned.

"Don't put a dampener on it."

"I'm not. Well done. Your big test will be the interview with Kitty Mulcahy tomorrow. Now let's go through it again to get it word perfect."

It was approaching midnight and Lynn was curled up on the couch watching an old horror movie. She was irritated that Peter wasn't back yet. Of course they had always worked unsociable hours without either of them complaining, but he had really gone overboard since Spinner started. Her phone rang and expecting it to be Peter, she answered it.

"Hi Lynn, it's Rory, I'm in Lillies. Come on in and join us."

"No. I'm chilling in front of the TV."

"Don't be a bore. Put your glad-rags on and grab a taxi here."

She thought for a moment – what *was* she doing sitting in on a Friday night?

"I'll be there in twenty minutes," she said.

CHAPTER 35

"Hazel will hit the roof when she finds out" said Leslie. She was having a coffee with Audrey in the Powerscourt Restaurant.

"Yes, she probably will. But what do I care? I modelled for Boom for years. I earned them a huge amount of money and when things went bad for me, all Hazel said was that we wouldn't bother having a post-mortem and that my career was over. There's your hat; what's your hurry?"

"Hazel Harte isn't known as Hazel No-Heart for no reason. What did you expect?"

"Nothing better, I suppose. But it should be better. I want to try to run things differently. Look at you, Leslie."

"Me?"

"Yeah, you're a fantastic model but Hazel won't give you the breaks or the push you deserve because you aren't one of her favourites. Which basically means kissing her ass, and projecting the right image and being seen out with the right men at the right parties. You never bothered with that bullshit and your career suffered for it. I got so caught up playing the game and I allowed Aran and his family and others like them make me feel bad about myself because I so wanted to be one of them. Well, not any more. I'm back but on my terms."

"Which is great. But with Peter Reynolds?"

"I know how much we clashed, but I saw another side to him when he looked after me. A side I haven't seen since and which he keeps totally hidden. What I'm saying is, he's not that bad. And great at PR. Leslie, I would love if you came to model at Spinner."

Leslie blushed. "I'm flattered but . . . I know I'm not a top earner at Boom, but it pays my way."

"I'm not going to put you under any pressure, but think about it."

Kitty Mulcahy ordered a coffee and settled into a sofa at The Westbury Hotel.

She expected it to be a long wait for Audrey. She couldn't believe it when Audrey strode towards her five minutes early. She did a double-take when she noticed Audrey's style was completely different from usual. On Peter's instructions Audrey wore the minimum make-up and had her hair pulled back off her face. She wore a simple cream dress. Despite the lack of her usual glamour, Audrey looked naturally beautiful, Kitty conceded.

"I expected to be waiting longer." Kitty got her dig in as Audrey sat down.

"I look on time differently now since I gave up modelling."

"How?"

"Before I was cramming so much in to my life that time passed me by without me noticing it. I was late for everything, as you well know, Kitty. I took too much on myself. We're all human at the end of the day."

"You must have been enjoying it or else you wouldn't have done it."

"Of course, I enjoyed it. I love this business. But you need to keep things in perspective. You need to take time out for yourself. It's easy to lose your head when you work in this business. And when that happens you can be led on to drink or drugs."

"Were you?"

"Drugs, never. And I never drank that much. But when you are constantly going to parties and are expected to be witty and look well all the time, you can use these substances as a crutch. It came to an end for me the night of the Childwatch Show. I was so caught up in everything I became a drunken mess."

"That ended your modelling career, didn't it?"

"Sure, I lost my American contract. But it was time for me to move on anyway. Now I'm starting Spinner, my chief concern is looking after the welfare of the models and clients we represent. I want to build their self-esteem."

"Peter told me you are becoming a patron of some charity?"

"The temptation to hide in drink and drugs is in every walk of life. We at Abacus are hoping to help rebuild lives when people hit rock bottom."

"Like you have?"

"Exactly like me. We are having an Open Day next week for potential models at Spinner."

"Yeah, yeah. Peter's given me all the background info. And what about your love life, Audrey? I hear Aran Murphy is dating somebody new."

CHAPTER 36

Chloe spent the whole of Saturday relaxing and preparing for the dinner party.

She bought a new outfit in the morning and had her hair done in the afternoon. Then she relaxed in a long bath so by the time Aran arrived to collect her she looked and felt great.

"I'm sorry about this," he said, kissing her when she stepped into his car.

"About what?" She was puzzled.

"My mother. She insisted on meeting you."

"Don't be silly. I'm looking forward to meeting your family socially."

When Aran drove into his family home she was taken aback by the size and grounds of the Murphy house. She made no remark.

"You look great," he whispered in her ear as they walked across the gravel driveway and up the steps to the house. "Good luck!"

"Aran," she took his hand and squeezed it gently, "will

you relax! There's nothing to be apprehensive about. I'm having dinner with your family, that's all."

Muriel sat next to Larry in the drawing-room. She adored Larry. She found him amazingly intelligent, charming, a true gentleman. She considered him to be the same class as themselves, mixing in the exact same circle and with the same connections. The fact that he had never married only added to his appeal. It made him more part of the Murphy family, the fact he had none of his own, Muriel reasoned. His numerous and various dates, always of an impeccable pedigree, were easily tolerated. Muriel knew Larry never stayed long with his girlfriends – nobody had ever come close to bagging his fortune. She often wished Aran could be as circumspect. Larry's date that evening was a friendly woman called Julianna, aged around forty, Muriel guessed. She was an accountant and hailed from a well-respected hotelier family.

The group were engrossed in conversation when Aran entered with Chloe.

"Ahhh, you've arrived." Muriel rose and, walking to her son, kissed his cheek. "And you must be Chloe." She arrested Chloe's arm and led her into the room.

"Thank you for inviting me, Muriel," said Chloe.

"Yes, and of course you know Reginald and Larry?" Chloe was greeted warmly by both of them and shook their hands. "And this is Larry's friend, Julianna."

Chloe was surprised, having expected Larry to be with Danielle, the girl he seemed close to in The Burlington.

"Now, take a seat." Muriel propelled Chloe to a chair. "And your drink is?"

"Just a white wine would be lovely, thank you."

"And a brandy for you, Aran," Muriel said, fixing the drink.

"Busy at work this week, Chloe?" Reginald enquired.

"Very busy. We had three launches."

"Chloe runs the Macken PR company," Reginald informed Julianna.

"I hardly run the company," laughed Chloe. "I'm a Director."

"That's not what I hear," said Muriel handing Chloe her wine and taking her seat again. "I hear you keep the show on the road."

"Not at all. Brendan and Vincent Boyer are very much hands on."

"Brendan's a good friend of ours," smiled Muriel.

"I know." Chloe smiled back.

Dinner was served in the dining-room by two household staff.

"Public Relations is just something I could never get my head around," said Muriel cutting into the duck on her plate. "I just think, what's the point of it?"

First test, thought Chloe. "That's because, Muriel, you're a trained solicitor and have a legal mind. So you are used to dealing with legalities and actualities. PR is more of a creative industry." She paused, taking a sip of her wine. "Also, when you left the business world, PR probably wasn't as important as it has become. Today, image is everything." A perfect measured response, Chloe thought. She had paid Muriel a compliment but also managed to slightly undermine her.

Muriel raised an eyebrow. "Left the business world? You make me sound prehistoric. I still do have a little say in the running of Murphy Hennessy, don't I, Reginald?"

"You have a say in the running of everything," said Larry, causing the party to laugh loudly. "Julianna, your firm is looking to change its corporate image – you should give Chloe a call"

"Yes, I hear you are excellent," Julianna smiled at Chloe. She knew Muriel Murphy of old, and knew what Chloe was up against.

Chloe reached into her purse and handed Julianna a card. "Please, do call me."

Muriel had been intently studying Chloe all evening. She was well aware of how intimidating her own presence was, and had turned it on full blast against Chloe to see what she was made of. Chloe hadn't faltered once.

"Who are your family, Chloe?" inquired Muriel.

"My family? My father recently retired as a Bank Manager."

"Ah, the bank! The preserve of the middle classes. And your mother?"

"Like yourself, a housewife." Chloe smiled, but the comment was cutting.

Muriel smiled and lowered her eyes, acknowledging she had been outplayed at her own game.

"We didn't get a chance for that meeting this week, Chloe. Definitely next week," said Larry.

"Whenever you are available and I'll put it in my diary."

Muriel continued to subtly direct the conversation through a variety of topics ranging from art to politics. She found Chloe articulate and informed on all subjects.

After dinner they retired back to the drawing-room for brandies and Muriel suggested Aran give Chloe a guided tour of the house.

Once they had left the room Reginald said, "You are certainly giving her the once-over."

"I'm just interested to know the company my son is keeping, that's all."

"I think you've met your match," Larry chuckled.

As they strolled through the house, Chloe came across as unimpressed, but was actually amazed by the extent of the art and antiques on view.

"I'm really sorry about my mother," Aran apologised.

"What's there to be sorry about? She's lovely. We got along fine."

"I'd hardly describe her as lovely."

"Well, I think she is," said Chloe.

They mounted the stairs.

"This is my room." He opened a door and she walked in.

It was actually two rooms, a sitting-room that led into a bedroom through a double door. He closed the door.

"I think she was impressed," he said and, taking her hand, led her to the luxurious bed. He sat and drew her down beside him. Then he kissed her and started to unzip her dress.

"No, Aran, not here," she objected, but he ignored her.

"Aran, stop it! Your parents are downstairs."

"So?"

Five minutes later, Aran was fastening up his shirt while Chloe tried to retouch her make-up in the huge mirror on the wall. Her cheeks glowed red.

"My dress is all crinkled," she snapped.

"So what?"

"So, I don't want your parents knowing what we just did." Her voice was cold, as she smoothed down her dress.

"That would blow the good impression I've just made. That was such a stupid thing to do."

He looked hurt and sat down on the bed.

Realising what she had said, she went to him and kissed him. "But worth it. Let's go back downstairs."

When Aran and Chloe said they would like to go on to a club, Julianna expressed an interest in going too.

"Oh, Larry, it would be fun," she pleaded.

"I think I'm a bit too old for nightclubs," he objected.

"Nonsense," said Muriel. "You might as well go out and enjoy yourself"

Larry finally agreed and they ordered a taxi.

"Thank you for having me," Chloe said to Muriel in the hallway before leaving.

"It's been a pleasure. Hopefully, we'll see you again."

"Well?" asked Reginald, closing the front door and re-entering the drawing room with his wife.

"Well, indeed. She's everything you said. Intelligent, professional, good-looking, a class act."

"And what we are looking for."

"Not from a moneyed background, I suspect."

"Purely a detail. She's earning the big money now, and she knows everybody."

"She seems very strong." Muriel sat down.

"Perfect breeding stock. But most important, she's not Audrey Driver"

"Where to? Lillies or Renards?" asked Larry.

"I'd love to go to The San Juan Club," suggested Julianna.

Chloe checked Aran's face for any change of expression, but there wasn't any. She remembered Aran had only glanced through the article in *The Sunday*

Independent and so probably didn't know Audrey worked there.

"Oh, that place can be such a bore," she objected.

"I love it. Please let's go there!" Julianna was determined.

Aran squeezed Chloe's hand. "C'mon, San Juan's always fun."

Maybe Audrey wouldn't be working that night. Or, more likely, Noel Flynn might have already fired her. "Sure, the San Juan is fine by me," Chloe conceded.

"It's quite late – will we get in?" Julianna looked worried.

"Of course. I know the owner," said Chloe.

"Is there anybody you don't know?" Aran smiled.

Noel was on the door and gave Chloe a big hug. He personally showed them into the members' lounge.

"If you want anything at all, Audrey will get it for you," Noel said before heading back downstairs to the door.

"Audrey?" Aran asked, confused. Then he spotted Audrey carrying a tray of drinks to another table.

"Isn't that your ex-girlfriend, the mad model?" asked Larry, bemused.

Aran froze as he observed Audrey sitting down at the table she had just brought drinks to, laughing and joking with the guests there.

"She's come down in the world," continued Larry. "A nightclub waitress"

"The term is hostess," corrected Julianna.

"Are you OK? Would you prefer we left?" Chloe reached over and took Aran's hand.

"Course not. It doesn't matter a damn to me if she's here."

Audrey cringed when she saw them. How could she

face Aran and Chloe? They were sitting there waiting for their order to be taken and she knew there was no way she could avoid it.

Standing up, she flicked back her hair and walked over.

"Hi, how are we tonight?" she said in a cheery voice.

Larry stood up and shook her hand. "I met you a few times before, with Aran."

Ten out of ten for discretion, Larry, thought Aran.

"Of course, I remember you, Larry. Hi Aran, hi Chloe," said Audrey.

"Audrey." Chloe acknowledged with a smile.

"What can I get you?"

"A bottle of champagne, please," Larry ordered.

"Coming right up." She flounced off to the bar.

"She's gorgeous, isn't she?" said Julianna.

"Isn't she?" Larry agreed, smiling at Aran and Chloe's discomfort.

"We really don't have to stay, if you don't want," Chloe repeated.

"I said I'm all right. She means nothing to me. It's in the past, all right?" Aran snapped.

Audrey came back with the champagne, which she uncorked. She then filled their glasses.

"Have you been working here long?" asked Chloe.

"A few weeks. I was bored, so decided I'd give this a shot."

"It suits you." Chloe smiled.

Condescending bitch, Audrey thought, resisting the temptation to pour the champagne all over her.

"And Aran. Mustn't forget Aran," Audrey said, filling his glass. She put down the bottle. "Give me a shout if you want anything else." Then she went and joined a group of wealthy businessmen at a neighbouring table.

"Her attitude seems to have improved," Larry commented.

"She's waiting tables. It would have to improve or else she'd be fired," said Chloe.

Aran couldn't help observing Audrey from the corner of his eye. He felt himself tense more and more as she flirted with the businessmen.

"Just going to the bathroom," Chloe said, standing and waiting for Aran to stand up to let her out. "Aran, can I get by you there?"

He didn't even hear her, transfixed as he was by Audrey.

"Aran!" Chloe called loudly.

"Sorry!" He was snapped out of his trance and jumped up. "Sorry, love"

The ladies' bathroom was large, marble and luxurious. Chloe was the only one there. Then, as Chloe reapplied lipstick, Audrey walked in.

She stared at Chloe's reflection in the mirror and slowly applauded.

Chloe looked around, and put her lipstick in her handbag.

"Well, I have to hand it to you, you don't waste time," Audrey said.

"Aran was finished with you," said Chloe. "I wasn't doing anything illegal."

"And you pretending to be my friend all along!"

"Let's face it, men like Aran don't come along every day. And I never considered us to be friends."

"I'm sorry, I just didn't realise what a false bitch you are."

"Look, you fucked up your life; you fucked up your relationship. Don't try to blame me for it. And you certainly didn't treat Aran with the respect he deserved when you were going out with him."

"That's his story. But you know, Aran isn't plain sailing either. He's possessive and extremely jealous – or maybe he just hasn't shown you that side of him yet. Maybe he doesn't care enough about you to be jealous if you so much as talk to somebody else. As for his family –."

"I know the Murphy family and get on very well with them."

"Figures, you deserve each other."

"Do you really think they ever took you seriously? They would never have allowed you to settle down with him."

"You know nothing about my relationship with Aran. You're just a rebound job."

"At least my job is not clearing tables in a nightclub."

"Well, watch this space!"

Chloe walked to the door. "Get out of my way, or I'll have you fired out of this place quicker than you can imagine."

Audrey stepped aside. "I have no doubt you'll be on the phone to Noel first thing Monday trying to try to do just that anyway."

Chloe slammed the door after her.

Back at their table Julianna was pleading with Larry. "Come on, let's dance!"

"I'm too old to be dancing in clubs. Aran, you go dance with her."

"Want to join us?" Aran asked Chloe.

"No, you go ahead."

Aran and Julianna walked out of the members' lounge and onto the dance floor.

"It seems to be going strong," said Larry. "The two of you."

"Yeah."

"I think you got the family seal of approval, which is the main thing."

"How does Danielle feel about Julianna?" Chloe was curious.

Larry raised an eyebrow, laughed and refilled his glass.

"I'll be over in a minute," Aran said to Julianna after they finished dancing and she was returning to their table.

He waited in the shadows, observing Audrey. After a while, she rose up and headed towards a small side bar.

He followed her. She was pulling a pint.

"You've moved on to beer now, have you?" he asked.

She looked up, surprised. "It's for a customer."

"Is this what you've come to? Chatting up leering middle-aged men?"

"It's my job and I enjoy it. You are showing that famous jealous streak of yours. And I don't know why, because isn't that your girlfriend out there waiting for you?"

"Where did you go to? I kept ringing your phone, but it was always off."

"I took some time out for myself. I needed to sort things out. Did you really think I was going to let you treat me the way you did?"

"And what about the way you treated me during our relationship?"

"If I did treat you badly, I'm sorry, but I felt smothered by you sometimes.

"And what kind of support did you ever give me?" he asked.

"Actually loads, if you think about it, but you just wanted me there all the time pandering to your every need and whim. I'm just happy now you have such a kind and caring partner who will give you all the support you need." She took the filled glass and pushed past him.

Shortly after, she gathered some rubbish from tables and went into the back kitchen to get rid of it in the bin.

Suddenly she was grabbed from behind and held tightly.

"What the –" She turned and was shocked to see it was Larry Hennessy who was holding her. "What the hell are you doing?"

"Just came in to say hello," he said.

"This is staff only." She struggled free. "Get out!"

He went to kiss her but she pulled back. "What are you doing?"

"Just being friendly."

"I'd prefer if you weren't!"

"Are you trying to tell me you won't be going home with one of those businessmen tonight. Come home with me instead," he urged.

"I'm not going home with anybody, especially you. My God, you are Aran's father's business partner!"

"Yes and you are now finished with Aran. He wouldn't mind. I'm practically family."

"I'm going to scream for security if you aren't out of here within five seconds!"she blazed.

Larry reached out and touched her chin and then, laughing, he walked out of the kitchen.

He rejoined the group. They were all sitting in stony silence, each thinking about his or her individual encounter with Audrey that night.

Except, of course, for Julianna. "Isn't this night so much fun!" she exclaimed.

CHAPTER 37

On Monday morning, Chloe had her secretary send flowers to Muriel with a thank-you card, before phoning Noel Flynn.

"Chloe! Did you enjoy yourself on Saturday night?" asked Noel.

"I had a great time. Lots of people are telling me they now prefer San Juan to Lillies or Renards."

"Really? That's great."

"I always recommend San Juan to anybody I know."

"Well, if you ever need anyone to get the VIP treatment, let me know."

"I'll do that. Bit surprised by your choice of staff though," said Chloe.

"Huh?"

"Having somebody like Audrey Driver working there."

"Audrey's OK."

"Oh, I'm not saying she isn't. But her attitude mixed with all the stories about her, remember? If she wasn't having a public brawl with some footballer boyfriend she was falling down drunk."

"I think she's moved on from all that now. Anyway, I always admired her spirit," Noel laughed.

"I just think from a PR point of view she's bad news for you and the club." She laughed. "There, I'm giving you a consultation for free."

"Quite the reverse. We've got loads of mentions in the press since she came to work here. Anyway she's only here a couple of nights a week."

"Well, it's your call. But I think she's lowering the tone of the place."

"The kid needs a break. She's had a tough time recently."

"All her own doing. Anyway, I won't detain you. Call me and we'll do lunch." She slammed down the phone.

There was a knock on the door.

"Come in!" she shouted.

Peter walked in and hovered.

"What is it?" she snapped.

"Just wondered if you had a free minute."

"I've got a hectic day. What?"

He sat down on the chair across from her.

"I hope you've been working on the Murphy Hennessy account over the weekend to try and catch up," she said. "I'm meeting them this week."

"I'd like to hand in my notice." Peter's face remained expressionless and he placed an envelope containing his resignation letter on her desk.

It took her only a split second to mask her shock. She leaned back in her chair and joined her hands "I see. This is all very sudden. Where are you going to?"

"I'm not at liberty to say." He knew this lack of information would infuriate her.

Chloe leaned closer and rested her arms on her desk.

"Do you realise this company gave you a chance when nobody else would? Even though we had those doubts about you, we took that chance on you. Because you have started to show your worth a little . . . what would you say if I had a word with Brendan about a salary increase?"

"Very kind, but I'm definitely going."

"But you don't know what I'm offering."

"It wouldn't matter. My mind is made up."

"How does Lynn feel about this move?"

"She's totally in agreement with me."

Chloe sat in silence, thinking about what to say next. "There's nothing I can do to encourage you to stay?"

"Not a thing."

"OK." She sat back in her chair. "By the terms of your contract you'll be expected to work out a month's notice."

"Month's notice?" Peter laughed. "I don't think so."

"It's in your contract. We need you to finish the projects you're working on"

"I'm leaving Macken today."

"Today! You can't give that kind of short notice!"

"I have no choice."

"If you don't work out your full notice, I'll have no choice but to give you a bad reference."

"That's immaterial in my present circumstances. Besides, Chloe . . . sorry, *Ms* Gallagher, I wouldn't rely on a reference from you. I'm going to clear out my office now." Peter got up and walked to the door.

"Peter!" Chloe called.

Turning, he saw she was smiling.

"We wish you every success in whatever ventures you have planned."

He nodded and left.

It took Peter ten minutes to clear out his office. As he

walked to the front door, he listened one last time to the building's eerie silence. And then he was walking down the steps onto the streets and away from Macken. Suddenly he was running and laughing.

Chloe went through Peter's contract in Vincent Boyer's office.

"He's obviously breaking his contract, so we can sue him," she said.

"Hardly worth it. Our legal costs could be high, not to mention the bad press we would get," said Vincent.

"It would be worth it as a warning to other employees who think they can just swan out when they feel like it."

"Very few employees serve out their full notice anyway."

"Well, they should do! It's an agreement and they should be made to stick to it."

Vincent was taken aback by the severity of Chloe's reaction. It was usually he who was overly strict on personnel protocol.

"Does it matter?" he asked. "We wanted to get rid of him since the takeover at Blast. Good riddance, that's what I say."

"It was you and Brendan who wanted to get rid of him," Chloe accused. Her tone was too harsh. She adapted her tone to a softer one when she saw the surprise on Vincent's face. "It's just that I'm very annoyed with this situation. Reynolds was in the middle of working on some important projects and he's left me in the lurch big time."

"I see. I'll contact employment agencies tomorrow and put adverts in the papers to find a replacement for you."

Chloe nodded and returned to her office.

"No calls till I tell you," she barked at her secretary. She remained in her office undisturbed for the rest of the day.

"I'm outta there!" Peter roared as he raced up the stairs to the Reception at Spinner.

"I'm in here!" Audrey called from her office at the back of the building. He found her putting files up on her shelves. "How did she take it?"

"She offered me more money."

"Were you tempted?" Audrey was alarmed.

"Not a chance. Then she got nasty when she found out I was leaving today. Then, typical Chloe, she tried to smooze up to me when she realised there was nothing she could do to stop me going. What have you been up to?"

"I met with Matilda today, the photographer."

"She's the girl from London?"

"Yeah, I've worked with her a lot. She's really cool and down-to-earth. She had a big studio in London and worked for *Vogue* and *Cosmopolitan* and them all."

"Why did she come to Dublin?"

"She fell in love with an Irishman and moved here. Anyway, the deal is we send models over to her looking to do up their portfolios, she photographs them at a discount and Spinner gets a cut. She will also give us any advice we need concerning a model's potential or look."

"Sounds good. So why the worried look?"

"I'm terrified about what Kitty Mulcahy's going to write about me in the paper tomorrow . . . I'm also terrified that Spinner will be a flop. That we won't get any good models or work."

"Hey, hey, too late for doubts now. We've both risked everything for this. We have to go full force ahead and not even think about negatives." Peter was suddenly reminded of how unstable Audrey had been to work with in the past. He searched her face for signs of this instability.

"It's easy for you to say. You've worked in PR for years. I haven't. All I've done is modelling. I'm not sure I'll be any good at this side of it."

"It will come naturally to you. You say you've never worked in PR. How many times have you been in the papers? You know this business inside out. Trust yourself and go with the flow." He sat down on her swivel-chair.

"Thanks for the vote of confidence."

"Hey, I wouldn't be sitting here if I didn't believe in all of this. And that means believing in you too," he said.

"I know you've risked a lot and I don't want to let you down." She sat down and looked at his smiling face, which always had a trace of arrogance. Even though she had got to know him a lot better over the past weeks, he still came across as the tough Peter Reynolds she knew of old. But every now and again he showed this other side to him. The side that had looked after her the night of the Childwatch Show. "You know, I never properly thanked you for taking care of me that night."

Peter swivelled around in the chair. "Please, Audrey, spare me. I can't stand this softer side of you. Give me back the old Audrey Driver. The selfish, scary bitch!"

Audrey saw red. "Well, fuck you! That's the last time I try to be nice to you."

"Good!" he laughed. "At least I know where I am then."

"You shouldn't have waited up." Peter found Lynn watching television when he got home after midnight.

"There was a good movie on."

"Ahhh, right," he said, pouring himself a glass of milk

in the kitchen. "You should have seen Chloe's face when I handed in my notice. She was horrified." He decided to hold back the fact he had been offered more money to stay.

"I thought you'd call me earlier to tell me how it went. I was dying to know."

"I'm sorry, love. I was busy trying to get everything right for the opening of the office tomorrow."

"You've hardly told me a thing about how everything is going. Coming in after midnight every night."

"Setting up is always the hardest part. It'll get easier after this and I'll have more spare time."

"I hope so," she said.

"Anyway, you've never worried about me working late before. As I haven't with you." Peter gulped down his milk.

"But every single night?"

"As you said to me, no room for failure."

"Whatever. Is Audrey putting in these hours as well?"

"She is. In fact, she was still working away when I left," Peter informed her.

"That's because she has nowhere to go now Aran has dumped her."

"I'm sure she'd never be short of a date."

"Oh really?" Lynn's expression was one of amusement. "You think she's attractive then, do you?"

Peter was about to be defensive when he realised Lynn was being sarcastic.

"Oh, shut up!" He threw a cushion at her and they both laughed.

Chapter 38

Audrey didn't dare read Kitty Mulcahy's interview until she was safely in her office. Then she took the paper from under her arm and spread it out on her desk. As she scanned through it she was greeted by a big photo of herself and a heading: *Audrey Driver – The Perils of Modelling.*

She held her breath and read through the article.

"As we look at beautiful models, it's all too easy to see them as superhuman. Audrey Driver demonstrates that this often isn't the case. Audrey had it all, looks, fame and a contract with an American cosmetic firm. Then it all went sour. It's a more relaxed, natural and confident Audrey sitting beside me in The Westbury Hotel today. Audrey is normally a teetotaller, but she tells me the pressure of her work literally drove her to drink. We all remember the press stories and rumours about Audrey at the Childwatch Fashion Show. It's been a tough journey, but Audrey has finally got her life back on track. She has retired from modelling, has become patron of the Abacus Charity and has just set up a new agency, Spinner, with former Blast and Macken PR guru, Peter Reynolds. It's a fascinating story Audrey begins to tell me . . ."

As Audrey read on, she blessed herself when she saw it was all positive.

"Well?" said Peter, leaning against the door of her office.

"It's brilliant. Really, really brilliant." There were tears in her eyes.

"Consider yourself rehabilitated. Most importantly, she gave Spinner a big plug and as promised gave our phone number and address for the Open Day."

The phone began to ring on Audrey's desk.

Startled she picked up the receiver. "Good morning – Spinner – how can I help you?"

"Hi, I'm just enquiring about the Open Day mentioned in today's paper. Could I come in for an interview?" a young girl's voice enquired.

Audrey winked at Peter. "Sure. Are you available to come in today? Twelve o'clock? Bring in a head-and-shoulder photo and a full body shot, as natural as possible. You have the address from the paper? Good, see you then."

She hung up and the phone rang again. "Good morning, Spinner . . . That's right. Are you available for an appointment today?"

Every morning the papers were delivered to Chloe's office. It usually took her twenty minutes to speed-read through them. It kept her up to date with what was happening and also allowed her to check for any positive or negative press her clients were receiving. Although Macken employed a media-monitoring company gathering such information, she liked to read items first-hand. She often managed to pick up things the media monitors didn't. That morning she flew through the papers, noting nothing much of interest until she came across a huge photo of Audrey. Absorbing the headline she quickly read the interview.

"The bastard!" she shouted when she read that Peter had gone into business with Audrey, then slumped back into her chair staring at Audrey's photo.

One of Aran's cousins rang him telling him to get a copy of *The Independent* quickly and look at Page 10.

"I don't believe it," he said to himself when he read the Kitty Mulcahy interview. "She couldn't even run her home properly, let alone a business." He read on. "With Peter Reynolds!"

"I just feel they concentrated too much on Audrey and only mentioned you in passing." Lynn expressed her opinion down the phone to her husband as he sat in his office.

"Darling, the interview was about Audrey, not me. We were just using it to give Spinner a plug too. I think it's brilliant PR, don't you?"

"I suppose."

"The phones haven't stopped hopping with people wanting to join up."

"It's easy to get young people to chase dreams, Peter. It's selling those dreams on to real clients who'll pay real money is the difficult part," warned Lynn.

"I know that." Peter raised his eyes to heaven.

"And I hope Audrey is grateful to you. That interview managed to make her look like a victim of the system instead of the silly little cow she really is."

"Now, Lynn, we're in business with her now, so let's all try and be nice. There's some more calls coming through, I'll call you later."

As Peter hung up and glanced down at Audrey's interview, he tried to imagine Chloe's face when she saw it.

Audrey answered the phone. "Hello, Spinner."

"I can't believe what you've done!" Hazel's harsh voice shrilled down the phone at her. "Setting up in competition to me, without as much as a phone call warning me!"

Audrey sighed. "I was actually going to ring you today. But I couldn't until the article was printed."

"This is how you repay me after all I did for you?"

"I needed to get on with my life and this is the only business I know."

"When you modelled you couldn't get yourself anywhere on time to save your life, so what says you can manage other people's time schedules? I built you into what you are and you've stabbed me in the back!"

"Hazel, you had me on your books all those years because I made you money and you kicked me out the minute I stopped earning you money."

"I gave you another chance in the commercial section, which you fucked up as well."

"I had to beg for that chance. And what a chance! Dressed up as a tart for leering businessmen."

"I hear you are doing that at The San Juan Club anyway."

"Actually, I have never dressed like a tart in my life. In any case, I don't see what your problem is – there's room enough for everyone."

"The problem is, apart from your disloyalty, you told Kitty Mulcahy that your ex-agent, i.e. me, didn't give you any emotional support."

"Well, you didn't. How many years have we worked together? I considered you a good friend and you didn't ring me once since leaving to see how I was."

"It's defamation!"

"I mentioned no names."

"Oh, Reynolds checked out every angle for you, did he? You'd better not try to poach any of my models. Not that any of them would be bothered with you. Most of them can't stand you anyway."

"Charming as ever," said Audrey.

"Put Reynolds on the phone. I see his handiwork written across this article."

"He's in a meeting."

"I said put him on the phone!"

"Goodbye, Hazel."

Hazel was ready to explode when she heard the phone click.

Seeing a second number printed at the bottom of the interview for Spinner, she dialled it. As she expected, Peter answered it.

"Reynolds, you really must have sunk to the bottom of the barrel to get into business with someone like her."

"It's nothing personal, Hazel. It's business."

"Stay away from my patch, I'm warning you."

"I've no intention of going near your patch. I want fresh new faces not the same ones you keep peddling out because you know they'll earn you money."

"I've warned you." Hazel hung up.

Audrey had walked into Peter's office and heard the last part of the conversation. "She's furious."

"She's worried," said Peter. "Which is a good sign. I'd be worried if she wasn't."

"I'm expecting the first of the interviewees in a few minutes. We'll interview them in the front office, OK?"

The Kitty Mulcahy interview caused quite a stir and the other newspapers were soon phoning, looking for further interviews with Audrey. Peter carefully negotiated with the individual journalists to ensure their interviews would be flattering to Audrey and give Spinner maximum exposure. He followed this up with calls to the TV stations and managed to get Audrey on TV3's Breakfast Show on the Friday morning and on the Maeve Kelly's afternoon show on RTE on the same day. Maeve had been the compere the night of the Childwatch Show, a fact which caused Audrey some trepidation at the thought of meeting her again.

"We can't let an opportunity like this pass," explained Peter. "Do you know how many people watch Maeve's show?"

"But she saw how I was that night."

"Then she should be even more sympathetic towards you."

Spinner was to be divided into a number of sections: Female Model, Male Model, Children's, Commercial (including Promotions) & Celebrity Management. Each of these areas came with its own problems attached. Audrey had always found that male models fitted one of two types: they were either very vain and obsessed with themselves, or the type who viewed it as a way of earning some extra cash and didn't take it too seriously. Children's work tended to be mainly in catalogues as legislation had to be strictly adhered to and stage mothers and fathers always caused much hassle. The Commercial section dealt with everyday people – people to play the housewife in a detergent commercial or a bank manager in a mortgage advert – and the clients' demands were usually very specific. Celebrity Management could be a nightmare. Nevertheless all these areas were very lucrative.

But it was the female models who kept the industry rolling. This was the glamorous and well-paid area. It was also extremely tough and very fickle. Many of the girls who came through the doors of Spinner that week, nervously clutching their photos and their dreams, believed they only needed the right break to make it to the top. But, as Audrey and Peter well knew, trends and styles constantly changed in the modelling world. For a while conventional glamorous beauties are in. This then gives way to more unconventional looks. One month heroin chic may be what grabs people's attention. The next a healthy glow is what the public wants. In addition to this, a model needed to have the genetics right in the first place. Designers need to fit clothes on the figure that will most flatter their products: a tall and slim frame. Secondly, the camera must love the girl. She doesn't have to be beautiful. In Peter's experience, many girls he considered beautiful took a bad photo. A top model needed that quality that made them photogenic. Excellent bone structure, an unusual look, a chameleon look, a certain appeal in their eyes – something that made them special. This quality was thin on the ground in all the girls who came through the doors of Spinner those first few days.

The photographer they affiliated themselves with, Matilda, told Audrey that she used a model in her studios in London who lived on a very rough council estate. She was a part of a street gang and never came in for a photo session wearing anything but jeans and a T-shirt, and often she'd have cuts or bruises from some fight. You could pass her in the street and not look twice at her. But something happened that made this girl mesmerising as soon as she got in front of the camera.

"We've got loads for the commercial section," Peter said on the Thursday evening.

"But we haven't got one really good fashion model," complained Audrey. "And that's what we need to establish ourselves. That's what will get us media coverage and profile and earn us the big bucks. I suppose any girl worth her salt will just go and sign up with Boom or one of the established agencies -- why bother with a little upstart like ourselves?"

There was a knock on Peter's door and a blonde head popped inside.

"Am I too late for an interview?" came a strong Derry accent.

Her name was Tiffany Cooper. Five foot ten with a perfect slim figure. She had very blonde hair way past her shoulders. Her skin was pale and soft. Her face was interesting as well as beautiful.

"What age are you?" asked Peter as he and Audrey looked through her photos.

"Eighteen next week. I thought I'd have missed you. I'm just down from Derry for the day to go around the agencies."

"Have you modelled before," enquired Peter.

"Aye, in Belfast. I've done catwalk and some photo assignments when I was at school."

"You obviously plan to move to Dublin permanently."

"Aye, as soon as possible."

"Planning on going to college here?" asked Peter, thinking she was viewing modelling as a handy way of earning money to put her through her education.

"No, I aim to be a full-time model. My heart and soul are in it. It's all I've ever wanted to do. I'll be honest with ya, I've been around all the agencies today and thankfully they've all wanted me to join them. I was heading to the train station back to Belfast when I read an interview with yourself," she nodded to Audrey, "and thought I'd drop in."

They brought her into the front office and asked her to walk up and down.

"She's gotta lot of presence," whispered Audrey.

"Take a seat, Tiffany. We'd like to sign you up," said Peter. "So the ball is in your court, if you've received other offers."

"Aye." She shook her long hair back and looked at the floor. "I was very impressed with what you said in that interview, Audrey. And I've followed your career over the years. I always liked your style."

Audrey found herself blushing. "Thanks."

"The problem is I would be depending on money I earn from modelling to survive, and I'm just not sure, with you not being established yet, if you can get me enough work. Hazel said she would have me working every day."

"Hmmm." Audrey raised her eyes. "Hazel tends to promise new models a hell of a lot, but she likes to concentrate on her established models. Take it from me, I had a difficult time getting to the top and I really had to push myself all the way. Here we would give you one hundred per cent of our attention."

"Damn, I'd better grab a taxi or I'll miss my train. I'll give it some serious thought."

"I'm about to leave. I'll give you a lift," offered Audrey.

"He seems nice," said Tiffany in the car.

"Peter? Yeah, he is."

"Are you two involved?"

Audrey burst out laughing "With Peter? Are you joking? No, we certainly are not!"

"Oh, sorry!"

"Where will you live in Dublin?"

"I have to sort all that out."

"It's not that easy to find a nice place. I meant what I said in the interviews about providing support for the models. We'd help you find a place."

"I am getting a good vibe from Spinner. I found a couple of the agencies snobby and Hazel was very overpowering." Tiffany looked at her watch "Damn, I really am going to miss my train!"

"Not with me as a driver." Audrey swung her car into a narrow side-street.

"Is this the right way?" Tiffany asked nervously.

"Short cut. Just trust me!"

That night Audrey got a call on her mobile from Tiffany.

"Hi, I got back to Derry safely, thanks. I've made a decision. I'm going to join Spinner, if that's all right."

Audrey was up very early the next morning and made her way out to the TV3 studios for her interview. The presenters kept the interview light and Spinner got a big plug.

Back at the offices Audrey told Peter about Tiffany's decision.

"She has something very special," said Audrey. "She's very Scandinavian, or Germanic-looking. She would do very well abroad. In the Mediterranean, for instance – real blondes are in big demand there."

"As soon as she gets to Dublin, get Matilda to do her photos. Speaking of which, Matilda's sent all the commercial people's negatives to the printers, so we should be getting the first of their model cards today." His phone rang. "Hello, Spinner . . . uh huh, sure . . ." He grinned at Audrey. "Absolutely. We have a variety of people we can send you. Sorry, your name again was? Give me your number and I'll set up a casting for you." He scribbled down the number. "Fine. I'll get back to you." He put down the phone and shouted, "Result!"

"Who was that?"

"The marketing department for a coffee company. They are looking for a middle-aged man and a young kid for a casting."

"Great – I'd better head over to RTE to do the Maeve Kelly show.".

"You know what you're saying?"

"We've gone through it enough times."

He walked her out to the Reception.

To their surprise they saw a tall tanned girl, with a cascade of golden-brown hair falling over her shoulders, coming up the stairs. She had a chocolate-box beauty with big innocent eyes.

"Leslie? What are you doing here?" asked Audrey.

"I wondered if I could have an interview. I'd like to join your agency," she smiled.

"You're leaving Boom?"

"Yeah. You're right what you were saying. Hazel has done nothing to help promote me. My career should be much more advanced than it is."

"You're so welcome!" Audrey embraced her in a big hug.

CHAPTER 39

As Audrey walked through the RTE main doors to reception she felt happier than she had in ages. She really felt she was getting her life back on track. And this time it was on her terms. She was thrilled her friend Leslie had put such a vote of confidence in her.

"I'm here for the Maeve Show," Audrey informed the glamorous blonde on Reception.

"Take a seat and somebody will be out to you in a minute."

A few moments later, a researcher emerged. "Audrey, thanks so much for coming," she gushed, shaking her hand. She led her through a double door and through a maze of corridors to make-up. "I've been reading all about you in the papers. It's great what you've been doing."

Researchers are paid to gush, thought Audrey. This one obviously had no interest in her whatsoever, but still felt the need to flatter.

After make-up, Audrey went to meet Maeve. Although still cringing at the memory of the Childwatch debacle, she remembered Peter's advice – charm offensive.

"Maeve, great to see you again."

"Good afternoon, Audrey. Back to normal now, are we?"

Before Audrey could think how to respond to that, Maeve had to resume her seat on the set.

"And that was the St James's choir who will be performing at Galway Cathedral this Saturday evening."

Maeve was sitting on the sofa in the studio, which in true afternoon-chat show style was made to look like somebody's sitting-room. "Thanks for making the journey today to sing for us."

It was Maeve's relaxed and informal manner that made her the country's favourite female presenter. Her live show attracted huge audiences and she was continually featured in layouts for magazines with her husband and two children in their idyllic home.

"My next guest this afternoon will probably be very familiar to you. She has been a very popular face in modelling over the past few years. However, it all went tragically wrong for Audrey Driver. She's here to tell us about that and how she's rebuilt her life. Good afternoon, Audrey."

Audrey managed to conduct the interview word-perfect as rehearsed.

"And your work with Abacus is very important to you?" asked Maeve.

"I think it's so important to help people under a lot of pressure who are turning to drink, and that is what we are trying to do at Abacus."

"Audrey, we wish you the very best of luck with Abacus and with Spinner and thank you for joining us today." Maeve turned to the camera. "Have a nice weekend and join me Monday for some more warm conversations with myself, Maeve." The music started up.

As was customary Maeve talked to her guest as the credits rolled, unheard by the viewers.

"Thanks for having me on," Audrey smiled, conscious they were still going out live, if unheard, because of the loud programme music.

Maeve laughed lightly for the benefit of the cameras. "I'll tell you one thing, Childwatch certainly wouldn't have you as a patron, the way you fucked up their night."

Audrey was taken aback by the switch in Maeve's personality from the warm woman she was on screen. She was even more surprised to hear Maeve, the nation's favourite mother, swear.

When they went off air, Maeve got up abruptly and walked off.

"Maeve!" Audrey called. "I'm not sure who's representing you, but we'd love if you came into Spinner for a chat. We have a Celebrity Management section, as you know"

Maeve smiled before her face went sour "Darling, the chances of that happening are slim to none."

Audrey furiously grabbed her bag and stormed down the corridor. Maeve, all sweetness and light in public, was an ace bitch in reality.

As she slammed through a door, she hit a girl on the other side, almost knocking her to the ground.

"Why the hell don't you look where you're going?" shouted the girl.

"Why don't you?" Audrey shot back. Audrey recognised the girl as the front receptionist she had spoken to earlier.

The girl stood up and burst into tears.

Audrey was immediately contrite. "What's wrong?" she asked, concerned.

"Another fucking rejection!" The girl threw the video she was holding to the ground.

They went for a coffee in the RTE canteen. A few months ago, Audrey thought, she would have just stormed past this girl without a thought, too busy trying to get to her next appointment. Now, here she was having a coffee. Having said that, she did have an ulterior motive.

The girl's name was Vanessa and she told Audrey she had graduated from drama school the previous year. She was desperate to get into acting but was having no luck. That afternoon, she had been rejected for another role.

"I got the job on reception here because it pays the bills and I thought I could hear about all the jobs coming up. But I'm just not getting the break."

Audrey studied Vanessa's pert prettiness and her flowing honey-blonde hair.

"Have you ever thought of modelling?" she said.

Aran and Chloe spent Friday evening at the theatre and afterwards went back to Chloe's where they drank wine while curled up on the sofa.

Aran hadn't been particularly communicative that evening, or for the whole week for that matter.

"Everything all right?" she enquired.

"Just a bit tired. A lot on at work."

"It's the same for me." She began to massage his shoulders. "Celtic Vodka are driving me to distraction with their demands. And then there's the ever-demanding Maeve Kelly, who thinks I should be at her beck and call 24/7. I'm her PR consultant not her PA."

Aran sat quietly, with a far-off look in his eyes.

"Speaking of which, Audrey was on her show today," Chloe ventured.

Aran quickly turned to her, his eyes alive. "Was she? Did you see all the press she got this week? I can't believe she's gone into business with Reynolds. I thought his career was dead and buried."

"I thought she was dead and buried as well."

"Will they be any good in business?" There was an urgency in his speech.

"I doubt it. She won't be able to keep it together for long."

"You don't know Audrey. She can be very determined when she wants to be."

"There's a difference between being demanding and selfish and running a successful business."

Aran lapsed into silence for a while before saying "The rumours must be true about the night he spent at her place. They must be having an affair."

"Well, she's just the type of girl who would mess around with a married man."

"As if he could ever be good enough for her." Aran spoke harshly and too loudly. Embarrassed, he quickly looked away.

Chloe stared at him silently. She reached over and picked up the remote control. "There's a good film on," she said cheerily. "More wine?"

CHAPTER 40

Larry's girlfriend, Julianna, had decided to become Chloe's new best friend, ringing her up all the time and inviting her out to coffee or lunch. Chloe reckoned Julianna saw her as a way of ingratiating herself further with Larry.

"You've nothing to worry about with Muriel and Reginald," said Julianna as they finished a Caesar salad lunch. "Larry told me they thought you were great."

Chloe laughed. "I haven't even given it any thought."

"Oh sure!" Julianna said sarcastically.

"So how serious are you and Larry?" Chloe quickly guided the conversation to safer waters.

"Let's put it is this way. I'm very serious and he's not as serious as I'd like him to be."

"Doesn't the age difference worry you? He must be mid-fifties at least."

"Not in the least. I've always gone for the older man. And before you say anything I'm not just interested in his money and power."

"I wasn't going to." Chloe was well aware how much

Julianna's hotelier family were worth. She had no need to go fortune-hunting.

"When he talks to you he makes you feel you are the most important person in the world to him. Then suddenly, the next day he can treat you like shit. But when he is treating you like shit, which can be a lot of the time, you're just waiting for him to be nice again because it feels so good."

Chloe sighed. "Sounds sadomasochistic to me. Give me a straightforward old-fashioned relationship any day, where I know where I am."

"Where you are in control, you mean. That's not the same as being in love so much that you are completely vulnerable to the other person."

"I don't think I like the sound of that." Chloe winced at the thought.

"Larry dates so many women, but when you're with him, you feel special. Regardless of how cruel he is being, you don't care because he's with you."

"Good God, I think you need counselling." Chloe was genuinely perplexed.

"If you are going out with someone and everything is just nice and easy-going with no ructions, that's not a relationship, that's a convenience. And I don't want that."

They paid the bill and as they were leaving the restaurant, they bumped into the girl Chloe had met with Larry in The Burlington – Danielle.

"Hi, how are you?" asked Chloe, feeling very uncomfortable with two of Larry's dates face to face.

"Fine, thanks," answered Danielle and walked on to join a man at a table.

"How do you know her?" asked Julianna as they walked down Grafton Street.

Chloe opted to be diplomatic and keep Larry's name out of the equation. "I met her briefly through an acquaintance."

"My dear," Julianna stopped and put her hand on Chloe's arm, "she's a hooker!"

"What?"

"A high-class hooker! And a well-known one at that."

Chloe remembered watching Larry and Danielle get a room key and go upstairs at the hotel. "I don't believe it!"

Chloe said goodbye to Julianna and, her head still spinning, made her way to The Gallery.

On entering and seeing Lynn with a customer she just waved over to her and started to study the paintings.

Having finished with her client, Lynn came over and they greeted each other with a kiss on the cheek.

"I'm looking for a Rory Ryan," said Chloe.

"Isn't everybody?"

"I thought if I could get one anywhere it would be here."

"I can put you down on a waiting list. Anything I had was snapped up by the UK market."

"I'd appreciate that."

Lynn went to her desk and started writing Chloe's name in a book.

"How's Peter doing?"

"Really good. They've received lots of press."

"I saw that. His job is always waiting for him back at Macken if it should all go pear-shaped."

"Really?" Lynn closed her order book, surprised.

"I was very disappointed to see Peter go. You know how fond of him I am. We even offered him a pay rise to stay. But he couldn't be enticed."

"A pay rise?" Lynn's eyes opened wide.

"That's what I admire about Peter. He makes his mind up and goes for it."

"Stubborn is the word you're looking for." Lynn frowned.

"I hope it works out for him, because he's a nice guy. I just hope Audrey doesn't drag him down and mess things up for him."

"I believe she's changed. More focussed and happy in herself," said Lynn.

Chloe laughed "She must have the love of a good man then. I have to say, Lynn, I think you're marvellous."

"How so?"

"For letting your husband work in close contact with a woman like Audrey. She is very beautiful and you know how she always gets what she wants."

Lynn crossed her legs "I'd say if she was coveting any man, it would be yours, Aran being her ex and all."

"And I think you were marvellous the way you rose above those rumours."

"What rumours?"

"How they spent the night together at her apartment. You know, the night of the dreaded fashion show. I'd better get back to work. Do call when you get anything from Rory in."

Peter was very busy ringing all his old contacts. Audrey spent much of her time grooming the models they had signed up. Some were naturals; others were hard work.

"When you're on a photo shoot," she informed Tiffany and Vanessa."Never stare blankly into the camera. Focus in and concentrate on one part of the camera, usually the corner of the lens. This will give your expression direction."

That night when she was working in The San Juan Club she spotted Alison Flatley, Ronan Flatley's daughter, in the members' lounge. Alison was a favourite on the social scene. Audrey guessed she was about twenty and very striking with long red hair. Because of whose daughter she was, combined with her looks, she was a regular in the social pages of the magazines. Audrey studied her for a while before approaching her.

"Enjoying the night?" asked Audrey.

"Yeah, thanks, having a great time." They knew each other to see but hadn't spoken before.

As Audrey talked to her she discovered Alison had recently dropped out of college and was taking time out, mainly partying, while she decided what to do next. Audrey did some quick thinking. She had the looks and build to be a striking model, with some training and grooming. But more importantly, because of who her father was, the press and clients would be very interested in her. She already had a profile which would be a big advantage in establishing her. Audrey invited Alison into Spinner on the Monday morning. Alison flattered, readily agreed.

"Is she not some spoilt rich girl who may be prone to diva demands?" cautioned Peter before he met her.

"Maybe. But you have to admit, she'd be an easy sell. Flatley is one of the most well-known politicians in the country."

He agreed and, as soon as he met Alison, they signed her to the Agency.

CHAPTER 41

Chloe was stressed from work. She now worked exclusively on the Murphy Hennessy account herself since Peter had left and she found it complicated, tiring and involving many meetings. She quickly made her way to the boardroom for a meeting with Maeve Kelly.

She was in no mood for Maeve, but she would have to grin and bear it.

On entering the boardroom, she found Maeve seated across from Dermot, who was red-faced and looking worried.

"Maeve, and how are you today?" Chloe beamed.

Maeve stood up as Chloe sat.

"I could be better. As I was just saying to Dermot, I'm not happy with what I'm getting from you. All these proposals you sent me. . ." She picked them up dramatically and flung them on the table. "Well, frankly they bore me!"

Chloe exchanged an exasperated look with Dermot "I think we should adopt a fresh approach –."

"Don't sidetrack me with your PR bullshit," Maeve interrupted as she paced up and down. "How old would you say I am?"

Chloe, feeling very uncomfortable, smiled and shook her head in confusion. "I couldn't say."

"I said – guess what age I am."

"I – I would say forty . . . er, mid . . . er, early forties?" Chloe chose to be kind – and safe.

"I'm fifty-two." She continued to pace. "You know when I started off in this business, women didn't become presenters like I am now. They became secretaries, or air hostesses until they got married and then disappeared into suburbia. But I didn't disappear. Oh no, I did whatever I had to do to get to the top. And that's where I am . . ."

"Without a doubt. You're a national. . ." Chloe searched for the right word, ". . . treasure."

"I'm at the top of my profession, but do you know how many young women are snapping at my heels prepared to do anything to get my job? Every day I go into the studio, I feel I should take out life insurance, in case one of them tries to push me down a stairs or something. And then I go to a board of directors meeting and they tell me I am stale. Can you believe that anybody would describe a woman as if she were a loaf of bread that was gone off? And why am I stale?" She took up the pile of proposals and flung them across the room. "Because of your goddamned PR!"

Chloe cleared her throat "Maeve, I understand your concerns –."

"No, you don't! And I can't afford to risk my future because of your PR."

"Dermot, I'm sorry but your work obviously isn't up to scratch on Maeve's account. I propose appointing a new Account Manager for you –."

"Cut the crap, Chloe. I know he's the best you've got. Don't kid a kidder," snapped Maeve.

252

"Well, what do you suggest we do?" Chloe was exasperated with the woman.

"Nothing. Because I'm terminating my contract with Macken Communications."

Chloe paled. "Maeve, you're a very important client to us. I think you'll find us very accommodating to maintain your contract. We can look at giving you a sizeable discount."

"It's not a question of money. It's the lack of return I'm getting for my money that is the problem. I'm sorry, I have no choice." With that, Maeve turned and left the room.

Chloe and Dermot sat in silence until Chloe slammed the table.

"What the hell went wrong, Dermot?" she demanded.

"N-n-nothing was ever good enough for her," Dermot stammered. "You know that yourself. You sat in on all the meetings."

There was a knock on the door and a receptionist came in holding an envelope which she handed to Chloe, explaining it had just arrived by courier and was marked urgent.

Chloe tore open the envelope and as she read it she paled further.

"It's from Celtic Vodka . . . they are formally terminating their contract with us. What the hell is happening here? First of all Maeve and now Celtic Vodka. One of the reasons we bought Blast was to bring Celtic Vodka back into the fold. To lose a client once is bad enough, but now to lose them twice!"

"If you don't mind me saying I think that was part of the problem," said Dermot. "Celtic Vodka chose to leave us and they weren't comfortable to find themselves back with us after the takeover at Blast."

"I do mind you saying! Leave the business planning to me. If the work was good enough they wouldn't have left."

"Well, you worked on the Celtic Vodka account as well, and there wasn't any inspiration coming from you to keep them here."

"You're on very shaky ground, Dermot – I'd stop right there if I were you."

Peter jumped out of a taxi outside Spinner and was bounding up the steps in a happy mood. He had been successful in setting up castings. Out of the corner of his eye he saw a girl waiting nervously down the street. He smiled at her and she smiled back. She was tall and willowy with very high dramatic cheekbones. He saw she was carrying a folder.

"Are you here for an interview at Spinner?" he called.

She nodded nervously, surprised he had spoken to her.

"Well, come on up then," he encouraged.

She was from Latvia and her name was Ivanka. "I've been here about a year and I work in a bar," she explained.

"You have all your right work permits?" Audrey enquired, glancing through her photographs which were cheaply shot but managed to show the girl's amazing bone structure.

"Yes, I'm legal," Ivanka said. "It has always been my dream to model. It's the reason I came to the west."

Over the next two weeks Audrey concentrated on grooming the girls who would be their showcase models. They brought in a team of hairdressers, make-up specialists, exercise instructors and dieticians to get a full, all-round opinion. Tiffany needed to lose half a stone.

Alison Flatley needed to spend time at the gym toning up and to cut down on late nights out smoking and drinking. Ivanka had her hair cut short which further emphasised her bone structure and started a whole new make-up routine. Leslie had further highlights put in her hair and had further tanning sessions. And Vanessa, the RTE receptionist and actress, had her teeth whitened and her hair enhanced to a Californian blonde colour.

Peter organised a Press Call in Stephen's Green. Tiffany, Leslie, Ivanka, Alison and Vanessa looked stunning in eye-catching designer outfits which were borrowed. When the Press photographers arrived they had a field day. Editors like nothing better than to fill their pages with beautiful girls. And Peter knew exactly how to work the situation. He informed the serious broadsheets who Alison's father was and they zoned in on her. The tabloids went for Leslie and Vanessa's glamour; whereas the style magazines were attracted to Tiffany and Ivanka.

At the end of the shoot the five girls posed together, with Peter and Audrey standing in the middle of them.

CHAPTER 42

Chloe looked down at the photo of Peter and Audrey on the front page of a newspaper surrounded by their stable of models. The caption read: *Peter Reynolds and Audrey Driver launching their new agency Spinner in Stephen's Green.* It went on to name the models. She crumpled the paper and tossed it across the room. She then steadied herself as she went for her weekly meeting with Brendan and Vincent. She was not looking forward to their reaction on hearing the recent loss of clients.

"I'm afraid it's just one of those things. There was nothing we could do," explained Chloe. "Reading between the lines I suspect Maeve is feeling vulnerable about her career, her age, everything. And she was looking for a scapegoat to blame."

"But to lose a client of her profile!" Vincent's eyes widened. "And she's been with us for so long!"

"I did try everything to keep her here. But there was just no way of pleasing her. She's a difficult woman."

"And it's a big blow to have lost Celtic Vodka," said Brendan. "Gaining them back as a client was one of the reasons we took over Blast."

"I know, but to be honest, they were always going to be a tricky customer. They are losing ground to the competition and again are blaming their PR. But I can assure you, all of Blast's other clients are very happy with the takeover situation and the service they are getting from us."

"I see Peter Reynolds is getting a lot of press with his new company," said Vincent.

"Yes, what's that all about, Chloe?" asked Brendan.

"Some silly new agency. I don't give it long."

Lynn had rung Peter and suggested meeting him for a drink after work.

He looked hassled when he arrived at the Octagon bar in the Clarence.

"Everything OK?" she asked.

"I'd arranged to meet a Fashion Editor but I'd forgotten when we arranged this evening. I tried ringing you but your phone was off."

"Why? Were you going to cancel me in favour of a Fashion Editor?"

"Of course not. But I could have arranged to meet you a little later."

"I suppose. Well, it didn't take you long to get back to your old self, did it?"

"What do you mean?"

"Oh – busy, working day and night."

"Oh. So any particular reason you wanted to meet me this evening?"

"Only the fact that we are married and we haven't seen each other since Spinner came on the horizon, " said Lynn. "I thought you might like to tell me how everything is going."

"I do tell you."

"Peter, the only thing I've heard about Spinner is what I read in the papers and most of that revolves around Audrey."

Peter drank from his pint. "What do you want to know?"

"Everything!" She was frustrated.

"It's early days, but so far so good. The commercial section is flying. And we're sending the model cards to all the Ad agencies and PR companies and marketing departments. We're trying to establish our five main models. Huge demand for Alison, her dad being who he is. You know how people like a connection like that. Audrey was really clever to sign her up."

"And how are you finding Audrey?"

"She's working really hard. And she knows so much about this business. I couldn't have done it so far without her."

"Isn't she the clever one? I meant to tell you, I had a visit from Chloe Gallagher. She came by The Gallery to buy a painting."

Peter was surprised "What did she have to say for herself?"

"Why didn't you tell me she offered you a pay rise?"

"Because it wasn't important."

"You're telling me all the time to cut down on our expenses and that we should move to a smaller place and you didn't think being offered a pay rise was important?"

"It was probably only a small pay rise."

"That's not what she led me to believe. She told me you could have had a big future at Macken."

"That's a lie. I told you how I was treated there."

"It could take years before Spinner shows a profit, whereas we could have had a lovely lifestyle if you'd taken the rise at Macken. I just can't cope with this living-on-the-breadline mentality."

He reached out and took her hand. "I'm sorry, I should have told you. We've taken a risk, but it'll be worth it in the end. Trust me. Why not come by the Spinner office tomorrow and meet Audrey."

"That would really make me feel better! Meeting the lovely Audrey! I just can't trust her."

"Stop stressing yourself. We haven't got drunk in ages. Let's get drunk and talk about us. Not work, just us."

CHAPTER 43

Chloe knocked on Aran's door at Murphy Hennessy and slipped into his office. Seeing he was talking on the phone she crept over to him and kissed his forehead.

"OK, I'll have it over to you today." Aran finished his conversation and hung up the phone. "Do you have a meeting with Dad and Larry?"

"Yes, I just thought I'd drop in to see my favourite boy first." She ran a hand through his hair. "Why don't you come over to my place tonight. We'll send out for a Chinese and watch some TV."

"I thought you wanted to go to an opening?"

"We've already been to three this week. So I figured a quiet night in." Especially when you haven't been in good form recently, she thought.

"That sounds good."

She fished her keys from her handbag and gave them to him. "My meeting will probably go on late here, so I'll see you back at mine. Just let yourself in."

Reginald and Larry looked through the numerous press clippings Chloe had brought with her.

"We have been using our press contact to actively

promote the idea of a shopping centre in the area. These articles we organised showing that the area is in dire need of services and employment."

"They are all excellent," complimented Reginald.

"Using the press is a sure fire way of changing people's opinions and attitudes," said Chloe. "Which is what PR is all about"

"So what is the timescale we are looking at now?" questioned Larry.

"As you know, planning is a long and drawn-out process but we are getting there. The key is Ronan Flatley. What he says goes in this area. If we can get him on our side we are home and dry," Chloe said.

She tried not to stare at Larry, remembering the revelation about Danielle's profession. "Also, Larry, I need those original deeds you promised me."

"Damn, I left them at home."

"I do really need them for my eight o'clock meeting in the morning."

Larry looked at his watch. It was almost seven. "Drop by my house on your way home to collect them."

Driving down the long tree-lined avenue Chloe squinted, looking at the house numbers on the gateways. The houses were large and Victorian in the heart of moneyed Dublin 4. Having spotted Larry's number, she pulled into the gravel driveway. His house was a spectacular three-storey-over-basement. She climbed the steps up to the front door and rang his door bell.

Larry, dressed in casual chinos and a blue shirt, answered a minute later.

"You found the place all right then," he said.

"I think everyone knows where Aylesbury Road is."

She stepped into the hallway. There were black and white tiles on the floor and at the end of the hallway was a winding staircase with a long window over the landing. He showed her into a room with leather couches and book-lined walls.

Going to his desk he reached for a file and handed it to her "This is what you are looking for. Would you like a drink?"

"Aran's waiting for me back at the house." She knew she sounded rude, and after a pause conceded. "Sure, I'll stay for one"

She took a seat on the couch and he poured them both a red wine.

"It's a very big house to live in on your own," Chloe said after speaking about work-related issues for a while.

"Well, I'm never short of company." He had sat beside her on the couch.

"So I believe."

"What have you heard?"

"I'm talking about Julianna . . . and Danielle."

"Hmm. I heard you had met Julianna for lunch a couple of times."

"She's a very nice woman and she's very fond of you. And she'd be a great catch, her family being who they are."

"All those lovely hotels! Chloe, I don't need to marry for money or prestige. I have it already"

Chloe sipped from her drink. "What's Danielle's background? Is she wife material?"

Larry stared at her. "She's well connected, in her own way".

"You obviously enjoy the company of too many women to settle down with just the one."

"I'm very happy the way I am." He took the bottle of wine and refilled both their glasses. "So tell me all about you and Aran".

"What's there to tell?"

"Do you love him, for instance?"

"Aran's a wonderful man."

"That doesn't answer my question."

"I wouldn't be with him if I didn't care about him."

"I've known Aran since he was a baby. I suppose he's like a son to me. They're just looking for good breeding stock, you know, Muriel and Reginald. She couldn't have any more children after Aran. So that put an end to their dream of having a house full of over-achievers like themselves. That's why all their attention is focussed on Aran. It's his responsibility to continue the dynasty."

"I think every parent wants the best for their child."

Larry laughed. "Your PR skills serve you to the last. I'm not sure they give a toss about what's best for Aran. They aren't concerned with what makes him happy, just how he can make them happy."

"I thought you were their best friend," said Chloe.

"I am. I think you deserve to know what you're getting mixed up in, that's all."

"And you never wanted a child of your own to pass all this on to?" she gestured to the room's grandeur.

"I have never met anybody who impressed me sufficiently to marry them." He shifted over on the couch beside her and began to rub her knee. A moment later he went to kiss her.

"I think I'd better go," she put up her hand to stop him proceeding.

His hand travelled up her leg. "Nobody need ever know. As I said, Aran's as good as family."

She abruptly stood up. "I'm complimented, Larry, really I am. But I have to go."

Larry put down his drink. "Of course."

Picking up the file she walked to the hallway. "I'll let you know how tomorrow's meeting goes."

"Do that. I do hope this little indiscretion will not affect our professional relationship."

Opening the door Chloe turned to face him. "Of course not. It's forgotten already."

"You're late," said Aran when she arrived home.

"Sorry. I got tied up with Larry over this file. Have you ordered the Chinese?"

"I was waiting for you first. Did Larry have anything interesting to say?"

"Not a thing," she said, picking up the phone to dial the Chinese.

CHAPTER 44

Quest was Ireland's most established and respected fashion magazine. And if *Quest* was the temple of Irish fashion, then its editor Jackie Davenport was the high priestess. For Spinner to establish itself successfully, Jackie would be an indispensable ally. During her modelling days, Audrey had undertaken numerous photo sessions for *Quest*, and had been on the cover four times.

And since Audrey and Jackie had become friends, it only took a phone call to arrange a meeting, instead of going on the usual waiting list.

Audrey brought Tiffany along to exhibit, as well as Spinner's model book. As they sat in the reception, Audrey noticed Tiffany was trembling, which made her more nervous as well. She felt like a model going on her first interview too.

Finally they were ushered into Jackie's office.

Jackie was a woman in her early forties, perfectly groomed, dressed conservatively and with an accent so plummy it bordered on the affected.

"Thanks for fitting us in," said Audrey. "This is Tiffany. We've just signed her up to Spinner."

Jackie didn't bother saying hello to Tiffany but rose from behind her desk and approached the girl. She inspected every inch of her. She took her hands and looked at her nails. She opened her mouth and looked at her teeth and ran her hands through her hair "You're a natural blonde? Do you use anything to help it along?"

"No, nothing." Tiffany was trembling even more now.

Jackie finished the inspection by getting Tiffany to walk up and down her office several times.

"You can wait outside," Jackie said to her, having completed her inspection.

"I remember you giving me the once-over at the beginning of my career," said Audrey, once they were alone.

"There were never any nerves from you, even at the beginning. So you've opened your own agency?"

"Took the plunge and did it."

"Hazel's not too pleased with you. She's been on the phone to me and I daresay every other editor giving out about you."

"How dare she!" Audrey saw red.

"The temper's still there, I see," observed Jackie.

Audrey calmed herself. "What do you think of Tiffany?"

"She's good . . . obviously. Where did you find her?"

"She walked in off the street on an open day."

Jackie took Tiffany's card from Audrey and studied it "All the right attributes are there and I can see you've put work into her . . . I suggest she lose a half a stone and cut her hair."

"Half a stone! We've already got her to lose weight and I'm thinking she's a bit too thin now. And her hair is one of her best features."

"Her hair is too long and makes her look circa 1985. Cut it to just below the shoulders. And if she loses more weight, it will enhance her face. She has the look of a farm girl about her. Make these changes and you could have a very dramatic-looking fashion model on your hands."

"I feel funny about asking her to lose more weight."

Jackie thought for a while before speaking. "If she does what I suggest, I'll consider her for a photo shoot, maybe a front cover. And also House of Opera are looking for a new face to front their Ad campaign. I may even recommend her for an interview."

Audrey became excited. House of Opera was a very exclusive Parisian fashion house which was popular in Ireland and the UK.

Jackie looked through the rest of Spinner's model cards.

"I go out scouting a couple of times a week. Trying to find new faces the traditional way."

"It's the way that works the best." Jackie stopped when she came to Vanessa's photo. "What are you trying to sell me here? She looks like a Barbie doll."

"I know she isn't what you'd be looking for, but she's in big demand for photo-calls"

"Yes, for *The Sun* maybe." She moved on to Leslie's photo. "She's lovely. I've seen her before."

"She was buried at Boom, but has joined us."

"She's lovely, but too lovely for what I'm looking for. She's not cutting edge enough for *Quest*. This one is interesting." She held up the card for Alison Flatley.

"C'mon, Jackie, she's stunning. Look at that amazing hair."

"Send me more photos of her." Then Jackie's face lit up when she saw Ivanka's card. "Now she has something.

The cheekbones and glacial eyes. A classic beauty with something a little quirky. That's the kind of look House of Opera want."

Tiffany was in tears as Audrey drove them back into town.

"I don't know why you're crying. She was very impressed by you," admonished Audrey.

"How could she be impressed when she said I was fat and dated-looking?"

"You're overreacting. She suggested you lose half a stone and shorten your hair, that's all."

"Do you think I need to lose weight?"

Audrey cast her eyes over Tiffany's slim frame. "Personally, no."

"My mum would kill me if she found out I went on another diet. And cut my hair! I couldn't bear to."

"Look, Tiffany, Jackie Davenport is just one fashion editor. Her word isn't Gospel."

"But you told me she could make or break a model."

"She is a very powerful figure, yes. But you know when I started modelling, somebody advised me to go blonde, but I ignored them. What I'm saying is never do anything you're not happy about. Always go with your instinct."

Vanessa sat at the reception at Spinner. She had a copy of that morning's *Mirror* newspaper spread out and was admiring her large colour photo in it – holding a can of a new brand of soft drink which she had been employed to endorse at a photo-shoot. She was delighted with the response since she had joined Spinner. She seemed to be in demand for photo-calls. And though it was the acting profession she really wanted to make it in, this was a similar field which would get her noticed and known. And that had to be a help getting her the big break. Vanessa had decided to give up her reception job at RTE which had been driving her mad. And now she even helped out Peter and Audrey a little, covering reception or taking general bookings, which earned her some extra cash along with her modelling assignments.

The phone rang and she answered it. It was a PR looking for another casting.

"Sure, could you fax me the details, and I'll show it to Peter and get things in motion this side. Thanks." She hung up and, looking up, she saw an elegant woman in her early thirties waiting for her attention. "Hi, can I help you?"

"Is Peter here?"

"Who's asking?" questioned Vanessa.

"His wife."

"Oh, I'm pleased to meet you. I'm Vanessa, model and," she gave a little giggle, "part-time receptionist."

"I hadn't realised they had taken on staff already." Lynn didn't return Vanessa's smile.

"Follow me down," said Vanessa setting off down the corridor to the back of the building. Lynn took in the fabulous photos of girls in various poses dotted around.

Audrey had popped next door into Peter's office to discuss Jackie's verdict.

"I just don't feel comfortable about Tiffany losing any more weight," she said.

"But would it get her the front cover of *Quest?*"

"Probably, but that's not the point –."

"This is a business and if she's as ambitious as she says she is, she won't have a problem with this," said Peter.

Vanessa knocked on the door and showed Lynn in.

269

Very surprised, Peter jumped up. "Hi!" He walked to her and kissed her cheek as Vanessa left the three together. "Er . . . you remember Audrey, don't you?"

"Could anyone forget?" Lynn's eyes were ice.

Audrey cringed. She had been dreading this moment but it was up to her to try and make amends. Audrey wrung her hands together as she stood. "Lynn, I am so sorry how I reacted that night. I'm sorry for insulting you the way I did. I had no right –."

"No, you hadn't."

"It was nothing personal. You were just in the firing line."

"And nothing could be fairer than that," said Peter.

"I hope in time we can be friends," offered Audrey.

Lynn stopped herself from treating Audrey to a variety of sarcastic remarks, feeling Peter's eyes bore into her. "Of course," she said as her gaze remained cold. "So, Peter, are you going to give me the grand tour?"

"Sure. This is my office, and Audrey's is next door. . ."

As Peter led his wife away, Audrey's first impression of Lynn being aloof was confirmed.

"You could have been a bit more friendly," said Peter as they entered the large front office.

"Why should I? It's only because she's in business with you that stopped me from telling her exactly what I think of her." Lynn cast her eyes around the large space. There were five models there, either on the phone or discussing jobs with each other and she found herself impressed with the progress they had made in a short space of time. "I'd better get back to the Gallery."

"When we are more established we're going to have bookers working from here as well," Peter explained.

"I'll see you tonight," said Lynn and left without kissing him goodbye.

When Peter walked back into his office, Audrey was still there talking on the phone. As she hung up and saw his downbeat expression she said, "I don't blame her after how I acted to her."

"She's fine with you."

"Peter, it's obvious she hates me."

"Just give her some time."

Vanessa knocked and walked in. "These are details of castings that came through to reception. You can look through and see who you think is suitable for which." She placed the papers on his desk. "I've marked the ones I think I'm suitable for." She winked and left the office.

"She's doing a great job out there," commented Peter.

"Maybe we should think about employing her full time?"

"We're still only paying ourselves minimum wages. Let's hold on a bit."

CHAPTER 45

Chloe sat in Ronan Flatley's constituency office.

"I will leave you this survey to look through. You'll see that it shows eighty per cent of people in this area in favour of the shopping centre" she said.

"That's strange. Most of my constituents are telling me the opposite. They want houses not shops."

"The reason for that is people don't come off the street to a politician's office to ask for a shopping centre. They only come in to ask for something personally beneficial to them, like housing. You need to go out into the streets to get a general view of how the public is feeling about an issue. I'd be grateful if you gave me a call once you've digested this information." She got up.

"Chloe, I wonder if I could ask you a personal favour?" asked the politician.

"Name it."

"My daughter, Alison, you met her in The Burlington when we were having lunch, remember? Anyway, she has just started a career in modelling. I'd appreciate any work you could put her way."

"Of course. In fact I plan to interview models shortly

for a department store we represent for their new catalogue. Maybe Alison will be suitable for that."

"I'd appreciate it if you gave her the opportunity to try for it."

"Is she with Boom? I'll give Hazel a call."

"She's actually with Spinner, the new agency."

Chloe felt a headache coming on. "Why is she with them? They are small fry. Hazel is a good friend of mine. I'll put in a call to her and we'll have Alison signed up with Boom today."

"No, Alison would hit the roof if she knew I was interfering in any way. Besides, she seems to be happy at Spinner. They are doing a lot for her."

Chloe rang Dermot as she drove back to town.

"Have we got a model book for Spinner? Well, get me one in that case and by this afternoon." She hung up.

No sooner had she hung up than her mobile rang again. "Yes?"

"Chloe, this is Muriel Murphy. I was just wondering if you are available for lunch?" she purred down the phone. Chloe felt it was an order as opposed to an invitation.

Chloe's headache intensified at the thought of meeting Muriel.

Why did she want to meet her? What did she want?

"I hope I haven't interrupted any plans you may have had," said Muriel as soon as they were seated at the restaurant in The Four Seasons.

"Not at all. I tend to work through lunch, unless it's a business lunch."

"Your dedication is admirable. It's no wonder you are so successful. I just thought it would be nice if we got to know each other a little better."

"Absolutely." Chloe nodded.

"What do you think of Audrey Driver?" Muriel was obviously not one for beating around the bush, Chloe mused.

"To be honest, Muriel, I didn't mix in the same circles as her. I prefer to mix in more stable circles."

"Quite. I couldn't stand her. Her very presence brought on my blood pressure. The way she treated Aran was disgraceful. He would often come home in foul form after they had some row or other. Of course he couldn't see anything wrong with her until the end. Aran has the potential to be a brilliant lawyer. But he has always had the same problem. He's easily distracted and so can often be sidelined into the wrong company. Something tells me, Chloe, that you never get distracted from your goals or never keep the wrong company."

"That's a compliment, Muriel."

"What Aran needs is a brilliant wife who will direct him to realise his full potential. We have plans for Aran to enter politics. With our backing he could go far. And his personal life must be irreproachable . . . did you ever give thought to being a political wife?"

"Have you ever considered politics?" Chloe questioned Aran in the back of a taxi that night, en route to another function. They had been to so many over the previous week that they all seemed to gel into the one, as far as Aran was concerned.

"How could I help but think about it with a family like mine? They've been telling me I'd make a great President since I could talk."

"But you wouldn't like to go down that road?"

"It's putting too much pressure on a person. It would be a huge invasion of privacy and put loads of pressure on a wife and kids too."

"Some women might like that kind of role."

"I suppose." Aran started laughing "Could you imagine Audrey as a political wife? She'd hurl abuse at the press and tell the voters to fuck off!"

"What the hell has Audrey got to do with this?" Chloe raged.

"Nothing." he looked alarmed. "I'm just pointing out how some people would be useless in that kind of role."

Chloe quickly softened her attitude. "We're here," she said as the taxi pulled up.

Later, Aran watched Chloe work the room as only she could. Her confidence amazed him. She had them on every guest list in town. Anything he wanted to attend, she organised it. She never tried to mess with his head and they had fun together. In many ways she was perfect. But there was something else about her. She was almost clinical in the way she treated their relationship.

And she was cold, he realised. Yes, she was nice, but also cold. He had always tended to wear his heart on his sleeve, but Chloe's heart was buried away somewhere. To be fair to her, Audrey had always been open with her heart as well.

Chloe saw him looking at her and waved.

A guest sidled up beside Aran and asked "When's the wedding?"

"Wedding? You mean me and Chloe? We haven't even begun to think like that."

"Really?" said the guest. "I think she was more hoping for next June or July."

CHAPTER 46

Dermot had managed to get his hands on one of Spinner's model books and Chloe sat at her desk admiring it. The presentation, colour and photos were all superb. She had heard rumours that the office interior at Spinner was visually stunning. If this book was an example of their style, she well believed it. What impressed her more was the quality of the models they had signed up.

Impressed her and disturbed her.

She studied Alison Flatley's card. The girl was good. However, she was too striking for the girl-next-door image she sought for the department-store catalogue. But with the right stylist they could create the look with her.

But she was in a dilemma. She hated the idea of giving work to Spinner. But she had no option but to employ Alison if she wanted to keep Flatley sweet.

"And they say nepotism is dead," she said, snapping the book closed.

She was worried about Aran. She had made considerable headway with the Murphy family who seemed to think she was wonderful. And on analysis, she was unable to pinpoint any particular problem with their relationship.

But a distance had emerged between them and she was unable to bridge it.

He seemed lost in his own thoughts when they were together, not really listening to her. But one thing she knew was that she was very happy going out with Aran. She enjoyed the respect that went hand in hand with being his partner. The whole relationship excited her.

"Yeah, they want her to go over to L.A. to do some screen tests." Peter swung around on his chair speaking to Kitty Mulcahy on the phone. "He mentioned a couple of projects to her, a big budget film coming up later this year or a new soap opera. She's very interested in both projects obviously. Great, thanks, Kitty. I'll let you know as I get more details." He hung up and rubbed his hands together.

Vanessa had attended a film premiere the night before and had spoken to a well known director for all of three seconds. It had been enough for Peter.

He had been on to all the press that day having invented the story of Vanessa being asked to go to Hollywood by the director to be his next star. It would make all the papers the next day and do wonders for Vanessa's profile. He constantly made sure the models were mentioned in the papers which in turn generated bookings. He didn't care which angle he could use or find as long as he could get one. Vanessa was fast becoming a tabloid favourite, always making sure she turned up in revealingly sexy outfits. The week before he had faxed out a press release from Spinner denying the rumour circulating that Leslie was seeing a well known actor. Of course, the rumour, which till then had been non-existent suddenly became the talk of Dublin and the work offers poured in to a delighted Leslie. Audrey was amazed by

Peter's mind. He never stopped coming up with different ideas and knew how to execute them to perfection.

Alison's love life was colourful enough to make news anyway. But Peter put his own spin on it and was always coming up with dramatic stories for her, like how she narrowly escaped injury when she lost control of her car on a coast road. The journalists were hungry for stories, and Peter gave them just what they wanted. However he did not believe that all publicity was good publicity.

He made sure no stories circulated about Tiffany or Ivanka. Realising they had the potential to be top fashion models, he guarded their reputations closely.

He knew that these kinds of stories would damage their chances of making it to the top in that market on merit. The image of the models outside their work was equally important in building their profiles. Peter made sure Leslie, Tiffany and the other girls were put on all the PR firms' VIP guest lists. Audrey organised free membership to all the top clubs for them. Everyone they contacted was happy to oblige; it was good for their image to have models attend as well.

"There's no need to give them membership. Any time they want to come into the club just get them to ask for me at the door," explained Noel to Audrey,.

"No, that means all that will happen once they introduce themselves to you is you'll spend the rest of the night chatting them up. I want them being seen out socialising, not fighting off your advances. When they come to The San Juan with their own membership, they won't have to lick your arse all night to get into the members' lounge."

"You are one bitch," he frowned before laughing loudly, "but you're a clever bitch!" he conceded.

Audrey had no intention of giving up her couple of

nights a week working at The San Juan, even though sometimes she was exhausted after a full day's work at Spinner. But she enjoyed it thoroughly and it kept her mind off how disastrous her love life was. She didn't need a date to go into work at The San Juan, but she still got the fun of being out and interacting with lots of people.

Not that her mind thought much about love. She was just concentrating on work.

Audrey was in the club office sorting out membership on the computer when Noel walked in.

"Don't you think you should wait until June gets a chance to sort that out tomorrow?" recommended Noel. June was the girl who looked after the office during the day. "You tinkering with the system like that might fuck it up."

"It's hardly Nobel prize stuff." His attitude irritated her.

"It still took a long time to establish it and I don't want you destroying it."

"I don't know the last time you paid any attention to membership but this system is a mess and totally outdated. A lot of these people have either left the country or put their clubbing days behind them. And the membership numbers aren't corresponding to the names and addresses. June's too busy during the day to give this the attention it needs."

"If you don't mind me saying so, Audrey, I don't think I need any advice on running a nightclub from you or anyone else."

"Of course you don't. But let's face it, The San Juan is packed from Thursday through to Sundays, but pretty quiet the rest of the week."

"It's the same everywhere."

"But you could improve your trade on those nights by running a proper members' system."

"I don't have the time."

"But I do."

"You!" he roared laughing. "Audrey, you look great and the customers love you, but don't try to suddenly re-invent yourself as –"

"As what? A businesswoman? Well, fuck you, Noel, because that's exactly what I am. I've just set up my own agency, haven't I?"

"One that has yet to prove itself."

"Thanks for your vote of confidence. Spinner will be a huge success, Peter is a brilliant organiser . . ." She was irritated with herself for bringing Peter into the picture. She should be taken seriously for herself and not just rely on Peter's reputation.

"Look, sweetheart, I'd love to see you succeed, but don't be too upset if it all goes wrong, OK?"

She ignored him and continued working on the membership file.

"I don't know why you're angry with me. I gave you a chance when you were *persona non grata*," he said.

She turned around to him. "I know you did, and I'll always appreciate you being a good friend to me. But I will never allow anybody to try to talk down to me or undermine me again. And if that means sacrificing a job or a friend or even a relationship, then I'll do it."

There was an awkward silence while Noel contemplated the situation and Audrey carried on at the computer.

"I thought it was a modelling agency you had set up. What you're talking about is more PR," he said.

Audrey swung around, her face alive with enthusiasm.

"We are also Celebrity Management. If we took you on as a client it would be perfect marketing. We would ensure as many celebrities as possible came here, made sure it was known in the papers as the celebrity haunt, have all the models come here all the time. Get this . . ."she pointed to the computer, "sorted out. And we could even work on your image."

"My image?"

"Yeah. You are a big man in this town and you should have a profile to match. You need your image promoted as well. If you thought you were a hit with the women before, wait till we're finished with you. And the price would be right."

Noel lit his cigar. "What price is that when you say the price is right?"

CHAPTER 47

"I found us a client." Audrey bounced into Peter's office.

"Who?"

"The San Juan Club." She beamed.

"Doing what exactly?"

"Their PR."

He frowned. "But we aren't a PR company. We are Model and Celebrity Management." He frowned. "By taking them on it will be confusing our branding."

"No, it will enhance it. The San Juan is the place where stars like to go, and we will be representing the stars so the two go in hand in hand. I need you to take a look at the members' list and tell me what to think." She flung the computer disk on his desk.

"I really wish you had discussed this with me before agreeing to it."

"You are the one who says we need to make a profit, so this is money coming in, isn't it?"

"How much is Noel Flynn paying us?"

"Well, I had to go in low at the beginning – till we prove ourselves."

"Which means we are expected to do a lot of work for

little money." He rolled his eyes to heaven. "And while we are on the subject of rates, did you take this booking for Vanessa for that photo shoot for the swimwear collection?"

"Yeah, why?"

"I can't believe you agreed that price. You went in way too cheap." He frowned.

"That was as far as their budget would go."

"And you believed them?"

"Actually, yes, I did. And if I didn't agree to that price they were going to take their business to Boom. So isn't it better to have some money coming in than none?"

"We aren't a charity, Audrey. Check with me next time someone tries to quote you so cheap, OK?"

"Yes, sir," she snapped sarcastically. She dropped a pile of papers she was carrying in front of him. "I was going to ring these about bookings later, after I'd been to the hairdresser with Tiffany. But why don't I just let you do them all, since you're the expert?"

Tiffany was smoking in reception while she waited for Audrey.

"This is a non-smoking building." Audrey took the cigarette out of Tiffany's mouth and stamped it out. "And when did you start smoking anyway?"

Tiffany ignored Audrey as she followed her downstairs and out of the building to Audrey's car.

"Is this a non-smoking car too?" Tiffany asked sarcastically sitting in.

"Oh, go on then and have one. But open the window fully down."

"Didn't you ever smoke?"

"When I started modelling I used to. But it ages you. Besides, with my addictive personality, it was all or

283

nothing. It was a case of fifty a day or abstaining totally. No moderation with me."

"Everything in moderation, including moderation, that's what I say," giggled Tiffany. "So how did you manage to keep thin?"

"The healthy way. Exercising. Remember, we all get the face we deserve eventually."

"Just cut it to about here," Audrey informed the hairdresser.

"That's too short!" wailed Tiffany with tears in her eyes.

"That's the length Jackie recommended," reminded Audrey.

The hairdresser neared with her scissors ready which made Tiffany burst out crying.

"Just give us a couple of minutes," Audrey asked the embarrassed hairdresser.

"Let's just get up and go away. You really don't have to do this."

"Then I'll never be on the front cover of *Quest* magazine." Tiffany wiped away her tears.

"There will be other magazines."

"But I'd have lost this opportunity."

"Then it's a case of priorities." Audrey placed a comforting hand on her shoulder.

After Tiffany's hair was cut, she and Audrey went for a quick drink before returning to the agency.

"I don't know what all the fuss is about," said Peter. "So she had a couple of inches taken off her hair, big deal."

"The big deal is, she's a young girl who feels insecure about her looks."

"If she feels that insecure she should have become an accountant or something else."

"Peter," Audrey became angry, "all models feel insecure about their looks. They think their whole identity is tied up with it. People have always given them attention because of the way they look and that makes them insecure in themselves."

"Most models I've ever worked with come across as arrogant rather than insecure."

"That's just a mask."

He sat back in his chair and fiddled with his pen. "Were you insecure?"

"In the beginning, very much so. Try to imagine sitting there and waiting for some editor or PR guy to tell you whether he considers you attractive enough for what they had in mind. It can be soul-destroying. And that's why we are running this agency differently and more supportively."

"Audrey, this is me. Peter Reynolds, not Kitty Mulcahy giving you an interview. You can drop the 'I want to help others' routine."

Audrey was incensed. "I know you finely tuned those interviews I gave, but I did believe in what I was saying. I said from the start I wanted to run Spinner differently from the others and I meant it."

"Good for you! My main concern is getting Spinner up and running successfully. So I'm glad she cut her bloody hair."

"Arrogant shit," Audrey whispered to herself as she left his office.

When Audrey had re-evaluated her life, one of her decisions was to control her temper. She didn't want to be known for her outbursts, but rather be respected as someone who was able to argue in an intelligent and adult fashion. But as she pulled into the carpark at her home that evening, she really felt like having a go at Peter Reynolds.

He was beginning to show the same kind of disregard he had when he was flying high at Blast. The kind of attitude that had helped them to clash so much in the past. She had thought he was showing a different side to him, particularly after the Childwatch Show, but he was keeping it well hidden now. She had to learn to handle him differently. They were partners now, she reminded herself, and they had to find a way of working well together. Audrey got out of her car and walked across the carpark.

"Audrey!" whispered a voice in the shadows.

Audrey screamed with fright.

"It's me! It's me!" said Aran, quickly coming into view.

"You nearly gave me heart failure!" she shouted. "What the fuck were you doing there?"

"I was waiting for you."

Audrey steadied herself and regained her breath. "What do you want, Aran?"

"Just a chat, that's all."

"We've nothing to say to each other."

"You could give me five minutes at least."

"Not interested." She turned to walk away.

"Either we can talk privately in your apartment or I'll just shout up to your window what I have to say and all your neighbours can listen too."

She knew he wasn't bluffing and decided to allow him up. Besides, she wanted to know what he had to say.

As he entered her apartment he was overwhelmed by nostalgia, the scent of the place and all the different memories flooding back.

"Does Chloe know you're here?" asked Audrey.

"No."

"You'd better make it quick. I have to get ready soon to work at The San Juan."

"You still working there? I thought you would have given it up once you became an agency boss."

"I enjoy it. When you are not seeing anyone, it's a perfect job. Gets me out at night and I meet lots of interesting people."

"Not seeing anyone? Peter Reynolds might not like to hear you say that."

"Peter Reynolds?" she was confused. Realisation dawned and she laughed and sat down. "I'm supposed to be seeing Peter, am I?"

"You tell me. You are on record as having spent the night together here. And then suddenly you are business partners. If you could call it a business."

"Spinner may not be as big a company as Murphy Hennessey, but at least we did it ourselves instead of hanging on to Daddy's coat tails." She knew she was touching a raw nerve with him. He hated being viewed in that way.

His face reddened. "Are you with him?"

She was infuriated. "No, I am not!"

"Well it's the rumour going around."

"Put out by Chloe, no doubt."

"I never thought you'd get mixed up with a married man. Just shows how low you've gone."

"I am not having an affair with Peter," she shouted.

"So why did you go into business with him? You used to hate him."

"Because he is good at what he does."

"Good in bed, you mean."

"This is ridiculous. I have to get ready for work."

"And I think that's pretty dodgy too – you working for Noel Flynn. Everyone knows what a womaniser he is. You're probably having an affair with him."

"Absolutely." She folded her arms and nodded her head. "I'm sleeping with Noel and also with Peter. Alternate nights. Now does that make you happy?"

She wondered why was she entertaining him. Why was she bothering even to talk to him? She should tell him it was none of his business and throw him out. Then she realised she still cared for him. She may have blanked it from her mind, but the feelings hadn't gone away. And that was why she had to be very careful. She couldn't let him hurt her again.

She softened her tone. "Aran, what are you doing here?"

"I wanted to talk to you about this."

"But why, Aran? Really, why? You're in a relationship with somebody new. I've started a new life as well. We don't have a say in each other's lives any more."

Aran began pacing. "I just don't want to see you used by someone like Reynolds."

"He's not using me. It's Audrey Driver here, remember? The one who always puts herself first. At least that's what you always told me."

"You always suited yourself when we were seeing each other."

"Maybe I wasn't always the kindest. But, Aran, you used to try and dominate me especially when you were jealous over imagined things. I used to just try to assert myself, that's all. But you've no reason to be jealous any more, because we are out of each other's lives."

"You can't just shut someone out like that." He snapped his fingers. "We were together a long time."

"I think, Aran, you've probably seen a lot of me in the papers recently and seen what I'm doing with my life. You see me back in control. If I was still the same way I was after Childwatch, you wouldn't care less about me."

"That's not true. I came to see you after that."

"Oh, sure," Audrey smirked. "You eventually came over, made me feel even worse, when I really needed you. Let's face it, Aran, we were never suited to each other. We come from different worlds, as your parents were only too anxious to point out."

"You know how much I cared . . . care for you."

"So what are you proposing? That we start seeing each other again? That you dump Chloe and defy your parents and we are out seen as a couple?"

Aran looked silently to the floor.

"No, I didn't think so," said Audrey. "I don't know what you're doing here . . . I don't think you know yourself." She walked over to the door and opened it for him. "See you around."

Slowly he turned and left the apartment.

She stood leaning against the closed door for ages.

CHAPTER 48

Lynn had just closed The Gallery and was waiting for Rory to call by. They were going for dinner with some of his friends. She had thought about asking Peter if he wanted to join them, but thought better of it. He was probably working late.

Besides, although there was no antagonism between Peter and Rory, her husband did find some of his more arty friends hard to take. She sat thinking at her desk.

She had subtly investigated Chloe's comments among her more trusted friends. Sure enough, there was a rumour that Peter had spent the night with Audrey. She didn't know how to react. She didn't believe the rumour in the least. She knew her husband and, with all his failings, unfaithfulness wasn't one of them. He wasn't a vain man, in that he didn't need constant female approval.

He got a sense of worth from his work, and if she allowed herself to be less than modest, through her. Peter was proud to have an attractive wife, the golden girl, who could hold her own in any intellectual company. She supposed he loved her. He may have dated many girls before her, but she was 100 per cent certain he hadn't since they settled down. Besides, he was always too busy with work to stray. He barely had time for her, let alone a mistress.

Nor did she think Audrey would be bothered with Peter. Audrey only went after very wealthy, high-profile men, and to Lynn's constant consternation, Peter wasn't in that league. No matter how drunk Audrey had been that night, she still felt assured nothing happened. And even if Peter had been willing that night and Audrey drunk enough and something did happen, Audrey would have run a mile from the situation and not contacted Peter to set up Spinner.

No, Lynn didn't know what Audrey was up to and she certainly didn't trust her, but she was sure of one thing: Audrey wasn't after her husband.

What concerned Lynn more was this rumour going about and how it made her look. The cheated wife role was not one she relished. Yet, in a strange way, it amused her. It added a certain kudos to Peter that people were saying he slept with a gorgeous ex-model. It amused her to think Peter would be horrified if he knew, instead of complimented. She would ignore the rumours.

She would probably have put her foot down if she had discovered it before and refused to allow Peter to start Spinner. But it was too late now. And she was much more concerned about Spinner being a success at this stage, so they could eventually start making their way up the ladder.

Rory knocked on the front door and she let him in.

"We'd better hurry or we'll be late," said Lynn.

"Sorry, I had to stop off to buy a little present," Rory smiled as he took out an envelope.

"Something tells me it's because of that," she pointed

to the envelope, "that you're so far behind in providing me with any new work."

"This helps my work," he objected and pulled the blinds over the windows.

Going to her desk he emptied cocaine out of the envelope onto the glass top.

He diced up the cocaine with a credit card. Rolling up a note, he bent over and snorted.

Lynn shook her head. She hadn't had any for a long time, and she had only very occasionally taken it anyway. If Peter even knew she had tried it, he would go mad.

"Go on." Rory handed her the note.

Lynn hesitated before bending over to snort.

CHAPTER 49

"Morning – Spinner." Peter answered the phone

"Hi, Peter. Chloe Gallagher here."

Peter froze on hearing her voice.

"Peter?"

"Er . . .yes, Chloe. How can I help you?"

"I'm just looking through your model book."

He wondered how she got her hands on a copy. He had deliberately not sent one to Macken. "Yeah?"

"I need a model for a client, a department store. The usual thing, catalogue and in-house posters. Maybe TV adverts, not sure yet. I haven't finished the full budget."

"I see."

"Could you set me up a casting. The models I would like to see are Tiffany, Alison, and, hold on a second," she flicked through the book, "and Leslie."

"No problem."

"Today at four. I'll drop by your office."

The phone went dead. He felt stressed. All the bad memories of Macken came flooding back. He had hoped he would never see her again. But he also reasoned that was impossible. She was too powerful a figure in Dublin to ignore.

"What's her agenda?" asked Audrey when he explained the situation. "She doesn't do anyone any favours."

"But she is also driven by wanting to be the best. Maybe she just realises that we have great models whom she can't ignore," suggested Peter.

"Peter, she is going out with my ex. She would love to damage Spinner, even if it entailed cutting off her nose to spite her face."

"We have to handle her with care. Maybe she's just coming by to be nosy. Anyway, I think it's a good idea for you to stay out of the way."

"Why should I stay out of the way in my own office?"

"Because at the end of the day, she's a potential client. If you are present there will be antagonism, to say the least."

"Peter, I don't like this. I'm an equal partner who should not be hidden away from clients."

"I'm not saying that –"

"You are!" Audrey slammed her fist on his desk.

"Fine. Stay here and have a big cat fight with Chloe. Because that's what will happen. She'll wind you up and you'll explode and then she'll tell everyone that you are as unstable and temperamental as you always were –"

"I was never unstable or temperamental." She stood up and shouted, "I just gave assholes like you and Chloe Gallagher as good as you gave."

Peter jumped to his feet. "Stay here and meet her then. See if I give a fuck."

Audrey glared at him but said nothing, and he suspected he had won.

Chloe was having a busy day. First of all she had to go over to the Blast office and finally close it down. She executed the mission quickly and efficiently. It had been a gradual process with most of the accounts having already been shifted over to Macken, so now all she had to do was transfer the remainder of the business over and tell the remaining staff whether they did or didn't have jobs any more.

Then she had met Muriel for lunch who requested her advice on a charity luncheon she was organising. After that she had hailed a taxi to take her to Spinner. As she climbed the stairs up to Reception, it irritated her beyond belief that she had to give work to them. But she was meeting Ronan Flatley the next day and wanted to have already employed his daughter by then.

Like everyone, she was struck by the dramatic colour scheme and waited for the blonde receptionist to finish her phone call.

Then she announced, "Chloe Gallagher here to see Mr. Reynolds."

"Please take a seat," said the receptionist and buzzed in to Peter.

Peter steadied himself before going out. She's no longer your boss, he reminded himself. She has no say over you. She's just a business contact.

"Peter, good to see you again," Chloe rose when he entered Reception, smiled warmly and looked genuinely pleased to see him, all her outrageous outbursts long forgotten. She was good, he thought.

"Love your interior. Who did it for you?"

"We came up with it ourselves."

"Really?" She raised an eyebrow. He was very familiar

with that expression which was supposed to indicate a mixture of surprise and disbelief.

Peter had ensured the front office was empty and now showed Chloe in.

"A coffee?" he asked,

"Black, no sugar." She watched him go to the coffee machine and fetch their drinks. "Give you a couple of years and you'll have someone to make the coffee for you."

"Don't think so. I'm too informal for stuff like that. You know I even insist on everyone being on first-name basis here, regardless of their position." He couldn't help himself from getting the dig in. But he had to be careful: she was a potential client, he reminded himself.

"Different horses for different courses." She took the coffee. "Will we begin?"

Tiffany came in first. "Are you getting much work?" Chloe asked her, riffling through her portfolio.

"I'm doing a lot of castings at the moment."

"Not quite the same thing, is it?"

Alison was next up. Chloe held her breath in anticipation. She found Alison to be elegant, self-assured with an unhurried approach to life. And she was dramatically good-looking.

"Nice to see you again." Alison remembered Chloe from the Burlington.

"You too. Are you fitting in here OK?"

"I'm having a ball."

Peter was uncomfortable with the fact they knew each other, and figured the link must be Alison's father.

Being objective, Chloe felt Alison was not the look the department store wanted. Alison's looks were too threatening for the middle market who were the chain's customers. Similarly, when she met Leslie, she thought her chocolate-box beauty would be too much for her client's needs. It was Tiffany's wholesome blondness that would appeal most to the department store. But this wasn't about being objective; she was doing the politician a favour.

"Definitely Alison," Chloe announced to Peter when they were alone.

"Really?" He hoped that whatever Chloe's connection with Alison was, it had nothing to do with her selection process.

"Without question. I need some changes though. Her hair tone will need to be different, more gentle. Also her skin is too pale – I want that healthy tanned glow. A few sun-bed sessions would sort it out. Not any fake-tan stuff – it's so obvious."

"I'm not sure she'll agree to go on a sun-bed, with her being so pale."

"That's the deal. I need to know now."

He really couldn't stand this woman. But, he was delighted they had got the job. Hurriedly he checked with Alison who had no problem amending her looks to their needs.

"Good, consider her booked," said Chloe.

"Don't you need to check with the client first?" asked Peter.

Chloe just smirked at him and, without another word, left.

Alison was told the good news. Leslie shrugged it off – she had another photo call in the morning. However, Peter was worried about Tiffany's reaction to the rejection, as her eyes became red.

Peter immediately rang Audrey to tell her the news.

"This job pays big bucks. Imagine how pissed off Hazel will be."

But Audrey was still smarting from their earlier run-in. "Yeah, great."

"You could sound more enthusiastic."

"See you tomorrow, Peter." She hung up.

CHAPTER 50

Next day, Peter slotted the San Juan membership disk into his computer, and spent the next two hours analysing them.

Eventually he rang Audrey's office next door and asked her to come in.

"I can't make head or tail of all this," he complained.

"What's wrong?"

"It seems really outdated and entries made in such haste they are obviously wrong. It would be easier to start from scratch."

"OK, so we start from scratch," she said.

"For the amount of money Flynn's paying us, it's really not worth the effort."

"You've become very cocky all of a sudden. You think we're in a position to turn down clients?"

"I'll be honest with you. I don't know if we should be associating Spinner with someone like Noel Flynn anyway."

"And why?"

"Everyone knows he's a crook, with connections with some seriously dodgy people."

"That's a false rumour actually." Audrey's voice rose in spite of herself.

"Let's put it this way. If Noel Flynn's house ever went up for sale, the Criminal Assets Bureau would be the estate agent."

"Noel's always been a good friend of mine, and I'm not going to listen to idle gossip. Talking of undesirables, you're nobody to talk! Chloe Gallagher snaps her fingers and you run," Audrey accused.

"So you'd have me turn down Alison's job for Macken?"

"No, but I am a co-director here and I've accepted San Juan as a client and so we deliver the goods."

"When you say 'we', you mean me."

"No," she reached over and took the disk out of his computer, "I'll do the damned thing myself."

Chloe was disturbed after her visit to Spinner for a variety of reasons. Spinner seemed to be operating very slickly. She had to admit the models were good. If she had neutral feelings towards Peter and Audrey, she would probably use them regularly. As she looked around the Macken Building's traditional grandeur, it looked slightly dated compared to Spinner's bold chic. However, she could hardly compete there. If Chloe ordered the building to be splashed in red and white colours and wooden floors, Brendan and Vincent would drop dead as would half their clients.

She phoned Ronan Flatley.

"Just letting you know I was really impressed by Alison today. Think she has a big future ahead of her."

"I appreciate you giving her the job," he said.

"I intend to use her quite a bit in the future. I like to pride myself in spotting talent and nursing it along."

CHAPTER 51

It was the scandal of the year. Maeve Kelly, the nation's favourite television presenter. Maeve Kelly, married for over twenty years with two teenage children. Maeve, who managed to combine glamour with a homely and kindly image. Maeve, who enjoyed everybody's respect and cultivated her image as an ordinary housewife who popped into RTE to present her afternoon show each day, before running home to put on the dinner for her family. She was usually photographed with her perfect family at home for glossy magazines. But now Maeve had been photographed going into a hotel bedroom with a handsome stranger on a Saturday afternoon, and emerging two hours later looking dishevelled.

The photos were all over the front of *The Irish Sun*. Peter read the accompanying article in his office. He read how an undercover reporter had been following Maeve over a six-week period and she had ten of these liaisons with the same stranger over this period of time. Peter felt sorry for her. She had hosted a few shows for him and he always found her true to her image, pleasant and warm.

"Did you see this?" he asked Audrey as he passed her in the corridor.

Audrey looked at the newspaper he was holding up. "Good enough for her."

"That's not very charitable. Wasn't long ago since you were in the same ship suffering bad publicity," he reminded her.

"I always knew that sweet image of hers was phoney. She was a bitch to me off camera when I was on her show."

Peter knew Audrey was still angry with him. Somehow their personalities were reverting to the way they used to be before Spinner, clashing all the time.

As long as Spinner was a success that was the main thing, he reminded himself.

He looked down at the unflattering photo of Maeve. He had heard she had dumped Macken as her PR, and he wondered who she employed now.

Chloe was relieved Maeve Kelly had walked out as a client. She wouldn't have relished doing damage limitation, trying to rescue Maeve's image from this mess she had found herself in. The reception at Macken was being hounded by journalists looking for a statement about Maeve. Chloe had instructed reception to respond to any enquiries by saying that they no longer represented Ms Kelly. Chloe wasn't too surprised at the disclosure of the affair. Over the years she had got to know the real Maeve, who she believed to be fiery, insecure and frustrated. Having just finished a meeting with Reginald, Chloe made her way to Aran's office.

Aran was sitting at his desk massaging his temples. He had been getting headaches that wouldn't go away. His doctor had suggested stress to be the cause, and recommended he cut down his workload. But as Aran looked at the stacked papers in his tray which he had ignored for days, he knew work wasn't the problem. At night he would either lie awake unable to sleep, or wake up after having a terrible dream. And he knew the root cause of his problem. He was completely stressed about his private life.

Chloe felt wrong. He didn't love her. Everything seemed perfect with the relationship on the surface, but his heart wasn't in it. Since he could remember, people, especially his family, had been trying to direct him, push him. Expecting him to go to the right university, choose the right career, get the right grades, pick the right relationships. And then along came Audrey, and she didn't want to push him anywhere. She didn't care if he was late or what he had been doing. Suddenly it was Aran trying to control Audrey. But now he felt he had lost control of his future as he felt he was being slowly marched up the aisle by Muriel, Reginald and Chloe.

His door opened and in walked Chloe.

"Just had a meeting with your dad, so thought I'd drop by." She sat on his desk. "You look awful. Is it those headaches again?"

"Afraid so."

"Come by tonight and I'll cook us something nice and give you a massage."

"No, this headache is too bad. I'll just go home and sleep."

"I insist. I'll look after you."

Every PR worth his salt has a guest list, a list of people whom they invite to their various different events, a kind of rent-a-crowd. When Peter went out to lunch, Audrey sneaked into his office and photocopied his list.

Then she got Vanessa to show her the rudiments of how to work her computer and she started to type up a new file for The San Juan, adding in the people from Peter's list and the people she knew herself who would value membership and use it. She met Noel in the evening and got his permission to give free membership for the next twelve months and then to charge an annual subscription after that. In this way the new members had nothing to lose.

Despite all Chloe's best efforts, Aran's headache was getting worse as he sat in her living-room.

He willed himself to say the words he knew he had to, but couldn't bring himself to.

"Often a hot whiskey and a good night's sleep is the only solution," advised Chloe.

Aran rubbed his temples. Say it, say it, he silently screamed at himself.

"Chloe, we need to speak."

"That sounds ominous." Chloe smiled.

"First of all I'd like to apologise for my behaviour this past couple of weeks. I know I haven't been good company."

"You're always good company, Aran."

"Truth is, I haven't been happy for a while."

Chloe straightened her back and leaned forward, but maintained an expressionless face.

"Chloe, you are a wonderful person. You've been really good for me. After Audrey, it was lovely to be with someone who respected me . . . it's just . . . it doesn't feel right any more."

"I see."

"You are an amazing person. You have such ability and

talent, but . . . well, there's no spark there, really, is there? Between the two of us?"

Chloe didn't know how to deal with this. She didn't know how to react or what to say. She just wanted this scene over and him gone out of her home.

"I just don't think we are suited, do you?" he pushed.

Stop asking me questions, she wanted to scream. I am a strong and confident person, she repeated to herself. I can and will do this.

Smiling, her tone had no emotion. "In a way, yes. I thought we were suited. We are both high achievers –"

"You're a much higher achiever than me. I was just born into it. From your point of view I don't think you were looking at us as a relationship, but it felt more like you were trying to land a client . . . does that make sense?"

"No."

"What I'm trying to say is that I wear my heart on my sleeve, but yours is buried away somewhere . . ."

Stop it, stop it! she thought.

"You are nice," he continued, "but you are also cold."

No!

"Maybe it's the business you work in. But I do think you are cold."

"Hmmm, maybe. And I suppose lawyers are known for their warmth and sensitivity?" she allowed herself one cutting remark.

"When I say cold, I mean you won't allow yourself to open up to be hurt. But I guess that works two ways insofar as you wouldn't hurt anyone either."

Wouldn't I? She wished he would leave.

"I don't think you are looking for a marriage," Aran concluded, "more like a merger."

If anyone else had even attempted to say a tenth of

what he had said she would have destroyed them. And yet here she was maintaining her composure. Relationships did really make people vulnerable, she thought.

"Is there anything you want to say?" he questioned.

"I guess you've said it all." In the same manner she would conclude a business meeting, she stood up and walked to the front door. Even now, he thought, not a glimmer of emotion.

Smiling she opened the door. "No doubt I'll see you when I'm at Murphy Hennessy at some stage."

"Sure . . . I'd like us to remain friends." He went to kiss her and she accepted his kiss on the cheek. Then she closed the door firmly after him.

Feeling numb, she walked out to the patio and gazed out at the sea under the twinkling stars. She couldn't understand what had gone wrong. She had dealt with the whole situation with such expertise. She had charmed his family and impressed him with her lifestyle and connections. Goddamn it – she was a great catch! She had the same feeling as when she lost a big client – and she hated that feeling more than anything else in the world. She had her own way of doing things, her own methods to ensure people remained in line. But she was unable to think of a thing that would work with Aran. He was beyond her reach, beyond her power. She would recharge her batteries with sleep and consider the whole situation in the morning. She fell into a troubled sleep and awoke in the early hours with a frightening thought. It had suddenly just dawned on her. Audrey! Aran was still in love with Audrey.

CHAPTER 52

Peter braced himself before dialling Maeve Kelly's mobile number. Having enquired around he had discovered she hadn't replaced Macken with any other PR yet. And one thing Maeve desperately needed at the moment was PR. He picked up the phone.

"Maeve, hi, Peter Reynolds here."

There was a long pause before Maeve responded in an irritated voice, "Yes, Peter, what is it?"

Might as well go straight for the kill, he thought. She wasn't in the mood for any small-talk.

"I actually wanted to have a meeting with you about representing you here at Spinner. I have some very good ideas about handling your present . . . situation. And also about the direction your career should now be taking."

"Peter, there's a lot of shit going on at the moment, and I'm not really in the mood to talk about this."

"Exactly. That's *why* you need to talk about it. If you don't strike soon, everything you've built over the years will be lost. You can't hide away from this situation –"

"Thanks for your concern, but –"

"Ten minutes, that's all I want. I'll come and meet you anywhere you want. Trust me, you won't regret it."

"You look fantastic!" Audrey said to Tiffany who had just waltzed into her office.

Jackie had been right, Audrey conceded. Losing that half a stone had made Tiffany's cheekbones and bone structure dramatically beautiful. And now with her shorter hair, Tiffany was the epitome of stylish chic.

"Are you happy with the way you look?" asked Audrey.

"Honestly? I couldn't give a shit as long as Jackie Davenport is impressed and I can get my career rolling."

"I'll set up another appointment with her immediately." Audrey found Peter typing furiously on his computer.

"Just letting you know I'm setting up another meeting with Jackie Davenport for Tiffany. She looks great now. I'd say Jackie will snap her up."

"Good. But don't talk money when you are over there. Leave that to me."

"Sure." Audrey nodded. Then she was angry with herself for agreeing to this. She was well able to negotiate money as well.

"What are you doing?" she questioned, noticing Peter hadn't taken his eyes from the computer screen for a second.

"Just trying to finish this proposal for Maeve Kelly. I'm trying to get Spinner to represent her."

"You never discussed it with me."

"You must have been busy."

Seeing how he was trying to concentrate she was about to leave when her temper got the better of her. She had enough.

"What time are we meeting Maeve at?"

"Tomorrow at three . . . We? It's just me going."

"No, both of us are going. We are partners, remember? I won't be sidestepped like this," she blazed.

Peter raised his voice too. "What have you got to say at this meeting? You haven't got any ideas about how to handle her present situation, do you?"

"I'd have plenty of ideas if you had given me some notice."

"Well, I'm giving you notice now. Give me five ideas straight away about how you would handle Maeve Kelly's present negative press and how to save her career."

"You are such an asshole, Peter. I'd need more time to think about it and read more about what's happening to her."

"Well, I know the whole situation already, so it will save us time if you just leave me to it, OK?"

"No, not OK. I am more to this business than just a beauty consultant and a chaperone to castings."

"I don't have time to argue about this." He forced his voice to calm down. "Maeve Kelly is a woman in a very insecure period of her life. Her career could be over, her marriage could be over, her glamour is fading. She feels vulnerable. The last thing she wants to see is a woman like you, twenty years younger and a former model, walking in the door to her."

"Fine." Audrey threw her hands in the air. "Just ignore me." She walked to the door before turning to face him again. "You know, you've turned back into the smug bastard you always were."

It was two o'clock in the morning and Peter was still working on ideas for his proposal for Maeve on his laptop at home.

309

He heard Lynn put the key in the front door and let herself in.

"Are you still working?" she swayed over to him.

"I have to get this finished for tomorrow? Had a good night?"

"Great night." She sat on the couch beside him and kissed him. She pushed his papers on the floor.

"Hey!" he objected.

"Leave it till the morning." She put her head in his lap and started stroking his face. "Peter, when was the last time we went out socially?"

He couldn't think offhand. "Don't know. Why?"

"It's just we used to do things, didn't we? Go places, weekends away. Now it's just all Spinner, Spinner, Spinner."

"You're the one who warned me there was no room for failure with Spinner."

"I know." She stretched out her arms.

"And we never put demands on each other before. What's brought this on?"

"It's just gone to such extremes recently. We never spend any time together any more. Everything is such a struggle, isn't it? I never wanted life to be a struggle. I just wanted everything to be easy. No hassles. Safe. I just feel we are losing our way . . . don't you, Peter? Peter?" Looking up she saw he had fallen asleep.

"I heard Chloe Gallagher had cut off your balls, marked them up and sold them on," said Maeve Kelly. He had driven out to her home in a plush suburb. She sat in her large airy conservatory opposite him, smoking. He recognised the interior of her home from all the photo shoots she had conducted there with her family for magazines.

"You always had a nice way of putting things." He smiled at her.

"And you've started your own little firm." She sat back in her wicker chair. "Called Spinner, I believe. A one-man-and-his-dog set-up, I hear. The dog in question being Audrey Driver." She laughed aloud at her own humour.

He laughed lightly out of politeness. "Spinner is a Model and Celebrity Management company. We promote, create or salvage images, reputations and careers."

"Very interesting." She looked bored and then looked him up and down. "You look as if you work out. Do you?"

"When I can. I don't have much time at the moment."

"You don't like it, do you?"

"Like what?"

"Me sizing you up like a piece of meat."

"I wasn't aware that you were doing that."

She reached forward and touched his leg intimately.

Peter joined his hands together, smiled and looked at her curiously. "Maeve, what are you doing?" His voice was non-hostile, friendly but slightly bemused.

Maeve roared with laughter and quickly sat back. "Trying to seduce you? No, trying to intimidate you, maybe. Or maybe trying to be sexist. At least letting you know what it felt like being a young girl starting in the media all those years ago."

"Well, it didn't hold you back."

"Of course it didn't. I used it to get ahead. All that's gone now. Sexual harassment claims have taken the romance out of the office. Is there any romance in your office, Peter? Not tempted by the lovely Audrey?"

"I'm a happily married man, Maeve."

"Well, I haven't met many of those. My husband certainly isn't one, anyway. Our lives have been a charade for years. But I guess the game is up now. People don't want to think that the nation's favourite housewife is not playing house. That the nation's favourite TV presenter is having an affair – a no-no. I've been having an affair for a number of months and now the blue-rinse brigade think I'm a slut."

"But we can change that with the PR campaign we'd run –"

"Sorry, Peter, I've wasted your time. I'm tired of discussing this situation. I've already been hauled in front of the powers that be in RTE and been read the Riot Act. It's only a matter of time – they'll wait for this to die down and then I'll be quietly ejected."

"It doesn't have to be that way –"

"My career is over. I may as well face it," she said and put out her cigarette, indicating the meeting was over.

CHAPTER 53

Chloe called in sick that day. She could count the number of times she had done that on one hand. But that morning she couldn't face going in. Which was odd, because she usually got her strength from work. It was what defined her.

A million thoughts ran through her head as she sat on her patio gazing out at the sea. The feeling that continued to develop that day was worse, much worse, than losing a client. Regardless of what Aran had said about her not leaving herself open, she had. And left herself open to ridicule. It would soon get around that Aran Murphy had dumped her. The impending public ridicule was what kept going through her head. She could have handled just Aran. All she would have done was make sure she never bumped into him again. But the thought of everyone knowing, of thinking, that in some way she wasn't good enough for him, was soul-destroying. They would all speculate about what went wrong. About what was wrong with her. She had achieved and succeeded in so much, but had stupidly allowed herself to be set up . She had played for big stakes and lost. Her previous eligible dates had never been allowed close enough, long enough, for this situation to have arisen. They had merely been interesting company, good for her image, whom she had practised on until she met "the big one". She had thought Aran was "the big one".

She had thought everything was perfect and hadn't seen this coming. Her enemies would enjoy this. And she was convinced Audrey was the prime cause. She imagined Peter and Audrey laughing at her in their red and white offices.

What did Aran see in Audrey that he couldn't see in her? That awful feeling crept over her. The one she had banished for years. The feeling of being second-rate, of being inadequate compared to others. She tried to quickly think positively. She would not allow herself to ever think like that again.

Chloe wasn't a plain child. But nothing in particular stood out about her. Being an only child, she was quiet and content in her own company. Her mother had been a housewife since marriage. She prided herself on keeping their suburban house clean and respectable-looking. Her father had a supervisory position in the bank. He never reached the much-coveted management title he dreamed of. This had made him bitter for a while, before time mellowed the anger. Chloe was never sure why he had been passed over for promotion. Both her parents were very intelligent. She presumed he lacked the confidence in himself that was needed. And this was a family trait passed on to herself. She passed through her teenage years in an unassuming fashion. Concentrating on her studies, she was never top of the class, but she was a good student. Her friends were similar to herself, not standing out in a crowd. From afar she would listen to other girls talk about their boyfriends, their wild weekends, or watch their display of fashion and hairstyles. Her parents, always quietly supportive of her, suggested if she wanted new clothes or anything else she could have them. But the interest wasn't there. She lacked the confidence to experiment. And she didn't want to draw attention to herself by arriving into school with her light brown hair in any other style that the ponytail she always sported. Or to be seen in anything else but the green school uniform.

She was delighted to be offered a place at university. She decided she would work hard and do something academic after graduating, maybe in research.

She was overwhelmed by the sight of the students. They all seemed so exciting and carefree and full of youthful confidence. She quickly found some friends with similar dispositions to herself. There was always safety in numbers. And that's how she spent her college years, studying in the library, classes, or talking to her friends in a quiet corner of the canteen. Very occasionally they would venture to the student bar, more because they felt they should rather than any desire to go. Of all the interesting and glamorous characters she spotted around campus, none was more so than Peter Reynolds. She spotted him in the first few days of starting college. He stood out with his looks and confidence. He seemed to be everyone's friend and everyone wanted to be his friend. She couldn't believe anybody could be that confident and popular. He never noticed her. She was fascinated by him as she looked on from afar. In second year, he began dating Lynn. Chloe became equally mesmerised by Lynn's style and the way she held herself. Chloe followed their on-off romance with great interest. She could tell when they had argued. Other times she knew straight away when they were being romantic. She tried to sit near them to listen into their conversations. Other times she picked up breadcrumbs of gossip about them. In her naivety, she thought of them conducting a big-scale glamorous romance equal to one in a movie. All the time neither of them was aware of her existence. Chloe left college with an excellent degree. She wasn't sure what she wanted to do, so went on a secretarial course and began temping. She was assigned to a big company and from the first day she loved it. She loved the environment, the office banter and most of all the politics. She temped for two years. She rarely stayed longer than two weeks at any one firm. And it was this constant changing of environments that allowed her to change herself. Meeting so many new people in new work places all the time forced her to become more confident. It also allowed her to experiment with her image. Because people didn't have any preconceptions about her as the quiet studious girl, she could try different images. She started experimenting with make-up and clothes. She began to realise she was good-looking and had a good figure.

All she needed was the right colours and styles to enhance her. One Saturday, in between temping jobs, she went into a hairdresser's and had her hair dyed blonde to complete the transformation. Before going into work on the Monday morning, she looked at her blonde tresses, her expertly made-up face, her smart outfit and set off feeling great. The company she was temping in that week was a PR company. She had found her niche. She was fascinated by the idea of creating something out of nothing. Of creating image. She realised it mirrored her own life. She began a PR course at night, applied for an administration job at Macken, worked her way up and the rest was history.

Still gazing out at the sea, Chloe realised she had come too far to allow herself to be undermined by the likes of Aran Murphy, Audrey Driver or Peter Reynolds. And she had no intention of going back.

CHAPTER 54

An uneasy atmosphere fogged Audrey and Peter's interaction. Audrey knew it was ridiculous and certainly self-detrimental, but she was almost glad when Maeve Kelly hadn't entertained Peter's proposal. She was sitting on Reception sorting through some faxes when the mainline phone rang.

"Afternoon, Spinner, Audrey Driver speaking."

"Audrey? It's Maeve Kelly here."

"Oh . . . er, hi, Maeve."

"Peter was out at my house the other day, and I . . . did you see the papers today?"

"No, haven't had the chance."

"They've axed my show."

"I can't believe it!" Audrey was genuinely surprised. It was like a piece of fabric of Irish society being got rid of.

"I'd like to meet with Peter again, and yourself, of course. I don't really want to be seen out at the moment. Could I come round to your offices this evening, when there's nobody else around?"

Maeve arrived that evening wearing a headscarf and dark

glasses. Peter showed her into the front office where Audrey waited. He would have preferred to have met Maeve on her own, but he knew Audrey would explode if he suggested this.

"Thanks for meeting me again," said Maeve, removing her scarf and glasses.

"That's no problem." He held a chair out for her to sit.

"Good evening, Audrey, and how are you?"

"I'm fine." Audrey gave what she hoped was a sympathetic smile.

"If only I had been more discreet. That bloody photographer following me around everywhere, waiting to capture my next tryst."

"They'll do anything to get their story," sympathised Peter.

"I've been sticking my head in the sand hoping it would all go away. Refusing to deal with it. My marriage isn't the issue – we've had an open relationship for years. But my career is now over. What can I do?"

"Initially, I see you having three options," said Peter.

"Which are?"

"You could deny everything."

"And say we were playing chess in those hotel bedrooms?" Maeve raised an eyebrow.

"Why not? There's no photographic evidence – I hope."

"Of course not!"

"But who is going to believe that?" asked Audrey.

"Or you could adopt a contrite approach. Say it was a moment of madness. Pressure had been building at work, you felt unloved and uncared for. You could blame your husband, say it was his fault, that he drove you to it with his cruelty."

"You can't expect her to blame her husband!" Audrey was incredulous.

Peter gave her a warning look. "I'm not endorsing these options, I'm simply pointing them out. Maeve, you've come here for advice, and I'm covering everything."

"No, I couldn't do that to him. Love might have left our marriage, but we still respect each other. And I couldn't do that to my children. They are suffering enough."

"It would be a cruel thing to do," agreed Audrey.

"Or thirdly, you could reinvent yourself."

"Go on." Maeve perked up.

"You've lost your homely image. Even if we ran a big campaign of contrition, you will now always be seen as an adulteress. You've lost your market. Your market was always a very judgemental one anyway," said Peter.

"When are you going to give me some positive news." Maeve was in despair.

"That is the positive news. We re-invent you. You find a new market. I've heard a lot of people talking about you since this broke who never gave you a second thought before. I'm hearing lots of comments like 'I didn't think she had it in her.'"

"Charming!" Maeve said, annoyed.

"This scandal has awakened a lot of interest in you. Let's go with the flow. If your marriage is over, finish it officially. Then let's have you out and about in a wardrobe of new clothes. Let's have you posing in magazines draped across a swing in some seductive pose, instead of in a back garden with Labradors,. Let's show this country that Maeve Kelly isn't perfect, she's a flawed human being like everyone else. But she's not ashamed either. Let's get you a new show. Not that trivia you produce in the afternoons but a late-night show dealing with real people with real issues. Grown-up stories"

"But will I get such a show?"

"We'll negotiate it for you. And after the PR campaign we run for you, the channels will be fighting with each other to get you."

They spent a further two hours planning and talking. Maeve went through every emotion from fear, to sadness to excitement. By the end of the evening, she trusted them.

"I'll call you first thing in the morning," said Peter as they said goodbye.

"Thanks for everything." Maeve kissed them both on the cheek, put on her scarf and left.

"I feel really sorry for her," said Audrey as soon as the door closed on Maeve. "I used to think she was such a phoney. But it was only because she was trying to be something she wasn't."

Peter walked straight up to Audrey. "Don't you ever contradict me like that again!" he shouted at her.

"What?" she asked, shocked.

"Everything I said, you questioned it. Saying things like 'Don't blame her husband, that would be cruel'," he mimicked her voice. "Why were you interfering like that?"

"Because I'm a partner too," shouted Audrey. "I can say what I want. And where do you get off saying stuff like that, anyway? The poor woman is at the lowest ebb of her life, and you tell her to finish her marriage."

"She didn't come to us for marriage counselling, she came for PR."

"You can give PR without being unkind."

"It's her choice what she does in the end. I was only giving her the options."

"You're a cruel bastard," she spat.

"It's a cruel business. If it was up to you, we'd be sitting here handing out tissues to sacked TV presenters, and models who had to, shock horror, cut a couple of fucking inches of their hair. Do what you want, but stay out of my way. You've fucked up my career and life once in the past. I'm not going to let you do it a second time." He stormed off.

Audrey shook with anger all the way home. How dare he talk to her like that?

Who did he think he was? She now remembered why she had despised him in the past. He was arrogant and unfeeling. He allowed nothing to get in his way. She knew he had a rough time at Macken, but there was no excuse for his carry-on. She was very disappointed because they seemed to gel so well when they were starting Spinner up. As she let herself into her apartment, she realised it was his dedication to work and his brilliance at it that had made her pick him as a business partner in the first place.

She did a double-take inside her apartment. There were ten vases of red roses placed all around the lounge. There was a beautiful smell of cooking coming from the kitchen and soothing music coming from the CD player.

She backed towards the door. In her confusion she wondered if she had entered the wrong apartment. Or had she a burglar? But what kind of burglar would fill the place with roses and cook themselves a meal in her kitchen?

"Hello," she called out, with one hand on the front door, ready to dash out if needs be.

"Ah, you're home." Aran popped his head around from the kitchen. "Take a seat at the table, dinner will be served in five minutes." He approached holding out a full glass of wine for her.

"What the hell are you doing here?"

"Cooking your dinner after a hard day at the office." He handed her the wine.

She ignored it. "How did you get in?"

"The caretaker remembered me and let me in."

"Well, damn him!" She was consumed with anger and confusion. "Aran, I want you to leave right now –"

He put his two hand on her shoulders. "Let me cook you one meal, as an apology. An apology for my atrocious behaviour, when you needed me."

"No, I really don't want to –"

Ignoring her protestations, he led her to the beautifully set dining-table. "What does Chloe think of all this?" she asked, as he pulled out a chair and forced her to sit.

"It doesn't matter because I've finished with her." He returned to the kitchen.

"Finished with her? When?"

He emerged with a great-looking Italian dish and began to serve it on her plate. "Does it matter? I'm not here to discuss Chloe. I'm here to make your evening pleasurable."

"But you aren't making it pleasurable. You're just confusing me big time."

She was starving, and she couldn't help raising a fork and beginning to eat.

"It's very simple, really. My relationship with Chloe meant nothing to me. I only went out with her to make you jealous."

"Make me jealous? But it was you who didn't want to be seen out with me."

She was angry with herself, but she liked what she was hearing.

"There's no spark between me and Chloe. Not like us. Most of the time I want to kill you, but at least they are strong emotions I always have for you. We aren't just passing time with each other, know what I mean? There's nobody else for me but you."

"Aran," Audrey was exasperated, "you can't just waltz back in here and expect me to –"

"Enough for now." He filled her glass. "Just eat."

Later, they were curled up together on the couch listening to Al Green singing "Let's stay together".

"I just missed you so much," said Aran. "I miss just this. Lying with you and just being with you."

"Didn't you cuddle up to Chloe?" asked Audrey.

"Sometimes, but her house was a like a bloody museum or art gallery. Not a home. I never felt easy there."

She knew from a lot of experience that people were always critical when talking about recent exes, especially to their potential next partner. It was a way of reassuring them. She didn't care. It made her feel good. She couldn't believe what was happening. But she had missed this, missed him.

"I really am sorry for not supporting you. But my parents were giving me such crap. And we were going through a nasty patch at the time."

"I'm not saying I was an angel, Aran. I know I let you down a few times, but you stifled me sometimes."

"I was jealous and possessive. I'm just happy to be back with you now."

"Are we back together?"

He kissed her. "Could we keep it low key for a while? I hate appearing in those social columns. I just want to spend time alone with you."

Audrey was alarmed "That sounds like what you were suggesting before. Just visiting me but not wanting to be seen out with me."

He squeezed her tightly. "No, love, of course we can go out. I just don't want to be a socialite couple with our every move watched. Is that all right?"

She remembered how much she had missed him. How lonely she had been, even if Spinner filled her life now. "OK," she said.

"Thanks."

Then, remembering their last confrontation Audrey sat up slightly. "You'd better hurry and leave."

"Why?"

"I'm expecting Peter over in twenty minutes."

"What?" shouted Aran.

"Only joking!"

CHAPTER 55

Chloe requested a board meeting that afternoon.

Herself, Brendan and Vincent went through the normal examination and discussion of the progress of the company.

"So, now we've totally closed the Blast offices, we are saving on rent there as well," said Brendan.

"And the staff we kept on are settling in OK here," commented Chloe, and then she paused before continuing. "There is something I think we need to discuss." She sat upright.

"Yes?" asked Brendan.

"I have been receiving feedback from clients and different people like journalists, business people etc. about the image of our company."

"And?" asked Brendan.

"Our image," continued Chloe, "is what we are. One of the big three. A PR company that deals with blue-chip clients. We represent corporate clients."

"Well, that's fine then," said Vincent.

"Sure. We have our market cornered. But I think we

have also pigeon-holed ourselves to a large degree. There is a danger we will be seen as too serious, too corporate and so put off younger and more fashionable clients."

"We are happy with our market," stated Brendan.

"I don't think we should be. I think we need to expand our abilities."

"So what are you suggesting?" Brendan placed his hands together. "That we dumb down our organisation?"

"Of course not. We don't want to risk alienating our clients. The last thing we want is to scare people by letting them think that Macken Communications is becoming radical," said Chloe. She nearly had to stop herself from laughing at the thought of anyone ever thinking such a thing. "I'm suggesting we branch out into a new area and build it up. Basically what I'm saying is we are being regarded as too stuffy to represent celebrities, to do magazine deals for celebrity weddings, to put together sponsorship deals for sports stars –."

"But we do represent some of the country's finest personalities," objected Brendan.

"Some, yes, but not many. And I fear because we aren't specialising in that market, we will lose them, like we lost Maeve Kelly."

"Our miss was our mercy in her case, in light of recent revelations." Brendan's puritanical expression crept over his face.

"Whatever Maeve's personal problems were, and I know none of us here approve of the lifestyle she was leading . . ." Chloe actually couldn't give a damn what Maeve got up to, but expressing a conservative view always impressed Brendan, "but the fact is, we've missed representing a major star during a major crisis, which equals us losing money."

"So what are you suggesting?" Vincent sighed and folded his arms. "Another takeover?"

"Actually, Vincent, yes."

"Why doesn't that surprise me? And what company do you suggest?" Vincent was irritated. Chloe certainly was living up to her nickname of The Takeover Queen, he thought.

"Boom."

"The model agency?" gasped Vincent.

"Yes, the model agency. I've looked around all the companies in this area and they are the best with an excellent reputation. What we can do is slowly move all our celebrity management over there and run it all together."

"I think we should stick with what we know best," advised Vincent.

And what would you know? thought Chloe. All Vincent had ever done was ride on the back of her and Brendan's coat tails. All he did all day was think up new stupid personnel rules that alienated the workforce even further.

"Vincent, I think adopting that attitude is setting ourselves limitations and that in turn is setting ourselves up to be overtaken at some stage in the future. A company must always be on the run, constantly looking over our shoulders, to make sure we are ahead. If a company stands still, if it doesn't expand, it is only a matter of time before it starts contracting."

They sat in silence for a couple of minutes.

"And it makes financial sense," continued Chloe. "Instead of booking models all the time and paying commission to agencies, we will control the market ourselves. We can do so much with Boom, giving it a bright young image and expanding business there, without interfering with our image here at Macken."

Again, silence for a couple of minutes.

Chloe felt exasperated. "Let me tell you something. A new company called Spinner has been set up, have you heard of it? It's an agency run by an ex-employee of ours. From what I'm hearing it's going to emerge into quite a force and evolve into a threat to us."

"How can a small company like that threaten us?" Vincent snorted.

Chloe savoured her golden nugget of information, courtesy of a contact at RTE.

"Well, they've already landed Maeve Kelly."

"Are you serious?" Brendan was surprised.

"Yes. Say you are a charity putting on a fashion show or event, how many of them do we do a year? Spinner offers the full service, supply of models and arranging of the event. Why come to us who'll charge our fees and the model agencies' fees as well".

"And who in their right mind would trust those two to run a fashion show after the Childwatch fiasco?" Vincent asked.

"Once they put on a couple of successful shows, that will be forgotten."

"Well, maybe if Reynolds is such a threat, we should have treated him better when he was with us," suggested Vincent.

"If you remember it was I who insisted on keeping him –"

"Only to treat him like muck when he was here," Vincent finished off triumphantly.

Brendan was very uncomfortable. Chloe and Vincent usually treated each other with cold respect. That was now threatening to be destroyed and their true feelings emerge. Brendan knew they had nothing in common. "I think we should explore all avenues," Brendan intervened. "This is a very interesting proposal and should be looked at carefully. But my first response about going into this new area is to have reservations."

CHAPTER 56

Jackie Davenport was impressed with the transformation in Tiffany.

"I have to hand it to you, you were absolutely right," Audrey said to Jackie, once Tiffany had left them alone in Jackie's office at *Quest*.

"I know," Jackie smiled smugly. "Now she's a classic. I'll sign her up for a photo session for our cover."

"Great." Audrey managed to contain her excitement.

"Rules are – I don't want her appearing in any other publication beforehand, and I mean that. I want an embargo on her until that cover is on the stands. I want an exclusive on her."

"Absolutely!"

"Double-cross me at your peril!" Jackie narrowed her eyes. *Quest* had a litany of bad experiences of having spotted a new face, and after investing in her, both the girl and the agent got greedy and she was booked out to other magazines leaving Jackie with egg on her face.

"I'll keep her hidden until you go to print," Audrey promised.

After going for a lunch-time celebratory drink with an

overexcited Tiffany, Audrey headed back to the office feeling good about herself. Everything was at last coming together. Suddenly, herself and Aran were back together, happier than ever. The agency was going nicely and now she had signed a major deal with Jackie. She'd achieved it herself, with no help from Peter. She had taken Tiffany, advised and groomed her through the process and now she was about to become a big name. Peter's door was ajar as she walked past and she overheard him on the phone.

"Sure, that's fine," he said. "I'm glad you like her. I agree, she has the right look for an exercise-bike commercial. I'll book her into that day now. Her name's Tiffany. OK, talk later." He hung up.

Audrey rushed in. "What was that about?"

"A booking for Tiffany. She'll be happy, her first job."

"But Jackie's just booked her for *Quest*'s front cover."

"That's great too," Peter smiled.

"But she can't do that exercise-bike thing, because Jackie's insisting on an embargo on her doing any work till the cover comes out."

"You can tell Jackie Davenport to piss off," snapped Peter. "I'm not turning down any work. She's already changed Tiffany's looks, now an embargo – she'll be looking for blood next."

"In that case Jackie won't go ahead with the photo shoot for *Quest*." Audrey folded her arms.

"Just don't bother telling Jackie about the bike commercial."

"You don't think Jackie Davenport would find out?"

"Well, I'm not cancelling the bike booking."

"Peter, you know once Tiffany appears in *Quest*, she'll work non-stop. You are prepared to risk that because of

some lousy bike advert? You know what this is about?
This is about the fact that you can't stand I got Tiffany this
far on my own."

"Yeah, sure," he said, raising his eyes.

"You are becoming so driven and out to prove yourself
that you can't give anybody else any credit. You've
become a control freak. You're becoming like Chloe!"

"Oh, grow up!" He went to walk past her. "You know,
I don't know how we ever thought this could work. Let's
face it, Audrey, we clash."

"I honestly thought you'd changed after everything
that happened, or at least you were allowing yourself to be
your true self. But now you are more regardless of people
than ever before," she said.

Peter paused in front of her. "If we are honest, we don't
even like each other. I'm going out for lunch, a late lunch."

"Trouble in paradise?" Leslie came into Audrey's office
and closed the door behind her.

Audrey had been working on The San Juan file but
switched off her computer.

"You heard us argue?"

"Vanessa told me. I think everyone who was here
heard you two."

"I just don't know why we rub each other up the
wrong way so much," Audrey confided.

"Maybe you are too similar," suggested Leslie.

Audrey raised her eyes. "I hope we aren't! You know,
Leslie, I actually genuinely like the guy, when he's being
himself. There's another side to him I've glimpsed and you
couldn't meet a nicer guy. But now, it's like he's trying to
prove himself all the time and he's so defensive."

"Maybe he's under a lot of pressure."

"Aren't we all! He hasn't come back from lunch, and he left three hours ago."

"Vanessa said he went to meet Maeve Kelly."

"Nice of him to include me, as usual. I've something to tell you, Leslie: I'm back with Aran."

"You're joking me." Leslie's face was full of concern.

"Keep it strictly to yourself. We are taking it very slow and seeing how it goes."

"But after the way he treated you!"

"We were both guilty of a lot of things in our relationship. We are trying to iron them out."

"What about Chloe?"

"He dumped her!" A grin spread across Audrey's face.

"Oh, be careful, Audrey," she said.

The phone rang and Audrey picked it up.

"Hi darling, how are ya?" asked Aran.

"OK, I suppose." She waved goodbye to Leslie who closed the door after her. "I've just had another row with Peter."

"Really?" He sounded concerned but he was delighted. Since getting back with Audrey he heard all the low-down on Spinner from her. He laughed at himself for even contemplating anything could ever have happened between her and Reynolds.

"He's such a bully. He may be good at what he does, but I've been in the modelling business a long time. Long enough to know you don't upset Jackie Davenport," she said after explaining the whole story.

"Stand your ground," Aran urged. He would indulge her this little hobby with the agency for now, he thought.

"But I don't want to make matters worse. I don't want to jeopardise everything."

"He has more to lose than you."

"How exactly? This is both our livelihoods."

"But not to the same degree. You've got me," he said.

She knew his words were meant as comforting and supportive. But it gave her the old feeling of feeling suffocated and trapped.

"I'll see you after work," he said.

"Look forward to it. But I can only see you for a short time as I'm working in The San Juan tonight."

He tried to keep the irritation out of his voice. "Haven't you given that up yet?"

"No, and I'm not going to." Her voice was firm.

"I don't know how you can stick working so late at night."

"Noel Flynn was good to me when –"

"I know, I know, when nobody else was and you aren't going to let him down now." He tried a different approach, "I just wonder if you are doing your image any favours. One minute you are trying to promote yourself as a serious businesswoman and the next you're serving drinks in a bar."

"I never thought of it like that," she said, pondering.

He smiled to himself recognising this approach worked much better. "Gotta go. I'll collect you from work. It will be a bit late though. Love ya." He hung up.

"I'm just off now," Vanessa popped her head around Audrey's door. "I have that audition tonight for Fair City, the one Peter set up for me."

"Best of luck!" Audrey meant it. Vanessa would be worth a lot more as a successful actress on their books rather than someone who looked after their reception and did part-time modelling. However, another part of her hoped Vanessa wouldn't get the part. She had become indispensable in the office. Audrey became annoyed with herself. She was beginning to sound like Peter, judging everybody on their value to Spinner. She hoped Vanessa got the part because she deserved it, she corrected herself. Looking at her watch and seeing it was nearly six, she was surprised that there was no sign of Peter back yet. She got up to get herself a coffee while she waited for Aran to collect her.

The door to the front office was open and she could hear two female voices – Alison and Ivanka.

"I've got this shoot with Macken Communications in a couple of days" Alison was saying.

"Really, that's good" said Ivanka.

"Did you know the head woman at Macken is going out with Audrey's ex?"

"No, I didn't!"

"Aran Murphy. My dad is friends with his family. Aran's a great guy. I've been out socially with him a few times. I'm not surprised he dumped Ms Driver. I'm surprised he went out with her in the first place."

"Why? Don't you like Audrey?" asked Ivanka.

"It's not that. But she can be a pain, can't she? Just look at her. She struts around as if she's the hottest thing around, when, let's face it, she's well over the hill and past her sell-by date," said Alison.

"She still looks good though."

"She does herself up well, if that's what you mean. She'd been modelling for years before she had to give it up. She'd been on the scene so long she'd become a joke. I think that shampoo commercial she supposedly landed in America was made up to make people think she was still in demand. And all that 'I care about my models act'! Audrey Driver never cared about anybody but herself. Ask anybody who knew her when she was at Boom –

selfish spoilt bitch. She's been whoring around this town for near on ten years trying get any fella with money to marry her."

"Well, she's always been nice to me."

"That's because she's good at promoting herself. Pretending to be a socialite when everybody knows she's a hick from a one-horse town."

"We can't all be the daughter of a famous politician," Ivanka said sharply.

"Just give me time to establish myself. I'll make Audrey look like an amateur."

Audrey hid in the doorway as Alison and Ivanka made their way out into reception and down the stairs.

CHAPTER 57

Peter's meeting with Maeve had gone well. She was warming considerably to the image he was creating for her. He had been touting her story around the papers and there was immense interest in it. He and Maeve were due to meet the programme chief at TV3 that week to discuss the format for a late-night talk show. Pleased with himself, he was about to go into his office when he heard the sound of someone sobbing in Audrey's office. Concerned, he edged to her door and looked in. "Audrey?" he questioned, seeing her sitting at her desk and wiping away tears with a bunch of tissues.

She tried to stop crying but was unable to.

"What's wrong?" He quickly moved over to her.

"Nothing," she managed before continuing to sob. Sitting on her desk, he held her shoulders. "C'mon, tell me." He felt his heart crumble. It was the same the night of the fashion show. He hated seeing someone who was usually very strong be vulnerable. "It's really nothing," she insisted.

"Is it the argument we had earlier?" He felt guilty. He

had effectively told her he didn't like her. He reminded himself to think before speaking in future.

"No," she paused. "Oh, I heard a couple of the girls talking about me earlier"

"And?"

"Well, Alison wasn't saying very nice things about me." She wiped away her tears.

Peter was concerned. "What was she saying."

Audrey started crying again. "She said I was past my sell-by-date . . .and that I had become a joke!"

Peter was angry. "How dare she? The cheeky little bitch . . . after you got her into modelling and did so much for her."

"I know! I could take the knocks over the years, from people who didn't know me and judged me. But hearing from someone I've only tried to help was hard . . . She's probably right . . .I am past it!"

He started laughing. "You're still young!"

"But I'm not a model any more. I'm past it. And now I'm surrounded by all these beautiful young girls. They remind me of how I was and I'm jealous of them. I'm jealous because they're at the start of their careers and mine's over.

"I'm jealous because I'm at these meetings and everyone is talking about what style suits the models, what clothes suit them and I don't matter any more. I'm now immaterial. And my looks are fading and what will I have left?" The sobs started again. "Who'll bother with me?"

He had always imagined her as vain before, but now he realised she wasn't at all. She really was insecure. Her looks had obviously counted for a lot in her life. And now the fear of losing them was too much for her to bear.

He got down on one knee to be level with her. "But you're maturing in different areas. You're at the beginning of a new career as an agency boss. People now will respect you in different ways."

"Like you do? You just ignore any contribution I make. You never include me in anything. Nobody is taking me seriously in this job and they all expect me to fail."

"I don't want you to fail. I'm sorry if I've been hostile. Just so much rests on Spinner succeeding. So I've put everything in it, heart and soul. I didn't mean to exclude you." He got a tissue and wiped at her tears. " Please stop crying. We're doing good here. Spinner's taking off. We're on our way. And we don't really dislike each other, even though I give you plenty of reason to." He tried to joke. Her tears kept falling, but silently now.

"You're still more beautiful than any of the models. None of them could hold a light to you."

"What's this? Peter Reynolds being kind?" She managed to stop crying.

He held her shoulders. "No, just being truthful. You're a beautiful woman."

"That's not what I overheard Alison Flatley say about me earlier."

"She's just jealous of you," assured Peter.

They said nothing, just looked at each other. They both made the move at the same time, inching closer to each other until they kissed. It was a careful, almost frightened kiss. Then slowly they became more confident, until it became a hungry and passionate embrace.

"What are we doing?" she gasped between kisses.

"I'm a married man," he returned.

"We can't!" she muttered, her arm around his waist.

"I know," he said.

The loud insistent beeping of a car horn outside the office surprised them and they pulled away.

"Aran!" she said quickly.

"What?" He stood up abruptly, jolted into reality.

"It's Aran. He's collecting me from work. He's waiting outside." She buttoned her blouse that had become undone.

Peter ran his fingers through his hair, not believing what had just happened.

"Why's Aran Murphy collecting you?" He was confused.

"We are back together." Her mobile rang and she quickly answered it. "Hi, hon . . . yeah, I'll be down in two seconds." She hung up and quickly set about applying her make-up, using her compact-mirror. He stood there feeling stupid.

Reality was hitting both of them fast and furiously and they avoided eye contact.

Audrey threw her make-up bag into her handbag and walked out to reception without saying another word.

Peter watched as she ran down the stairs.

Audrey slammed the front door of the building behind her and ran to Aran's car, jumping in.

"You took your time," Aran said.

"Did I? Sorry."

"Do you want to get something to eat or go back to your place?"

"Back to mine, I think," she said.

He leaned forward. "Don't I get a kiss?"

"Of course!" Hesitating for a second, she reached forward and kissed him.

"Is everything OK? You seem flustered."

"Everything's fine. Just want to get home and relax."

Aran had tried his best to persuade Audrey not to go to The San Juan that night. But she went, as she had to keep herself busy. She couldn't stand the idea of staying in with Aran after what had happened. She felt too guilty and she was sure it must be written all over her face. Thankfully the club was packed that night. It was only when she was sitting in the back of a taxi going home in the early hours of the morning, that she allowed herself to think.

She couldn't believe it had happened. Where had it come from? How did it start? How could she have allowed it to happen? He was a married man, for God's sake! He was Peter Reynolds, for God's sake!

The man she spent most of her time arguing with. She hadn't even thought about him in that way before. But maybe in the recesses of her mind she had found him attractive . . . well, she obviously had found him attractive or else what happened wouldn't have happened! Married men had always been way off the Richter Scale as far as she was concerned. She would never even have given a married man a second thought. It was just the moment, she reasoned. Damn, why did she have to destroy everything when things were going great? Just when everything was falling into place she had to go and do something like this.

She cursed herself over and over again. Something like this would never have happened to Chloe Gallagher. Why couldn't she keep level-headed like Chloe? But she lived for the moment, she realised. She never weighed up the pros and cons. If she had, she would have never have left Ballyabbey to pursue her dreams. She would never have become a model. And when the going got tough she would never have started Spinner. Or approached Peter as a partner.

As the taxi pulled up outside her apartment block, she paid the taxi and got out. Seeing the lights on, she realised

Aran had waited up for her. How could she face Peter in the morning? Sighing, she entered the building.

Peter had never been unfaithful to Lynn. Never even contemplated it.

Sure, he had dated a lot before marrying, but he thought marriage was for life. He loved Lynn. So why the hell had he ended up in a clinch with Audrey? He sat in his office for a couple of hours, brooding. She was trouble. Always had been and always would be. He should have never have gone into business with her. All they did was argue and now this had happened. That's so convenient – just blame her, he thought. He knew he had done wrong. He was racked with guilt. God knows, his marriage had its ups and downs, but they had ultimately always been loyal to each other. Until that evening. At least it had stopped before it had gone any further, he reasoned. But he had to admit to himself that at that time he hadn't wanted it to stop. And just to confuse matters totally, Audrey announced she was back with Aran! He half wondered whether Audrey had a hidden agenda. Was she up to something? Now he was being paranoid, probably after spending too much time in Chloe's company, thinking everything had a hidden meaning. Audrey wasn't like that. She had many faults, but she wasn't manipulative. In fact, she was one of the most straightforward people he had ever met. Hence her temper. No, the situation had come from nowhere and surprised both of them. He was also now in a vulnerable position. If it ever got out, Lynn would finish with him forever. And also, did this jeopardise Spinner? How would they react to each other in the morning? He thought all the way home.

He found Lynn stretched out on the sofa reading *VIP* magazine. There was a feature in it about Alison and her father, Ronan Flatley, which he had organised. It was great PR and Alison was receiving more bookings than anyone else at the agency.

"The Flatleys have a beautiful home," commented Lynn, scrutinising the photos. "She was a bit of a coup for you."

"Yeah, well, people like a famous surname," he said. Lynn cast the magazine aside and stretched her arms in the air. "Oh, to have a famous surname!"

"Someday, maybe." He was in the kitchen pouring himself a coffee.

"You're back early."

He glanced at his watch and, seeing it was nine, realised how late he had been working recently. "My meeting with Maeve Kelly finished early." He knew Lynn was impressed that they had landed Maeve as a client, tarnished image and all.

"I have to make some calls." She got up and went to the study, leaving him sipping his coffee on the sofa.

He thought about their marriage and the lack of communication that was there at the moment. They shared a bed, spoke for a bit in the morning and again late at night and that was it. If they attended a function, and since Spinner had taken off the invitations were arriving in plentiful amounts, they spent the time talking to other people. He wondered whether the situation with Audrey would have occurred, if everything had been right in their marriage,. There had been so many changes over the past months, he felt he had lost himself. After losing all his confidence at Macken, and trying so hard to regain it and become a big success, he had forgotten that life was also there to be enjoyed.

CHAPTER 58

Aran sped back to Howth the next morning to change suits for work.

Then he ran down the stairs hoping to avoid his parents.

"Aran!" Muriel called from the breakfast room.

Groaning to himself, he went in to find his parents seated at opposite ends of the table reading newspapers.

"Good morning, Aran," said Reginald.

"Morning."

"Would you care for some breakfast?" enquired Muriel.

"I have an early appointment."

Muriel put the paper down. "Chloe has been helping me somewhat recently with the charity lunch I'm organising. I was considering inviting her to dinner on Saturday in gratitude."

"Ahhh!" Aran scratched his head. "Could be awkward."

"And why?"

"We've taken a break . . . well, we're finished really," Aran explained.

Reginald, too, put down his paper and both parents' faces frosted over.

"That's unfortunate. What exactly happened?" asked Reginald.

"Just didn't work out. She wasn't my type really."

"When you say she wasn't your type," Muriel's voice was ice, "do you mean she's clever, educated, intelligent, witty and good-looking? It leaves one to wonder what exactly qualifies as your type."

"I'm just not ready to make big commitments," said Aran.

"You will never be taken seriously in law if you persist with this playboy image," warned Reginald.

"I don't have a playboy image," Aran defended himself.

"Yes, you do! Out drinking and socialising all the time. We have been very tolerant of you at the firm with your late starts and early finishes. Not to mention your slap-happy approach to work."

Aran concentrated on the tiled floor and said nothing.

"You are setting a bad example to the others," Reginald kept his voice controlled. "You are heir apparent. Larry has no children, so Murphy Hennessy is yours in the future to run and control. At the moment I can't see you ever having the interest, motivation or ability for that role."

Why don't you adopt? was one of the many sarcastic replies Aran wanted to voice, but didn't dare to.

"You used to be good," Muriel contributed. "You used to be much steadier and have great interest, until you were distracted." Muriel placed her napkin on the table and closed her eyes. "Aran, I don't want to ask the question because I'm frightened of the answer . . . but I hope Audrey Driver has not resurfaced in your life."

"Of course not. I wouldn't dream of going back out with her." Aran grabbed a slice of toast. "I'd better run. As you said, set a good example and all that." And he dashed out the door.

As Chloe looked around Boom's interior, she decided it could do with a revamp. But still, the place had a great buzz about it, and they were still the most established in Dublin.

Brendan had given her the go-ahead to have a preliminary meeting with Hazel to see if they had any interest in selling. Brendan was lukewarm about the idea of moving into the modelling world. Vincent was simply dead against it.

However, Chloe had railroaded the idea through. It was crucial for her to control Boom in order to eliminate Spinner. Brendan knew Chloe was an excellent businesswoman. He also knew Vincent, though part owner, was useless at business. He realised Vincent was often jealous of Chloe's ability and power. So he had sided with Chloe after much thought. When Chloe spoke, Brendan listened.

"I'm not at all happy with you," Hazel warned as Chloe came into her office.

"What have I done?" Chloe took a seat.

"Booked a model from Spinner, that's what." Hazel's loud voice was unforgiving.

"Ah, Alison Flatley." Chloe nodded her head. "For reasons I won't go into, I had to book Alison. If she were with Boom, I'd have gone through you."

"Mmmm." Hazel was unconvinced. "What's she like?"

"Alison? Very good actually."

"It helps of course that her father is who he is. She can't be that good or else she'd be with Boom."

"Audrey Driver discovered her," Chloe said.

Hazel hooted laughter. "Just don't get me started on

that bitch. Anyway what can I do for you? I've a brilliant new girl on the books if you are looking for a fresh face."

"I'm hear to discuss something more serious."

"Go on."

"This is strictly confidential. Macken Communications are thinking of expanding into the modelling world."

"Why the hell does everyone suddenly want to be a model agent? So you've arranged this meeting to inform me you will be one of my competitors? Very kind of you. Now if you don't mind, get out!"

Chloe's smile didn't waver for a second. "We don't want to start at the bottom, we want to start at the top. Have you ever thought about selling Boom?"

"Sell?. . . No."

"Would you consider selling Boom?" Chloe pursued.

"Macken are interested in buying my company?"

"Yes, we are. We would run Boom as a sister company. There would be no changes. No firing of staff. We would like you to remain as MD. There would be no change of direction or policy. I might become involved in the day-to-day running of Boom, but that's all."

"I'd be a salaried MD?"

"Of course," assured Chloe.

"And what kind of figure did you have in mind?"

Chloe was very pleased after finishing her meeting with Hazel. She would have the whole proposal ready to present to Brendan that afternoon. As she walked back to the office she bumped into Julianna who looked pale and drawn.

"You've been keeping a low profile recently," commented Chloe. Julianna was usually out and about at functions.

"Well, things happen." Julianna looked very uncomfortable.

"Everything OK?"

Julianna was trembling slightly. "Fine, fine." She pushed to get past Chloe.

"Wait, what's wrong?"

"Nothing – I don't want anything getting back to Aran." Julianna almost looked scared.

"There's no fear of that. Aran and me are history."

"Are you?" Julianna visibly relaxed.

"Let's grab a coffee."

Julianna had insisted on a quiet little coffee shop, off the beaten track.

"So what happened between you and Aran?" she asked as she heaped sugar into her coffee.

Chloe breathed in. "It just had gone its natural course. It was a mutual decision."

"Too bad."

"So are you going to tell me what's the matter with you?"

"It's Larry." Julianna waited a while before continuing. "He's such a bastard. Such a sick bastard."

"Tell me what happened."

"He was always cruel to a certain degree. Remember I told you before?"

Chloe nodded.

"He just became crueller and crueller. He seemed to know no limitations. I know I should have dumped him. But I couldn't help myself. I thought I was in love.

"The longer I stayed the worse he became. I knew he was seeing other women. He didn't even try to hide it from me. In fact, he flaunted it. He had never been even-tempered. But suddenly he was going way over the top. One night he stood me up. So I went around to his place. It was so obvious another woman had just left. So I got angry and started to call him names. And then he . . . attacked me. It was really bad. And he was in control throughout, enjoying it."

"What did you do?"

"He eventually left me. I was covered in bruises, cuts . . . I called a taxi and went."

Chloe placed a hand on Julianna's. "Did you tell the police?"

"How could I? You know who my family are . . . They couldn't cope with that kind of publicity . . . I couldn't cope with it. Besides, my family did try to warn me away from him. It isn't the first time he's done something like this, by all accounts."

"But you can't just let him away with it."

"What else can I do?"

"As I said, go to the police," urged Chloe.

"He's Larry Hennessy of the highly respected Murphy Hennessy, who was trying his best to get rid of a persistent girlfriend. They would just portray me as a woman scorned."

Chloe arrived back to the office late after lunch. She had continued to try to advise Julianna as best she could. But Julianna was adamant that she would not report the attack. Thinking about Larry, Chloe remembered Aran saying something about having to cover up for him in the past. She thought about Larry's reputation as a ladies' man and the mysterious Danielle. Most significantly, she remembered how he had made a pass at her in his house. All the pieces fitted together very easily to show what kind of a man Larry Hennessy was.

"I still say we should stick to what we know best," advised

Vincent at the board meeting that afternoon, having gone through all the figures regarding what a takeover at Boom would cost.

"And I say that Boom is a lucrative acquisition that brings Macken into a new but similar field," said Chloe.

Brendan asked to bring the documentation home before giving a final decision.

That night, he relaxed in his manor style house in the country just outside the capital. Because of his religious beliefs, Brendan and his family lived a quiet life. They shunned the glamorous lifestyle associated with most PRs. This had helped give Macken Communications its serious and no-nonsense image. Chloe was a fantastic asset to the company. Putting aside her amazing ability, she presented a glamorous and friendly image for Macken. Her work had impressed him so much over the years that he had made her a director. That spoke for itself. As he studied her proposal, he thought if she hadn't chosen PR for a career, she would have made a fantastic investment banker dealing in mergers and acquisitions. He discussed the plan with his wife Rose. She was a quiet woman, whose interests stretched to gardening and dressmaking, but he valued her opinion.

On Sunday night he rang Chloe at home.

"Make the offer to acquire Boom," he authorised.

CHAPTER 59

Peter had arranged a spate of interviews for Maeve the following day and so decided to avoid going into the office in the morning. He rang and informed Vanessa who relayed the message to Audrey. She was glad at first, but then realised it was only prolonging the agony. A series of journalists anxiously awaited their turn to interview Maeve that morning, all burning with questions about her infidelity and future. Peter had carefully coached Maeve with the correct replies. Yes, she had had an affair, conducted in hotel bedrooms. No, she regretted nothing. She was a woman who had been trapped in a wrong marriage for a considerable time, despite the great mutual respect she and her husband had for each other. Now, she no longer wanted to live the lie. Her career as an afternoon presenter was over and now she was looking forward to new challenges and being her own woman. The journalists couldn't go anywhere with what she was saying. Her brutal honesty left them with nothing to dig for. Sure, there would be the attention-grabbing headlines the next day, but nobody could any longer accuse her of being a cheat, liar or hypocrite. After the journalists scurried off to write their articles, Maeve and Peter headed over to the photographer's studio where a photo session had been arranged. Audrey had spent some time working on restyling Maeve's image, and now she looked better than ever. At the photo session, Peter had arranged for Maeve to be photographed in a number of infamous poses. First Maeve adopted the classic Christine Keeler pose astride a chair. Then she was photographed in the Marilyn Monroe shot in the white dress blowing over the subway grating. A replica of "that dress" worn by Liz Hurley, complete with safety pins, was borrowed for another photo still. Finally they drove out to the beach and Maeve was photographed coming out of the sea in a retake of the Bo Derek shot in the film "10". Peter knew all these photos were at variance with Maeve's normal image, but it would be the shock value that would make them sensational. He had promised the journalists exciting photos to accompany their articles and that was what he would deliver.

Audrey too had been busy that day. She accompanied Tiffany to the photo shoot for *Quest* magazine. Jackie Davenport dropped by and started to supervise all aspects of the work, much to the photographer's obvious fury. He liked being alone with the models, believing he could get more out of them, but Jackie was too powerful to offend. Audrey had gone along to support Tiffany, but it also kept her out of Peter's way. Every time she thought about what happened she started blushing deeply, even prompting Jackie to ask if she was feeling all right a couple of times.

"I'll head off now," said Audrey, looking at her watch and seeing it was nearly five. There was no sign of the shoot coming to an end soon.

"Sure," said Jackie. "I was right, wasn't I? About the changes with Tiffany?"

Jackie was never shy at singing her own praises.

"Thanks for the advice."

"I've also recommended the Latvian girl, Ivanka, to be seen by House of Opera."

"Thanks a million, Jackie."

"If they weren't good, I wouldn't be doing it. Congratulations, Audrey, Spinner is doing great work so far."

Until she had to go and fuck it up by getting off with Peter, thought Audrey.

She was back in the office by six and checking her messages at reception, when she heard Maeve and Peter talking as they came up the stairs.

Audrey closed her eyes tightly, then she swung around and beamed a smile at them.

"I've had such a brilliant day," Maeve exclaimed.

"That's great," answered Audrey, allowing herself a fleeting glance at Peter who looked embarrassed.

"I just feel so liberated," Maeve went on. "I don't have to live that lie any more – afraid of upsetting RTE or the viewing public with the truth. Here I am, with nothing to hide. My marriage is over, and hopefully I'm on the verge of a new career. Hopefully. No more smiling at the camera and asking dull guests boring questions! And it's all thanks to you two: Peter, for masterminding it all, and you, Audrey, for making me look this good and being a role model. You are a great team!"

Peter and Audrey glanced at each other and then smiled at Maeve.

"Well, let's see how our meeting goes with TV3 tomorrow before we start opening the champagne," said Peter. "Could you come to my office? There's lots of enquiries about bookings for you and I just want you to look through them and see what you'd like to do."

Maeve marched off down to his office.

Peter was about to follow her when he stopped and turned to face Audrey.

She took a deep breath and tried not to blush.

"Audrey, I was thinking, if Alison really pissed you off yesterday – we can kick her out of Spinner."

"Em . . . no, I wouldn't go that far. It's a bitchy business and I should be more hard-skinned."

"Well, if you're sure . . ."

"Besides, she's a good model. If we let her go, she'd just go straight over to Boom and they'd sign her up there." Peter nodded and went to join Maeve in his office.

Grabbing her handbag, Audrey rushed out of the place. At least the ice was broken. Peter seemed willing to pretend it had never happened. Which suited her fine. And why wouldn't he pretend it didn't happen? He was a married man. And she could imagine Lynn being quite vicious when the mood took her.

As Maeve sifted through the bookings, Peter's mind wasn't on the meeting.

He had rung around all the press to make sure they'd received the photos of Maeve taken that day. After agreeing to some work commitments, Maeve went home and Peter sat back in his chair and sighed. Audrey seemed to be as embarrassed as he was. The best thing was to get on with things and pretend it had never happened. He had rung Lynn and asked if she wanted to go to dinner, but she had already arranged to go to a concert with Rory. The tickets were like gold-dust, she had explained, so she had to go.

CHAPTER 60

Maeve Kelly's interviews with the accompanying photos were the talk of the country the next morning. Her image was transformed.

As she swept into the TV3 studios with Peter she looked a million dollars.

"You certainly have set tongues wagging," commented the TV3 executive during the meeting, "and obviously we accept that you have a very high profile. It's just we're not sure you can make the transition from daytime queen to the kind of late-night show we're talking about here."

"Have you seen the amount of publicity surrounding Maeve?" asked Peter.

"How could we miss it!" The programme planner looked at his executives.

"Maeve is so controversial right now, anything she touches is guaranteed huge viewership," argued Peter.

"But can you manage this kind of programme?" The executive looked at Maeve straight in the eye. "You won't be talking about cooking titbits any more. You'll be talking about everything from contraception, abuse, and of course infidelity."

"I've been broadcasting for twenty-five years," said Maeve. "Same deal, different shit. I can manage it just fine."

The next week passed with the same whirlwind itinerary. They tried to keep out of each other's way as much as possible. When Peter and Audrey did speak they kept it polite and short. They were overly polite to each other, something they never had been before.

Hazel looked through the contracts from Macken Communications. She was overwhelmed by a sense of sadness. She had built Boom from nothing. It was a big part of her life. But she just couldn't afford to turn down this offer from Macken. She must put her future and her security first. And this takeover would mean she would never have to worry about money again. She knew she was tough and experienced enough to fight Boom's rivals. But the cheque from Macken meant her life didn't depend on it any more. She knew she could see off Spinner, but she had been surprised by their success to date.

Of course, Jackie Davenport had helped them a lot and given them clout. Hazel was aware that Jackie had never liked her much, seeing her as a rival who was as respected in the industry as herself. Jackie was known for being very fickle, often throwing her weight behind a new kid in town. She was renowned for liking to take credit for "discovering" new faces or trends. So Hazel wasn't particularly surprised at Jackie's support for Spinner. It was true Hazel did like to rely on established models who were always in employment. What was the marketing term – cash cows? Did the term ever apply itself so deservedly as to her models, she chuckled to herself.

She didn't actively promote new models because she had always felt if they were good enough they would establish themselves. But as she looked on and saw Spinner aggressively promote all their girls, she realised her policy was working to her disadvantage now. Also, she knew that Spinner was undercutting competitors' rates. She imagined this could be just down to Audrey's inability to do sums. However, if it was their long-term policy, it could also threaten Boom. The cheque from Boom meant she didn't have to have sleepless nights about all this. She quickly signed the contracts.

"I'm just bringing Ivanka over to that casting for House of Opera that Jackie set up for us," Audrey informed Peter.

"Have you any price got yet?"

"No, I thought there was no point in discussing money until they saw her and decided if they were interested."

Peter was about to advise to talk money straight up and let them believe Ivanka was worth being interested in. However, he just smiled and nodded.

That afternoon, an executive from TV3 rang Peter and offered Maeve the late night programme. It was to be no-holds-barred, hard-hitting television. The first programme would deal specifically with Maeve's own affair, guaranteeing a huge audience. Peter was elated and so was Maeve when he rang her.

House of Opera had been impressed with Ivanka, and signed her up. Audrey was nervous about telling Peter. Although she had negotiated hard over the price, she had settled for less than she had hoped for. But in the end of the day, they were a new company, and the idea of one of their girls being the face of a respected Paris-based fashion house was too tempting to resist.

She knocked on Peter's door. "Are you busy?"

The adrenaline was rushing through Peter's body over the news from TV3 and he was busy drafting a press release to announce it.

"Yeah, er, no – I have great news – Maeve got the show." He looked up, his eyes flashing happiness, his excitement banishing the awkwardness between the two of them.

"I've got news too. House of Opera accepted Ivanka."

"Well done. I'll call them tomorrow to discuss rates."

"I've already done that." She blushed.

He was immediately worried. "What did you agree on?"

"They'll fax it through later."

"Well, you must know off the top of your head what you settled on?" Realising from her silence she was embarrassed to say the amount he slammed the table.

"Goddamn it! I told you to let me negotiate prices. We are not in the business of selling models cheap!"

"The word is hiring not selling!"

"This is no use. I don't have the time to go around watching your every move. We're going to have to hire in a professional that I can work along with. Someone like – Dermot from Macken."

"The guy who tried to dress me up in a bunny outfit? Forget it! I'm not having one of your cronies in here so you can gang up on me."

"Someone who'd be excellent at their job," Peter pushed.

"We can't afford to pay a guy like that. We're just beginning to make some money. We aren't going to piss it away on that prat. No, Peter, I've had enough of your attitude. Don't ever try to put me down again. I don't need you to watch what I'm doing. I'm the person who thought up the idea of Spinner, who pushed it along and who does just as much work as you do. And if that's not enough, then remember I'm 50% owner as well."

Audrey sat at Reception taking calls. She had spent a couple of hours in her office trying to calm down after her run in with Peter. She felt she had asserted herself and felt the better because of it. When she heard his door open she quickly picked up the phone and pretended to be having a conversation.

"Sure, no problem. I think I've got just the girl for you. I'll send you over her details." She hung up.

"I'm going home," Peter mumbled.

"See you tomorrow."

"You needn't worry in future. We won't be having any more arguments like today. I think from now on, we'll just stick to a purely professional way of interacting. We'll just do our work, get on with it, and have regular meetings where we can update each other. Probably the less we talk to each other in a non-professional way, the better all round." He sounded sullen, a little cold.

Audrey thought he looked like a scolded schoolboy. She stood up from behind reception and walked over to him, suddenly smiling. "Peter, why be so uptight all the time? Stop taking yourself and everything else so seriously."

Thrown by her warmth, he nodded and quickly left.

CHAPTER 61

Lynn had left a brief message on the coffee table saying she would be out until late. He couldn't blame her really. She was hardly going to stay at home watching soaps while he worked all hours. Thoughtfully, she had prepared him dinner and left it in the oven. Peter was unnerved by Audrey's reaction when he was leaving the office. He had become increasingly angry after their argument earlier in the afternoon. He had decided enough was enough and hence his speech when he was leaving. But, in typical Audrey style, she had reacted unpredictably and had been warm, leaving him looking inflexible. With one sentence and a smile she had dismissed his speech as being impractical and stupid. Of course partners needed to be in constant dialogue, and if arguments were a part of that, so be it. Maybe he hadn't been treating her as an equal partner. It was a self-acknowledged fault that he liked to do everything himself. And maybe because of her lack of business experience, he had been dismissive of her, he mused as he ate his dinner alone.

Spinner had been her idea, that was true. And she was

also right when she said she had been the driving force behind it. He also had to admit that her knowledge of the modelling world, her natural flair for image creation and her contacts, especially Jackie, had all been crucial to their success so far. In fact, he had to admit to himself when analysing the situation, it was true for Maeve, they made a good team. Audrey's talents complemented his business and PR skills.

God, where was Lynn? He needed his wife there to discuss the situation. He had always relied on her cryptic advice. It dawned on him he barely mentioned Spinner to Lynn at all. This was because of her negative opinion about the whole business, not to mention her ultimatum that it had to succeed.

He hadn't wanted to give her any scope for thinking anything could be going wrong. And, of course, Lynn had informed him that she didn't want to push him or carry him any more. Maybe he would like to discuss with his wife what had happened between Audrey and himself the previous week, he teased himself. Overcome with guilt, he downed another glass of wine.

"Well, you sound much better than you were," Kathleen said down the phone to her daughter.

"Oh, I feel great, Mum. I'm enjoying every minute of Spinner. And I'm really happy being back with Aran."

"I'm still worried about that after how he treated you last time."

"That's all in the past now. We are both treating each other better second time around."

"Glad to hear it. Does his family know yet?"

"Not yet, no," Audrey confessed.

"Audrey!" Kathleen was exasperated. "Then nothing has changed! He has you back on the terms he wanted before. Seeing you when it pleases him and hiding your relationship from the world . . . as if he's ashamed of you"

Audrey cursed herself for telling Kathleen the truth. "We do go out, all the time. But to local restaurants."

"Look darling, every relationship you've ever had has been in the papers, so why aren't I reading about you and Aran now?"

"Probably because I'm not a top model any more."

"Rubbish! They would still print who you are seeing."

"We just want this time to ourselves. What's wrong with that? It's nobody else's business but our own . . . and you don't know how awful his family are. I don't want to meet them again, anyway. This suits me, too."

"You can convince yourself of anything, Audrey. A man like Aran Murphy is used to getting what he wants and on his terms. Unless he is willing to stand up to his family and say this is the woman I love, then there is no future in this relationship."

After another ten minutes of Kathleen's well-meaning rants, Audrey managed to skilfully switch the conversation to local gossip from home before saying goodbye.

She should have known better than to confide in her mother the ins and outs of her love life. She had never understood and subtly disapproved at the best of times. Kathleen would only be happy if she had married Shaun and was living down the road and pushing a pram. Of course, Aran wasn't ashamed of her. What was wrong with wanting time to themselves? Before breaking up last time their lives had been such a flurry of being seen in the right places and going to the right functions, and everyone having their say, that their relationship wasn't given the space to develop naturally. And if she were one hundred per cent honest, their relationship had probably been based on and hindered by who they were. It was only after they had broken up that they realised there was much more to it than that, that they did have strong feelings for each other. And now they were enjoying those feelings in private. Kathleen, whose advice she mostly respected, was wrong on this one.

Audrey tasted the rich sauce she was preparing to go with dinner. She put on her earrings and smoothed down her black cocktail dress. She was expecting Aran any minute. It was nice to stay in and relax rather than heading out all the time, especially now she worked at San Juan. Stirring the sauce, she contemplated Peter's little speech that evening. She hoped she had defused the situation. She allowed her mind to think back to how she used to think about him before their first major fallout about her timekeeping during the Childwatch Show. It was hard to remember because so much had happened between them since. But she remembered thinking of him as intriguing. When he asked her to go to Lynn's exhibition, she had gone out of sheer curiosity to see what his wife was like. But in all honesty, he had never occupied more than a passing thought in her mind. Little did she know then that he would become such a central part of her life. The doorbell rang and she pressed the button to let Aran up.

He greeted her with a kiss and chocolates.

"I may not be modelling any more, but these," she put the chocolates on the coffee table, "are still out of bounds . . . most times!"

"I'll have them then," he joked, pouring himself a brandy.

Later, as they ate dinner, the candlelight sparkled on Audrey's diamond earrings and necklace.

"So I told Peter straight that I wasn't going to be shunted to one side."

"Too right. He's an idiot anyway. I'll never know why you picked him as a partner."

"Because they weren't exactly banging on my door at the time, remember? And I told you before, he's good. And he isn't an idiot, for the record."

"I can't understand you. You used to hate him with a passion and now you defend him."

"That was before I got to know him."

"And do you know him now?"

"He's kinda hard to get to know. But I think I understand him." Noticing Aran's worried expression she quickly distracted him by saying sarcastically, "Unlike your friend!"

"My friend?"

"Chloe." She pulled a face.

"I've told you a million times. She was just a stop-gap."

"I'm quite intrigued by this relationship you had with her." Audrey smiled wickedly.

"As if I hadn't guessed! You've quizzed me about everything from what colour bathroom towels she has, to what she's like in the sack!"

"Well, a girl needs to know about her competition."

Reaching over to take her hand, Aran said, "She's no competition for you, baby."

She bent forward and kissed him. "Still, knowledge is power. Did she ever talk about marriage?"

"She never came out and talked about it. But it just hovered there in the air like an unspoken agenda."

"I bet it did. She would have loved getting her hooks into you."

Aran adopted a childish voice, "And I didn't have you there to protect me."

"Well, I'm here now, so she had better steer clear. I bet Muriel liked her."

"Oh, they were the best of friends. Even meeting up for lunch to discuss ideas for Mother's charities."

"How cosy!" Audrey hated herself for hearing Kathleen's words of warning echo in her mind. "Your parents haven't guessed we are back together yet?"

"No. They did make some derogatory comment when they found out Chloe and I were finished"

"What derogatory comment?"

"Just that they hoped we weren't seeing each other again."

Audrey threw her napkin on the table. "I just don't get it – why do they hate me?"

She adopted a haughty self-mocking voice. "I'm not bad-looking."

"Without equal!" he laughed.

"And I'm clever," she continued.

"More like cunning, I'd say."

"And talented."

He reached over and kissed her. "Many talents!"

"And now I'm a successful businesswoman," she concluded.

"I'm such a lucky man. I don't know why they don't love you, like I do."

"Do you? Love me?"

"Of course I do." They began to kiss again.

She drew back and looked at him seriously. "But what

happens when they do find out? When are you actually going to tell them?"

"Let's just take one step at a time, eh?"

"All right . . . one step at a time."

Chapter 62

Peter knocked on Audrey's office door. "Come in!" she called. Then on seeing Peter she said, "You don't have to knock, you know."

"Just making sure you weren't on the phone."

"Even if I was, it wouldn't matter. We are partners and shouldn't have secrets."

"Yeah, I know. I was thinking a lot last night and I suppose we have been pulling in two different directions. I would like us to be more of a team."

"I want that too." Audrey felt the conversation would have been more comfortable if it weren't taking place in the very place where they had kissed passionately.

"So from now I propose we keep each other more informed, take mutual decisions and respect each other's ideas."

"And negotiating skills," she added.

"And negotiating skills. So maybe we can get together this afternoon and talk about Maeve's new show and also this House of Opera deal for Ivanka."

"That's cool."

"I'll see you later then. I'm off now with Alison for the

photo shoot for Macken. I don't want to leave one of our models with Chloe for one second."

"Chloe will be there? Give her my love," Audrey joked.

"And will I give her Aran's love?" He could have kicked himself as soon as he had said it.

Audrey was taken aback. "No. Myself and Aran only have love for each other," she said pointedly. She was glad of the opportunity to obliquely say what happened shouldn't have. To point out they were both in committed relationships.

"That's good. I'll see you later."

Peter was relieved to have it confirmed Audrey was back with Aran; it helped him to forget about their indiscretion. He had so much more to lose than her if it ever got out. And he thought Aran and Audrey were well suited. They were similar types. But what he couldn't understand was that he didn't feel totally happy at hearing this news. He was experiencing a strange irritation at the thought of Audrey and Aran back together. And he didn't know why.

He prepared himself for seeing Chloe again. On arriving at the photo studio he found her and Alison deep in conversation.

"Peter!" Chloe called on seeing him approach. He admitted to himself she looked good in Roberto Cavialli. She seemed to have elevated power-dressing to an art form. "So good to see you again."

He wasn't taken in by the beaming white smile or charm. "You're looking well, Chloe."

"So are you. I've just been talking to Alison here. I think she has a big future ahead of her."

"That's why we have her at Spinner," answered Peter.

Chloe turned to Alison. "I'll leave you to go into Make-up and get this show rolling."

Alison was taken away by both make-up and hair stylists who had received specific instructions from Chloe.

Peter and Chloe sat down on two wooden chairs at the edge of the studio.

"So you're keeping well?" asked Chloe.

"Very well. Couldn't be happier with Spinner."

"I'm happy for you. You deserve it."

"Thanks." Peter nodded.

"I met Lynn at her shop. I was looking to buy a painting."

"Yeah, she said. Don't rise to the bait, he thought. Keep professional.

"Told her what a loss you were to Macken. Still, I wouldn't hold anyone back from getting on."

Like hell, he thought, you are all heart.

"And how are you finding Audrey?"

"She's a great girl," Peter nodded.

"Isn't she? She's keeping a low profile at the moment. Not like her," said Chloe.

"Well, she's run off her feet with the agency."

"And is she still doing bar work at night?"

"She's still a hostess at San Juan, yes." He couldn't help himself from smiling. Chloe was definitely a class act, he thought. Her subtle manipulation of words was excellent. But he could see right through her now.

"I have to say," continued Chloe, "I think she's amazing. The way she recovered from alcoholism. I read all about it in the papers."

"It wasn't alcoholism," he corrected.

"Oh!" Chloe looked surprised. "You must have delivered the wrong message to the media then."

Don't rise to the bait, he reminded himself.

After being styled, Alison emerged from the dressing-rooms and Chloe selected the first outfit for her to wear. After she had changed into it, the photographer got to work.

"I think Alison is a trouper for letting us change her hair colour," said Chloe.

"It's only a temporary measure. It'll wash out," said Peter. "Audrey did it for her."

"Audrey sounds likes she's being really hands-on. Which is good, you need to be in this business. Planning any holidays?"

"Too busy at the moment. Especially since we landed Maeve Kelly's account."

"Yes, poor Maeve, how is she? It must be hard for her to come to terms with the fact her TV career is over."

"Over? We've just landed her a new talk show at TV3." He savoured the moment and studied her face for a reaction. There was none.

"I think if I get a chance I might try and organise a sun holiday. Recharge the batteries," she said. A new talk show, she thought, how the hell did they manage that? "You should try and get away too – if you feel you can trust Audrey enough to leave her in charge."

"I have total confidence in Audrey. She's quite a businesswoman."

Oh please, thought Chloe before saying, "I'll be after her to join Macken next!"

"You'd be wasting your time. There's nothing like being your own boss, owning your own company. No matter how high you go, it's not the same as working for yourself, is it?"

You are treading on very dangerous ground, Peter, thought Chloe, recognising the thinly veiled dig at herself.

"True," said Chloe. "Lynn never thought of branching

out and starting up her own gallery? I believe the crowd she works for pays terribly." Chloe fired the ball right back into Peter's court.

"I think one entrepreneur is enough in the family at the moment."

"Wise of you. You don't want to put too much of a strain on your marriage. Lynn is a very understanding wife with you working with such a beautiful woman as Audrey."

Now you really have left yourself wide open, he thought. "I think I have enough willpower to stay away. Unlike Aran, who came running back to her."

Touché! He thought.

Chloe's expression didn't falter. Inside she screamed: so my suspicion was right!

"Audrey and Lynn are good friends as a matter of fact. The four of us regularly meet up for dinner," Peter lied.

Chloe began to feel nauseous. She was suddenly transported back in years to be the one left out, looking in on the cool kids having fun.

Time for the *pièce de resistance*, she thought.

"Friends are important," she said. "I hope the new situation won't affect our friendship, Peter."

Like we were ever friends, he thought. "New situation?"

"That we are competitors."

"I don't see Spinner and Macken as being in any way direct competition. I know you manage some celebs, but you are primarily blue-chip PR."

"But that's what I mean. We are in direct competition now that we've taken over at Boom."

Chloe slammed the door behind her as she stormed into her office. Sitting behind her desk, she buzzed her secretary.

"Ring Hazel at Boom and tell her to get those signed contracts over to me this afternoon."

She was infuriated. Firstly Peter had been so smart with her with his backchat and smart answers. She should have finished him off when she could have. She shouldn't have given him a second chance after the Childwatch fiasco. Now he was on his feet again. But what infuriated her most was the confirmation about Aran being back with Audrey. What did he see in her? And the thought of them all forming a cool circle to her exclusion was too much for her to bear.

She had to attend a function that evening. Ever since entering PR she had no qualms about going to events alone or with an inconsequential date. Her personality, position and many contacts meant it was more favourable to go like that because she was freer to mix and mingle. But now she had become used to going to places with Aran. She was comfortable being out with him and being seen out with him. She would ring one of her contacts and see who was free that evening to go with her. But first she had to make another call.

She quickly dialled a mobile number and got through to the gossip columnist at *Ireland On Sunday*.

"Hi, Chloe at Macken here. I've got a scoop for you. But it's very sensitive. It has to be handled exactly as I say. My way or no way."

Arriving back at Spinner, Peter was unnerved by the news of Macken's takeover at Boom. Unnerved and scared. This was a different field from their normal business. What was their agenda? Did they perceive Spinner as a risk because they had taken Maeve as a client, like when they lost Celtic Vodka to Blast? Or was it a personal issue? Whatever the reasons, he was frightened of the thought of having Macken and Chloe as a competitor.

"How did it go?" Audrey asked.

"The shoot went very smoothly."

"And how was the lovely Chloe?"

"Same as ever."

"Everything OK?" She noticed he was a little pale.

"Macken have bought Boom. They are going to run it as a subsidiary." He saw the shock register on her face.

"Hazel selling out? I don't believe it."

"When Macken wants something, money is no barrier. They go after it till they get it. I know, I've seen it close up."

"What does it mean for us?"

"It means we have a bigger and more powerful competitor. They believe in destroying anything that stops them from being the best. And they have huge resources."

"OK, so why don't you try and tell me something positive now."

"Can't think of anything. Apart from the fact I nearly managed to knock the smile off Chloe's face when I informed her you and Aran are back together."

"You did what?" She was incredulous.

"I told her Aran had come running back to you."

"You had no reason or right to talk about my private life with her or anybody else."

"I didn't realise it was a secret," Peter said.

"Well, it is. Or it was till you opened your big mouth. We didn't want people to know." Audrey was furious.

"God, I'm really sorry, Audrey."

"You just don't think before you speak. You never think of the consequences, do you?" Grabbing her handbag, she pushed past him and left .

He sat on the edge of the desk and buried his head in his hands.

"Another fight?"

He looked up to see Vanessa leaning against the door.

"Looks like it."

"I've never met two people like you. Just when you call a truce it all erupts again," she observed.

"Crazy, isn't it?"

"Is there anything going on between you two?" She raised an eyebrow.

"Of course not," he snapped.

She held up her hands. "I'm not accusing you of an affair. You just might have stronger feelings for each other than you have realised. There's a thin line between love and hate."

"Vanessa, I'm happily married. And Audrey is in a happy relationship. I'm afraid what you get is what you see with us. And I think that could be mutual dislike."

"He did what?" roared Aran.

"I know. I lost the head with him," said Audrey.

"What kind of moron is he?"

"I guess I never told him to be discreet."

"For fuck's sake! If Chloe knows, she'll make sure everyone else knows."

"I know, I know. I'm as pissed off as you are." Audrey sat down.

"How stupid is he? I've a good mind to have a go at him."

"Oh, Aran, that would be silly. He didn't know. It's not his fault."

"Standing up for him again?" Aran was inflamed.

"I'm not! I'm as angry as you. But maybe it's not a bad

thing. I mean we had to let people know sooner or later we are back together."

"My parents will go mad when they find out."

"To be honest, they are just going to have to live with it. I'm a bit tired of being disapproved by them all the time. This is our relationship and it should matter only to the two of us."

"Not out somewhere?" Peter was surprised to find Lynn at home.

"I'm tired out. I had to bring some clients for lunch and they were hard work"

"Sell any work?"

"I did OK. But I would do a lot better if Rory would get his finger out and finish some paintings he has promised me." Lynn observed her husband taking off his tie. She knew that expression on his face. It was a defeatist look.

He was either full of energy and very positive. Or when he suffered a major blow he tended to feel a failure.

"What's wrong?"

He sat down. "I met Chloe Gallagher today. At a shoot she'd hired one of our models for."

"And how was she?"

"That woman could pass through a tornado and her smile and every blasted hair on her well-groomed head would stay in place."

"She's a strong character all right."

"She told me Macken have bought Boom."

It all fell into place for Lynn. Hence the defeatist look on Peter's face, she reasoned. "And how does that affect you?" she enquired, already fully aware of the consequences.

"You know what Chloe is like in business, vicious. She'll try to wipe us out."

I see, thought Lynn. You've been flying high since Spinner began and now with the first big cloud on the horizon you are losing confidence in yourself again.

"So what are you going to do about it?" she enquired.

"What can I do?"

"What does Audrey think about it?"

"I don't think she understands the full implications. She doesn't know them like I do."

"I think you are, as ever, jumping ahead of yourself. So what if Macken has taken over Boom? So what if they take over Ford in New York? You've established yourselves enough to keep making a success out of it."

"Anybody but them." Peter shook his head.

"You are allowing yourself to be intimidated."

"I saw how they operated when they took over Blast."

"A different situation. They owned Blast; you were at their mercy. And they may act the same at Boom. But you are an independent company. You are the boss."

"I suppose." Peter didn't sound convinced.

"Do you consider Chloe to be more talented than you?"

"No, just more ruthless."

"You can be ruthless too, when you need to be. Don't let her intimidate you."

Peter nodded. "I'm going for a bath . . . thanks." He got up and walked off.

As she heard the bath run, she put her head back and closed her eyes.

She had managed to bolster his confidence and give him support. But she felt drained and exhausted.

CHAPTER 63

The social column in *Ireland On Sunday* read:

"They say the course of true love never runs smoothly. Never has this been more true than in the case of Aran Murphy, heir apparent at Murphy Hennessy, and our favourite girl about town, Audrey Driver. We can exclusively reveal that the pair have established themselves as an item again. Readers may remember Aran was seeing PR boss Chloe Gallagher. But they have now parted company and Aran is back in Audrey's arms. So far the couple have been keeping a low profile as they rekindle their love. But it will only be a matter of time before they emerge from hiding to become Dublin's most popular couple on the party circuit again. I believe there are no tears over at Macken Communications, where Chloe reigns supreme. She has been seen out around town with a number of eligible men. As if this didn't occupy Chloe's time enough, in another exclusive, we can reveal that Macken have taken over Boom Model Agency. Chloe has many innovative ideas where she wants to take Boom in the future. This should be fun, as Audrey runs Spinner, Dublin's newest agency."

"The bitch!" shouted Audrey.

"Of course Chloe was going to get it printed once she got the info – to put her own spin on it," snapped Aran. They lay on Audrey's bed reading the papers.

"She made sure she was shown in a good light."

"She was hardly going to say she got dumped. She didn't get where she has by being stupid. My life is going to be hell." Aran had been in foul form since discovering Chloe knew about them. Audrey had tried to be understanding but she was becoming annoyed by his attitude.

"Well, at least now we can go out to restaurants and things without feeling like criminals," she said.

"I wondered how long it would be before selfish, think-of-myself-only Audrey would reappear." His words were like a slap. It was the first time either of them had been unkind to each other since getting back together.

"Well, I was becoming to feel like a mistress the way you have hid our relationship away," she shot back.

"Even a wife would be more understanding than my parents are when it comes to you."

"For God's sake, Aran, what age are you? Isn't it about time you told your parents to piss off?"

Muriel's phone had been hopping all morning long with friends and relatives advising her to get *Ireland On Sunday*. With dread she sat down to read the social column. And there it was, her worst fears confirmed.

"What kind of strange hold does she have over him?" Muriel demanded of her husband as she entered their lavish bedroom from her dressing-room that evening. "To pass over such an intelligent and talented girl like Chloe for *her*?"

Reginald was putting the cufflinks on his tuxedo. They were due to attend a hunt ball at Muriel's cousin's country estate.

"And the fact that he deceived us for so long by denying going back to that girl" Muriel, seated at her dressing-table, was putting on her pearls.

"I would like to say Aran is an intelligent and sensible young man. That I am sure he will see through her eventually and marry someone suitable. But I'm not sure he will. He seems besotted by Audrey."

Muriel turned quickly. "What are you saying? That we may have to accept her."

"At the end of the day, what choice do we have?" said Reginald.

"I can't believe you are even contemplating it."

"I deplore the idea as much as you. But I suppose, to some she may be considered a good catch. She can be charming and well, you know, attractive."

"She's flashy and devious. Imagine our grandchildren with her breeding. I simply won't stand for it, Reginald. We'll be a laughing-stock."

"I know. I know," Reginald approached his wife and put his arm around her. "We won't let it happen."

"But what can we do?"

"Everything we can," he assured.

The social column only managed to compound Peter's guilt. Damn it, why hadn't he thought before speaking? He had bad nights' sleep over the weekend, tossing and turning and having nightmares. In his dreams he was back at Macken, being humiliated by all and sundry. Then in his dreams he was suddenly kissing Audrey only for him to look down and see it was Chloe with her saying, "We are now in direct competition." He woke up with a shout a couple of times. Lynn had tried to soothe him, but in the end, she'd despaired of getting any sleep herself and moved to another room.

Peter was cooking a fry for them on Sunday morning, while Lynn was reading the culture section of *The Sunday Times*. There was an interview with Rory in it.

"Fancy going down to my parents today?" he asked while serving the food.

"Not really, no." She was tired from lack of sleep.

"I might pop down myself for a while. Take one of the horses out riding."

"That's fine." She continued reading the article as she ate.

But even riding through the countryside didn't make him feel much better. Driving to work on Monday morning, he still felt tense. He had been working too hard, he thought. Maybe Audrey was right; he was taking everything too seriously.

Audrey was on the phone in reception when he got in.

"I agree, Ivanka is very unusual looking. But she doesn't come cheap. I'll email you her rate card and you can get back to me." She hung up. Word had spread that Ivanka was about to become the face of The House of Opera and was very much in demand. A good opportunity for Audrey to improve her negotiating skills, she thought.

"Morning." Her voice was ice.

"Audrey, I'm so sorry for landing you in the shit about Aran. I read the paper yesterday. I'd never deliberately do anything to cause you any problems." His face was earnest and sorrowful.

Her icy stare melted. "I know you wouldn't. I'm sorry I

flew off the handle with you. It was as much my fault as yours for not telling you to keep quiet."

"What's the problem anyway?" He was confused.

"Too complicated to get into . . . his family disapprove of me. Me? Little old sweetness and light me, can you imagine?" she laughed.

"No. I think Aran and his family would be very lucky to get you," he said. She waited for a sarcastic follow-up, but none followed.

She felt awkward and blushed. "Thanks, Peter – Will we have that meeting now about Maeve? Now Chloe has taken over Boom, we're going to have to be even more on the ball."

Getting ready to go in to work at San Juan, Audrey thought about Aran's reaction to their "going public". He was in bad form and seemingly his parents hadn't said anything but were being very frosty with him. Her thoughts drifted to Peter whom she had spent most of the day in meetings with. He seemed different – distracted and not bursting with the usual energy and coming up with great ideas that he usually did. He kept directing the conversation back to Macken's takeover at Boom. A taxi brought her to the club and she had a brief meeting with Noel about a rock group that were performing in Dublin the following week. She had contacted their tour manager and they had agreed to have the after-show party at San Juan. It would mean Noel supplying some free drinks, but it would be worth it, for the amount of publicity it would generate. It was a busy night at the club and a few of the models from Spinner were there. Tiffany was out with Vanessa, and Mark, a business student they had just signed up part-time. His looks were matched with a funny and witty personality and the girls were going for him big time. Audrey hoped clients would as well. Alison was out with her own crowd, who Audrey recognised as all part of the millionaire set. Alison always seemed to be socialising with the in-crowd. Her father's position as a senior politician allowed her entry to wherever she wanted. Audrey had acted in a professional way with Alison, pretending she hadn't heard anything of that conversation or the snide comments. But it left her with a mistrust of the girl. Tiffany's cover on *Quest* was due to hit the stands the following week. Observing Tiffany laughing away with Mark, Audrey made a mental note to have a word with her about her weight. She seemed to have kept on losing weight even after reaching Jackie's advised target. She was beginning to look too thin.

Lynn would have preferred not to have gone to San Juan that night. But Rory and the rest of the crowd they were with had insisted. She knew Audrey worked there and she would have preferred not to be put in a situation where she would have to talk to her. Arriving at the front entrance, they were quickly ushered into the members' lounge. Being out with Rory always ensured VIP treatment. He was famous and respected. Their mutual friends were the intelligentsia and she adored their company. More specifically, she adored how Rory put her on a pedestal. There were no arguments or pressure with Rory or their friends. No talk of nasty business dealings, frivolous models or backstabbing. No bouts of unbridled energy mixed with mood swings when the going got tough. Just an appreciation of the finer things of life. Many people had been complimenting Lynn on

Spinner's success. Before she might have revelled in the reflected glory. But she felt detached from Spinner. Almost as if it had nothing to do with her. Almost as if she was waiting for the bubble to burst. Judging by Peter's mood over the weekend, it looked like it just had.

"I just don't have the energy to boost him up any more," Lynn confided her woes to Rory. They were deep in conversation in the members' lounge.

"You've pushed him enough over the years. It's time he pushed himself," advised Rory.

"Just because Chloe Gallagher is giving him a bit of competition, I can see him crumbling."

"Why though?"

"Because he thinks she's better than him, that's why. And the funny thing is, she's not. If he could only believe in himself, nobody would be better than him." She had enjoyed a few glasses of champagne throughout the night, "If only life could be like a Constable painting."

"A Constable painting?"

"Yes, you know. Serene and safe and untouchable. No threats."

Audrey was busily chatting to a customer when she spotted Lynn. Her immediate reaction was guilt that she had kissed her husband. She wondered if she could avoid Lynn for the night, but decided that would be rude. She was her business partner's wife. Of course she should go over and have a chat.

"Hi, Lynn. Good to see you," said Audrey, sitting down beside her.

Lynn turned around. This was what she had been dreading. "Audrey! You're still working here? I'd thought you'd be too busy with Spinner."

"I enjoy it. It keeps me out of trouble."

"Well, that's a plus." Lynn tried not to sound too sarcastic.

"Peter not with you?"

"He's at home. He's feeling tired."

"Yeah, he seems under the weather these past couple of days," said Audrey.

"Well, that's the other side of Peter."

"What other side?"

"Peter is brilliant at what he does." Lynn nodded her head as she spoke, "but he doesn't believe he is. And this can make him turn on himself when he feels he isn't good enough."

"I've never seen that side to him."

"I am married to him. I think I know him better than you."

"So what can we do to help him snap out of it?"

"We?"

"All our futures depend on Spinner being a success," explained Audrey.

"Darling, Spinner is yours and Peter's. Nothing to do with me."

"I don't understand you. I thought you would be proud of your husband's success and that he is realising his talents. But, it's like you're jealous of him."

"My God, I more than anyone have pushed and pushed Peter to succeed."

"You never wanted him to start this company with me, did you?"

"Honestly? No. I think he's wasting his abilities. He was meant for better things."

"You are jealous of him." Audrey was incredulous. "You're jealous of his success at Spinner. And that he's done it without your help. Because he has me as a partner. That's why you said Spinner has nothing to do with you. You wanted Peter to be a success, but on your terms. And I make you uncomfortable because I'm in the limelight with Peter. You want all the attention yourself ."

"Darling, I think we had better stop this conversation before I say something I regret. Could you refill my champagne glass, please." Lynn left San Juan soon after her conversation with Audrey. She was angry with the familiarity with which Audrey spoke to her. Accusing her of being jealous of her own husband! The girl was mad as well as pathetic. Goddamn Peter for having anything to do with her and bringing her into their lives. She had pleaded with him not to, but he had just ignored her. And now they were associated with this frivolous, scandal-attracting idiot, who was trading on Peter's knowledge so she could play businesswoman. As if all this wasn't enough, there had been sarcastic little remarks from her friends in the art world about Peter's choice of business partner.

"Good night?" Peter asked as she let herself into the apartment. He was lounging on the sofa, scribbling some notes down.

"Fine." She walked into the kitchen and put the kettle on. She reached for her hidden stash of cigarettes and lit one up. He smelt the tobacco smoke drifting in from the kitchen and recognised the sign that all was not well.

"Peter, could you stop writing for a minute, please," she requested, sitting on the sofa opposite him, coffee in one hand and cigarette in the other. "I would like to talk to you about us."

Peter breathed in deeply. "OK. Go on."

"Well, we aren't exactly having a normal marriage, are we? We haven't been having one for a while."

"And what's a normal marriage like?"

"One where the husband and wife talk to each other occasionally. Even talk about something other than work occasionally. Where they spend time together and enjoy each other's company."

"I always enjoy your company. I asked you to come horse-riding with me on Sunday."

"You know I don't enjoy horse-riding. I would have ended up sitting chatting to your parents while you went galloping cross-country."

"I've asked you to meet me lots of times recently but you had other arrangements. The dinner the other night, for example."

"That's just the point. A husband doesn't ask his wife to join him for dinner. It's supposed to just happen."

"But both our schedules have always been busy. I know I've been spending too much time at work recently, but that's natural starting a new company."

"There's work commitments and then there's work commitments. You see much more of Audrey Driver than you do of me."

"So, this is about Audrey again!"

"It's about us. When I married you I thought we were going places."

"And we are, now that Spinner is being established –"

"Peter, I've seen the way you've been over the past couple of days. You've lost your confidence. And you will be relying on me to give it back to you. Just the same way I've pushed and encouraged you since the day we met. I don't have any encouragement left to give."

"You're being unfair. You're the one wanting a bigger apartment, a plusher car, exotic holidays. So when you push me it's for your benefit too. I might have shut you out from Spinner, but it was only because I was frightened you might think I was looking for just the kind of support you're talking about. Anyway, I thought that was what marriage was all about, supporting each other."

"I never rely on you to support me."

"How can you say that? I've always supported what you do. I know you like what you do, so I've never even suggested getting a better paid job."

She stubbed out her cigarette. "Peter, we could sit here trading snipes all night. The fact is I'm no longer happy with our relationship."

"So, you want me to change? To be more attentive? Spend less time at work?"

"The sad thing is, I don't think I want you to do anything. I don't feel the same about us any more."

"OK. I promise I'll cut down on my work hours."

"Peter, my priorities have changed."

"What are you saying? That you want to finish or something?" He said it half-smiling, frightened of the answer she would give him.

Lighting up another cigarette she said, "I guess I do. Not finish. I don't know. I want some space."

He began to panic. "But you just said we don't see enough of each other, so why then do you want space?"

"Exactly. I'm not suggesting anything other than what is happening already. I'm just making it more official."

Peter gasped and held the corners of the coffee table. "You want a divorce?"

"A separation. Some time for myself," Lynn spoke with certainty.

"But I . . . I love you."

"Oh, Peter, I guess you do."

"Come on. Come on, Lynn. How long have we been together? We can't let this go." His eyes were pleading.

"I didn't want to come out and say this . . . I'm seeing somebody else." Her words were like a knife going through his chest. "I still care for you a great deal. But we need a trial separation."

"I don't believe this. Who are you seeing?"

"Myself and Rory have been together for a while."

He flopped back into the couch. "Rory bloody Ryan!"

"I can't say when it started. I can't even remember. Not that long ago. In case you think I've been having a long affair, I haven't."

His desperation turned to anger. "Oh, your priorities haven't changed, Lynn. They've stayed the same. You have always been a self-serving woman. You married me because you thought I'd be big and successful. And because it hasn't been this steady story of success, you've cast your eyes around for someone else. And there's Rory Ryan. Acclaimed artist, who can command a few grand for that shite he calls art. So you can be at his side and be seen as the other half of this great artist. What were you saying the other week? Wanting a famous surname? His, by any chance?"

"You're talking rubbish. I'm with Rory because we get on. We have so much in common."

"What the hell have you in common?" Peter demanded.

"We live in the same world –"

"Cloud-cuckoo land?"

"The art world. I'm very comfortable with him. I'm tired of being part of your PR world and all its murky deals and underhanded ways."

"You just want to be cosseted in life. Protected from anything ugly. I said this to you before when I told you the real story of working for Macken. Do you know when our marriage really broke down? I think it was that night when I confided in you how unhappy I was at Macken. You didn't want me to confide in you. Not like the way normal couples do. You just wanted to hear that everything was great. Because you can't deal with real life. And that night you did your normal routine, shut out the truth, and took to your bed. You say you pushed me all those years. I say you lived in a fantasy world, giving me unrealistic targets. And whenever your fantasy world was threatened, you retreated. You've been looking for a way out of this marriage ever since then."

"I don't have to listen to this." She got up.

He jumped up. "You do have to listen! Don't shut out reality as usual!"

"This is what I mean. I do not like this kind of scene, and you should know that. That fact that you don't, shows how little we have in common any more."

"Oh, I know you don't like this kind of scene all right, but I don't care! You still think you are the golden girl. The girl destined for greatness. And you think you deserve it. The reason our marriage is over – is because you've got a better offer! Why do you think I work so hard? Push myself so much? Because of you. To give you what you want. To somehow get your approval. You always thought you were better than me. And I, for my part, have always gone way out to try and get your respect. For you to admire me – or just to think I was good enough for you . . . for you to love me back."

She picked up her cigarettes and went to the spare bedroom, gently closing the door behind her.

Peter stood, staring at the closed door. He couldn't believe what he had just said. All his thoughts and fears built up over the years had just come blurting out. He couldn't believe she was with Rory Ryan. He would wake up shortly and realise it was just one of those bad dreams he had been having recently. He poured himself a whiskey and knocked it back.

CHAPTER 64

Chloe found an empty office at Boom and ensconced herself there, studying all the model books for the agency.

Afterwards she confronted Hazel. "I'm not doubting for a second that you have the most established models in the business. But you haven't discovered anyone for a while. I recall booking some of these models when I started off in PR, and that's over ten years ago. They are all Audrey Driver vintage."

"They are tried and tested. They are the big earners here and keep Boom where it is," answered Hazel.

"But you are leaving yourself wide open to be overtaken." Chloe picked up a copy of that morning's *Mirror*. There was a huge photo of Vanessa and some accompanying story of some actor she was seeing.

"This is active promotion by Peter Reynolds. What he is doing is making these girls famous and they will quickly be overtaking our models."

"A model can't be invented through the media," said Hazel. "She has to learn the ropes and become slowly established."

"I beg to differ. At the end of the day a model is only a product, just like any other that needs the right PR. This girl I keep hearing about, Tiffany from the North. Have you seen her?"

"She came in to see me for an interview but went to Spinner instead. I did offer to represent her," said Hazel.

"And now she's going to be on next week's front cover of *Quest*. Why did she not come here? We have to see how Spinner are working, what they are offering. For a start this place is looking dowdy and needs a facelift. Let's get the painters and decorators in."

"I think you'll find that style never triumphs over substance. Spinner could never match the expertise we have here."

"We've invested a lot of money in Boom. I'm not prepared to take that risk. I'll be in my office at Macken, if you want me."

Hazel watched Chloe walk out, feeling very dissatisfied. She was used to giving the orders. Now she was up against the steely Chloe *et al*, at Macken. She was still Managing Director here and she was going to behave as one. She knew this business better than Audrey Driver, Peter Reynolds or Chloe Gallagher put together. She would not take orders from anyone.

Having spent ten minutes selecting a couple of shirts for Aran in Brown Thomas, Audrey gasped when she got to the till and realised the price. She bought them anyway, wanting to cheer Aran up. Peter was very quiet when she got into the office. Audrey felt she had overstepped the mark with Lynn the previous night and she had probably gone home and bitched all night about her, causing a further wedge between them, no doubt.

"I met Lynn last night at San Juan," she told him, testing the waters.

He looked up from his computer screen. "Who was she with?"

"That artist guy."

"Rory Ryan?"

"That's the fella, and some other people."

"What did she have to say for herself?" he asked.

"Nothing much. Just chit-chat, you know." She decided some damage limitation was in order. "She's really nice."

Peter's eyes flicked back to the computer screen. He had asked all calls that day to be diverted to Audrey, saying he was busy working on a new PR plan.

She was run off her feet. She wanted to ask Peter's advice on some of the enquiries, but decided against it, with him being in his present mood. She battled through and felt proud of herself by the end of the day. There hadn't been a whisper from his office, and thinking about what Lynn had said, she became worried. It was true she had only seen the energetic side of Peter, and this new side worried her deeply.

Peter sat in his office doing nothing. Waiting till he was sure the building was empty, he headed home. He had thought about phoning Lynn numerous times during the day, but couldn't bring himself to lift the receiver.

He was surprised to find Lynn at home waiting for him.

"I suppose we have to talk about things," she said.

"Guess so," he agreed.

"There are practicalities that need to be sorted out."

He wondered would it make any difference if he threw himself at her feet and begged her to come back to him. If he told her his life was empty without her.

"Practicalities?" He knew such behaviour would only make Lynn despise him. And as she had pointed out – she hated scenes.

"As I said last night, I haven't thought about divorce. I just need time to myself. I think we both need to assess our feelings for each other."

In other words, you want to keep all your options open for now, he thought. He wondered what she would say if he told her he did want a divorce. If he told her his life with her was over. He wanted to say it just to see her reaction, to hurt her as she had hurt him. But it would be a lie.

"If we could just for now sort out living arrangements etc."

"Fire ahead," he nodded.

"Since, as you hinted last night, you pay the lion's share of the mortgage –"

"I didn't mean it like that." Guilt swept over him. But why should I feel guilty, he asked himself. She's the one being unfaithful.

"Whatever. I can't obviously expect you to move out. What I suggest is that we both still have use of the apartment as a base for now. I won't be here much, if at all. I'll be back at my parents . . . or at Rory's."

You really are keeping all your options open, he thought. Still he couldn't object; she was telling him he had the run of the apartment for now.

"That sounds fine," he managed.

"Good. I've moved some of my stuff out. The rest is in the spare bedroom." She went into that room and emerged ten minutes later dressed in a cocktail dress.

"All right then," she said. "I'll see you whenever." Putting on her coat, she left.

He did feel empty sitting there, and a failure. He had failed at his marriage. He had tried so hard to make her happy and proud of him, but it had never been enough.

"Audrey, I've Maeve Kelly on the line, I'm putting her through to you," Vanessa said.

"Hi, Maeve, and how are you?" asked Audrey.

"Pretty pissed off, actually."

Audrey still wasn't comfortable hearing Maeve swear, in spite of her new daring image.

"I was supposed to have a meeting with Peter this morning with these make-up people who want to employ me and he stood us up. He left me there with these people, none of us knowing what to talk about. Now the bastard is avoiding my calls."

Audrey thought fast: what would Peter say in this situation?

"So sorry, Maeve. Peter's wife had a small accident and he had to look after her."

"Oh . . . it's still unprofessional of him. I'm shit scared because my new show is starting tonight."

"I know, I know, I really apologise. It was just one of those things."

"I hope I haven't lost that make-up contract because of Peter's incompetence."

"Of course not. They have already been on the phone saying how impressed they were with you," Audrey lied.

"Really?" Maeve's sour mood suddenly turned sweet and she gave a little laugh. Oh, vanity, thy name is Maeve, thought Audrey.

"Damn Peter!" shouted Audrey, once she hung up the phone. She dialled into reception. "Vanessa, have a huge bunch of flowers sent to TV3 for Maeve Kelly wishing her luck for tonight. Where the hell is Peter?"

"Don't know. I've loads of messages for him."

"Keep trying his mobile, please."

Audrey's mobile rang and she answered it.

"Audrey, Jackie here. I've just had a call from House of Opera. Ivanka was supposed to be over there for a shoot this morning. She didn't go. Peter assured me she'd be there on time when I booked it the other day. I've put my head out for you; I at least expect good timekeeping."

"Leave it with me a couple of minutes and I'll call you back."

Audrey quickly phoned Ivanka's mobile. "Where the hell are you?"

"Shopping, why?"

"Why the fuck aren't you over doing the House of Opera shoot?"

"I didn't know it was today."

"Didn't Peter tell you?" Audrey asked.

"No, he didn't."

"Quickly take down this address and get over there pronto."

After much grovelling to Jackie, Audrey managed to calm her down. Audrey was exhausted covering for Peter all day and was ready to go home for a long soak in the bath when Alison knocked on the door and marched in.

"Hi, I'm just letting you know I'm finishing here from today."

"Finishing? Why? You've been doing really well."

"I got talking to Chloe Gallagher and she convinced me I'd be better off at Boom."

"I see." Audrey was furious. "I think we've worked

really hard to establish you and I think it's a lousy trick to swan off to the opposition now. You've been getting loads of work with us. It was me who even convinced you to try modelling in the first place."

"At the end of the day, I guess it's a case of who I have more faith in. You just don't cut the mustard."

"I can't say I'm not annoyed, but there's nothing I can do to stop you."

"Not really. Could I have my portfolio, please?" Alison requested.

"Actually, no. We paid for those photos so they are our property. I'm sure with all Chloe's big plans for you, she won't mind investing in some new photos for you."

Audrey knew she was being petty but didn't care. Alison was joining the opposition and she wasn't going to help them. Business was business, as Peter would say.

On the way to San Juan that night, Audrey took a detour to TV3,

"No Peter?" asked Maeve, who was visibly shaking before the show was due to go out live.

"He can't leave his wife, but he sends his very best wishes to you and he'll be watching you at home."

"Oh, Audrey, this is so different from the usual stuff I do."

"You'll be great. Don't worry."

"Easy for you to say. I'm about to discuss my affair in front of the country. You try talking about your dirty linen in public."

"I did, remember?" Audrey reminded her.

Maeve reached out and squeezed Audrey's hand. "I'm sorry. And I wasn't very supportive when you were on my show that time."

Audrey noticed how Maeve had become dependent on

Peter since he had rescued her career and image. She noticed a lot of people became like that with him. Was she herself, she wondered.

The format for Maeve's show was a live talk show involving five different guests discussing a certain issue. The guests were a mix of famous and ordinary people. It was an interesting blend and the guests were informed beforehand that no question was off limit.

The cameras began to roll. "Welcome, tonight we are talking about an old story that seems to never go out of fashion: adultery," began Maeve looking into the camera. "I myself am guilty, if that's the right word, of having an affair. I'm going to start tonight by talking about my affair and then sharing my experience with my guests who have all been in similar situations . . ."

Audrey listened intently from the studio sidelines. The blatant honesty made it compulsive viewing, and Maeve managed the programme perfectly. Audrey breathed a huge sigh of relief.

Arriving an hour late to The San Juan, Audrey spotted Tiffany there.

"Out partying again?" she asked.

"Why not? *Quest* is coming out any day. I'm about to be famous." Tiffany was genuinely happy.

"You heard about Alison leaving?" Audrey asked.

"I told her she was mad. I told her after all you and Peter had done for her, she should stick with Spinner. But there was no talking to her."

"Well, her loss," said Audrey.

"Speaking of Peter, he's here."

"What?" Audrey was shocked.

"I never had him down as a clubber. And he's had a few drinks as well," Tiffany giggled.

"Where is he?" Audrey demanded.

"Up in the members' lounge."

Audrey rushed upstairs and sure enough found Peter with a group of friends, laughing and joking.

She marched over to him. "Where the hell have you been?"

"Audrey!" He laughed loudly. "Everybody, this is my business partner, the very beautiful Audrey Driver!"

Audrey smiled briefly at them. They were very similar to Peter, all suited.

"Audrey, these are all friends of mine."

"Can I speak to you for a minute, please?"

"Sure you can." He got up and followed Audrey over to a quiet corner.

"You'd better make it a quick one then," shouted one of his friends after them.

"I hear it's always quick with him," responded another.

Audrey ignored their comments. "Where were you? I was looking for you frantically. Appointments have been missed. Maeve's been having a nervous breakdown."

"I've been on the piss with my mates most of the day, if you must know."

"On the piss! Chloe has grabbed Alison from under our noses and looks like she's all out to try and destroy us and you've been on the piss!"

"Yeah. You know you were right when you said I was taking things too seriously." He looked over at his friends, anxious to rejoin them.

"There's a time and a place, Peter. There's too much at stake here."

"I'm sure you were able to handle anything that cropped up. Anyway you always said I don't trust you enough. So now I'm trusting you, what's to complain about?"

Audrey was horrified by his reaction, "It's true for Lynn, you do give up in the face of adversity."

"Lynn?" His mood changed from jovial to anger."So, you were having a little girls' chat about me, were you? Comparing notes about what a rotten bastard I am?" He marched back to his friends and was immediately laughing and having fun again.

The club was finished and Audrey was trying to clear out the customers. Peter's crowd looked like they were stationed there for the night as some of them were chatting up women.

Peter, very much the worse for wear, was talking to a young blonde.

"Come on, guys. Finish your drinks and go home please!" Audrey called over to them. If she didn't know Peter better, it looked like he was chatting up the girl.

I'm just going to rescue you from one big mistake, she thought, going over to them.

"Peter, isn't it time you went home to your wife?" she said, interrupting their conversation.

His bleary eyes looked up at her and she knew he was out of it.

"Who are you, his mother?" snapped the blonde.

"Yeah, a very well-preserved sixty-year-old. Now, goodbye!"

The blonde grabbed her jacket. "You aren't half as good-looking in real life," she huffed at Audrey before strutting off.

"Peter, c'mon, I'm putting you into a taxi home," said Audrey.

"I wouldn't let him go home to Lynn in that state," said his friend standing up. "She'll hit the roof. You know what she's like. I'd bring him home to my place, but I'm, er, taking a detour first." He smiled, slightly embarrassed, and nodded his head to the woman he had been chatting up.

Thinking about Lynn, she knew he was already in her bad books. She would flip if she saw him in that state.

"C'mon, Peter," she said and nudged him awake.

She would bring him home to her place. Aran would freak if he found out, but she had no option.

Driving home to her apartment, Peter was fast asleep in the passenger seat beside her.

"I suppose this is payback time," she said, knowing he wasn't listening. "You looked after me and I'm returning the favour. I've never seen you like this before. You're such a control freak, I never thought you'd allow yourself to lose it like this. You were probably wild when you were younger. What changed you – Lynn? And what were you doing chatting up that tart? You are happily married. You aren't the kind of guy who has affairs or one-night stands." Remembering their own indiscretion, she double-checked he was still sleeping. "I'm not counting what happened between us. That was nothing really. Just a kiss. A mistake, that didn't mean anything," she whispered as she pulled into the carpark.

Opening the passenger seat she tried to wake him to no avail.

"You are bloody heavy," she complained as she started dragging him from the car. He half woke up and with one of his arms around her she guided him into the building.

"Where am I?" he mumbled, as they climbed the staircase.

"My place. You were too drunk to go home."

"My head hurts."

"I'll give you something for it when we get in. I don't know why you're behaving like this. Avoiding work and going on a bender all day."

He pulled away from her. "Why shouldn't I?"

"Because you are far too responsible a person for that. You have a company and a wife -"

"What a great wife I have!"

"Yes, she is. She's intelligent and beautiful and –"

"What's she doing with me? Is that what you mean?"

"Of course not. You are ideally suited," Audrey said quickly.

"Tell her that."

Audrey put two and two together and realised something was amiss in the Reynolds' household.

"Is everything OK?" she ventured.

"No, it isn't. She's left me for that stupid bastard, Rory Ryan, if you must know. Our marriage is breaking down."

Audrey was stunned. "I'm so sorry." She meant what she said.

"No, you aren't. That's just words. It's just another bit of gossip to you." Peter suddenly lost his footing at the top of the stairs and staggered backwards.

"Peter!" she screamed as he toppled down the stairs. She ran down to him. "Don't move. Don't move!"

"I'm fine," he said angrily and sat up. She helped him to his feet. The caretaker came to his front door. "You again!" he snarled as he saw Audrey help Peter up the stairs.

"A whiskey. A strong whiskey," he demanded, once they were inside her apartment.

He gulped it down after she handed it to him.

"Another," he demanded. "Why do I always seem to fall when I'm at your place?"

She watched him knock back the whiskey. Then he grabbed the bottle. She pulled out the couch and made up a bed there for him and he immediately fell fast asleep.

The bottle of whiskey he was holding was in danger of spilling and she tried to rescue it.

As she did this, he put his arm around her in his sleep and she found herself trapped beside him, under his arm. She tried to get out without waking him, but couldn't. She lay still for a while and she drifted off to sleep herself.

The light flooding in through the windows the next morning awoke her.

It was almost six. He had moved in his sleep, releasing her, and she got up. She sat in the chair beside the couch and looked down at his sleeping frame. Pushing the hair back from his forehead she stroked his chin, before bending over and kissing him on the cheek. Then she made her way to her own bed.

CHAPTER 65

The aroma of food frying woke Peter. His head was thumping and his body aching. Sitting up and looking around, he saw Audrey cooking in the kitchen.

"Ah, you're up! How do you like your eggs?"

"What am I doing here?"

"I rescued you from The San Juan last night. You were too pissed to go home." She walked into the main room and set the dining-table. She poured two glasses of orange juice.

He vaguely recollected coming home with her.

"That was quite a binge you were on yesterday," she commented. "Your eggs?"

"Scrambled . . . but I don't think I can eat anything." He crawled off the bed. "My God, I'm bruised all over!" Wincing, he pulled on his shirt with difficulty.

"That would be from the fall. You fell down the stairs outside. I think you're OK, but no harm in getting yourself checked by a doctor."

After serving breakfast she sat down. "Come and eat. You don't want it going cold."

He staggered over and sat. "Thanks for looking after me."

"One good turn deserves another. I didn't want you going home to Lynn in the state you were in."

He looked up briefly. "Yeah . . . thanks."

She put her fork down and looked at him. "Peter . . . I know. You blurted it out when you were drunk."

"Oh." He studied the tablecloth.

"You should have told me. I would have understood. We are partners. And in spite of my image as being self-obsessed, I'm actually a good listener."

"There's nothing to tell. We're on a trial separation."

"I know how it feels to be left. Now, eat your food. We have a very busy day ahead of us and a fry is a great cure for a hangover."

"I'm not going into the office today," he said, pushing his uneaten plate away.

"You have to. You probably can't remember but I was telling you last night, Chloe has taken Alison over to Boom. Maeve Kelly is having a nervous breakdown without you. I've had to lie to everyone, saying Lynn had a small accident and you had to care for her – an unfortunate choice of cover-story as it turns out. But I don't intend to compound it by adding to the story today – especially if Lynn is out swanning around with Rory Ryan. Peter, there's so much going on, we can't afford to slip up now."

"You can handle things for a while. I have confidence in you. I'm having . . . personal problems and need to take some time off."

Audrey kept her voice calm and understanding. "You can't hide away. You have to drag yourself in, Peter. We all do. Day after day. Life goes on."

"For the first time for as long as I can remember I haven't got Lynn here. She's the reason why I pushed myself so much, why I worked so hard. She's left me and now I want to take some time for myself."

"Which means getting pissed every day?"

"If that's what I feel like doing, then yeah. It was you who said I took myself too seriously."

"Oh, Peter, but what happens if Spinner goes bust? You've lost your wife and your business. What will you do then?"

"Face that bridge when I come to it. Go and raise horses at home. Or go work in a bar on a Greek island. Explore the Amazon. I could do anything I wanted."

"Why don't you try doing something for yourself for a change? This company is yours. Yours and mine. Forget about Lynn and concentrate on yourself. If you had wanted to raise horses you'd have done that years ago when you had the option. You'd last two minutes on a Greek island without being bored daft. You love this business and that's why you are in it."

"How do I know I love it? I may loathe it."

"Bullshit. It's written across your face, in your eyes. Even when you are stressed stupid you still love the buzz. Admit it to yourself."

"No."

"Imagine yourself doing something else. Being an architect, or a solicitor or a bus driver . . . see, you can't. Imagine yourself on a Greek beach with no fax, mobile or clients to meet – you'd go mad. You love this business."

He pushed the bacon around his plate with a fork. "And if you love this business, then there's nothing to fear. Fuck Chloe Gallagher and all of them. What do you care if they are better or worse than you? Because you aren't in this business for them. You're in it because you want to be. You do it for yourself. Now eat your breakfast and go and have a shower. I've laid some clean towels out for you in the bathroom."

The phones were busily ringing as Audrey and Peter walked up the stairs to Reception. Vanessa and Mark were hard at work.

"Peter," hissed Vanessa covering the mouthpiece with her hand, "Maeve's on the phone demanding to speak to you."

He took the phone from Vanessa. "Maeve, so sorry about yesterday! Of course I saw you on TV. You were brilliant. Absolutely brilliant. My phone has been hopping all morning from people congratulating you – lots of offers coming in – who? Well . . .writing an advice column for a magazine, for instance . . . I thought you'd like that, all right . . . sure, lunch at one would be perfect. The Shelbourne is fine. My wife's accident? Oh, she's fine now, thanks for asking." He hung up "Why in God's name did you choose to say that? Couldn't you just have said I was unavailable?"

"I had to think of something to say." She blushed. "And you're in no position to judge white lies. Look at all the crap you make up about our models to get PR."

"I've an Ad. exec on the phone insisting on speaking to you," said Mark.

"Give me a minute and put them through to my phone."

"I'll leave you to it," Audrey said, collecting her mail and going into her office.

As she opened the envelopes, photos of different girls fell out. They were constantly receiving photos and details from aspiring models. She made a point of studying all photos. Sometimes a gem was hidden away amongst them.

She could hear Peter speaking rapidly on the phone and gathered her own thoughts. She was genuinely shocked that Lynn had left. They seemed happy and suited. For now, her main concern was that Peter didn't lose interest in himself or Spinner.

CHAPTER 66

Chloe looked through the interior-design books in her office at Boom while she spoke on the phone to a PR. An interior designer hovered nearby awaiting her decision.

"I've a fabulous new model on my book, Alison Flatley – that's right, Ronan Flatley's daughter, which means you are guaranteed column inches. If you want her for any work, call me and I'll see if I can slip her to you." She pointed to a colour in the book, a mauve, and covering the mouthpiece said to the interior designer, "I like this one for the carpet." Then returning to her phone conversation, she said, "Great. I'll book her for that. Thanks, bye." She hung up.

"And the colour for the walls?" asked the designer.

"Something rich. It's just got so drab-looking here. I want to wake the place up. I can't close down the offices while you redecorate, so you'll have to work at weekends. Is that a problem?"

"It would be an additional cost."

"Fax me through your quote, all inclusive, furniture and all."

In stark contrast to Spinner, Chloe had opted for a rich *fin de siècle* Parisian look for Boom.

Ben, who headed Commercial, knocked on the door after the interior designer had left. "Sorry, it's just I got that early copy of *Quest* you asked for."

"Give it to me." So far she liked Ben. He was polite and good at his job and also in awe of her.

"So this is the girl they're making all the fuss about," she said, studying the image of Tiffany adorning the front cover. "She's good, don't you think?"

"She's an unusually exciting new face," said Ben.

Chloe was about to say something sarcastic about his pretentious choice of words, but stopped herself.

"So why isn't she with us then, Ben?" she questioned. "Ring Jackie Davenport for me and set up a meeting."

Chloe had been shifting through all the paperwork and bookings at Boom and was alarmed to see that *Quest* hadn't used any of their models for at least six months. And she was fully aware of the support Jackie had shown to Spinner. Macken's accountants had been examining Boom's accounts, which appeared to be in more of a mess than the perfect accounts facade Hazel had presented to them during the takeover. Their accountants were finding creditors and debtors unpaid, tax bills ignored and some legal cases that were not settled.

Basically, Hazel was a contradiction to her own belief that substance was always triumphant over style.

From what Chloe could see, Hazel was an excellent model manager, but a hopeless business manager.

Ben buzzed her. "Jackie Davenport's secretary said she's in a meeting and won't be taking any calls."

"Keep trying her till you get through."

"I'm delighted Alison has joined you," said Ronan Flatley.

"I plan to put a lot of work into Alison. I believe she is

going to be one of Boom's leading future stars," said Chloe, seated in his constituency office.

"I appreciate favours greatly."

I'm glad to hear it, Chloe thought. The whole planning process for the shopping centre was stuck in a rut while local opposition grew stronger.

No politician had so far pushed the project along.

"I'm afraid your shopping centre isn't becoming any more popular," sighed Ronan.

"We are trying everything to appease opposition," Chloe said, slightly exasperated.

"I know, I know. I just can't see a quick fix solution to this. It would mean a politician putting his head out quite a bit." He began to chuckle. "And as a rule, we aren't known for doing that."

"I do appreciate all you've been doing."

"I still feel I could do more," Ronan said seriously.

"Really?"

"It is in the realm of my influence to push this through quickly. But I would be risking putting myself into the firing line," he confided.

"Anything you could do would be so much appreciated."

He paused for a long while, thinking. "I would need to protect myself if I put this project onto the fast track. It would have to be worth my while."

"Anything we could do to help you wouldn't be a problem."

"As I said, I appreciate favours. And I look after my friends."

Realisation began to dawn on Chloe." And would a donation from my client to your political fund help them become a better friend of yours?"

"I think it might just."

The choice was simple. A sizeable cash payment to Ronan Flatley would mean he would take care of the whole matter of the shopping centre in months. And Chloe knew that Flatley had the power to ensure the project got full go-ahead, regardless of the opposition.

As Chloe explained the offer to Reginald and Larry at their offices, she knew what she thought would be the safer and more efficient answer. If they paid Flatley off, it would release her from this difficult and time-consuming account, so she could spend more time building up Boom. Also she would no longer need to come to Murphy Hennessy for these meetings and risk bumping into Aran all the time. Or receiving constant sympathetic smiles from Reginald. "It's bribery and it's illegal," stated Larry unhappily.

"It's a quick solution to a difficult problem," said Chloe.

"I thought the whole idea of hiring a PR firm for this project was to change people's opinion about this shopping centre," Larry stated.

"No," corrected Chloe. "The reason you hired us was to make sure your shopping centre became a reality."

"I'd just be concerned this would ever get out," said Reginald.

"Outside ourselves the only other person who would know about it would be Flatley. And as one of the most respected politicians in this country he has more to lose than anyone."

"I don't like things like this," said Larry.

No, thought Chloe, you just prefer attacking women. "It's a lot of money he wants," said Reginald.

"But how much more will that land be worth with a shopping centre? I consider it a small price to pay. I'm not advising you one way or the other. But I have been informed of this offer and it's my job to pass on that Information."

"I know, Chloe," said Reginald, "but it's something that needs a lot of thought."

"I completely understand," Chloe agreed.

Chloe left the meeting and bumped straight into Aran.

"How are you?" He looked embarrassed. He, too, would probably be happy if she didn't have to come over here any more, she thought.

"I'm great. Just at a meeting with your dad."

"Everything going OK with the shopping centre?"

"I hope to have a breakthrough soon. I read in the paper you are back with Audrey."

"Yes." He contemplated tackling her about his suspicion that she was the one who broke the story to the newspaper, but thought better of it. "Yes, back together."

"I hope it works out for you. Anyway, I'd better run." She walked off.

He sensed no bitterness or bad feeling from her. Watching her stride down the circular staircase in her white trouser suit, he thought she seemed as confident as ever.

CHAPTER 67

Ben had eventually managed to set up a meeting with Jackie for Chloe.

Chloe shook Jackie's hand at *Quest*. They knew each other vaguely.

"What can I do for you?" said Jackie. No time for chit-chat.

"I just thought I'd give you a courtesy call now that we are the new management at Boom."

"I see."

"I'm just a little concerned as I've noticed we haven't done much business for a while. I wondered if there was any reason for that?"

"No," Jackie shrugged.

"I had heard there was some sort of rivalry between you and Hazel. I'd like to assure you, we are the new management at Boom now. So feel free to deal with us in the future."

Jackie decided she disliked Chloe nearly as much as Hazel. "I'll keep you in mind," she said, lifting her phone to indicate the conversation was over.

Chloe was enraged. She was not used to being dealt with like that.

"You do realise, we at Macken advise our clients who they should advertise with. A great deal of them place adverts with *Quest*."

"I consider *Quest* is able to stand on its own two feet without giving favours out. People advertise with us because they want to."

"I think you are giving too much support to Spinner. I consider that to be unfair and biased."

"I give work to Spinner because they give me what I'm looking for. I don't want the tired old formula at Boom."

"We are developing the business in a new direction. I've just signed a great new model called Alison Flatley –"

"Who you poached from Spinner," Jackie accused.

"I don't have time to sit here arguing with you. When I say I want models booked from Boom by your magazine, I mean it."

"Or maybe you'll buy us out and fire us? That's what you're known as, isn't it? The Takeover Queen?"

"If I have to, I will. For now," she stood up, "you'll probably find your advertising revenue considerably reduced. My way or no way."

Driving back to the office, Chloe had to admit the meeting with Jackie had gone badly.

Back at Boom, she found Hazel giving one of the models a dressing-down.

"I don't care what the client says to you, you are never, ever rude back. It reflects badly on you, on me and the other models. Now go and apologise," demanded Hazel and the girl left tearfully.

"That Jackie Davenport has a big attitude problem," Chloe complained.

"She's got worse with age," Hazel agreed.

"I hate how she gives all that support to Spinner."

"She always had a soft spot for Audrey. Even when I fired her she rang looking for her number. She gets a big kick thinking she is at the cutting edge."

"But she did confirm to me what I've been saying about Boom. We need a major update. In the meantime, I've come up with an idea. Instead of waiting until the clients pay us and then we pay the models, we pay the models as soon as their work is done, in advance."

"That means a lot of money going out. Sometimes it takes three months for clients to pay up."

"Macken will fund the payments. Watch those models come running over to us from Spinner."

Peter turned off his computer after a meeting with Audrey.

"I'd better go home," he said, looking at his watch.

"I'll go down with you. Aran's collecting me." She turned off the light and they walked down the stairs.

Before Peter opened the front door, he turned to her. "And thanks for everything, helping me through . . . well, you know."

"Any time."

Aran was parked outside.

Audrey opened the car door and sat in.

Peter bent down and nodded. "Hi, Aran."

Aran tried to give a civil smile, but it was obviously false.

"See you tomorrow," said Audrey and they sped off.

Peter set off walking home. Between his drinking binge and the hard work over the past couple of days he felt exhausted.

When he got home, the lights were off and the

apartment felt lonely and cold. He put a Marks & Spencer dinner in the microwave and sat down in front of the TV to eat.

"Welcome to the life of a singleton," he said to himself. He wondered what Lynn was doing, while he tried to come to terms with what had happened. It wasn't easy.

CHAPTER 68

There was a long queue of models waiting to be interviewed by Chloe and Hazel. Word had spread quickly that Boom would now be paying models in advance of client payment.

"I just have no option but to go over to Boom," Leslie told Peter and Audrey. "With the new mortgage and everything, things are tight. To be paid upfront, I just can't turn it down."

"But you've been getting loads of work from us," said Peter.

"I feel really bad." Her eyes were dewy.

There had been a steady stream of models telling them that morning that they were heading over to Boom. The temptation was too much for them to resist.

However, Leslie was one of their high-profile girls and her loss would hurt.

Seeing Leslie was getting upset, Audrey asked Peter to leave them alone.

She went over and put her arm around Leslie and hugged her.

"Don't cry. I totally understand. You're in this business

419

for the money, not the bullshit and so I don't blame you for going to Boom."

"I just feel like I'm letting you down."

"Nonsense. Look, you took a chance when we started up here and came to join us. I'll always thank you for that."

"It won't affect our friendship, will it?"

"Don't be silly! We've been friends for years," said Audrey, hiding how really upset she was.

Once Leslie had left, Audrey shouted, "Damn that bitch, Chloe Gallagher!"

"We knew she'd play nasty," said Peter.

"Handing them a carrot like that, of course it's hard for them to refuse. We've lost two of our best girls to her, Alison and Leslie."

"I've checked with the others. Vanessa, Tiffany and Ivanka are all safe with us."

"For now," sighed Audrey.

Peter raced down to his family home after work. It was his parents' wedding anniversary. His brother David and his long-term girlfriend were present. Peter explained Lynn's absence by saying she had a work commitment.

Nobody even raised an eyebrow when he said this, and he wondered if they had become immune to hearing it over the years. He studied his parents over dinner and knew they were still in love with each other. In spite of the ups and downs. Peter's mind drifted back to his upbringing and he remembered mostly very secure and happy memories. At the end of the day, his family had always been very supportive of him and encouraged him fully. He knew he was lucky to have had that. It could have been different, he realised, if his father had let drink take control of his life permanently. Peter had always been sociable and had lots of friends. He had imagined life would just work itself out perfectly for him. He never could have thought his own career would go so astray along the way. And he never could have imagined his wife would walk out on him.

After the dinner, Peter informed his family that he and Lynn were having a trial separation. He saw the worry written across their faces, and quickly reassured them that he was fine and they weren't to fret.

After the Club closed, Noel offered Audrey a lift home as he was visiting a friend near where she lived.

"Funny time to be visiting a friend," she teased knowingly, as he drove them through the deserted Dublin streets. They talked about PR plans for San Juan, mainly arguing about how they saw the image of the Club developing.

When he got to her place, they sat in the car for ten minutes trying to reach a compromise.

Aran had waited up for her. He happened to glance out the window and spotted Audrey in Noel's car. He observed from behind the curtain and felt himself become enraged as she seemed in no hurry to come in. Audrey opened her apartment door as quietly as possible so as not to wake Aran, but was surprised to find him sitting on the couch looking irritated.

"You seemed to have spent a long time sitting out in his car," he said.

"Were you spying on me? I was talking to Noel about work. I do have a life, you know." She felt her temper rise. She hated when he was like this – controlling. Seeing him sulk, she continued,"Do you just want me cooped up here all day at your disposal? Well, I'm sorry, Aran, but I'm not wasting my life like that. I know what it feels like to be down and I'm not going back there. You have no choice but to accept who I am and what I do . . . or leave." She went into her bedroom and sat at her mirror removing her make-up.

Aran sat thinking. He hadn't seen that fury in her eyes for a long time. He knew how far he could push it or risk losing her again. He crept into her room, came up behind her and hugged her.

"I'm sorry, baby," he whispered. "I just care about you so much. I can't help it if I want you with me all the time."

Despite her anger she was taken aback by this soft approach from him.

"You've just got to learn to trust me, Aran. I can't be at your beck and call all the time. I'm trying to build my own career."

"I know. Tell you what, I think it's about time we started going out in town again. Being seen as a couple."

"Really?" Audrey started smiling.

"Thanks to Chloe, everyone knows we are back together anyway, so why not show them?"

"What about your parents?"

"I'm a big boy now. Who cares?" She felt a pang of guilt and fear at the thought of him ever finding out Peter had just spent a night at her place again.

Tiffany's face blazed down from the cover of *Quest* throughout the country. The phones were hopping with bookings for her. At the same time, Ivanka's adverts for House of Opera were beginning to appear in the press and she was equally in demand.

Peter and Audrey worked closely together. Being so

busy on the phones, making bookings and running into each other's office to discuss an idea or make a decision, they quickly became very familiar and comfortable with each other. Of course there were the usual flare-ups that ended in brief screaming matches. But they didn't have time to ponder who was right or wrong. They had to quickly get on with it. And after an exhausting day they developed the habit of having a quick glass of wine in the office before heading off in their different directions. Peter realised that when Audrey quit her star act, she was very down-to-earth and had a great sense of humour. And Audrey got to know that other side of Peter, other than the bully-boy workaholic she had dismissed him as. In fact, when he let his guard down, she found him generous to a fault. He could suddenly play a joke or a prank that before she never would have thought possible of him. She was even more surprised, because she knew he was going through such a hard time without Lynn. This was something he never mentioned.

CHAPTER 69

Spinner's long-term business plan had always entailed launching Irish models abroad. And they now felt in a comfortable enough situation to start moving in that direction. They contacted all the major agencies in London and Paris: Models 1, Storm, Elite, Regency and of course Ford. Then they sent photos of their models to them and got a positive response. They decided to go over to London for a day and see the head bookers with the agencies.

They caught a plane from Dublin Airport at seven in the morning and got a taxi from Heathrow to the West End and were in time for their first appointment at 9.30 at Models 1, off the King's Road. When they saw the size of the offices they quickly realised just how small an outlet Spinner was. The booker was a Kate Moss look-alike who knew the business inside out.

"It's not just about being beautiful any more," she said, sharing her knowledge. "It's about being interesting-looking as well. I want something raw. Leave me your book and I'll see what I can do."

It would be a simple arrangement. The big London

agencies would book a girl through Spinner, the home agency, and they would get a commission as well. Audrey adored London. She could spend days wandering around the stores and begged Peter for just one hour in Harvey Nichols, which he refused.

As they hurried down Sloane Street, late for their next appointment, Audrey stood statue-like directly in front of Gucci's window, mesmerised by the outfits on display.

"If they try to bargain with us we have to hold firm," Peter continued talking as he rushed down the street unaware he had lost Audrey to Gucci.

When he turned around looking for his missing companion and saw her peering through the shop window he roared, *"Audrey!"* People stared as he ran back for her and pulled her away by the arm.

"Just ten minutes in there, please!" she begged.

"Forget it!" he said, secretly enjoying her frustration. She was like a kid trying to get into a sweet shop.

He noticed that Audrey was attracting many admiring glances, dressed in her sixties-style suit. She seemed oblivious to the stir she caused.

As they flew back to Dublin that evening, they felt satisfied they had achieved a lot and made many contacts.

"I could sleep for a week." She stretched her arms out.

"Me too," he stifled a yawn, "but we have to be back in the office at nine in the morning."

"Wouldn't it be nice to take the day off and go to the pub instead."

"I don't think either of us wants to see the other drunk again, do you?" he asked.

"Do you know what's funny? We've both seen the other drunk, but we've never been drunk together," Audrey said.

"It's probably just as well. Imagine the mayhem we'd cause."

"We would probably end up being arrested or something," she giggled. "Could you imagine Aran's face coming into a prison to rescue me!"

"Could you imagine Lynn's!" he laughed, but his face quickly clouded over.

Her heart went out to him. "It'll be OK."

"Everything is OK," he smiled brightly. "Spinner is a success. What more could I want?"

"A decent haircut," she joked.

He ran his fingers through his dark hair. "And what's wrong with my hair?"

"Nothing – that a good barber wouldn't sort out!" she laughed.

"Charming!" he said.

"Yes, I know I am."

He laughed with her and put his hand on hers where it lay on the armrest. There was a moment of awkwardness and he pulled his hand away quickly.

Chapter 70

Audrey had been invited to the opening of a restaurant.

"I don't know. I'm kinda tired," said Aran, when she rang him at work and asked would he go.

"I thought we weren't going to hide any more," she snapped.

"I'm genuinely tired," he complained.

"Well, I won't see you tonight then because I'm going anyway."

He thought for a second before saying, "OK, I'll collect you after work."

The restaurant was packed with guests. Waiters were circulating with trays of delicious food and glasses of wine.

"How I missed these events," he said sarcastically. He was screening the room looking for acquaintances of his parents to avoid.

"Well, I love them," stated Audrey, as she mingled with guests, many of whom hadn't seen her for a while and were congratulating her on Spinner's success.

"I'm surprised your ex-girlfriend isn't here," said Audrey.

Aran ignored her comment.

"Hi, mate, how are you?" A hand suddenly grasped Aran's shoulder. Turning around he saw it was his cousin, Galen.

Galen Murphy was from the poor-relation side of his family. Unlike all their other relatives, Galen's father, Reginald's brother, had not pursued a career in law but had become a scientist, a highly respected, but poorly paid scientist. Galen's mother wasn't of the usual pearl-and-tweed set like Aran's other aunts, but had a bohemian style. They had inherited a large house but no money, and lived in genteel poverty. They were popular with their relatives and included in all family events, but were still regarded as the poor relations. Because both Aran and Galen had been only children, they had spent a lot of time together growing up. Reginald and Muriel had always been very fond of Galen, and because of his parents' lack of funds, they had helped out financially in his upbringing – a fact that both Aran and Galen came to resent for different reasons. As the boys went through their teenage years, they realised they didn't like each other much and tried to stay out of each other's company.

Galen quickly fell back in line with his extended family's choice of career and studied law at Trinity. He was now regarded as a brilliant young solicitor, a fact that didn't make Aran warm to him any more. Nor did the fact that Galen was smart, intelligent and popular.

"Hi, Galen," Aran tried to appear friendly. He knew Galen was bound to carry stories back to his parents that he was with Audrey. Then their family grapevine would quickly carry the story to Reginald and Muriel.

"This is Jessica," Galen introduced the girl beside him.

She was the usual type Galen went for, Aran thought, a pretty socialite. "And this is my cousin, Aran."

"Pleased to meet you." Jessica shook Aran's hand. There followed an uncomfortable silence as both Galen and Jessica looked at Audrey, standing by Aran's side, and waited for an introduction. "Busy at work?" questioned Aran, who turned slightly away from Audrey.

"Er . . . yes," said Galen, aware that Audrey was beginning to blush. He felt embarrassed for her. "Very busy, you know how it is." Galen worked for a rival firm.

"Sure do," agreed Aran.

"Anyway, I'll talk to you later," said Galen. Both he and Jessica smiled at Audrey sympathetically and moved on.

"Want another drink?" Aran turned back to Audrey.

"What was that about?" blazed Audrey.

"What was what about?"

"Leaving me standing here like I didn't exist."

"I didn't think you'd want to meet my boring cousin."

"It was the height of bad manners. You all introduced each other and ignored me. How dare you?" thundered Audrey.

"You're overreacting."

"I'm not! You were embarrassed to introduce me in case your parents found out," she accused.

"That's not true."

"You are so obvious. Why the hell are we going out together if you don't want to be seen with me?"

He held her arm. "Darling –"

"Just fuck off!" she shouted, shaking off his arm and making an exit.

He raced after her. "Slow down and listen to me," he pleaded.

She kept walking and refused to say anything. When she got to the door he grabbed her and turned her around to him.

"Will you let me explain?" he pleaded.

"Smile!" said a woman's voice. They both turned to see the speaker was a press photographer holding a camera which she clicked as they gaped at her.

Chloe looked through some notes before leaving her office for a meeting in the boardroom.

Brendan looked a little sterner than usual and Vincent a little grumpier. She took her usual seat.

"I was speaking to Reginald Murphy this morning and it looks like they will go ahead with the pay-off to Flatley," Chloe began the meeting. "Larry Hennessy is uncomfortable with it, but Reginald is very enthusiastic."

"Chloe, there is a very important issue to discuss before anything else," said Brendan.

Chloe looked up from her file and raised a quizzical eyebrow.

Vincent and Brendan looked at each other momentarily before Brendan began.

"We've got the auditor's report back from Boom. We've just left a meeting with our accountants."

"Yes?" said Chloe.

"We have been told some very disturbing news. It looks like we paid way over the odds for Boom. Their business affairs have been in some disarray for some period and Hazel Harte seems to have a peculiar aversion to paying taxes."

"We rushed into Boom before checking it out first," said Vincent. She could detect a certain smugness lying just below the surface of his seriousness. "Something I did

430

caution strongly about at the time," he continued and his smugness was confirmed.

Chloe was speechless. In all her years in business she always had the upper hand, had always been in control. And now here were Brendan and Vincent, her two bosses, telling her she had screwed up big time.

"As if all this wasn't bad enough," continued Brendan, "our own audit has delivered us even more frightening news. We have run into financial difficulties ourselves."

"But how could that be possible?" Chloe was shocked and horrified.

"Quite simply, we have overreached ourselves. Mainly because of our aggressive takeover policy. Firstly we paid an enormous amount of money for Calder Media, then there was Blast and now Boom. All over a period of less than two years. In that same period of time we have lost key accounts. Calder and Blast are no more, and the majority of their clients have decided not to stay with us."

"I would like to say that this was a policy that was entirely thought up by and overseen by yourself," said Vincent pointedly to Chloe.

Chloe felt the walls closing in on her.

"Myself and Vincent built this company from nothing, and then you joined us as a director. We have enjoyed huge growth, but that has now turned. We must take whatever steps we can to ensure our survival," said Brendan.

"What can we do?" asked Chloe, finally managing to speak.

"It is your priority to turn Boom around and make it into a success. We can't afford to let this takeover be a disaster."

"Not after the money we paid for it," added Vincent.

"This, for now, is to be your chief responsibility," said Brendan.

"If you fail, then we'll have to make some serious cutbacks," said Vincent.

"No calls," snapped Chloe as she barged into her office and locked the door behind her. She leaned against the back of the door and closed her eyes.

She couldn't believe this was happening. How could Macken be in financial trouble? It was a huge company. They had some of the biggest clients in the country. OK, so they had spent on takeovers, but they had been strategically based business plans, approved by the three of them. But it had been she who had come up with the plans, and now they were looking for a scapegoat.

Vincent had always resented her. In reality she had more power in the company than he had. He had always been jealous of her talent. It was Brendan's reaction that had shocked her the most. He had been like a father figure to her, albeit a very stern Victorian-style one. It was because of him she had been allowed to mature and grow and become so powerful. He always backed her, no matter what. But now he had issued her with an ultimatum. She would not allow herself to be dragged down because of other people's inadequacies. If they were losing clients it was because the account managers were not doing their jobs properly. If Boom was a mess it was because of Hazel. She would do whatever it took to remain on top.

"You're fired." Chloe sat coolly on the other side of Hazel's desk.

"Fired?" screeched Hazel. "We have an agreement that I stay on as MD!"

"That was before we realised what a crap MD you are."

"I've been in this business for twenty years."

"Then you've obviously lost your touch. Why did you never pay those taxes?"

"It was the accountant's fault," explained Hazel.

"That's not what he's saying. Besides, I've noticed you've built up quite a ferocious reputation."

"You have to in this business," Hazel defended herself.

"People don't want to work with you. Jackie Davenport, for example."

"She's a bitch and you know it."

"All I know is Boom needs to start making big profits, without any baggage. This means restructuring the whole company, which I will oversee myself. You have till the end of the day to remove all your personal belongings from the building." Chloe stood up.

"What goes around comes around," Hazel spat.

"I'm taking these measures to make sure it doesn't come round to me."

CHAPTER 71

Muriel's Mercedes glided through the Howth hills. She never drove more than forty miles an hour. She was after leaving a very successful charity lunch she had helped organise.

The car drove through the big gates and came to a halt in the driveway.

She walked up the steps and retired to the drawing-room. Her daily brought some tea to her and she settled back to read the racing results in the paper. As she flicked through the paper trying to find the sports pages, she was greeted by a photograph of her son and Audrey in the social page. He had his arms around her and both of them looked startled.

The caption read: *Agency Boss Audrey Driver with boyfriend Aran Murphy at the opening of The Cedar Tree restaurant*. She stared at the photo in horror, feeling pure loathing for Audrey. She placed the paper down and dialled Reginald's number on her phone.

"Have you seen that photo in the paper? It's time to act, Reginald."

Lynn had no regrets since leaving Peter. She adored Rory's

home, which was an old Victorian three-storey-over-basement terraced house not far from the city centre. Her family had been furious with her for leaving her marriage. Her parents were very fond of Peter. Also, she had received some concerned calls from Peter's own parents trying to get them back together. However, she had been surprised that she had received no calls from Peter himself. She had expected him to be constantly on the phone to her, but so far he hadn't been. Whenever she needed to get something from the apartment she made sure to call at a time she knew Peter wouldn't be there. Life with Rory was the polar opposite to life with Peter. Rory was so relaxed and laid back. He wasn't concerned with money in the least, and spent lavishly on the good things in life. He didn't even bother with a mortgage on the house, but rented it. And he didn't need to strive for recognition through his work, because he already had it. He was the famous artist Rory Ryan. They shared many mutual friends, but since becoming his partner, she had become a part of his whole set. They were the intelligentsia, and she fitted in a treat. They were constantly entertaining. When they were having their regular big dinner parties, Rory would pay a catering company to come in and do all the work. She could sit back and talk with the guests about politics and art, and not even have to worry about the washing-up. This set had a relaxed attitude to everything, including drugs, and a couple of joints would be passed around after the dinner. Sometimes cocaine made the rounds as well. She avoided it, as she didn't particularly like the whole drug scene. Besides, she could still hear Peter's screaming disapproving voice. And when they went out at night they were treated like VIPs. Which, Lynn had to remind herself, they were.

Rory passed the joint to Lynn and she accepted it and placed it between her lips. All their guests from an earlier dinner party had gone, leaving the two of them alone, stretched out on a pile of cushions in the lounge, wearing only Japanese-style kimonos. Lynn had indulged in a line of Coke earlier, and it now mixed pleasantly with the pot. Her head was spinning as she started kissing Rory and they started tugging at the belts on their kimonos.

"You have a great body," Rory complimented as his hands ran over her thighs.

"I'm holding up well," she laughed. It was so nice to be with someone she hadn't just spent three hours arguing with. They were totally at ease with each other's body.

And all the sensations were mixing together and suddenly Lynn was seeing lots of colours as the pot started to have an effect.

"Renoir . . . Constable . . . Van Gogh," she said as she abandoned herself to the moment.

"What are you talking about?" Rory managed to ask.

"Hush! You're ruining it for me . . ." she gasped. "Picasso . . . Da Vinci . . . Rory Ryan!"

Chloe, exhausted when she got home, ran a very hot bath, peeled off her clothes and sank into the steaming water holding a glass of cool white wine.

She had gone through Boom like a tornado. Having examined the salary scales and personnel files she had gone on to fire half the staff. People that she deemed too well paid or not productive enough had been dismissed. And that would only be the beginning. She was in the tightest corner ever in her career, and she would do what it took to survive. Although she was not one for regrets, she wished she had never touched Boom. Everything had been going fine until then. Why had she gone after the bloody place? She knew she had allowed her emotions to get in the way of good business sense. Her emotions which she usually kept so well hidden and cool had somehow managed to bubble to the surface. And this was the result. Aran dumping her had made her feel vulnerable. She knew Aran had been in love with Audrey, so she had decided she would crush Spinner out of existence, and Boom was the tool that would do it. But there was more to it than that. Audrey had gone into business with Peter Reynolds.

She remembered the first time seeing Peter Reynolds at university. She was on her way to the library holding some books. He was sitting in the sunshine with a group of friends, all laughing and enjoying life. She was hiding behind her glasses and her frizzy hairstyle, and he never noticed her. But he caught her eye immediately. She suddenly found herself looking out for him, and began to observe him from afar. She observed what he wearing, who he was talking to and who he was dating. She was mesmerised by him. She would arrange to be standing in a queue in the canteen or at a shop when he was nearby, just wanting to be close to him. But he never even said hello. She wasn't surprised when Peter started dating Lynn. Lynn was beautiful, Chloe thought, and popular and they made a glamorous couple. It was approaching exam time and she had been studying very late in the library. It was nearly eleven as she walked home across campus to catch her bus. There was a dance on in the Students' Union, and she spotted Peter and Lynn emerge from there. They both seemed very drunk and were arguing. She hid behind a tree and watched.

"Look, I swear I wasn't flirting with her," he was defending himself. "It's your imagination."

"I saw you!" Lynn shouted back.

"Grow up."

"You can go back to her, because we are through," Lynn spat and stormed off. He called after her but she ignored him. And then he was alone. He seemed very drunk and was staggering across the green. He suddenly fell over.

Gasping, Chloe ran over to him, "Are you OK?"

Looking up at her bleary-eyed he said "Just one too many."

"I'll help you up." She helped pull him onto his feet. "I'll bring you back to your friends."

"No, I don't wanna go back in there," he objected and sauntered over to a bench and sat down. She followed nervously and hovered beside him.

He took a small bottle of vodka from his jacket pocket and slugged some back.

Then he offered it to Chloe, but she shook her head.

"Who are you anyway?" he questioned.

"My name is Chloe Gallagher. I'm in some of your lectures."

"Go on and drink." He pushed the bottle to her again. She nervously took it and raised it to her lips, allowing her mouth to touch where his just had and take a sip.

"Sit down," he ordered and she gingerly sat beside him. She felt great. This was what going to university was supposed to be about. Here she was sharing a drink out on the green with the guy of her dreams.

"I'm sorry. I've had a bad night. I'm going out with this girl called Lynn and we had a big bust-up."

"Yes, I saw you arguing."

He looked up from the bottle. "Did ya?"

"She's very pretty."

"And doesn't she know it. She thinks she's better than everyone else. Better than me."

"You must like her though."

"That's none of your business."

"I'm sorry," she apologised.

"No, I didn't mean to snap. I'm sorry. I've had enough of her though. I don't want to see her again, ever."

"Ever is a long time."

"Well, I mean it. What did you say your name was again?"

"Chloe Gallagher."

He looked into her face intensely and removed her glasses. Then he reached forward and kissed her. She was terrified and delighted all at the same time.

Maybe he meant it. Maybe he didn't want to see Lynn again and she could become his new girlfriend and it would be just like she dreamed about.

"What subjects do you do?"

"The same as you."

"How come I never saw you before?" he asked.

"Because you sit at the top of the lecture halls and I sit at the bottom."

"You seem like a very nice girl." He reached over and they kissed again.

There were roars of laughter and shouting as a group of people came out of the Students' Union.

"Peter!" they roared.

"Yeah, over here," he shouted. They came across the green to them.

"We're going on to a club in Leeson Street. Come on,"

said one his friends who grabbed his arm and pulled him up. The happy group staggered off across the green, leaving Chloe sitting on the bench.

Peter turned around and shouted, "See you . . . whoever you are."

The next day she felt confused, happy and scared all at the same time.

After lectures in the morning she went to the bathroom and combed her hair.

Seeing Peter at a Coke machine she nervously went up behind him and waited for him to put the money in and get his can.

As he turned around to go she said, "Hi," and smiled.

He looked at her blankly and said, "Hello," and walked off.

Looking after him, she felt mortified. He was ignoring her, but then she realised he wasn't. He just couldn't remember her. He hadn't a clue who she was.

An hour later she saw him with Lynn, walking hand in hand and kissing.

She raced home, the tears stinging her eyes. She cried the whole night long.

Why could he not remember her? She was a nobody to him. Finally she fell asleep in exhaustion.

The humiliation stayed with her for a long time. But she had learned a valuable lesson. She had followed Peter's career throughout the years, with the satisfaction she had achieved much more than him. When the opportunity arose to acquire Blast, she had been unable to resist. Even though he never did remember her from college, she had the immense satisfaction that he would never forget who she was now.

The hot water soothed Chloe's muscles and she felt better. She had not put a foot wrong since those days. She had become the golden girl. She was a different person from whom she was then and she knew she could take care of Peter, Audrey and Aran. It would be no bother at all.

CHAPTER 72

Aran had been having a bad week, what with Audrey going mad over his not introducing her to Galen. She had screamed and screamed about it back at her apartment and threatened to finish their relationship there and then. There was no point in arguing with her, so he just continued to apologise, finally managing to calm her down. He was poring over some documents in his office and couldn't get to grips with them. Deciding he needed a coffee, he got up and set off down the corridor. Suddenly he came face to face with Galen, carrying a folder.

"Hello, mate. How are you?" asked Galen.

Aran was surprised to see him. Judging by the folder he was carrying, it wasn't a social call to Reginald either. Perhaps Galen was asking for some advice over a case.

"I'm fine," said Aran. "What has you here?"

Galen shifted awkwardly before speaking, and adopted the embarrassed smug look Aran had grown to hate in him.

"I've started working here today," said Galen.

Aran stormed up the stairs and into his father's office, slamming the door behind him.

"What the hell is going on?" he shouted.

Reginald casually looked up from his work and removed his glasses, before questioning, "Anything the matter?"

Aran marched up to Reginald's desk and slammed his fists on it. "Why is Galen working here?"

"He is working here because he is a brilliant solicitor."

"Why wasn't I consulted about this?" Aran demanded.

"You probably missed the meeting. You had probably left early that day."

"I don't want him here."

"That is your problem. He is just what this firm needs, talented, ambitious and dedicated."

"You are undermining me by having him here."

"You've undermined yourself. You show no interest in this firm. You swan around as if it's your birthright."

"It is my birthright!" Aran pointed out.

"My main concern is for this company to be in safe and capable hands in the future. Larry has no heirs, so I need to ensure Murphy Hennessy has somebody capable at the helm. You are not inspiring me to believe you are that person, Aran. You are not hungry enough. Galen, on the contrary, is very hungry. I think he would make an excellent partner in this firm."

"I know why you are doing this," Aran pointed a finger at his father. "This is because of Audrey. You don't want me seeing her and this is your warning, isn't it?"

Reginald sat expressionless, but he didn't deny it.

"You can't do this," shouted Aran. "I won't let you do this." He stormed out of the office roaring, "You can't dictate who I see."

"They would do this to me!" said Aran, lying on the couch at Audrey's.

Audrey sat beside him, full of concern at his white face.

"Maybe they have no plans to make Galen a partner," soothed Audrey.

"Bullshit. I know my parents. This is because I'm seeing you."

She also had to admit, she also knew them, and knew them to be very capable of such a stunt – regardless of the pain it would cause their son. She felt so sorry for Aran, and guilty for having given him such a hard time. She knew what he was up against.

"They've always loved Galen," continued Aran. "It was always Galen this and Galen that. They always wanted me to be more like him."

"I'm sure they don't. They love you for who you are," she said, wondering why she was defending the Murphys.

"And of course that penniless fucker has always wanted what I have. And now they are handing it to him on a plate."

Audrey didn't know what to say or to advise. The best advice she could give him to secure his future would be to dump her. She didn't want that obviously. And besides, she was beginning to realise just how much he loved her to put up with all this.

Audrey was on the phone trying to organise a flight for Tiffany to London. A booking had come through Models 1. Tiffany sat on Audrey's desk, her legs swinging.

"OK, that's fine. I'll book that one," she told the telesales agent and gave her the company credit-card details. Since being on the front of *Quest*, Tiffany had worked solidly.

"All sorted," said Audrey, putting down the phone. "Your ticket will be at the airport at customer services. I've written down the address of the photo studios here so just grab a taxi there from Heathrow."

"Thanks, Audrey, you're the greatest," said Tiffany and she meant it. She was delighted with the way she had been represented at Spinner.

"Tiffany, I want to have a word with you about something." Audrey crossed her legs.

"Fire ahead."

"Are you still dieting?" It was a topic Audrey had wanted to broach for a while.

"No, not at all."

"It's just you've lost far more weight than Jackie recommended."

"Honestly, I haven't been dieting. I never stop eating!"

"Then you need to take more care of yourself." Audrey chose her words very carefully so as not to undermine the girl's confidence. "You've gone a bit too thin."

"No, I haven't."

"You seem to be out with Mark and the others every night. You need to slow down a little and sleep. You need rest and to eat good food. Promise me you'll start looking after yourself a bit more."

Tiffany laughed. "There's nothing wrong with me. But, OK, I promise."

She jumped off the desk and waltzed out. Looking after her, Audrey felt very uncomfortable about her weight. She was beginning to look unhealthy.

Peter came in. "Another booking for Ivanka just came through from London. That trip we did certainly paid off."

"Cool," said Audrey.

"I was thinking. We should do a similar trip to New York."

"New York? Don't you think we should learn to walk before running?"

"Why wait? We should strike while the iron is hot."

"How long are you talking about?"

"Just four or five days," he said.

"Can we afford to go?"

"Can't see why not. It's an investment in Spinner's future."

Audrey thought about Aran's reaction if she announced she was heading off to the States, especially with all the present hassle with his family.

"Sorry, Peter, I can't go."

"Why not?"

"I can't leave Aran and just take off to New York."

"I'm sure he could survive without you for four or five days." Peter raised a cynical eyebrow.

Audrey became hassled and slightly annoyed. "How would it look, the two of us going away together?"

"Er, Audrey, we are business partners. It would look perfectly normal."

"Well, it wouldn't to Aran. I'm sorry, Peter, but I can't go."

"So you're stopping our company from the opportunity of expanding because of what your boyfriend might say."

"I have commitments, Peter, that I can't just walk out on. If you were still with Lynn, I'm sure you wouldn't be able to just run off whenever you wanted either."

"Myself and Lynn always respected each other's work commitments."

"Perhaps if you hadn't, you might still have a marriage." She regretted saying it as soon as it was said.

The hurt caused was clearly evident. "Thanks," he said and walked out.

He could tell Lynn had been to the apartment that day. The clothes in her wardrobe had been moved around. She had probably dashed up during her lunch-hour, anxious not to bump into him. Settling down on the sofa, he devoured a Chinese takeaway. Plenty of invitations from friends had been flooding in, but he wasn't in the mood. He was aware he was throwing himself into work and had no reason to be angry with Audrey just because she had a life outside work. Thinking about her comment that day, he knew he should have spent more time with Lynn. But the whole irony of the situation was he had lost her trying to do everything to keep her. He was surprised that there had been no reason for interaction between them since Lynn walked out. Nothing was urgent enough to have caused them to speak. Some nights he sat thinking up excuses why he should phone her. But his pride wouldn't allow him to pick up the receiver. And besides he was hurt. Very hurt. He had thought they were unbreakable, but she had simply walked away because she had got a better offer. He tried not to think of her with Rory. One other reason why he avoided going out was the fear of bumping into them. He was sure they were painting the town red each night. He began to skim through the Sunday paper supplements he hadn't time to look at yet. He was suddenly confronted with a photograph of Rory and Lynn sitting on a very plush and ornate couch, his arm around her. Above the photo was the headline: *Artist Rory Ryan Supreme*. He quickly devoured the accompanying article which concentrated on Rory's style of painting. The article also spoke of Rory's "partner", gallery manager Lynn Reynolds. It was strange seeing his surname in print attached to another life. There was no mention that Lynn was separated; they were just presented as a hip trendy couple.

"Well," he said aloud, "you got what you always wanted: recognition, respect and a successful partner."

"We got so much work from that trip to London," said

Audrey. She was stroking Aran's hair, as they lay out on the bed.

"That's good," Aran said, half uninterested.

"Peter thinks our models have what it takes to make it internationally."

"Good for you."

"Of course, it's all about getting them seen by the right people."

"Like everything I suppose. Have you noticed Galen never has a permanent girlfriend?"

"Doesn't he?"

"No . . . just out with different rich girls. Probably shopping around for a bank balance that's big enough. Opportunistic bastard."

"Well, give me a couple of years and Spinner will be so successful, everyone will be saying that you bagged a rich girl," Audrey joked.

"Yeah." Aran still did not take Audrey's business career any way seriously. "I wished he had just pissed off and become a scientist like his father."

"Since nearly all his relatives are in law, I suppose it was in his blood too . . . Peter mentioned, because our trip to London was so successful . . . we should head to New York for a couple of days."

"Yeah . . . I suppose." Aran's head was full of Galen.

"You wouldn't mind, then?"

"Mind what?"

"If I went to New York for a couple of days?" Audrey spoke slowly.

"No . . . why should I care?"

CHAPTER 73

Shockwaves ran through the Irish fashion and media industry with the sacking of Hazel and half her staff at Boom. Chloe Gallagher had always been known as hard, but her bloody wipe-out at Boom was considered ruthless. However, when people got beyond their sentimentality, many admitted some kind of a change was needed there. Now, fully aware of Chloe's abilities, they sat back to watch the transformation of Boom.

"Sure," Chloe said down the phone, in Hazel's old office where she had installed herself. "I've got just the girl for you. A new model, Alison Flatley . . . yes, daughter of Ronan, so she'll guarantee you press coverage. I'll send her over to you for an interview . . . Yes, you probably could get someone cheaper at Spinner, but you get what you pay for. Give me a call after you've met Alison." She hung up the office phone and reached over to answer her ringing mobile.

It was a gossip columnist from one of the papers, fishing for information about a model.

"I'll tell you what," Chloe informed her. "I'll dish the dirt if you give me a huge photo and plug for her in your column this Sunday. Deal? Good. Yes, she has been seeing him. They met at an after-party at one of his concerts . . . I don't know, who can say . . . all I know is they are seeing each other and are pretty keen. I'll look forward to the plug this Sunday." She switched off her mobile.

Ben knocked on the door and came in. She had made sure to keep Ben on. Not only was he a good booker, but because he was easily controllable and she enjoyed the respect mixed with fear he showed her.

"Chloe, Sandra O'Brien is here to see you." Sandra O'Brien was a thirty-five-year-old model, who had been the biggest thing around in the late eighties. She was still highly thought of and had grown into a respected celebrity. She was now a regular on the party circuit.

"What does she want to see me about?"

"You know Sandra, just a chat probably. Talk about her career."

"What career? I don't have time to talk to Sandra O'Brien or any other has-been. I've seen how much she's earned the company over the past year and she isn't worth the effort. Say I'm in a meeting."

Ben went bright red. It was true what Chloe was saying, but she put it so bluntly. And Sandra was used to being treated with the utmost respect.

"Sure." Ben turned to go.

"And Ben, there isn't much point in keeping her on the fashion books any more. She's only taking up space. Gently ease her into – our catalogue section. I see you still have her down as available to do bridal wear, when it's plainly obvious she's at the stage where she should be Mother-of-the-Bride."

He nodded and closed the door after him.

She would turn that company around if it was the last

thing she would do. She wished she could find out what was happening over at Spinner. It would give her such an advantage. If only she could get her friends at the security company to wire up their phones so she could listen into their calls whenever she liked. But that was much too risky to contemplate in a company not owned by Macken.

Luckily, the industry was alive with gossips and big mouths and so she was somewhat aware of their comings and goings. She knew, for example, they had made contact with London agencies and were getting work via them. That would be a route she would need to investigate herself once things had settled down.

Her phone rang and she picked it up.

"Did you hear?" She recognised the voice as one of her contacts.

"Hear what?"

"Peter Reynolds and his wife have split up."

"I don't believe it." Chloe sat back in her chair.

"Believe it. She's taken up with Rory Ryan, no less. There was a big interview with them in *The Sunday Times*."

Maeve Kelly sat nervously at the end of the photo studio.

She had been signed to be face of a new make-up company. She had been styled and looked brilliant, Peter thought.

"This is madness. I'm not a model." She was very tense.

"Nobody is saying you are a model. You are being yourself, and they want you, as yourself, to represent their product," Peter encouraged. The photos they would take that afternoon would feature in a national campaign. Both Peter and the client felt confident Maeve would appeal to the target audience.

"I'm too old to be in an advertising campaign. This whole idea is ridiculous. I should never have listened to you." She was becoming agitated.

"You look great. Just have confidence in yourself."

"Don't bullshit me." She fed hungrily on a cigarette and, standing up abruptly, announced, "I'm going home. You can cancel the whole project. Send them over a selection of your twenty-year-olds tomorrow to choose someone new from."

"They don't want a twenty-year-old. You are the image they want."

"See you later." She walked off.

Peter panicked. The whole studio was set up and the photographer ready to begin. He must do something to stall her – anything.

He raced after her, grabbed her and kissed her full frontal on the mouth.

Maeve was taken aback. "Peter!" She ran a hand through her hair.

"Would I do that if you didn't look ravishing?" he asked.

"You'd do anything to get this make-up contract," she accused and then she smiled. "It was nice though."

"Now will you do the damned shoot?"

Peter stayed with her for the afternoon. Her initial reluctance was quickly overcome once she got started. Soon she was enjoying every minute. Peter looked on relieved.

"I don't have forever," Vanessa snapped at Audrey.

"But you've been working solidly since joining us. Why are you so upset?" Audrey was perplexed.

Vanessa flicked out her platinum blonde hair. "Tiffany

has gone over to London and no work has filtered through from there for me. You haven't bothered to promote me with the agencies over there at all."

"We did. But no bookings have come through yet."

"So what are you going to do today to promote me?" demanded Vanessa.

"There's a casting over at Heineken at three. Go over to it," Audrey said. She had seen the briefing sent over from their PR and she knew Vanessa wasn't what they were looking for. Ever since Vanessa had landed a small part in a soap opera she had become very big-headed and demanding. Audrey had seen it lots of times before, and had been guilty of it herself. When a degree of success came along it was natural for them to get carried away.

"I didn't join this agency to be stuck out there on reception sending faxes and answering phones all my life," Vanessa objected.

"But you were glad of that job."

"I am because I need an income. But I should be getting enough from TV work and modelling so that I don't need it."

Audrey bit her tongue and didn't say that if Vanessa managed to turn up on time for the past two castings she might have stood a better chance of getting the jobs. But she didn't want to fall out with Vanessa – she had been a great asset in the office since they started.

"What's wrong with Vanessa?" Peter asked coming into the office. "I just passed her in the corridor and she looked in fierce bad form."

"She thinks she's going to be the next Madonna and thinks we aren't doing enough to help her."

"Oh, I see."

"Her attitude is becoming a bit much. Anyway, about

what you were saying yesterday about going to New York. If we can set up some appointments, I'm game for going."

"What changed your mind?" Peter was surprised.

"Aran was fine with it."

"Great, I'll start making the calls then."

Peter's gift for the gab meant it didn't take him long to get past Ford's switchboard in their Manhattan office and find the right person to speak to. He did the same with all the other big agencies like Elite and Regency. Jackie was also helpful in giving contact names. Because the modelling industry relies on the new and the undiscovered, agencies are always open to enquiries. The agencies want to be inundated with photos from hopefuls. They want to be linked with smaller agents that could feed them the next supermodel. They know exactly what they are looking for. They can quickly cut through thousands of hopefuls who annually try to be a model and reach out for the star among them. Out of sixty thousand hopefuls that apply to Ford each year, only thirty girls are signed on to their books annually.

"You never said anything about going to New York," said Aran.

"I did! I told you we were thinking of heading over to tout for business. You said it was a good move."

"I was only half listening – I thought you meant send some photos over or something. Not actually physically head over."

"Well, it's all organised now. Peter's set up meetings and the tickets are bought."

"Oh, I should have known you'd be going over with Petey-boy."

"He's my business partner – who the hell else would I be going with?"

"He'd like to be a lot more than just business."

"Don't judge everyone by your own standards."

"Defending him again. Here I am going through all this shit with my family over you, I might add, and you are just fucking off to America."

She calmed her voice."I know the hard time you are going through. I know it's because of me. But I still need to make a success of my business. It will only be for four days."

"When are you going to wake up and smell the coffee? This business of yours is just a joke."

"Thank you for that, Aran."

"It's a small hobby for you. Can't you see the bigger picture. Me in charge of Murphy Hennessy and you by my side. That's what's important."

She knew she should be delighted by his suggestion. He was hinting at marriage. But it also unnerved her. This control he wanted over her, without any life of her own, scared her.

"There's nothing I can do. The airline tickets, the hotel rooms, they are all paid for."

"But I'm asking you not to go."

"And I'm saying I can't," insisted Audrey.

"I thought you had changed. I thought you might put me first for a change."

Tears sprang to her eyes. "And you still won't allow me to have any kind of a life or independence. What the hell is the big deal? Four days away which will be full of meetings. Can't you just let me go for such a short space of time."

CHAPTER 74

Chloe watched Leslie stride into her office and take a seat.

"I just wanted to have a word with you about the assignment I was on yesterday," said Leslie.

"Fire ahead." Leslie had shot a TV commercial for a soft drink.

"I just think the way they shot it wasn't good."

"How so?"

"They had me bouncing along a beach in pigtails and shorts. I just don't think that kind of work is for me."

"Leslie, you are a good model. Of course I'm glad you joined us from Spinner, but let's face it, you are no advertising mastermind. They pay advertising people lots of money to devise the right image for their brands. If they want you in pigtails, and are willing to pay the price, then who cares? Now why don't you stick to what you know best."

Leslie bit her lip and looked at the floor. She was used to popping into Audrey's office and having a word with her about anything. There was to be no such relationship with Chloe, she realised.

Lynn sat beside Rory listening to the vivacious piano

playing. A film producer who was a friend of Rory's had organised a private concert by the upcoming pianist in his Dalkey Villa. Lynn allowed the excellent playing to tantalise her. Studying the pedigree of the fellow guests, she was thrilled to be there. Rory was listening attentively, but had a glazed faraway look in his eyes. He had had a joint before leaving the house and was slightly stoned. And she was irritated. He had promised to complete a painting two weeks ago for a customer in London, and he hadn't been even near a canvas. She had gently encouraged him, but he had objected by saying he wasn't in the right mood. As the music stopped, the small audience burst into applause. As the pianist began his next rendition, she spotted one of Rory's paintings hanging on the wall, and on seeing this settled back smugly into her chair.

Aran's silence and stony expression as he drove Audrey to the airport indicated how annoyed he still was about the New York trip.

She tried to make small talk but came up against a brick wall. Finally, exasperated she said, "I'll tell Peter to go on his own. If it upsets you this much, I won't bother going."

"And so then you can make my life hell accusing me of being possessive and not trusting you. No, you're going," he said stubbornly, pulling up outside the terminal. They got out and he put her case on a trolley for her.

"Aren't you coming in?" she asked

"I'd rather not see your business partner, thanks all the same," he sniped,

"I'll ring you when I get there," she said, and leaning forward she kissed him.

"You know something, Audrey. If we are to have any kind of a future together, then you are going to have to start making choices." He sat into the car, put on his sunglasses and sped off without even a wave.

Sighing, she took out her mobile and called Peter. "Where are you?"

"By the Aer Lingus desk."

She found him talking on the phone to Vanessa and Mark.

"And don't forget to arrange that casting for Coca-Cola. And rearrange that interview with the PR guy I was supposed to meet tomorrow. And don't forget to send off the cheque for the phone bill. I'll call you when I land in New York." He turned off his phone.

"You do not realise the hassle this trip has caused me," Audrey sighed.

"It's only four days!"

"You don't know Aran. C'mon, let's check in."

"Audrey!" She suddenly heard a voice shout her name across the airport. She turned to see it was Leslie running towards them.

"What are you doing here?" Audrey was confused.

"I spoke to Vanessa and she told me you were heading to New York. It's just, I want to rejoin Spinner."

Peter was annoyed. "Leslie, even for this fickle business, you are being very fickle. Are you just shooting back to us because you think we're going to make lots of contacts in the States?"

"No. It's just . . . I can't stand Chloe Gallagher . . . and I missed you guys!"

Audrey looked at Peter and they both nodded.

"Welcome back!" Audrey opened up her arms and hugged her friend.

"And give me your model book quickly so we can bring it with us," said Peter.

"You see, I told you our approach with models and celebrities would work," said Audrey. They were high over the Atlantic after enjoying their meal and were now having a drink.

"Yeah, you're right," agreed Peter.

Audrey looked at him aghast. "You're agreeing with me?"

"Yes, I am. My earlier approach was wrong. You have to respect their feelings. And as you said many of them are insecure."

"Of course, none of this new sensitivity you are demonstrating has anything to do with the fact Superbitch is ensconced at Boom, and you now think the softly-softly approach would give us an edge over her?"

"Of course not," he smiled.

Peter told Audrey the story of how running up and kissing Maeve broke the ice and made her stay for the make-up photo shoot.

"I can't believe you did that!" Audrey was incredulous.

"I didn't even think about it. I had two seconds to keep her in the building or lose the whole contract," he laughed.

"But the poor woman fancies you. You doing that has probably fed her fantasies."

"She does not!" Peter was horrified.

"It's so plain to see. She adores you." Audrey was studying his reaction. He was being utterly dismissive. Some men would have loved having their ego fed, she pondered. But Peter was just embarrassed.

Arriving into Kennedy Airport and stepping off the plane

was like stepping into another dimension. The very bright sun was shining through the airport's massive windows as the airport staff directed them through Customs and into baggage collection. Then they ventured into the terminal building. As the door opened into the main area they were hit by the huge noise of people rushing around and talking loudly. They cut a handsome pair as they cut through the crowds, absorbing the atmosphere. Outside, the cabs came fast and furiously and they were directed to one by a porter.

And seated in the back of the yellow cab, they were transported through Queens to Manhattan. Audrey had been to the city once before for a brief holiday. Peter had been there on working trips a few times, which now gave him a useful knowledge of the city's layout.

The hotel was off 7th Avenue in Upper Manhattan. Feeling exhausted, they said goodnight and went straight to their rooms. Peter found his room was large and elegant. Switching on the television, he flicked through the channels before falling asleep.

The next morning, Peter opened his window and inhaled the smells and sounds. He was overwhelmed with the excitement of being in the heart of New York City. He was getting ready while watching Breakfast Television when his phone rang.

"Did you sleep well?"

"Great. Nearly ready now. I'll see you in the lobby in fifteen minutes."

As only a continental breakfast was being served in the hotel, they decided to skip it. Instead they stepped out onto the streets. Their senses were assaulted by the strong aromas circulating from delis and subways. They found a little diner and had a full breakfast. They knew it would be a long and tiring day and so ordered the full works, bacon, sausages, eggs, and pancakes dripping in syrup. Their itinerary was due to start at 12.30. This gave them a couple of hours to wander around first.

"I'm getting that temptation to go shopping again," warned Audrey as they wandered along Fifth Avenue. Sauntering along they took in the window displays of Tiffanys, Saks and Bergdorf Goodman. They ventured as far as Bloomingdales before returning to the hotel to collect their briefcases and model books and grabbing a taxi to the Ford Agency.

The Ford Agency was established in the 1940s by husband-and-wife team Jerry and Eileen Ford. It led the way in creating the modern agency business and its code of practice. The Fords were the experts at discovering and promoting a stable of models from Twiggy to Lauren Hutton, Jerry Hall to Linda Evangelista. It was the Fords who began to negotiate the big contracts for the models in the seventies which led to the phenomenon of the supermodel. Ford remains the most respected name in modelling. In the late nineties Jerry and Eileen took a back seat and let their daughter Katie take over the reins. Katie made some important changes to the company. Most notably she moved the head office from upper Manhattan to the more trendy Soho district. She also oversaw the company's expansion into Celebrity Management. Audrey stood outside the entrance of Fords in Greene Street, staring up at the building. "What's wrong?" asked Peter.

"I can't believe I'm here."

He smiled and took her arm. "Come on. Can't keep them waiting."

They walked down a quiet white corridor and into a lift that whisked them up to the fifth floor. They stepped out into the reception. Some young people, male and female, were sitting around, obviously waiting for interviews.

"We are here to see Gina Collins," Peter informed the receptionist.

Gina came to them five minutes later. She was a Director at Ford, responsible for business expansion. Business was obviously expanding very well, with new offices opening in Miami, Los Angeles and Paris over the past few years. A woman of about forty, attractive with shoulder-length brown hair, Gina was exquisitely groomed.

"Good to meet you." She was warm and friendly and shook both their hands.

"Since it's lunchtime, I think we should have our meeting over lunch, don't you?"

The venue for lunch was a short walk around the corner to a hotel. The restaurant, situated in the basement, was all black tiles and glass tables.

"You had a good flight?" Gina asked, settling down at the table after they had ordered lunch.

"Nice and calm, fortunately," answered Peter.

"You used to model yourself?" Gina addressed Audrey.

"For a long time, but I gave it up when we started our agency."

"And how's it going?"

"We can't complain so far," said Peter, "but we have so much talent in Ireland that is staying local. We want to link up with agencies like yourselves so we can launch them internationally."

"So, show me your books."

Gina took her time looking through the model photos, stopping and peering at some, virtually ignoring others.

"Their dimensions are all correct?"

"Of course."

Eventually Gina closed the books and concentrated on finishing her meal.

"Where do you scout? In the malls?"

"I go out a couple of times a week just to see what's out there," said Audrey. "And we've built up a good reputation at home so we get a lot of people just walking in to us for interviews."

"This is such a subjective business, as you know yourself. What's in this year is out the next. There's always a good market for a classic model, which a couple of yours are. And you have some with interesting looks that I'd like to see more off. And see what some of the bookers think."

"Please, keep that model book," urged Peter.

Gina thought hard as she pondered the dessert menu. "Banoffi pie," she told the waitress. Peter ordered ice cream while Audrey resisted.

"After lunch, I'd like you to come back to Ford, and I'll organise you to be taken around the place on a tour."

The whole agency was decorated in the colour white. Bookers from different departments were based in different offices, working around huge tables, all on the phones at the same time.

"This is where the serious money is made," informed Gina leading them into the office where the supermodels were managed from. They spent some time in meetings with the head bookers and talked about rate cards. Peter realised if they could break just one girl internationally they would be set up financially.

"That was brilliant," yelled Peter as they walked down Greene Street. "They were impressed. They want to do business with us!"

"If we don't hurry, we'll miss our next meeting at Elite," warned Audrey, as they jumped into a cab.

That night they were tired but happy. They had asked the reception at the hotel to make a booking in a restaurant for them and they walked the few blocks there.

Audrey was disappointed because she had tried to get through to Aran but had been unable to. She had checked with reception at the hotel and he hadn't tried to call her either.

"What are you thinking about?" asked Peter, noticing Audrey's pensive mood as they walked along.

"Nothing important. It's just this feels so real and yet unreal at the same time. You can't understand what today being at Ford meant to me. Ever since I was a young girl, I've been obsessed by this business. I used to dream about being a Ford model. And, OK, so I'm not one. But I still feel as if I've made it in a way. I got to Ford, albeit in a different capacity. But I'm feeling regrets."

"Regrets?"

"Of course, regrets. I haven't thought about it for a long while . . . but I fucked up my one opportunity to make it in the States. I'm finding it hard to forgive myself for that."

"You know, what's meant to be is meant to be. And if that hadn't happened, Spinner would never have existed."

"I know . . . but I can't help dreaming."

They managed to get a corner table with a view over the streets below. Peter ordered steak and Audrey ordered chicken.

"It's funny, isn't it, the dreams we have for ourselves? After a wonderful career in modelling I envisaged myself going into acting and being like one of those great actresses in the fifties. Pure glamour." Audrey laughed at herself.

"Well, you have the right look. Why didn't you pursue it?"

"Because I can't act to save my life! I did go to acting classes a few years ago, but I was pure crap. Stiff as a board! And of course I couldn't take criticism. When the acting coach tried to direct me in a different fashion, my temper would explode."

"I feel sorry for your coach, having experienced your temper on many occasions. Remember the rows over the Childwatch Show?"

"I hated you then! If somebody had told me then I'd be sitting here with you in New York after opening a business together, I would have told them they were pure mad."

"But it's happened," he said.

"Looking back on me then, I could be obnoxious."

"Let's agree there were two of us in it. When did you stop hating me?"

"Who says I have?" she joked. "I suppose . . . I stopped hating you when you looked after me the night of the Childwatch Show. I only disliked you after that!"

"Thanks!"

"I just couldn't figure out why you looked after me. You hated me, I'd ruined your show – most other people, including me, wouldn't have cared less"

"Well, I couldn't let you take off on your own."

"I saw a different side to you then. You said earlier about things meant to be. If I hadn't had that big upheaval I would have continued the way I was. But now I think I'm truer to myself. I've allowed myself to develop in other ways. And you know what? Sometimes I even talk about things other than myself. What about you, Peter?"

"Me?"

"What got you into this business? Did you always want to work in PR?"

"No way. I spent my youth raising horses. But my

older brother took over the family stud farm. I suppose if I'd have been the eldest, I'd be on the farm now. So I entered the civil service and started applying for the jobs in the communications department. I built up my experience there. After a while, I decided I wanted to be in private business. Of course Lynn was pushing me big time to enter the business world."

"Have you heard from her?" Audrey asked cautiously.

"Not a word. Too busy living the life of Riley with Rory Ryan."

"How do you feel about her now?" Audrey couldn't help herself.

"I'm trying to get on with my life . . . but I still care deeply for her. She was always what I wanted, but I'm not what she wants."

She reached over and gave his hand a firm grasp of support. "Then she's mad. Will you get back together?"

He shrugged. "Let's order more wine."

CHAPTER 75

As Aran walked across the lobby at Murphy Hennnessy, he could hear talking from up the stairs. Hiding in a doorway and looking up, he saw Reginald on the landing with Galen and Larry, all of them laughing and joking.

"I just told them straight that our client wasn't prepared to stand for it any more and we'd be suing if they didn't sort it out quickly," said Galen.

"Good man," said Reginald. "They've been giving us hassle for ages."

"That showed them you meant business," agreed Larry.

"It's the only way to go," said Galen. "Give them an inch and they smell blood. You have to be really tough from the start."

They laughed and joked some more before they descended the stairs, Reginald clapping Galen on the back.

After work, Aran made his way over to Audrey's apartment. She had left him her keys, so that he could escape from the icy atmosphere at home. He was infuriated by the little scene he had witnessed that afternoon. Galen had ingratiated himself very quickly. And Reginald's fondness for his nephew was growing by the day. Meanwhile Aran felt excluded. His anger was stopping him being his normal self, which was excluding him even more. He sat on Audrey's bed, missing her, and feeling lost but also feeling angry with her for deserting him. He couldn't allow Galen to just walk in and take over his life. He would have to think very hard to stop him in his tracks. As the night wore on, his anger towards Audrey intensified, that she had left him at this difficult time. He decided it was time he started to think about himself.

Enterprise Ireland was situated in a skyscraper off Park Avenue. Their role was to promote Ireland in America. Audrey and Peter had a meeting there the next morning to look at ways of expanding their business. After this they made their way to The Regency Model Agency. This was a name nearly as famous as Ford. The two agencies had been battling it out for supremacy for the past thirty years. The company had been started by an Englishwoman named Helen Holden, working from a spare room in her house in Queens in the sixties. Regency quickly gained ground and now operated from a skyscraper in Upper Manhattan. Helen, who was now in her late seventies, left the running of the company to a board of directors. Regency was now a multimillion-dollar business with offices in Milan and London. Again the head booker there was enthusiastic with Spinner's Model Book.

During the meeting Audrey began to cough and excused herself to get a drink of water. Making her way back to the office she swung through a door and all but bumped into a man.

"Steady on there," he advised in a loud New York accent. Aged around forty, he had slicked-back black hair and mischievous eyes set in Clark Gable features.

"What's your hurry?" he asked.

"No hurry," she smiled.

He looked her up and down. "Here for an interview?"

"No, a meeting."

"That's an Irish accent. My grandmother came from the County Longford, kept her brogue the whole of her life."

"Everyone I've met here seems to hail from home."

"Never been there though," he confessed.

"You should try and visit."

He held out his hand. "Boris Stein."

She shook his hand. "Audrey Driver." Then, with a smile, she headed back to her meeting.

She became aware he was heading in the same direction as her, keeping just a couple of feet behind her which made her feel very ill at ease. As she reached the office he was right behind her.

Then an arm reached out and opened the door for her. Embarrassed, she walked in.

"Hi, Boris," said the head booker, looking up from the photos she was studying.

"What's going on, Melanie?" Boris asked.

"These guys have an agency in Dublin and are showing us some of their girls. Peter Reynolds, this is our Chief Executive, Boris Stein." Melanie looked at Audrey. "I guess you two have already met."

Audrey became flushed. Even more so, as Boris winked over at her and pulled up a chair asking, "Mind if I sit in?"

"Of course not," said Peter. Audrey sat down, feeling uncomfortable. She felt Boris should have made his position clear from the start. She could have said something that jeopardised their business.

"We had a meeting at your office in London a while

back and already got a couple of bookings from them," Peter said.

Boris took up a stack of model cards and looked through them. "Crap, crap, crap," he said out loud as he put photos on his left-hand side. "Maybe." He put a card in the centre. "OK." He put a photo to his right. "Crap, crap, crap, good, crap, potential."

He went through all the photos in this manner.

"What are you suggesting. Some kind of link-up?" he then asked.

"We want to feed our talent to the States, working with Regency. We would be the models' home agent."

"Most of these don't impress me." He glanced down at the cards.

"Well, they impressed everyone over at Ford," Audrey snapped.

"You've been busy doing the rounds then?"

"We didn't come all the way from Dublin for just one meeting with you," Audrey snapped again. Peter glared at her to shut up.

"I'm not saying they are all crap," Boris said.

"So nice of you," glowed Audrey.

"This one is very good." He held up Tiffany's photo. "While this one," he held up a photo of Ivanka, "has a look of Gracie Mondeo, who is our highest paid model at the moment."

"So is there enough potential for us to work together?" asked Peter.

"I was never comfortable with dealing with third-party agencies. You could start a nice little bidding war between us and Ford for the same girl, no? I prefer to have the girls under our complete control."

"Well, your loss is Ford's gain." Audrey stood up and gathered up the cards.

After they shook hands, Boris called after them, "Enjoy the rest of your trip." Then he turned to the booker and said, "You got their contact numbers?"

"You could have lightened up your attitude a little." Peter hissed at Audrey.

"Why bother? He had no intention of doing business with us and was acting like an asshole," she said as she swung open the front doors of the building.

Another day of watching Galen being hailed as a demigod snapped Aran into action. He had had enough. He hadn't had a wink of sleep the previous night from worrying about the situation. He spent the whole day thinking and then made up his mind.

After work he drove out to Killiney.

Chloe had left work early that afternoon to drop her parents off at the airport. They were heading off on a 'once in a lifetime' cruise of the South Pacific and were not due back for a long while. She hadn't seen them for ages and so volunteered to drive them to their flight. They had exchanged quick goodbyes and brief kisses on the cheek.

Now, she was at home, Chloe was busy reading though some contracts for new models. She was trying to figure out ways of earning more commission from them. She decided she would write a clause into their contracts that if they earned over a certain amount they would have to pay extra commission. The established models would never stand for it. But the younger, less experienced girls wouldn't know the difference.

The intercom rang and she answered it. "Yeah?"

"Chloe, it's Aran."

What the hell do you want, she thought. She waited there, thinking hard and without answering.

"Chloe?" Aran called again.

She pressed the button to allow the front gates to open and heard his car come into the forecourt. She steadied herself for a moment before going to open the door.

"Hi, Chloe." Aran stood there looking sheepish.

"Are you selling something?" She couldn't help the sarcasm.

"I wanted to talk."

"What about?"

"Not on the doorstep."

She thought for a minute and then stepped aside, allowing him in.

"You're looking well," he commented as he sat down in her lounge.

She stood some distance from him with her arms folded.

"So, how have you been keeping?" he asked.

"Fine. Busy."

"At work?"

"And socially." Her face remained expressionless.

"Seeing anyone?"

"That's private territory."

"I'll take that as a no."

"Take it anyway you want, Aran. I have a lot to do. So if you wanted just to meet up for a friendly chat, call my secretary and we'll do lunch."

"I'm here because I wanted to see you . . . I've missed you."

"I'm sure Audrey will be delighted to hear that."

"She's in New York."

Chloe saw a window of opportunity to get some information. "What's she doing there?"

"She's over there with Reynolds meeting agencies to get work from."

Very interesting, thought Chloe.

"So you decided to drop over for a chat, because you were bored without Audrey?"

"No. I've wanted to see you for a while. The fact is Chloe, I've missed you a lot. Me and Audrey are over."

She digested the information. "I acted as a rebound job for you once and I'm not in the mood to do that again."

"I never meant to hurt you."

Chloe laughed out loud. "You didn't hurt me, Aran, I can assure you."

"She contacted me when we were going out together and used all this emotional blackmail on me. You don't know what's she's like." He wrung his hands together. "Why couldn't she have left us alone? We were doing fine, weren't we?"

Chloe sat down and crossed her legs, refusing to say anything or give anything away.

"I can't deal with her any more, Chloe. I don't want to. You know how mad she is, her temper. Sometimes I'm frightened to be in the same room as her in case she throws a knife at me or something."

"That really isn't my problem, Aran."

"But it is. Because the reason she's acting like this is because she knows that I'm still in love with you. Audrey knew all the right buttons to push to get me back," Aran continued. "But I've been regretting it ever since. She's so jealous. Jealous of you and me. She was always asking questions about what we did together and about you. She even wanted to know what colour bathroom towels you had. I just want the chance to get back together with you. Is there any chance?"

"I don't feel I could trust you any more, Aran. I think you play games. And I don't waste my time on game playing."

"I'm not just talking about us getting back together for a fling here, I'm talking making it permanent. I'm talking marriage."

Muriel and Reginald were sitting having breakfast when Aran came in and joined them.

"It's been a while since we had the pleasure of your company at breakfast," Muriel commented frostily.

"I'll have to try and make it more often." He poured himself a cereal.

Reginald continued reading the paper without looking up.

"I didn't hear you come in last night."

"I was in very late." Aran paused before continuing, "I was over at Chloe's."

Reginald put down his paper and exchanged a glance with his wife.

"Chloe Gallagher?" checked Reginald.

"That's right." He continued eating his cereal.

"And what did your friend Audrey make of that?" asked Muriel.

"It's nothing to do with her. She's history."

"Happy as I am to hear you have finished with that girl, you are still coming across as a spoiled playboy," said Reginald. "Racing between one and the other."

"Actually, myself and Chloe are very serious about each other." Aran stood up and left.

Only when they heard the front door slam did they speak.

"He's finished with her." Muriel was delighted.

"But as I told him, he'd not coming across as dependable."

"Don't push him," urged Muriel. "He needs gentle encouragement at this stage. The most important thing is Audrey Driver is out of his life."

CHAPTER 76

Peter and Audrey had meetings with a fashion editor and a photographer that Jackie Davenport had arranged. When they got back to their hotel in the evening, a message had been left on Peter's phone.

"Hi, Peter. Boris Stein here from Regency Agency. Give me a call on my cellphone. Number is . . ." Peter grabbed a pen and scribbled down the number.

"What do you think he wants?" Peter asked.

"Well, there's only one way of finding out," said Audrey. It was nine in the evening and they were about to go out for the night . They were having a drink from the bar in his room first. Peter took up the phone and dialled. "Hi, Boris, this is Peter Reynolds, just got your message . . . sure . . . that's no problem. We aren't going back until the morning after . . . OK, see you at one then, bye."

"Well?" asked Audrey as he hung up the phone.

"He wants to meet us for lunch tomorrow."

"What does he have to say then that he couldn't have said today? He's far too arrogant if you ask me."

"He's the head of Regency; he has every right to be arrogant. Come on, let's go eat."

They found a bistro in Greenwich Village, and after

enjoying a sumptuous meal they walked around taking in the street life. They made their way down to South Street Seaport and sat out on a balcony over a bar where they could take advantage of the sea breeze.

"Isn't this the life?" mused Audrey, feeling the warm air blow through her hair. "Away from all the worries." This wasn't true – she was very worried that Aran had made no contact with her since arriving. "No models screaming about breaking a nail. No pressure organising castings." She smiled and closed her eyes, "No working late at The San Juan. No arguments with my nasty business partner . . . yet."

"Cheers!"

"No jealous boyfriend watching my every move."

"Does he watch your every move?"

Audrey's eyes shot open, realising she had said too much. "He just worries about me, that's all."

Peter drank his beer. "And how do you feel about him?"

"I love him." She sipped at her mineral. "I've had a lot of relationships over the years. And most of them meant nothing to me or them. I suppose it's better than being on your own, isn't it? I thought I had passed on my one true chance at having a happy relationship when I chose to pursue my career over staying with the guy. And I suppose I carried that loss with me over the years. I used to think I'd never have children. And then I met Aran, and you know, it started the same way as my other relationships did. He had everything, the looks, the money, the respect, so he was a good man to be with. But it's developed so much more now. If you knew what he is prepared to sacrifice to stay with me, you'd be shocked." Her eyes welled up with tears.

"So why the sadness?" He reached out and gave her hand a comforting squeeze.

"Because, I think I've made the same mistake. Like I did with Shaun all those years ago, I've put my career . . . myself . . . before Aran." She finished the rest of her water.

Later, Peter began to speak about his father. "I guess I never knew what was going on. One minute I was having this great life. My family were great, horse riding, lots of friends. Suddenly, my dad started acting kinda strange when I was fourteen. You know, there were suddenly mood swings. One minute he'd be jovial and really, really happy. The next he'd be in a rage, throwing stuff and shouting. Drink changed him. He would start picking on one of us or going into these black moods. Take to his bed for long stretches. My mother is a coper, so she just continued as if nothing was happening. Me and my brother kept the stud farm going. It took me two years to realise it was drink that made him that way, that he was an alcoholic. I found out he would get my brother to buy him vodka on his way home from school. And after a night of ranting or roaring, or whatever . . . he would wake up the next morning and couldn't remember anything. After a couple of years of it, he realised he needed help, and got the professional help he needed. He hasn't drunk since . . . I don't know where all that's come from, I haven't even told Lynn any of that, though I suspect she's guessed parts."

"Thank you for sharing that with me. I think I understand you a lot more now. I know how you knew how to handle me the night of the Childwatch Show. It was second nature to you to be in that position. You allow people to become dependent on you."

"Fancy going to a club?" Audrey asked as they strolled past brown-stoned buildings.

"Not really, no."

"Oh, come on. It'll be fun. A New York club." She hailed a taxi.

They went to Float, a club near their hotel in Upper Manhattan.

"This looks very trendy," said Peter as he surveyed the decor and people.

Audrey was receiving a lot of attention, and being asked to dance by numerous men.

"Put your arm around me and pretend we're a couple, to get rid of these assholes," she asked Peter.

Peter obliged and they ordered a bottle of wine. They had a laugh, enjoying the spectacle of the zany clothes and egos on show.

"I'm popping to the loo, see you in a second," said Audrey, leaving Peter standing alone at the bar.

"A double vodka." A voice beside him said to the waiter. He turned and saw the speaker was an attractive blonde who seemed to be in her mid-thirties.

"Hi." She nodded to Peter.

He smiled back.

"What you working in?" she enquired.

"PR, I'm an agent." He spoke loudly to be heard over the music. He thought it interesting she asked him this before his name.

"You?" he responded.

"I'm a buyer at Saks." She got her drink and moved closer to him, her eyes flirting. "Married?"

"Separated," he answered.

"You're still wearing your wedding ring."

"Force of habit."

"Wanna dance?"

"I don't really dance," he said.

She ignored his protests, grabbed his hand and pulled him to the dance floor.

Audrey came back to the bar but couldn't find Peter. Finally she spotted him on the dance floor with a mystery blonde. She was surprised and stood there observing them. The blonde was being very flirtatious. She felt herself consumed with a surprising jealousy. She thought about leaving them to it, but then without thinking she found herself walking across the dance floor to them. Audrey tapped the blonde on the shoulder. "He's with me," said Audrey, resting a hand on her hip.

The blonde looked irritated and stood her ground staring at Audrey.

"He's with me," Audrey repeated. "So get lost."

The blonde looked at Peter. "Looks like your wife has returned," she spat and walked off.

Audrey burst out laughing. "You looked like you needed rescuing."

"Er . . . thanks," said Peter, not sure whether he was glad or disappointed.

"I know her type. A user. You don't want anything to do with her."

"Yeah . . . thanks again."

He went to walk to the bar but she held his hand. "I thought you wanted to dance," she said.

A couple of hours later they were walking back to the hotel.

She had his jacket around her shoulders as the night air had chilled.

"What was that blonde's name?" Audrey asked.

"Don't know. She just told me she was a buyer at Saks."

"At Saks! I should have let you go with her and I might

have got a discount when I go shopping there tomorrow!"

"There was no chance I was going with her."

"It didn't look like that from where I was standing."

"Besides, who said you're going shopping tomorrow?"

"I am. It's my last day, and I've done no shopping yet," she complained.

"We'll see." They reached the hotel and got the elevator to their floor. "See you in the morning." She reached forward and kissed him on the cheek before going into her room.

Boris Stein bit into a huge cheeseburger. They were in a crowded fast-food restaurant around the corner from Regency.

"When Ford took us out to lunch they took us to a very chic hotel" said Audrey as she tried to delicately master the burger in her hands.

"This is more my style," said Boris.

Audrey stopped herself from saying something sarcastic as Peter had warned her to be on her best behaviour.

"Why exactly did you want to see us again?" Peter pushed the conversation along.

"From what I saw, you do have some talent on your books. And I spoke to our office in London who you met with when you were there and they just had a couple of your girls over doing some work. They were impressed."

"So you want to do work with us in New York too?" asked Peter.

"As I told you I don't like dealing with third parties. It can get messy. But there is an alternative." Boris devoured the last of his burger.

"We're listening," said Audrey. The noise of the place was annoying her.

"A partnership between Regency and Spinner. This is all at suggestion stage. We would have to do more investigation to see if your agency is worthwhile."

"A partnership?" asked Peter.

"We take over a share of Spinner and so we are part owners of your agency."

"To buy part of Spinner?" Peter was confused.

"I'm not talking big bucks here. A very nominal price. We own a third of Spinner, you guys keep a third each. What you would be getting is to be a part of Regency and all the respect, protection, and big markets that would give you. Your models would immediately have access to international markets and international rates through us."

"But we wouldn't be able to work with Ford or anyone else," commented Audrey.

"Since we would be part of the same company, obviously not. You wouldn't be dealing with our opposition. But Spinner would immediately go into a different league."

Peter and Audrey looked at each other. "We'll have to give it considerable thought," said Peter.

"Sure. As I said, it's only at suggestion level. If you are willing to go ahead, I would need to see your models personally and your set-up. I'm in London in a couple of weeks, so I could pop over to Dublin."

"Let me call you when we get back to Dublin," said Peter, unable to keep the concern out of his voice.

Boris turned to Audrey and winked. "I could visit the place my grandmother is from in County Longford!"

"I just don't think we should give away a third of our company," said Audrey as they walked up Fifth Avenue after lunch.

"We wouldn't be giving it away. We'd be selling it."

"You heard him, for half nothing."

They talked and talked about it for an hour till Audrey said, "Let's forget about it till we get home and argue the toss then. It's our last day in New York and I want to do that shopping."

"I'm not spending hours being dragged from store to store," he objected.

"You've no choice." She put her hands on her hips.

"I would like to see some art galleries."

She raised her eyes to heaven. "Why waste your time in those places?"

"Better to look at dresses in Bloomingdales, I suppose?"

She linked her arm though his and pulled him off walking down the street.

"Let's practise compromising," she suggested. Soon after Peter found himself standing in Bloomingdales laden down with clothes Audrey was about to buy. "Look at this. It's fantastic," Audrey said grabbing a gown off a rail.

"Can you actually afford to buy all this?" asked Peter looking at the price-tags on all the clothes he was holding for her.

"It's an investment, my wardrobe for the next year."

"Next month, more likely . . .C'mon, Audrey, we've wasted enough time shopping." His face was pleading.

"You just don't understand how important this is. I'm spotting designers here that I've never heard off, and that aren't available in Europe. I'm just going to try these on." She flounced off.

Fifteen minutes, she emerged from the fitting rooms, and to her surprise, found Peter anxiously rummaging through the racks of clothes with a notebook and pen.

"Er, Peter, have you found a new interest in life?" Her face was perplexed.

"It's as you said. A lot of these designers aren't in Europe. I'm writing down their names and we can look up their addresses later and send them our model cards. We might get some work out of it. Here," he thrust the notebook and pen at her, "I'll call them out and you write them down."

Some time later Audrey was standing beside Peter in the New York Municipal Art Gallery staring at a painting. Peter seemed to be enthralled by it. She found the whole excursion boring.

"I'm hungry," she whispered.

"We've only been here an hour."

"Let's go eat."

He ignored her and walked off admiring another painting as if he was in his own little world.

Sitting down on a bench she watched him and supposed that Lynn would have been in her element there too. She got up and yawned and sauntered into another room which was filled with Dutch masters. She was immediately struck by the rich colours of reds, purples, indigos etched thickly onto the canvases. She went up closely to them examining them. She supposed that these paintings were the witnesses and recorders of their society in the same way photography was today. Looking at the women in the paintings, she marvelled how the idea and shape of body beauty had changed through the centuries. And she became entranced by the gowns they had worn.

CHAPTER 77

Chloe had been in shock over Aran's appearance at her door and his declaration. She had greeted all that he said with cold indifference and told him to call her the following day. She had spent the whole night giving the situation serious thought. There was a part of her that would like to coldly show him the door and have nothing to do with him after the way he had treated her last time.

But Chloe knew she was far too practical to do that. The fact of the matter was Aran remained somebody that Chloe could see herself settling down with. And those men were few and far between. He had everything that she looked for in a man, and she felt good in his company. She felt good being out with him. And most of all he was choosing her over Audrey.

Aran phoned her at ten the following morning and repeated what he had said. He arranged to come to her house that evening and they talked and ended up in bed.

They both took the next day off work and climbed down the rock face at the end of her garden to the sandy beach below and spent hours walking up and down. As Aran walked on the sand, his arm around her, he mused as he had countless times before on how strange Chloe could be. He had expected accusations, tears and ultimata. He had been prepared to be called every name under the sun before a final emotional embrace. No such displays from Chloe. She had simply acted very coldly in the beginning, then she thawed and eventually pretended nothing had happened and they were the same as ever. But he still didn't know who she was behind that exterior and she still treated their relationship in a businesslike fashion. But as they climbed up the rock face back to the house in the early evening, he wondered if it really mattered. In a way it was perfect for him that she was how she was. He yawned and decided to have an early night. After all, he would have to be up early to collect Audrey from the airport.

The restaurant was very relaxed and they sat back enjoying a glass of wine after eating a sumptuous meal.

"Are you sure you should be drinking that?" Peter asked as Audrey sipped on her chardonnay.

"Don't worry – I'm, as ever, only having the one."

"Good, I couldn't cope with a drunk you in New York."

A band was playing in the corner and people were dancing on the small dance floor to the slow melodies.

"I'd love to stay here longer," she said looking out at the skyline. She had tried not to think about it, but the fact Aran hadn't phoned once must mean her relationship with him was over.

"It's been good, hasn't it?" asked Peter.

"I can't remember when last I enjoyed myself so much," agreed Audrey.

"If we signed that deal with Regency, it might mean a lot of trips over here."

"Is that supposed to be an incentive to make me agree?"

"Would I try to bribe you?" Peter smirked.

"Of course, you would. Do you feel like dancing?"

"I'm even worse at this kind of dancing than nightclub dancing," he admitted.

"C'mon," She stood up and they walked to the dance floor. They danced closely to the slow song. And when they kissed it seemed like the most natural thing in the world to do.

Walking back to the hotel, Peter held his arm protectively around Audrey as she nuzzled her body close to him. They walked in silence, not needing to speak. In the hall outside their rooms they stood looking at each other. Neither of them knew what to say or do. They both willed the other to say something, but nothing was said.

Audrey suddenly found herself becoming angry at his silence, and angry with herself for being there.

"See you in the morning," she said abruptly, turning the key in her door.

"Is that it?"

"What?"

"Nothing further to say or discuss?" he asked.

"Well, you haven't said anything."

"I don't know what to say," he said lamely.

"Goodnight, Peter."

"No," he raised his voice. "We need to talk about what's been happening here. We can't just leave it like the last time."

"What are you talking about?"

"In your office, when we kissed and then we pretended nothing happened. And you went back to your boyfriend –"

"And you to your wife," she reminded him.

"I've never mentioned anything about that to anyone."

"Probably because you were married at the time."

A door opened down the hall and a woman stuck her head out. "Keep it down!" she said.

Peter opened his door and took Audrey's arm, pulling her into the room.

"What the hell are you doing here?" Audrey sighed.

Peter closed the door. "We need to talk about what's been happening. Why we have this habit of kissing each other."

"I'd hardly call twice a habit. I'd prefer not to start analysing the situation. We are both feeling vulnerable at the moment. Your wife has dumped you, my boyfriend has dumped me, we got carried away being in New York and all the excitement . . . that's all there is to it."

"It feels like more to me," said Peter.

"If Lynn was still with you, you'd be running a mile from me."

"So what are you going to do now? Try and get back together with your rich boyfriend and pretend nothing happened again?"

"Nothing has happened. And stop calling Aran my rich boyfriend, as if that's the only reason I'm with him."

"Isn't it?"

"It's not" she shouted. "He is prepared to give up so much for me, and if I could just stop being so bloody selfish I might have . . . might still be able to save that relationship."

"So let's just forget about back on that dance floor? Or what was happening out in the hallway?"

She decided to be cruel to be kind. "Yes. Let's face it Peter. Why would I be interested in you? You aren't even in the same league as Aran."

"Good night, Audrey." Hurt raged through his body as he turned to the door.

"Wait!" she called. "I'm sorry!" She rushed over to him and put her arms around him. "I didn't mean it! I really didn't mean it! I was only trying to hurt you." She hugged him tightly.

He slowly put his arms around her.

"I didn't mean it," she repeated over and over again, holding him tightly, before they started kissing again.

There was something surreal about being in a hotel bedroom in New York together. It was as if reality was suspended and they had been given a licence to do whatever they wanted. They were nervous with each other. Both of them had only been with the one person for so long that it seemed strange. But as they continued to explore, they began to feel more comfortable as the momentum built up into an urgency. All thoughts of Lynn vanished, as Peter realised that in Audrey he felt totally natural.

All thoughts of Aran were gone, as Audrey was caught up in the moment. They didn't need to speak, as they realised they had found a physical soul mate. Neither of them spoke afterwards as they lay in the darkened room. It was only when the morning sun light started filtering through the window that Audrey turned to Peter and asked, "Does this feel wrong for you?"

He was surprised by her question.

"No, it feels right." He felt nervous of the question he was about to ask. "Why? Doesn't it to you?"

She pulled him towards her. "Yes, it feels just right."

Peter awoke the next morning to the sounds of sirens in the street below. He stretched out contentedly, as the memories from the night came flooding back. What they had stopped themselves from imagining had become a reality. He realised Audrey was no longer in the bed beside him and he called out her name a few times. There was no answer. Jumping out of bed, he checked the bathroom. No one. She had gone back to her room. For some reason, he felt this was ominous though he tried to tell himself she could have gone to her room for a dozen reasons. He threw on the robe provided by the hotel, crossed the corridor and knocked on her door. It took a long time for her to answer. And when she did, he found himself confronted by a pale and tear-streaked face. She was already dressed. "Audrey! What's the matter?"

"Everything. I feel so ashamed of myself. I've been unfaithful to Aran and you're a married man."

"I'm separated, and your relationship with Aran's over. What's the problem? We really like each other."

"When I think about what Aran is going through over me . . ." She started crying again and he hugged her. "I love Aran," she said as she clung to him. "Oh, please, Peter, let's pretend this never happened. I want to try and make it work with Aran. I'm sorry I led you on. You don't love me either. You were just lonely after Lynn." She raised her head and looked at him. "I saw you in the art museum. Tell me you didn't wish Lynn was there with you. If we don't forget about last night, it will ruin both of us. It will ruin Spinner. Please, let's never mention it again. Please, Peter!" Her eyes were pleading.

"OK," he said heavily. "Whatever you want is fine by me."

CHAPTER 78

Lynn spread the strawberry jam on a slice of toast and sat down at the breakfast table. She was surprised when she heard Rory plod down the spiral staircase. She had discovered that Rory was not one of life's early risers. He came into the kitchen in his dressing-gown and kissed her cheek.

"Morning," he said and then yawned loudly.

"Tired?" she asked. They had been out very late the night before at another exhibition opening.

"Yeah," he yawned again and scratched his head.

"Any chance you may do some work today?" she enquired hopefully. Customers in London and Dublin were screaming for orders she had promised them.

"I'll see. I don't feel very focussed today."

"If you could just finish one for me it would be a start," she encouraged.

"It's not like manufacturing cars, Lynn," he said pointedly. "I'm not an assembly line producing paintings."

"I'm aware of that, but you haven't gone near a canvas in weeks." Her frustration bubbled to the surface.

"Not in the mood . . . the mood has to be right." He

went out to the front door and collected the post. She followed him out and watched him open a couple of letters, yawn again, and throw them with a bundle of other unopened letters into a drawer in a cabinet.

"I'd better go back to bed. See you this evening. Remember we are meeting François and his friends for dinner." He padded back up the stairs.

When she heard the bedroom door bang she went over to the drawer in the cabinet and opened it. It was stuffed with envelopes, some opened and some left unopened. She read quickly through them and found them all to be outstanding bills. Very large outstanding bills. She was swept by panic as she realised the amount of money he owed.

She got the bus into town, thinking about nothing but the bills. How could he run up so much money owing and not give a damn? How could he allow himself to be in such financial chaos? Why wasn't he working every minute of the day trying to clear his debts? Yet, in spite of her constant encouragement, he refused to look at a canvas.

As soon as she got to her desk her phone rang. It was her and Peter's bank manager.

"Mrs Reynolds, I'm quite worried because I sent a form for insurance out to your home and it was supposed to be signed and returned immediately. I haven't got it and I really need it."

Lynn found herself becoming even more frustrated. "Did you phone my husband about it?"

"I can't get through to him. It really is urgent you return it to me."

Lynn felt like screaming as she hung up the phone. Why couldn't Peter have signed the lousy form and posted it off? Now she would have to phone Peter herself to make sure he did. What was it with the men in her life? Why were they all so dependent on her doing everything? All she craved was a comfortable life, with no worries and everything taken care of.

She picked up the phone and dialled his mobile which was switched off. She then tried his office.

"Lynn Reynolds speaking. Can I speak to my husband please."

"I'm sorry, Mrs Reynolds. Er, Peter's in New York."

"New York?" Lynn said it a little too loudly. "What's he doing there?"

"He and Audrey are over on business." Lynn couldn't believe it.

"When's he due back?"

"Should be back in the office tomorrow."

"Get him to call me." She hung up.

She digested the information and burned with curiosity.

Audrey was pale and drawn as the cab took them out to Kennedy Airport. Looking straight ahead, neither of them spoke. All through Customs, they remained silent, and when they took their seats on the plane. Audrey closed her eyes and pretended to fall asleep before take off. She sat there alone in her thought.

Had she been born stupid, or was it an art form she had just cultivated along the way, she wondered to herself. What had she been thinking off? She was uncomfortable with sitting so close to Peter for the journey home. His Polo aftershave was thick and strong and it was stirring up memories of their night together. Even worse it was stirring up good memories for her. In her wildest dreams, she would never have imagined when she met Peter

Reynolds at the beginning that they would end up sharing such intimacy. And yet it had been unspoken in the air for so long. And it hadn't been a disappointment, she thought. It *had* been a disappointment, she told herself. The whole shabby episode had been a disappointment. If her friends and family knew! A one-night stand in a New York hotel with a married man. She shuddered at the thought of Aran ever finding out. She dreaded the reception she would be getting from him when she arrived back in Dublin. He would be angry and hostile with her, if he even took her calls. He had been right all along, she acknowledged to herself, and she should have never gone to New York.

He couldn't keep his eyes off her as she slept. Even in her sleep, Audrey seemed troubled and upset. Peter wanted to reach out and hold her and make her feel better. Then he was overcome by guilt that he had been the cause of her stress. She had been happily going out with somebody else before he had brought up this New York trip. And whatever had been brewing between them should have been kept firmly under control. As he thought about Lynn, he felt ridiculously guilty for having slept with someone else. And he was mad with himself for getting personal with his business partner and in doing so, risking everything they had been building up. He couldn't even begin analysing his feelings for Audrey, if indeed he felt anything. As she had pointed out, maybe he was just lonely after Lynn. The only solution was her suggestion of forgetting it ever took place and getting on with their lives. But as he looked at her, he knew it had never been like that with Lynn.

After they had landed in Dublin Airport, they quickly and

silently reclaimed their bags and made their way into the main airport area.

To her shock, Aran was waiting there for her, with a huge bunch of roses and a big smile.

"Hello, my darling." He grinned and picked her up before giving her a big kiss.

Peter stood nearby, feeling uncomfortable.

"I missed you," he said, putting her down and giving her the flowers. He grabbed her case. "Come on, the car's outside." Taking her hand, he began to lead her away.

"Er . . . Peter," she said, stopping and standing still.

Aran had been oblivious to Peter and only saw him when Audrey mentioned him. Aran nodded politely at him, but coldly.

"Do you want a lift?" Audrey asked.

"No." He shook his head. "I'll grab a taxi thanks. We're going in different directions," he lied.

Aran smiled when hearing this. "We'd better hurry to avoid the traffic."

"See you tomorrow," said Audrey, as Aran rushed her away through the crowds.

Peter watched them disappear before heading for the taxi rank.

"I thought you would be furious that I went," Audrey said as Aran drove them into Dublin.

"How could I stay mad with you for long?"

"I . . . when I didn't hear from you, I thought you had finished with me."

"Nonsense, you're stuck with me, babe. Did you enjoy yourself?"

"Yes, but I'm exhausted. I'll tell you all about it later. What have you been doing since I went?"

"Nothing much, just over at your place mostly, watching TV and missing you."

"How's the situation with Galen and your parents?"

"Improved a little . . . I'm fighting back and winning."

CHAPTER 79

"You would be mad not to," said Jackie Davenport.

"Do you think so?" Audrey was unconvinced.

"Absolutely. You have a chance to be part of one of the biggest agencies in the world. You should jump at it."

"Peter feels the same way. We've been arguing about it ever since we got back. I just don't like the idea of giving away a third of Spinner."

"You have to speculate to accumulate. Being part of Regency would establish you big time. It will give you an international market and give you huge standing here in Ireland."

"And why are they interested in little old us?" Audrey voiced her concern.

"They obviously liked what they saw, and it serves their purpose to have a base here in Dublin and be part of you."

"What do you know about Boris Stein? He seems a self-assured charmer to me."

"That's exactly what he is," laughed Jackie. "I remember him well from when I worked as a fashion writer in New York in the early eighties. He tried his hand at everything, the chancer! One week he was a photographer, the next a journalist, the next he was a PR. I tell you he changed his jobs as often as his girlfriends. He was always dating the latest pretty young model. We were all madly in love with him."

Audrey giggled at the idea of Jackie being madly in love with anyone.

"Finally he tried his hand at the agency business. Helen Holden, who still ran Regency with a rod of iron at the time, took a shine to him big time and fast-tracked his career. Audrey, you've nothing to lose – you and Peter will still own two thirds of Spinner."

Audrey sighed. "He's waiting to hear back from us and then he plans to come over to see the set-up for himself."

"Now," said Jackie. "I'm always doing you favours. I want one back."

"Name it."

"When he comes over I want you to set up a lunch just for me and him?"

Peter attempted to catch up with the work he had missed while he was away. He was busy returning all the messages left for him. To their credit, Vanessa, despite her growing arrogance, and Mark had done a great job in their absence.

With Audrey, as agreed, it was business as usual. She continued to look strained, but they pretended nothing had happened. It was important to do so, especially as they had such a big decision to make regarding Regency.

"I forgot to tell you, your wife called," said Vanessa.

"When?" snapped Peter.

"When you were away."

"Why didn't you tell me sooner?"

"I forgot." She closed the door of his office after her.

He nervously picked up his phone, steadied himself, and dialled the Gallery.

"Lynn, it's Peter," he said confidently down the phone.

"You took your time returning my call. I thought you were supposed to be back four days ago."

"I only got your message now."

"What brilliant and efficient staff you have . . . I got a call from the bank manager saying you hadn't returned an insurance form."

"I know. I was rushed off my feet before heading away and I didn't get a chance then. I sent it off a couple of days ago."

"Good." There was an awkward silence. "How are you anyway?"

"Fine. You?"

"Not a bother. What were you doing in New York?"

"Meeting with agencies to try and do work with them. We got a great offer from Regency." He couldn't help boasting.

"I expect your business partner was more interested in the shopping."

"Actually, she was brilliant over there." He jumped to Audrey's defence, surprising them both.

"A customer has just come in. I'd better go." She hung up.

There had been much debate in the offices of Murphy Hennessy regarding Ronan Flatley's offer. Reginald and Muriel were very much in favour for paying Flatley the bribe to ensure the shopping centre. Larry was against it. He never had the taste for bribery. He had also become increasingly bored with the whole project, and so it was agreed that the Murphys would buy Larry's share of the land, making them the exclusive owners. The documents were signed and Reginald and Muriel became the sole owners of the property and they gave the immediate go-ahead to Chloe to pay Flatley his money.

Chloe was delighted to wrap up the whole deal.

Chloe was delighted full stop. Since she had got back with Aran, everything was perfect in her life. Aran seemed much more involved with her the second time around. He no longer appeared to be distracted when he was in her company. Aran's work schedule was very heavy and so he wasn't available every night, but this suited her fine as well. He had developed an aversion of going out to social events, preferring to spend time alone with her at her house or inviting her over to the Murphys. Reginald and Muriel made no secret of how delighted they were to have her back in Aran's life. Aran had wasted no time in inviting her over for dinner and Muriel had embraced her and given her an uncharacteristic kiss, as if greeting an old friend.

"You are looking wonderful," Muriel had said.

They had talked like best friends over dinner, discussing the land deal, and with Muriel asking for more help for some of her charities.

For his part, Aran seemed content and relaxed over dinner, giving Chloe reassuring smiles throughout.

Now, as Aran walked down a corridor at Murphy Hennessy, he overheard Galen speaking to one of the secretaries.

"You seem very ambitious," she said.

"You have to be, to get what you want."

"It's just that somebody with your background can sometimes sit back and enjoy life."

"My background?" questioned Galen.

"Being a Murphy and all."

He laughed hollowly. "I'm a Murphy all right, but that's as far as it goes. I'm the poor relation."

"Really? But you trained as a solicitor."

"Thanks to my thrifty lifestyle and some help by the way of crumbs thrown at me by my wealthy relatives."

"You were lucky then," said the secretary.

"If you call having to bow to wealthy cousins in the hope of being thrown those crumbs 'lucky'. It's not a position I enjoyed or planned to stay in. I plan to go all the way to the top."

"To be a partner here?"

"And more," said Galen. "See you later." Galen got up and started walking down the corridor. Aran pretended he was just coming out of an office.

"Hello, mate," said Galen, before walking past.

"Aran, you shouldn't have bought me this," gasped Audrey as she took out a necklace from a box and put it on. "It cost you a fortune."

"You're worth it," he said, holding her around the waist and kissing her.

She held him tightly back, consumed with guilt about Peter.

"I'm so happy right now," she said, surprising herself. "I don't want anything to change."

"Why would it?" he asked.

Reginald sat with his arms folded. "I have to say I'm impressed with the changes in you over the last while," he remarked to Aran.

"I'm doing my best," Aran answered, with a fake embarrassed look.

"All your mother and I ever wanted was for you to fulfil your potential. If I can make an observation, some people bring out that potential in you, while others don't."

"I realise that too," Aran nodded in agreement.

"Marriage makes or breaks a man, Aran. If you choose the right partner, somebody who can support you, they can be an asset to you and you are made for life," Reginald smiled whimsically and cast his eyes down at his desk, "like your mother has been for me. However, taking up with a bad one could ruin you. Your reputation, your head, everything left in ruins. And then she hightails off and takes half your money with her. Do you understand what I'm saying, son?"

"I do." Aran sighed in a fake melancholy fashion.

"The day you declare your engagement to a suitable girl is the day you become a full partner here."

Aran smiled as visions of Galen being fired raced through his head.

CHAPTER 80

"So we are definitely sure about this?" asked Peter.

"I think so," agreed Audrey.

"Think so, or know so?"

"I can't say I know for sure. Let's invite Stein over and see what he says. He might take one look at our operation and laugh and head back to the States as quick as he can."

"All right then." He dialled the number for Regency in New York and waited for an answer. "Is Boris Stein there please? It's Peter Reynolds in Dublin."

Peter and Audrey stared at each other apprehensively waiting for Boris to come on the line.

"Hi, what's the weather like in Dublin?" Boris boomed down the phone.

"Sunny. Managing to keep the rain clouds away."

"Good, good."

"I'm ringing, really, just about what you mentioned when we were over there. We're very interested in your proposal and would like you to come to Dublin to discuss it further."

"Good. You are in favour of a merger then?"

"Well, we'd like to talk about it further."

503

"I'll be in London next week, so I'll call you to make arrangements to come over to you."

Lynn clipped on her diamond earrings and went to the phone as it rang. They were on their way to a cocktail party at an embassy.

"I'm not here if it's for me," Rory shouted from upstairs.

"Good evening, the Ryan home." Lynn answered the phone.

"Is Rory there?" asked an aggressive voice.

"No, he's not, I'm afraid – may I take a message?"

"It's Principal Properties here – the landlord basically. I've been trying to get hold of Rory for weeks. I've left loads of messages for him and he never bothers to ring back."

"I'll be talking to him later, if I can pass on a message."

"You can tell him that the rent is four months overdue on the house there. If he doesn't ring back and pay up by the end of this week, I'll issue an eviction order."

Lynn went cold as she put down the phone.

Rory skipped down the stairs. "We'd better hurry, come on."

"Don't you want to know who that was?" asked Lynn.

"Who?"

"The landlord."

"Principal Properties? Moaning about the rent, I suppose. Ignore them. We'll be late, come on," he said, as he bounded out the front door.

The embassy cocktail party was just the kind of event Lynn adored, with a crowd she had always wanted to belong to. However, she wasn't enjoying the evening in the least. Her mind was elsewhere as she tried to mingle with people. How could Rory not have paid the rent for so long? How could he ignore all those bills? How could he not work, just because he didn't want to? As she watched him being fêted by all the guests, a resentment burned inside her. He was more attentive to her needs than Peter was, and superficially he was much more successful and very well known. But in reality, she now understood that she had swapped her old situation with Peter for exactly the same one with Rory. It was being left to her once again to be the driving force in the relationship. Again she found herself nagging, this time for Rory to paint. This was not a role she wanted in life. She didn't want to carry anybody. She wanted the reverse. In a way Rory was even worse. At least Peter had striven to be successful and wanted it. Rory was haphazard about everything and took his new-found fame for granted. His fondness for drugs had also alarmed her. To such an extent that she had abandoned her own occasional indulgence.

She had enjoyed Rory's carefree attitude to money as they lived the good life. But as soon as she realised how little money Rory actually had, his attitude frightened her. She needed security; she needed financial security. She needed somebody who could take care of her every need, so she could go through life without any stress. She was very stressed now. Depression was clouding in on her. Her headache was coming on. She wanted to go to bed and stay there a long time.

"Lynn Reynolds, isn't it?" an upper-class accent asked beside her. "Jackie Davenport. I bought a painting from your Gallery last year."

Lynn's eyes misted over as she tried to concentrate on the speaker. "Oh yes. How are you?"

"I'm fine. Is Peter here?"

Lynn felt awkward and embarrassed at the question. "No, he's not."

"I speak to him or Audrey every couple of days," said Jackie.

Lynn remembered that Jackie was the editor of *Quest* "Really?"

Jackie was taken aback. "Doesn't he discuss work at home?

"Of course he does," Lynn realised that Jackie hadn't a clue they were separated.

"I have to say I think Spinner has really put the oomph back into Dublin's model and PR world. I had my doubts at the beginning. Didn't everyone? Audrey has made the transition from model to agent perfectly, under Peter's guardianship, of course. They're a great team." She lowered her voice. "And I really think this offer from New York will put them in the big league."

Peter had met Dermot from Macken for a few drinks after work. Dermot had said there was a rumour going around that the Boom takeover hadn't gone as smoothly as expected. A thought that made Peter's day.

Peter had paid more attention to his social life since splitting up with Lynn than when they were together. Apart from work related do's then, he hadn't bothered much with going out. Marriage made people lazy on that front, he thought. But now he regularly enjoyed going out with friends. He thought a lot about Lynn and what she might be doing. He also thought a lot about Audrey.

Rory and Lynn arrived home.

"Want a drink?" asked Rory going straight for the drinks cabinet and pouring himself a vodka while lighting up a joint at the same time.

She shook her head.

"A drag?" he offered her the joint.

"No," she said, inhaling her own cigarette. He put on the music and sat down.

"I'm going to bed," she said, going upstairs and closing the bedroom door.

Aran started to put on his Prada suit that he had earlier thrown on Chloe's bedroom floor.

He looked at Chloe as she sat in bed. He would like to say she looked flushed from their session, but she didn't. She spun around and sat, facing away from him so he could only see her long arched back. She put on a dressing-gown and went to her dressing table. Sitting down, she put her blonde hair into a ponytail and started to do her makeup.

His thoughts drifted to what had just happened between them. He had been adventurous, which she had seemed happy to go along with. Well, she hadn't objected anyway.

He had paid attention to her, making her feel special. And she had done the same for him. But she was always slightly reserved, almost just going through the motions.

But she puzzled him greatly. Her huge confidence didn't extend to love. That barrier he had spoken to her about before was built even higher when it came to the physical side of things.

She was so straightforward, he wasn't even sure if she enjoyed being with him. Not good for a boy's ego.

"Was everything . . . all right?" he ventured.

She turned and smiled at him. "Yes – why wouldn't it be?"

She looked back into the mirror and continued with her makeup.

As Aran knotted his tie, his thoughts drifted to Audrey.

Now they *were* compatible. They totally matched each other's needs.

As he looked at Chloe, he realised that barrier didn't matter any more. Chloe was wife material. She had everything going for her in that area. It was true what his father had said, picking the right wife was the most important thing for a man. Chloe was obviously the right kind of wife. Her lack of emotional neediness just strengthened her qualities. The fact she was independent and strong meant she wouldn't be demanding, sulking or giving him a hard time.

Audrey, as much as he loved her, was obviously not wife material. But he wouldn't have to sacrifice her and he wasn't sure even if he could. She could still be a part of his life and the role of mistress would suit her perfectly. In time, when she got used to the idea. He would obviously have to play his cards very cleverly. The French went through their whole life with a wife and a mistress. Once he was married, his parents wouldn't care who he was seeing in private.

CHAPTER 81

"Do you want a lift in?" Aran offered as he watched Audrey run around the apartment getting ready for The San Juan.

"Could you?"

"No bother."

"Are you staying here tonight?" she asked.

"No, I think I'll head home. Put in an appearance."

Things were going so great between them, Audrey thought. For the first time Aran seemed to have lost his insecurity and his possessiveness when it came to her. Unfortunately, this made her feel all the more guilty about Peter.

"I was thinking," she joined him on the sofa, "about The San Juan. I might give it up. It's true what you said before about it taking too much time up and not leaving enough for our relationship. It served its purpose when I needed to rebuild my confidence, but I think I'll just tell Noel tonight that I'll call it a day."

Aran looked alarmed. "But you still enjoy it?"

"Of course, I like the buzz of the place, but it's stopping me from being with you half the week."

"Look, forget what I said before." He took her hand and held it tightly. "It's true what you used to say about me being too possessive, and I'm trying to get over that. I have to learn to trust you as you always said. So keep working at the club if you enjoy it. I'm trying to change for you.".

Audrey's eyes misted over and she leaned forward and held him. "I love you." she said. At last, she thought, she was feeling safe and happy with someone for the first time since Shaun.

"Come on, you'd better hurry," he said. He was supposed to be over at Chloe's in an hour.

Chloe sat in her office at Boom. She had tried all her contacts to try and find out what had happened over in New York with Peter and Audrey, but she had been unable to find out any information. There was a knock on her door and Leslie walked in.

"Sorry, Chloe, can I have a quick word?"

"What is it?"

"I'm just letting you know I'm going back to Spinner."

"Can I ask why?"

"I just don't feel I fit in here as much. I get on really well with Audrey and Peter. I guess I just prefer the atmosphere there." Leslie was being truthful.

"What gives you the right to think you can skip back and forth between agencies just because it suits you." Chloe made no attempt to keep the sharpness out of her voice.

"I made a mistake coming back here, and they are being good enough to take me back, that's all."

"I'm sure they are. It's up to yourself what you do. But I can assure you that you won't make it anywhere once you walk out of here. Boom is the most established agency in this country."

"That might be true now, but they're expanding into Europe and the States."

"Just get out of my sight," snapped Chloe.

Leslie shrugged her shoulders and left. Chloe slammed a fist on her desk. Leslie had huge potential and she was furious to have lost her. What had they been up to in New York? Then she had an idea. Why hadn't she thought of it before? Usually there wasn't a hope but it was worth a try. She took out her address book and dialled Audrey's mobile number, dialling a 5 after the prefix to gain direct access to her message minder. She then pressed the hash button and when asked for the code she put in four zeros. As she had expected the automated voice told her she had put in the wrong code. She tried the same format with Peter's mobile-phone number and to her great delight the four zeros allowed her into his messages.

"You have two new messages," said the voice. She was amazed Peter could have been so stupid as to not put a code on his message minder.

The first message was *"Peter, it's Lynn. Please call me at the Gallery when you get a chance."* Chloe was still in shock over their separation and wondered what the call was about.

Then *"Message for Peter Reynolds"* boomed a strong American voice. *"Peter, Boris Stein here at Regency. Hope to be in Dublin in a week's time. Our lawyer is faxing you through some documentation. It breaks down the proposed merger if we decide to go ahead with it. You might give me your thoughts after reading it. I'm in New York today, or the Regency office in London on Wednesday, thanks."*

Bingo, thought Chloe. Regency, one of the biggest

agencies in the world. And they were planning a merger!

Peter came out from a meeting with Maeve feeling happy. He was happy because Maeve was happy. In fact she was delighted. Her new programme was scoring better-than-expected ratings and work offers were pouring in. Maeve had been so happy with her management at Spinner she was strongly recommending them to friends in the business. A close friend of hers was a well-respected band manager who was launching a new band and she had pushed that he use Spinner. Since the guy had a very good track record with pop acts, Peter realised just how lucrative this would be for them.

He checked his messages on his mobile. One was from Lynn and another from Boris. He was intrigued by Lynn's message. What did she want? Bracing himself, he rang The Gallery.

"Lynn, you were looking for me?"

"Yes, Peter, thanks for returning my call. I just wondered if you'll be back in the apartment tonight?"

"I should be. Why?"

"Could I come round to talk?"

"I'll be home around seven. Is that OK?"

"Fine, see you then." She hung up.

He felt a headache coming on straight away as he wondered what she wanted. Everything went through his head from her wanting to stop paying her part of the mortgage, to wanting him to move out of the apartment. To be fair she wasn't living there any more, why should she pay? Even if her contribution wasn't that much. Maybe she wanted to sell the apartment and take her share? Not that there would be much profit, they had barely made an inroad in repaying the mortgage, it was so high. Maybe she wanted to talk about divorce. Maybe she wanted to free herself so she could marry Rory. This thought hurt him deeply. And now Audrey avoided eye contact with him most of the time and Aran collected her every night after work. How had his life become such a mess?

"I booked Caviston's for tomorrow night," Chloe said. She loved the little seafood restaurant. "Are you sure you can't make it over tonight?"

She was in Aran's office, about to go into a meeting with Reginald.

"Sorry, too much work to do." Aran pointed to the paperwork on his desk.

"I'll be late for your father. I'd better go."

"I want a coffee. I'll walk down with you," offered Aran.

As the two of them walked down the hallway laughing at some story involving one of Aran's clients, they came face to face with Galen.

"Galen, you haven't met my girlfriend, have you?" Aran beamed as he put his arm around Chloe.

"I don't think so." Galen was confused, wondering where the brunette he had previously met with Aran had gone to.

"Chloe, this is my cousin, Galen."

"Have I met you before?" For once Galen didn't have his usual smug look on his face as he checked Chloe out.

Chloe, who had been given an abbreviated outline of Aran's worry about Galen, gave him a slightly condescending but friendly look. "I doubt it."

"You two off to lunch?" asked Galen.

"I wish I had time, but I have a meeting with Reginald," Chloe said.

"We are representing you in a case?" asked Galen.

"Er, no, I'm representing you." Chloe was anxious to show Galen who he was messing with now. Smiling at Aran she walked off.

"How is she representing us?" Galen was confused.

"Chloe's a director at Macken Communications. I can't really talk about what she's working on. It's confidential to senior management only. See you later . . . mate."

"This is excellent, excellent," Reginald said, browsing through Chloe's documentation concerning his land being rezoned for the shopping centre. He signed at the bottom of it.

"The money has already been paid into Flatley's account. Now I know you have already bought Larry out and you and Muriel are the sole owners of this land, but I still need Larry's signature," she turned over the pages, "on this page so he acknowledges he no longer has any right to the land."

"I sincerely doubt Larry would ever come after us for money," Reginald chuckled.

"It's still better to protect yourselves," she advised.

Reginald nodded, admiring the girl's ability. "Of course, of course. But Larry's not here today. He'll be off for a few days."

Chloe forced the irritation out of her voice. "Abroad?"

"No, just taking a few days at home. Don't think he is feeling the best."

"It's just I really need this all done and dusted by first thing in the morning. Is he home this evening? I could drop in on the way home and get him to sign it."

"I'll find out for you."

CHAPTER 82

Peter felt like a nervous schoolboy as he put the key in his front door.

Lynn was seated on the sofa flicking through a magazine. It was the first time they had seen each other since she walked out and their eyes locked for a moment.

He knew when he saw her that he hadn't imagined that he missed her. It had been for real. Seeing Peter again made Lynn feel safe and comfortable.

"You're looking well," she said and she meant it. He looked refreshed and the dark rings under his eyes she had last seen him with had disappeared. He seemed relaxed, rested and happy.

"So do you," he complimented.

"You've kept the apartment spick and span."

"Hardly been here."

"Working late as usual?" she assumed.

"Sometimes. Out socialising as well."

"Good. You needed to enjoy life more."

"How's The Gallery going?"

"Ticking over as usual. I hear Spinner is doing very well."

"I'm pleased with it."

"You deserve the success, Peter."

As the two sat opposite each other, there was a spell of silence, and both felt awkward.

As Chloe pulled into Larry Hennessy's driveway, her mind was completely preoccupied with the revelation that Spinner was planning a merger with Regency. She found it a frightening thought, as it would establish Spinner forever and leave Boom very vulnerable. But what could she do about it?

She grabbed the Murphy Hennessy file from the seat beside her, marched up the steps and banged the heavy knocker on Larry's front door.

Larry took a while to answer and without speaking beckoned her in.

"Sorry for disturbing you at home, Larry. I'm sure Reginald explained it was crucial I got your signature on this tonight." She followed him into the drawing-room and he gestured for her to sit.

"You haven't been well?" she asked, not particularly interested in the response.

"I've had the bloody flu or something. I stayed at home and rested."

"How are you feeling now?"

"Much better and back to normal. I should be back in the office tomorrow."

"That's good." She handed him the file.

"Drink?"

"Er . . . just a red wine, please." She suspected it would take him a while to read through the document.

He gave her a glass and refilled his own with gin.

Sitting down he read through the papers with impressive

speed, and signed the document theatrically. "I'm glad I'm out of it, this land. Reginald and Muriel paid me very well for my share. I don't like this bribing politicians stuff, it's smells bad. But the Murphys wanted a quick fix."

"As long as everyone's happy, that's the main thing."

"So the great romance is back on."

She laughed lightly. "Me and Aran? Yes, what are we like?"

"Muriel is delighted, as is Reginald."

"I'm glad. I'm very fond of both of them."

"They certainly engineered the whole situation expertly. Bringing young Galen in to force Aran to comply with their wishes."

Chloe said nothing for a while and then put down her glass. "Larry, I don't know what you are getting at, but if you are trying to shock me then don't bother. Aran has told me about the difficulty he has been having with his parents and all about Galen."

"Oh good. You know then that they basically told Aran to dump the model or he would be out on his ear?"

Chloe didn't want to hear any more. As much as she was aware that her relationship with Aran was based to some degree on mutual convenience, she didn't want to hear it put into words.

"I must say that as much as I like Muriel and Reginald, I don't like how they manipulate Aran," said Larry. "If I had a son, I'd like to think I'd let him make his own decisions and mistakes. I certainly wouldn't threaten him."

"Well, you don't have a son," snapped Chloe.

"No," he sighed. "I don't. You know I was quite ill this past week. I had lots of calls from friends and acquaintances, but nobody there. Do you understand me? No real partner or children for me."

"No girlfriend of the moment?" Chloe asked.

"Sure, there's a girlfriend of the moment. Some spoilt little rich girl who was terrified of coming near the place in case she got flu herself."

"You should have stuck with Julianna. She cared for you a lot." Chloe felt ill thinking of what he had done to Julianna.

"Mmmh. Julianna. I've always been too much of a selfish bastard to commit. I treat them like dirt till they can't take it any more."

Not just treat them like dirt, but attack them and visit hookers behind their backs, thought Chloe. "You reap what you sow."

"And what are you reaping? A loveless marriage?"

"Larry, you know nothing of my or Aran's feelings."

"I know a sham when I see one."

"That's your opinion." She finished her glass of wine and stood up. "I'd better be going."

Larry stood up and walked over to her and handed her the papers. "Thanks." She took them and put them in her oversized handbag and swung it over her shoulder.

"You are much too intelligent to sell yourself into that kind of a marriage," he said and then to her shock he took her hand and went to kiss her.

"Larry!" She quickly turned her face from him. "I've told you before that I'm very flattered but not interested."

Larry's grip on her hand slid up to her wrist and he squeezed tightly.

"Larry, let go of my hand," she said evenly and confidently. "Now!"

He made no effort to let her go and his eyes bored intensely into hers.

"Larry, I'm going now." She tried to sound matter-of-fact. "You haven't been well. And that's what I'm putting this down to. There's no need to discuss this situation again."

She tried to walk away, expecting him to drop his hold on her wrist. He didn't, but instead pulled her back and pushed her against the wall, her bag thumping to the floor, his body pushing up against her.

Fear ran through her as she remembered what Julianna had said. As she looked into his face close up to hers, she didn't recognise Larry Hennessy.

Lynn crossed her legs and laughed.

"What's funny?" Peter asked.

"This! Us! How long have we known each other and we are treating each other like strangers."

"How are we supposed to act, in that case?"

"More natural, I'd say."

More silence until Peter said, "Was there anything in particular you wanted to speak about tonight?"

"We've a lot to sort out. We can't go on living in limbo, can we?"

"I suppose not."

"If we let things go on indefinitely, everything will just get more complicated and harder to sort out, won't it?"

"Yes, you're right. Better to make everything tidy."

"The most important thing is the apartment, to sort that out?"

"Yeah," agreed Peter.

"Can you afford to take over my share of the mortgage?"

"I doubt it. The bank wouldn't let me anyway. It would be too much of a risk for them."

"We'll have to sell it then," concluded Lynn.

Sadness crept over him and he felt his heart was breaking with the finality of it all.

"Then there's all the furniture and stuff. There's just a few sentimental items I would like to keep. After that you can have your choice of anything."

"Well, I want to be fair about it. Just say what you want and I won't object. Also, I owe you some money."

"Money?" she asked.

"From Rory's paintings that financed Spinner."

Lynn waved her hand briskly in the air. "Forget it."

"I can't just forget about it," Peter objected.

"You always paid the lion's share of the mortgage and everything else, so really, don't worry about it."

"Whatever profit there is with the apartment we'll divide it evenly then."

"That's fine," Lynn nodded.

They lapsed into silence again before Lynn spoke. "I guess the only final point then is organising the divorce."

Peter sighed. "I suppose."

The sadness kept creeping over Peter till he felt he couldn't cope. "We can just use my family solicitor . . ." Despite himself his voice broke and he buried his head in his hands.

"Peter, are you all right?"

He said nothing but kept his head in his hands.

"Peter . . . you're OK . . . with all this, aren't you? You want the divorce?"

Peter jumped up briskly and walked into the kitchen.

Lynn smiled to herself and waited a while until she followed him in. Peter had his back to her and he was holding the kitchen counter with his two hands.

"Peter?" She coughed slightly and walked to him, putting her hand on his shoulder.

As he turned around she could see his face was full of pain and she leaned forward and kissed him.

Chloe made sure no panic registered on her face as he continued to twist her hand and pin it against the wall.

"Larry! I didn't realise you were into these games," she smiled and gave a flirtatious little laugh.

His intensity softened. "You like these – games?"

She smiled and nodded.

Larry grabbed both her wrists and slammed them against the wall.

She laughed again, in spite of the pain.

The doorbell ringing was like a scream through the house's silence.

He looked surprised and worried but made no attempt to release his grip.

"Quick!" she hissed. "Get rid of them!"

He made no attempt to move.

The doorbell rang again.

"Who are you expecting?" she asked.

"Nobody," he said and she was relieved she had managed to get him to speak.

"Get rid of them quickly. They can see the lights are on and the car is in the drive. Whoever they are they know you've been ill and won't go till they get a response. Just go out and get rid of them . . . Send them away so we can continue"

Larry thought hard and then he released her. "I'll be back in a second," he said and walked out into the hall. She heard him open the front door and she grabbed her bag.

She heard children's voices, then Larry saying, "No, I've no change." Chloe rushed into the hall and pushed past him and two children holding collection-tins. She raced down the steps and jumped into her car. She started the engine and tore off down the gravel drive and out on to the street. She didn't stop till she got home and locked the front door behind her, closed the electric gates and put on the security system.

Peter and Lynn didn't say much as they lay on the sofa, his arm around her. In darkness apart from one candle. "The Look of Love" was playing continuously on the CD.

"What about Rory?" he asked eventually.

She didn't answer.

Chloe wasn't one for tears. She didn't respect people who broke down crying and she honestly could not remember the last time she had cried herself. But as she sat on her couch nursing a brandy, she did feel like breaking down. But the tears wouldn't come. As the initial shock of what had happened with Larry wore off, she began to re-emerge full force. She had found herself in a difficult and potentially very nasty situation, with a man who was obviously dangerous and a menace to society, despite or maybe because of his enormous wealth and influence. She had handled the situation expertly. She could not fault herself on how she had acted and how she had dealt with him, and that was the main thing. It passed through her mind to contact the police, but she dismissed the idea immediately. She would be jeopardising her own position. It was a sad fact that if the police became involved and she pressed charges there would likely be a court appearance, and this would undermine her position at Macken. Macken was a conservative company, dealing with corporate clients and was above reproach when it came to respectability. For a director of the company to accuse a client of an attempted sexual assault would make her position untenable. Then there was Aran. She was confident her relationship with him would not survive if this incident came out in the open. Muriel and Reginald would be horrified beyond belief. Not only would Murphy Hennessy be tainted by the scandal but so would their family name. Chloe would quickly be shown the door. What's more, she too would be horrified by any whiff of scandal. She didn't want to drag her own reputation through a legal procedure. She had fought too long and hard to let this man have any effect on her life. And she suspected that was why Larry had tried it on with her. He knew she was too ambitious to risk revealing him. That was why he picked on socialites like Julianna. They would never dream of bringing the unwanted attention on themselves or their families. She wouldn't forget what Larry Hennessy had tried to do. But she would strike back in her own way, when her own position was unassailable. When she was married to Aran Murphy. She was a strong and capable person. If Larry or anyone else thought this incident would in any way perturb her, then they were mistaken.

CHAPTER 83

"Could I speak to Mr Boris Stein, please?"

"Who is calling please?" asked the receptionist at Regency's London office.

"Chloe Gallagher from the Boom Agency in Dublin."

"One second please."

Chloe tapped her fingernails on her desk as she listened to the jazzy music play down the phone.

"Boris Stein speaking," said a sing-song American accent.

"Mr Stein, good afternoon. I'm Chloe Gallagher from Boom Modelling here in Dublin."

"Uh huh."

"I'm not sure if you've heard of us."

"Vaguely. You've been round for a long while, no?"

"Not me personally," she laughed. "But the agency is the most established here in Ireland, yes."

"And how can I help you?"

"Basically, we want to establish our models internationally. I have a few ideas I would love to discuss with you and wondered if I could pop over to London to meet you before you head back to New York?"

"Pop over to London? But by an amazing coincidence I'm coming to Dublin this weekend. But of course you knew nothing about that, huh?" Boris's voice dripped sarcasm.

"Coming to Ireland? For a holiday?"

"A working holiday. You knew nothing about that?"

"Of course not, how could I?" Chloe sounded innocent.

"All sounds like a bit of a coincidence to me. You know the Spinner Agency in Dublin?"

"Yes, they've a couple of good girls." She laughed lightly. "To be honest with you, Mr Stein, they are very new and very small. If you're coming to Ireland, I'd be delighted to meet up with you and show you around Boom. As I said, I've some very exciting ideas I know you would like."

Boris didn't say anything for a while. "OK, OK, Ms Gallagher. You've obviously heard something about us and Spinner."

"You and Spinner?" Chloe sounded confused.

"Playing games was never my scene –"

"Nor mine –"

"So you can drop the act. Yes, I will meet you. There's nothing like keeping your options open."

Tiffany's weight had plummeted drastically and Audrey was very concerned. Not only was she worried about Tiffany's health, but also the vacant look that seemed to be in her eyes most of the time.

"I can't see what your problem is. You were the one, along with Jackie, who advised me to lose weight," Tiffany defended herself when Audrey tackled her again on the subject.

"Lose weight, sure. But you've gone way beyond what we recommended."

"So what's your problem? I'm getting loads of bookings. I'm the most in demand model on your books if not in the country at the moment and I'm photographing better than ever."

This was all true, Audrey conceded to herself. "But is it worth it if you are damaging your health."

"I'm not damaging my health," Tiffany raised her voice.

"You aren't eating properly." Audrey became exasperated. "Boris Stein is over here next week and you are one of the girls that he is most interested in. If you don't start taking better care of your health from now, then I won't be responsible for pushing you further into modelling."

Tiffany's face burned red. "You can't not let me meet Boris Stein! You can't stop me from getting a break like that!"

"Then I want to see you putting on weight. Maybe if I rang your mother in Derry –"

"Don't even think about it! She's a worrier. Leave her out of this. This is a waste of time. You are my agent. You get me work and I do the work and that's where your role stops. Now please stay out of the rest of my life."

Audrey was upset and went in to Peter after Tiffany left.

"She just can't see that she is beginning to look unhealthy, Peter. She's disappearing before our eyes."

"Don't upset her before Stein meets her. She's a big selling point for Regency."

"Peter! She's a young girl and I'm worried about her."

"So am I. After Stein leaves we'll concentrate on Tiffany. We'll give her our full attention, getting her to realise she has to take more care of herself. I just don't want any upsets next week."

"I used to be really close with Tiffany. She was a really nice and likable kid. Remember when she came here first, all giggles and excitement. But she's changed so much."

"Look, it's understandable. She's earning good money, has a degree of fame and it's gone to her head. She's become egocentric. I've dealt with enough models over the years to recognise the process evolving."

"Like I was, I suppose? But she has this haunted look in her eyes –"

"Anyway, I'm off now." He stood up.

Audrey looked at her watch and saw it was 4.30. "It's a bit late for a meeting, isn't it?"

"I'm not going to a meeting. I'm going home."

"Home?" Audrey was surprised.

"Yeah." He looked sheepish. "Me and Lynn have got back together."

"Oh!" Audrey quickly tried not to look so surprised. "That's good to hear. I'm glad to hear it."

Lynn was relieved there wasn't any scene when she informed Rory she was leaving. He had greeted the news in the same relaxed manner as he lived his life. No recriminations, no tears, no attempts to keep her. But then she knew there wouldn't be. Rory was simply not motivated enough to make a scene. It took her minutes to pack her bags and load them into the waiting taxi. As she closed the front door of his luxurious, heavily indebted house behind her, she felt only relief. She had certainly misjudged that situation. As they say, if you want to know a person, then go and live with them. On the surface he could provide her with the social status she required, but none of the security she craved. And at least Peter now seemed to be heading in the right direction and he was turning into that person she needed. She knew what she was and she knew what she wanted. She wasn't one of those career women like Chloe Gallagher who was capable of earning big money and living life independently. She needed protection and status. And she knew she was incapable of achieving it herself. But she did know she was everything a successful man could need by his side. She needed to be the power beside the throne.

She felt very comfortable being at home as she prepared dinner. And both her and Peter's parents had been delighted they had got back together.

"But do you really think they will agree to be a partner in Spinner?" Lynn asked over dinner.

"Please God and then it will be the big time for us."

Just what I've always wanted, thought Lynn. "What's this Boris Stein like?"

"A big-headed New Yorker. Brash and arrogant, but buckets of charm. There seems to be no bullshit about him, which I like. He says it as it is."

Chloe wasted no time in putting forward her idea about a merger between Regency and Boom to Brendan and Vincent. Both men were very enthusiastic and agreed it would make Boom a much more profitable and valuable commodity.

Even Vincent had given a grudging smile when she informed them Boris Stein was flying to Dublin to discuss the merger further.

"If anyone can arrange a merger it's you, Chloe – that's your speciality," said Brendan.

CHAPTER 84

Chloe felt on top to the world as she went out to Caviston's for dinner with Aran, who had been having a very busy day. First he'd had lunch with Audrey and then gone into Weirs on Grafton Street to pick up an item he had arranged to have specially made.

He had then gone home and told Reginald and Muriel his intentions. They had been overjoyed and given their full approval. Chloe was already at Caviston's when he got there and was in great form, chatting away. After they devoured the first course of oysters, Chloe went to the bathroom. When she re-emerged she found a ring box in place of her empty plate.

"Is this what I think it is?" she said opening it, her eyes glistening in the candlelight as much as the diamond.

He smiled and nodded.

She kissed him, slipped it on her finger and ordered champagne.

The next day Aran was made a full partner at Murphy Hennessy law firm.

Peter breathed deeply as he listened to the city's distant

night sounds. Lynn, asleep beside him, had told him many times that he had changed while she was away. He was more relaxed and content in himself. She said he had found the real inner confidence that had always eluded him before. She had asked him if he had seen anyone in her absence. He had lied and said no. There was already a dislike between Lynn and Audrey, there was no point in adding further complications with the truth of what had happened. While he stroked his wife's hair, he wondered if he had changed. And if he had, did he owe it to Audrey? Audrey, the last woman he would ever have thought capable of changing anybody, let alone himself. But she had changed his life. If she hadn't acted the way she had at the Childwatch Show, he would have ridden along with his career and his life, never really fulfilled. He wouldn't have had to face himself. And then Audrey rescued him from despair with the idea of Spinner. Audrey, who had given him something to live for when Lynn walked out. She had insisted he keep going, and then as they gained each other's trust, he had opened up and said things he never had before. What had happened between himself and Audrey? A love affair? A one-night stand?

Aran was a quiet sleeper. Which was a blessing, because Audrey was a light sleeper. He only snored when he was very tired. He was snoring that night and Audrey put it down to the fact he had been working so much lately. However, it was stopping Audrey from sleeping. Slipping out of bed, she put on her nightgown and let herself out of her apartment. She padded down the corridor to the EXIT door at the end. She opened it and climbed the stairs up on to the roof. It was a beautiful warm night and she sat down on the ledge of the roof looking out to the city lights and across the sea to the boats slowly coming in. She often came up there to gather her thoughts. She never brought anyone else up there, not even Aran, as it was a private place for her. She felt content.

After all her disastrous relationships, she had settled into a caring and loving relationship with a man who was prepared to give up everything for her.

That was true love. And now she knew that was all she had ever wanted. She wasn't driven by money, or fame, or a rich man. She only ended up going out with those kinds of men because she was mixing in those circles. She was more happy with Aran, facing a penniless future, than she ever was with him being rich.

All she needed to know was how much he loved her. She wasn't being loved as a trophy, but for who she was. And after her turbulent modelling career, she was now in a job that she loved and where she felt in control. She tried not to think about Peter too much. He was a great guy, and they had both handled what had happened between them as mature adults. They had been there for each other when they needed each other but it was now time to move on.

They shouldn't have allowed their attraction for each other to develop. And she was glad he was back with Lynn. They suited each other. The sea had always allowed her to think clearly. When she was growing up she used to gaze out at the sea thinking. And as she looked at the sun begin to rise, she realised it had been a long time since she had dreamed or thought about Shaun.

CHAPTER 85

Boris Stein looked out of the window as the plane began to descend towards Dublin Airport. The journey from London had taken less than an hour, just enough time for breakfast.

After a smooth landing, he walked out into Arrivals and scanned the crowd for a familiar face. He spotted Audrey, waving and smiling with Peter beside her.

"Good to see you again." He shook both their hands. "I could have grabbed a cab, you didn't have to collect me."

"We wouldn't hear of it," said as Audrey as they helped him with his bags.

"So, welcome to Dublin," said Peter.

Chloe looked at her empty engagement finger, itching to put on Aran's ring.

She knew it was out of the question. He was insisting on a long engagement, and only their immediate families would know for now. She had been over to the Murphy house last night for champagne with his parents. Fortunately her own parents were away on their extended cruise. She wanted to shout to the world that she was going to be Mrs Aran Murphy, but she had to respect her fiancé's wishes. There was a time and a place when dealing with the class Aran came from. There would have to be announcements in the papers and a select party. He even refused to go out to any functions with her any more, saying his parents hated when his picture appeared in the papers and it stopped him from being taken seriously at work. He told her he wanted to kill off his playboy image and appearing at parties or in papers would not enable him to do that. She had to accept his wishes, and it was a small compromise to have to make.

She had heard Peter was back with Lynn. She was irritated by the news, but her own engagement had completely filled her mind and so even that hadn't disturbed her as much as it would have otherwise.

Ben knocked on her door at Boom, interrupting her thoughts.

"Can I have a word?"

"I don't have that long. Stein is flying in today and I'm trying to get everything in order for him."

"It won't take long." He shuffled nervously.

"Well?"

"It's just I was out on a stag night last Saturday."

Chloe raised her eyebrow as she found it amusing to think of Ben out on a stag.

Noticing her reaction, Ben went bright red.

"Ben, I'm not really interested in your social life."

"I know," he stammered. "It's just I saw something that was very interesting."

Indeed, it was very interesting. After Ben had left, she contemplated his news and how best to use it. Right smack in the middle of Boris Stein's visit, she decided. Now she just had to think of the right journalist to break the news.

Vanessa tightened her raincoat around her waist and stepped out of Spinner, locking the door behind her. She was in foul form. She was just after having another argument with Audrey who was refusing to introduce her to Boris Stein when he came to the office. They had told her she wasn't the look he would be interested in. How would he know till he saw her? Her frustration was reaching boiling point. She was getting a lot of photo-call work, things that required a busty blonde to pose and smile. But when it came to fashion, forget it. Tiffany, Leslie and Ivanka were all getting the good work. She still had her tiny role in a soap, but wasn't even getting any other auditions. At the same time she felt she was running the reception at Spinner. The money was good and needed, but it wasn't what she wanted to do. Why should she be answering phones while Tiffany was on the cover of *Quest*? Tiffany, who had become a physical and mental wreck and seemed to be losing her marbles. Vanessa decided she was going to do something about it. If Spinner couldn't give her what she wanted, she would go elsewhere. It was quite late, but she wondered if anyone would be at Boom. Taking out her mobile she dialled their number.

Chloe was about to leave the office and lock up when the phone on reception rang. She was going to ignore it but thought better of it.

"Boom Agency," she answered.

"Is Chloe Gallagher there?"

"You're speaking to her."

"Oh!" Vanessa was surprised to have got hold of her

straight away. "Hi, Chloe, my name is Vanessa McGrath, the model at Spinner."

"I've never heard of you. If you want an interview, call back in the morning and ask to speak to Ben Egan."

"I don't want an interview." Vanessa was annoyed at the lack of recognition,. "I was on Page 8 of *The Sun* on Tuesday and I'm in a soap on RTE."

"Good for you, but still call back in the morning and ask for Ben."

"Listen here, I have something that could be very beneficial to you, and so you had better make time to see me this evening," insisted Vanessa.

"Two hundred and twelve," said the receptionist at The Berkeley Court Hotel, handing the room key over to Boris. He had flirted with her as he signed his details. The girl felt overpowered by the man's magnetism, not to mention his gleaming white smile. Audrey observed the interaction, and remembered how he had used the same charm on her when they had met first. It hadn't worked on her, as she was naturally wary of men who were too sure of their own attraction. Audrey suspected she was one of the very few females it didn't work on. She knew Boris had quickly realised he hadn't charmed her and hadn't wasted any more time trying to impress her. He used a totally different approach, a business one, towards her now and that suited her fine. The hotel porters took Boris's luggage and he joined Audrey and Peter in the bar.

"If we all agree for this merger to go ahead, what time frame are we talking about?" enquired Peter.

Boris took an ice cube from his Jack Daniels and crunched it loudly. "Sooner rather than later, I'd hope. I'm glad you said the word 'if'".

"We wouldn't want to be presumptuous," said Audrey. "You haven't even seen our offices yet."

Boris sat back into his leather chair and joined his hands. "I've also had an offer from another agency in Dublin . . . Boom . . . ever heard of them?"

Peter and Audrey looked at each other in stunned silence.

"Chloe Gallagher?" Audrey managed.

"That's the one – you know her?"

"The bitch!" Audrey said, much too loudly, causing people to stare.

As Peter recovered from the news, he shot Audrey a warning look to shut up.

Boris' face had lit up in amusement, obviously enjoying Audrey's response.

He prided himself on being an excellent judge of character – you had to be in this business. He had suspected from the beginning, that Audrey spoke her mind and was a firecracker, and he believed he was right.

Audrey ignored Peter's disapproving look and continued, "How the fuck did she find out we were dealing with you? Did you contact the other agencies in Dublin to check out the scene?"

"Hey!" Boris threw his arms up into the air. "Not guilty. I didn't. Not that it wasn't my right to. I guess you guys over here aren't so good at keeping secrets."

"We're a tight set at Spinner. Nobody would leak it out. We're the only people who knew and," she remembered Peter's reunification with Lynn, "our partners."

"Look, who cares how they found out? Where does this leave us?" Peter tried to bring common sense back into the conversation.

"I'm still interested in a merger with Spinner, why else

would I be here? But I also have to investigate Boom's offer. I wouldn't be doing my job otherwise," Boris said, reaching for another ice cube.

Audrey slammed the car door after her in The Berkeley Court's carpark.

"Well done," Peter said sarcastically, starting the ignition."You really came across as professional. You really showed him what cool operators we are."

"I don't care!" shouted Audrey. "How dare Chloe Gallagher come after our deal. You have to tell Lynn to keep her mouth shut from now on."

"Whoa! Lynn? What makes you think it was her? It could have been Aran just as much."

"Aran! Please! Aran has no interest in my job. He never listens to a thing I say when I start talking about Spinner, in one ear and out the other. He wouldn't know or care who Stein is. And gossip just isn't his style."

"But it would be Lynn's?" Peter was annoyed.

"Yes, with that atrocious arty crowd she hangs around with. She was probably boasting as usual – I can just hear her – 'Yes, my husband's company is merging with an international one' in that stupid voice of hers and obviously word got back to Chloe and now the whole fucking deal could fall through."

Peter's voice became ice. "Don't talk about my wife like that."

There was a horrible silence as both realised the complexity of their relationship. They had been hugely supportive of each other and acted as a team. Their relationship had intensified when Lynn was out of the picture. But now there was a wedge between them, and they couldn't speak freely. Audrey had been speaking to him almost as if they were a couple. But now she had been quickly reminded that they weren't and she had gone way beyond the pale.

"So what are you going to do now?" asked Lynn that evening.

"Fight our hardest to get that merger," explained Peter. "We can't let Boom become part of Regency; it would undermine our position too much." Lynn was delighted with Peter's fighting spirit. He wasn't intimidated in the least by the competition. His new strength excited her.

"You must do everything you can to succeed, Peter." She paced up and down the apartment thinking. "We'll have Stein over to dinner and wine, dine and charm him. The personal touch."

"Wouldn't hurt, I suppose," agreed Peter.

"Stein needs to know what we are like as people. Give him the full picture."

"We would have to invite Audrey . . . and Aran as well." Lynn's face soured.

"She is my partner. It would look odd if she wasn't here too."

Reluctantly Lynn had to agree. Besides, as much as she despised Audrey, she was going out with Aran Murphy and that was a connection worth nurturing.

"I'd better start planning the menu. Maybe we should just bring caterers in." She looked around her beautiful home. "I told you we should have moved from here to a bigger place. I'm telling you now, Peter, if this merger comes through, this place is going on the market and we are trading up straight away!"

In the bathrooms of The Berkeley, Chloe ran her fingers

through her hair as she checked her appearance in the mirror.

As she walked through the lobby into the bar she took out her mobile and dialled Boris's number. Hearing a mobile ring in a distant corner she followed the trail and got to him before he had time to answer.

"Boris Stein?" she asked. As she smiled down at him, an unusual feeling came over her. He was one of the most attractive men she had ever seen. She had never been taken in by appearances. She was far too practical for that. Handsome is as handsome does, her mother used to say. It was a weakness that could too easily be exploited. And if she was totally honest with herself, it was something that never excited her too much. But this man was different. As she reached out and shook his hand, it seemed his touch created a small electric shock that ran through her. A little dazed, she sat down and they exchanged pleasantries. Quickly regaining her poise, she hoped he hadn't spotted her reaction. What had been her reaction? She admitted to herself it had been attraction. Pure attraction. She was not comfortable with this emotion, as it was handing power over to somebody else. And this unusual attraction she had to this stranger was not only unwelcome at this stage in her life, but it was forbidden.

"Drink?" asked Boris.

"I'll have a mineral water," Chloe said and ordered from a passing waiter. "You've settled in all right?"

"So far so good. I had a meeting with the people from Spinner earlier. They were surprised to find out I was meeting you."

"I admire what Peter and Audrey have done at Spinner, I really do. They've done well and have some good models. But to be honest, they're small fry. And neither of them have particularly good business backgrounds."

Boris crossed his legs. "Is that so?"

Remembering their phone conversation when Boris warned he didn't like game-playing she decided to be blunt. "I'm not going to be polite about it. Boom is the biggest and best agency in this country. We have the best models and the biggest contracts. A company of the size and reputation of Regency doesn't want or need to deal with anything but the best. If that sounds boastful, I make no apologies."

He nodded his head. "I appreciate your honesty."

"I'll be in the office from eight in the morning. Anytime you want to come over we'll get down to business. I have some of our top models –"

"Actually, I was going to take tomorrow off. I have a grandmother who comes from Longford."

"Longford?" Chloe repeated.

"Yeah, so I'm going to hire a car and check out the place she comes from. My roots." He laughed loudly.

She hadn't expected Boris to be the type of man to waste time on such sentimentality. "Yes, you should take this opportunity to see the country."

"I aim to."

"I have a friend who runs a car-hire firm. Leave it to me and I'll sort it out for you," Chloe offered.

"There's really no need – the concierge –"

"I insist."

Chloe didn't find it hard to get her own way with people. She could either charm, bully or fool people into getting what she wanted. She suspected Boris Stein was a different type of animal from what she was used to. She would have to be ultra-careful and clever to make sure she got this merger. It was a pleasant evening and she and Aran sat on the verandah at the back of the Murphy house. Aran was engrossed in a novel. She looked out at the extensive gardens, engrossed in her strategy for Boris Stein. That initial reaction she had to him had disturbed her but she was now back in control. As Larry Hennessy had pointed out, she and Aran weren't love's young dream. But she didn't want that. She was comfortable when she was in control of her emotions, her life and her relationship. That reaction she had to Boris made her realise it all the more.

"I have an important business associate over from New York," she said.

"Really?" Aran was uninterested.

"I hoped we could go out to dinner with him during the week. Brendan Macken and his wife could be there too."

He pulled a face. "I hate that kind of thing. Think I'll give it a miss."

Chloe's expression didn't alter. "It's entirely up to you. But it could be an enjoyable evening as well as beneficial to my career."

Aran considered if he had said the same thing to Audrey, she would have flown into a rant and reminded him of every function she had attended for his benefit.

Muriel stepped out onto the verandah. "Did I hear you mention going out for dinner?"

"Yes, I have a business associate over from New York. He runs the Regency agency."

"Sounds fascinating company. And you mentioned Brendan Macken as well. We haven't seen Brendan or his lovely wife in an age. Why not invite them over here to the house for dinner?"

"That's very kind, but I couldn't impose," said Chloe.

"No trouble at all," reassured Muriel, silencing any further objection from Aran with a withering look.

"A dinner party?" asked Audrey.

"Yeah, at our place. To help get Stein on our side."

"Just the four of us and Stein?" Audrey felt sick at the thought of the four of them being together. What with the natural animosity between Aran and Peter, and the obvious dislike between herself and Lynn. And the ghost of what happened between herself and Peter hovering over the whole evening.

"I don't think so." She shook her head.

"We need to secure this merger. He could get to know us all a lot better over dinner."

"That's what I'm afraid of!"

"It'll be fine. And Lynn could impress him with her charm."

How deluded thought Audrey.

After much more cajoling, Audrey agreed. Now the difficult part was convincing Aran to go, she thought, as she picked up her phone and rang him.

"Hi hon, how are you?" she asked,

"All the better for hearing from you."

"I've a favour to ask. You know the guy who flew over from London, the one we hope to merge with?"

"Not really, but go on."

"Peter is organising a dinner party for us at his place on Friday to help the deal go smoothly."

"Forget it!" What had he suddenly become, he wondered. Arm-candy for dinner parties?

"Oh, Aran!" she raised her voice.

"I'm not spending an evening with Reynolds, end of story."

"Why can't you just do this one small thing for me?" She knew there wasn't much point in arguing with him. Besides, it might be for the best as it would probably be less strained without him. "Suit yourself then. What time are you picking me up from work?"

"I can't tonight. I'm working late," he said, remembering he was going to the theatre with Chloe.

"Well, come by whatever time you're finished. I've marinated that steak for you."

He had forgotten about the damned steak! In fact, looking at his diary he was pretty much tied up with Chloe for the rest of the week.

"OK, I'll go for dinner at Reynolds' on Friday."

"Really?"

"It shows how much I care for you that I'm prepared to sit through dinner with that fool."

She was surprised. "Thank you, Aran."

"But I won't be able to go if I don't make some headway with this case I'm working on, so I'll be working late for the rest of the week."

CHAPTER 86

Reception rang up to Boris's room the next morning to inform him his hired car had arrived. He pulled on a sports jacket and headed downstairs.

"There's a car waiting for me somewhere here," he informed one of the doormen.

He suddenly heard a loud horn blowing and looking up he saw Chloe waving at him from a white Mercedes.

"Great car." He sauntered over to her. "You didn't have to deliver it personally."

"It's my car. And I plan to escort you to County Longford personally."

"Huh?" He raised a quizzical eyebrow.

"Sit in. I'm your chauffeur for the day."

"So, who's minding the office?" Boris asked as they reached the outskirts of Dublin and began to speed down country roads.

"Who's minding your office?" she shot back.

"Good point," he conceded. "But aren't you the one trying to impress me, not the other way around? Shouldn't you be showing me you are a workaholic chained to your desk?"

"I think we are both checking if we will be compatible with each other. As for being a workaholic, I actually am one. But if you get the same results for being an hour at your desk instead of ten, then I would consider the other nine hours to have been wasted. It's results that matter at the end of the day, don't you agree?"

"Couldn't agree more."

"So no Mrs Stein?" asked Chloe.

"There is somewhere. We're divorced."

"Nobody else?" She was genuinely curious.

"I am seeing someone, a photographer. Nothing serious. I don't like things getting overly serious. It makes it too painful for them when you move on."

"You are very sure of yourself." She manoeuvred a bend in the road. "I suppose you date lots of models."

"I did when I was younger. I like to think my tastes have matured. I see photographers now, or fashion editors, PRs . . ." He looked at her and she felt a tingle of excitement. "I need more than just a pretty face. I need someone to intrigue me and they are far and few between, I can assure you. What about you?"

"I have a long-term partner."

"He's in the business?"

"No, he's a lawyer."

Audrey looked incredulously at Vanessa and said, "But you can't leave!"

"Yes, I can and I am."

"But this week of all weeks! With Stein over!"

"That's your problem not mine. I'm going over to Boom."

"As a booker?"

"No. Working in the office here was only short-term,

something you have forgotten. I need an agent who will concentrate on my proper career."

"This is because we won't push you with Stein, isn't it?" asked Peter.

"One of the reasons, yes."

"He saw all your photos – he just didn't want to meet you," Audrey explained.

"I don't want to hear your excuses. Chloe Gallagher thinks I have a big future ahead of me. You are going to be sorry about this. I'm going to be a famous model and a great actress someday." Vanessa turned and trotted down the stairs, her head held high.

"A great actress?" said Peter. "She has a barely speaking role as a barmaid on a soap."

"I feel guilty – maybe we could have pushed her more."

"We've done a lot for her. She never thought about modelling before us and it was us that got her that soap part. Not to mention the good salary she was getting for working in the office," said Peter.

"She's just frustrated. She wants so much and her talent and ability won't allow it. But you never know, determination alone can get you there."

"Anyway, she's gone. So what are we going to do now?" asked Peter.

"Mark is really blossoming as a booker. Let's see if he wants to take on more hours, and I'll contact a recruitment agency for a temp."

They stopped off for lunch at a pub beside the Shannon. They tucked into salmon salad sitting out on a patio while the river swayed past below.

"I suppose I do know Peter Reynolds quite well," said Chloe. "He used to work for us at Macken Communications as a junior exec. Very nice guy, couldn't really say anything bad about him. I was surprised he had the confidence to branch out on his own. He never showed that kind of ambition or ability with us."

Boris drank some beer. "No?"

"He's from some farming background. I'd say he would have been quite happy down on the farm if he hadn't married who he married."

"And who did he marry?"

"An ambitious woman who pushed him to succeed all the time. I worry about him sometimes because I think it's all too much for him. They even had a separation recently – he's not good under pressure."

"He seems pretty on top of things to me."

"Oh, yes he is . . . for now."

"And do you know Audrey?"

Chloe gave a little laugh. "Of course. She was a fixture on the modelling and social circuit here for years," Chloe took a sip of white wine."Before her alcohol problem got in the way. It's a pity really because she could have gone a lot further. She's a beautiful woman, let's face it. But as I said she has a problem. Some people are like that, they can't take success. They reach a certain level and then press the self-destruct button."

"You don't make them sound very reliable people to go into business with."

"I'm sorry." Chloe held up her hands. "I'm speaking off the record. I don't want anything I am saying to affect your judgement in any way."

"Considerate of you . . . I guess there's no self-destruct button with you?"

"No, I believe that if you are frightened of success then success will be frightened of you."

He leaned forward. "You seem to be able to tell me a lot about them, but nothing about their competition."

"Competition? Me? What's there to tell? I just live such a boring life. There's just work and Aran, my partner, that's all." She laughed lightly. "I'm so dull I sometimes wish I had this exciting, unpredictable, dangerous personality like Audrey Driver, but I don't."

Boris's penetrative eyes tried to see beyond Chloe's mask, to see behind it, but he couldn't.

Finally finding the little village where Boris's grandmother came from, Chloe parked in the main street. Some locals directed them to a derelict cottage that was Boris's ancestral home.

Standing among the ruins Boris said, "She spoke with that Irish accent all her life, despite decades living in the States."

Chloe feigned interest as she examined the stone walls.

"She used to speak so lovingly of this place. She made it out to be like paradise."

"It has a pretty view." It was all Chloe could think to say, secretly wishing he would hurry up as she spotted rain clouds in the distance. Then she thought of a plausible question. "You were close to her?"

"Sure. She doted on me. All my family are close. Aren't yours?"

Chloe thought of the detached relationship she had with her family. And it suited her that way. Looking at Boris who seemed to have had a charmed and warm childhood and life, he would never understand that she was now a different person from when she was growing up. And now she enjoyed the distant but tranquil relationship she had with her family.

"I don't mean to rush you," she said. "But there are rain

clouds coming this way and we are quite a distance from the car."

The rain was teeming down by the time she drove up to The Berkeley Court.

"Thanks, you've been a wonderful tour guide," he complimented.

"Everything is ready for you in Boom whenever you want to come by."

"Wednesday OK? It's just I'm at Spinner tomorrow."

"Wednesday's fine. Also, Thursday night, you are invited to a dinner party with my partner and his family. Brendan Macken will be there as well so it would be a good opportunity for you to meet each other."

"Sounds good," he said, jumping out of the car. He sprinted through the rain into the hotel. He was tired and wanted a drink, so ordered room service when he got to his bedroom. As he dried his hair from the rain he thought about Chloe Gallagher. He had pried and probed but there was no way of getting beyond that wall she had around her. She was super-confident, that he was sure of. But strangely for an industry full of people who loved to talk , who were always happy to talk incessantly about themselves, Chloe was very clever at not giving away any personal information.

And for somebody like Boris who needed to know and understand people and know what made them tick, she was beginning to irk him. He was intrigued about meeting her partner on Thursday.

CHAPTER 87

A recruitment agency sent over a temp who was immediately installed behind reception at Spinner. They were expecting Boris Stein in that day and there was an exciting buzz about the place.

"Mark!" roared Peter.

Mark came bounding into the front office.

"Mark, show the new receptionist the ropes and when Stein comes in make sure it's you who greets him and shows him in, OK?"

"No probs, Peter."

"I like your colour scheme," Boris remarked as Mark showed him down the corridor to Peter's office.

"Pretty trendy, all right." Mark knocked on Peter's door and opened it.

Boris sauntered in and said, "So, show me what you've got to offer."

Boris pored over the model books, taking in everything from lighting, poses and the models themselves. Having started off as a photographer gave him a natural advantage in seeing whether a model was genuinely good or whether it was trick photography.

"I thought it best that you meet the models separately," said Peter as he and Audrey showed Boris into the front office.

"That's fine by me."

Tiffany came in first and Audrey could see the interest light up on Boris's face. First, he chatted away to her, asking her about her background and what she hoped for in the future. He asked her to stand up and peered closely at her face. Asking her to open her mouth and holding her jaw tightly, he examined her mouth as Peter and Audrey looked on silently. Finally he got her to walk up and down endlessly as he took down notes.

He put all the models through a similar process. He was grabbed by Ivanka's striking looks and taken by Leslie's glamour.

Audrey was surprised by Boris's reaction to a young fifteen-year-old called Catherine who they had recently signed up. Audrey was in the process of grooming her and believed she had a big future ahead of her.

"She could never make it with us," Boris said flatly.

"But why? She's gorgeous."

"Sure she is. But her upper lip is a fraction smaller than her lower one. It would look all wrong in photos."

Finally the procession was over.

"You have some girls who could make it straight away," Boris declared. "You know who I'm talking about. Tiffany and Ivanka are excellent. You also have a few that aren't there yet but will be soon."

Peter and Audrey were delighted and they spent the next couple of hours going through their work history, accounts and client base with Boris.

After that they brought Boris over to a studio where the band which Spinner was now consultant for, thanks to Maeve, were shooting a video. The band was called Backtalk and Peter had arranged for Tiffany to star in their video.

"Who are these guys?" Boris asked as he watched the teenagers being put through their motions.

"We are doing PR for them for their record label. They've had a couple of hits in the UK and on the continent, but their management feels their image isn't right and wants to make them more directed – that's where we come in. We're also deciding what kind of press they should be looking for."

"They are going to be the next big Irish pop act," Audrey said confidently as the five members danced around Tiffany as the cameras rolled.

"How did you get this job?" Boris was impressed.

"Contacts," Peter said honestly.

"Thank you both," said Boris as they dropped him back to his hotel. "Tomorrow I'm at Boom."

"We would like to invite you to dinner on Friday at my home," said Peter. "Just a chance for you to relax and get to know us a bit better."

Boris happily agreed and strode into the hotel.

"Well?" asked Audrey.

"Seemed to go all right. It all depends on what kind of a show Chloe puts on."

Chloe stood in front of the whole staff at Boom.

"I want to see everyone run off their feet when Boris Stein is here. I want everyone talking on phones and I want to hear you all agreeing to big deals, true or fictitious, I don't care. So get to work."

Noise zoomed around the office as everyone followed

orders. Chloe arranged for some of the established models to sit at reception to give the impression they were coming for first interviews.

"Are the girls we are introducing to Stein all set to go?" Chloe questioned Ben.

"Everything is under control," he assured her.

"Good." She was beginning to like Ben. He was one of the few people who managed to carry out her orders to perfection – something his quiet and slightly shy personality wouldn't have indicated.

Chloe's phone rang. "Yeah? OK." She put down the phone. "He's coming down the street. Make sure everyone is in place."

Ben dashed around to give a final check.

As Boris walked in to the reception at Boom he was struck by the noise level. Then he was struck by the gorgeous girls obviously lined up for interviews.

"One second and I'll put you through," said the receptionist as she manned the switchboard. "Good morning, Boom, and how can I help you . . . one second and I'll put you through." She looked up at Boris with a bright smile. "Can I help you?"

"I'm here to see Ms Gallagher."

"Certainly, and your name is?"

"Boris Stein."

"Take a seat, please," said the receptionist before ringing in to Chloe and then continuing with her flashing switchboard.

Smoothing down her white suit, Chloe walked into Reception.

"Boris!" she stretched out her hand.

As he shook her hand, again that electric shock ran through her body. She ignored it.

"Welcome to Boom. I'll start off by just giving you a quick tour of the place."

She took her time showing him around. He took in the enormous photos of their most famous models blazing down from the walls.

"That's my final offer," said Ben as Boris passed him by. "No way, I'm not lowering my asking price. That's the rate card, take it or leave it . . . cool, I'll book her in for Monday the eighth then. I'll fax you through the booking form." From what Boris could hear all the bookers were making similar exciting deals.

"Coffee?" asked Chloe as she showed him into her office and closed the door.

Noticing the glass walls around her office Boris said "I guess you like to keep an eye on what's happening."

"It's not my style to be cut off."

"I'll have that coffee. But you seem to rely on your staff a lot – do you do any bookings yourself?"

Chloe wasn't sure what the correct answer to this question should be. She didn't want to come across as removed from the deal-making but wanted to come across as a capable senior manager. Knowing that Peter and Audrey dealt with most of their bookings themselves, she chose her words carefully.

"Of course I do bookings. But we have far too many clients for me to be able to handle even ten per cent of them. I ensure this agency is run correctly which means having excellent models and bookers. But I do handle the bigger deals myself."

Boris nodded.

"So what do you want to see first. Models, photos, accounts?"

"Let's start with the models."

Boris put the models through similar paces as the routine at Spinner.

"Your hair is a great colour," he complimented Alison, admiring her flowing locks. "Natural?"

Alison looked affronted. "Yes."

"What kind of work have you been doing?"

"Everything from fashion shows to photo calls."

"You enjoy it?"

"Love it." She nodded happily.

"How would you feel if you got some bookings in New York. Would you be able to leave Dublin and head over?"

"Like a shot! Who'd miss an opportunity like that?"

"Alison is the daughter of one of our more famous politicians, Ronan Flatley," Chloe informed him.

Looking uninterested in this news, Boris continued, "How did you start modelling?"

"I joined the Spinner Agency, then I met Chloe on a fashion shoot and she asked me to join Boom . . ."Alison's voice trailed off as she saw the look of horror on Chloe's face.

"So you were actually discovered by Spinner?" asked Boris.

"Well, yes . . . I mean no. . ." Alison didn't know what to say, as she became very aware of Chloe's furious expression. Alison's confidence evaporated.

"Thanks, Alison," said Boris and once she had left he turned to Chloe. "Do you make a habit of poaching models?"

Chloe attempted to not look angry. "Absolutely not. We have no need to. Alison did some work for Spinner but was unimpressed by their unprofessional setup, so she joined us. Sorry, could you excuse me for a minute?" Boris looked after her in amusement.

"Tell all the girls," Chloe hissed at Ben, "if they came

from other agencies they are to say to Stein they came to us first because we are the best. Or we personally discovered them in the street, or a store or the fucking airport lounge, for all I care. As long as they say to Stein they owe everything to us, got it?" Swinging around and fixing a smile on her face, she walked back into her office.

Chloe cringed as she watched Vanessa. Her hair seemed to be bigger and blonder than ever, her make-up heavier, and she was squeezed into a ridiculously low top that was the colours of the American flag. In spite of the invaluable information Vanessa had given her about Spinner, how could she have allowed her to meet Stein?

"I'm mainly doing photo shoots," Vanessa informed Boris. "I star in a very popular soap opera here, so I'm big in demand for the tabloids. You know the kind of stuff, big smile and chest out. But that scene is beginning to piss me off. I'm a serious actress, Boris, and a serious model. I want to do *Vogue* and that kinda stuff." Vanessa also seemed to have adopted a strange American accent for Boris's benefit.

Chloe raised her eyes to heaven.

"And how do you feel about working in the States?" asked Boris.

Vanessa smoothed down her star-spangled-coloured top. "It's my dream to work there. I'd love to work on Broadway."

"Thanks for meeting me," said Boris, who had been grinning through the interview.

"The pleasure was entirely mine." Vanessa shook his hand, bending forward enough to give him an ample view of her cleavage. She winked at him and left.

"I'm so sorry for that. I told Ben not to bring her in to you –" explained Chloe.

"I like her," Boris interrupted. "The girl has sheer naked ambition. Sure, her image is over the top. But she's got plenty of chutzpah. She ain't *Vogue*, but with the right management she could go far. Word of advice, Chloe, never, ever, talk down your models."

Chloe fell into a silence before saying, "Do you want to see the accounts?"

CHAPTER 88

Whenever Chloe was due to spend a long evening at the Murphy house, Muriel always had a room prepared for her to stay in. It would be unthinkable for Muriel even to suggest Chloe stay in Aran's room. For the dinner party for Boris, Chloe selected a black cocktail dress to wear which she quickly changed into in her room at the Murphys. It was 7.30 and Boris, Brendan Macken and his wife were due to arrive at eight.

She put on her earrings and went to the bedroom's long windows that offered views of the extensive gardens. The Murphys seemed to take it for granted that Aran and his future bride would live with them in Howth. Chloe knew such an arrangement wouldn't be to everybody's taste, but she would enjoy living there. Muriel had made a few references about inviting Chloe's parents over, as it was about time they all met each other.

Luckily, her parents' once-in-a-lifetime world cruise was due to last a long time yet, an excuse that had impressed Muriel. Chloe would plan the meeting of the clans with acute precision. There would be so many people there that there wouldn't be much opportunity for the two families to talk very much. She would need a crowd to distract Muriel's excellent sense of observation from realising Chloe's parents were nice, safe but incredibly dull people.

Chloe was glad Brendan was attending that night's dinner party. It would make him realise how close she was now to the Murphys, which would help rehabilitate her in his eyes. And the merger between Boom and Regency would mark the end of all her troubles. Once she was freed from Boom, she would be able to resume her normal position at Macken. She would just act as a figurehead at Boom, leaving the day-to-day running of the agency to somebody else, somebody unthreatening, but excellent at their job, who was totally in awe of her. Ben seemed to be the best candidate for that job.

Aran knocked on her door and walked in, dressed in a suit.

"I'm sorry for putting you through this evening," she said, kissing him on the cheek.

"It's all right, I suppose." He was still sulking. "You ready?"

"Yes."

They held hands and walked down the main staircase.

Muriel watched them descend the stairs and felt content with their union.

"You make a very handsome couple," she complimented.

"Thank you, you look great yourself." said Chloe. It wasn't a lie – Muriel always looked elegant.

"I actually invited Larry Hennessy to join us this evening," informed Muriel.

Chloe froze. "Is he coming?"

"Unfortunately not. He said he had already made prior

arrangements. I don't think he's fully recovered from that flu he had."

Feeling relieved, Chloe followed Muriel and Aran into the parlour and was surprised to find Brendan and his wife already there. They greeted each other warmly, Brendan even trying to make a joke. Chloe knew it was his way of trying to smooth over the recent difficulty at work. She also immediately detected a change in attitude towards her from Brendan. She was Brendan Macken's protégée. He had given her all the opportunities she had received. Brendan had enabled her to become who she was. It was he who had first realised and respected her talent and rewarded her accordingly. But at the end of the day, no matter how powerful she had become, she was still his employee. That divide was always there. But tonight, in the Murphy house, that divide vanished. His wife, Rose, sat with a sherry perched on her knee. In all her time at Macken, Chloe had only met Rose on a few occasions. This very quiet woman shunned all kinds of glamorous settings. Her posture that night was stiff; her expression was uncomfortable. She was trying to smile, but the ends of her mouth drooped down. She had tried to dress up, but still looked old-fashioned in a black lace dress that reached somewhere between her knee and ankle. Chloe wondered if Rose had once been a carefree young girl, whose spirit had been broken by Brendan's sternness. Muriel was oblivious to Rose's shyness, and spoke relentlessly about a charity lunch she was in the middle of putting together. Rose's only socialising was to support charity events, and she knew Muriel quite well through her charity work. But the two were polar opposites. Reginald and Brendan chatted away like the old friends they were. As Chloe mixed freely with them, she marvelled at the divide she had crossed. The divide from a middle-class suburb to the elite who had serious power and money.

The rain poured down as the taxi negotiated the bendy roads of Howth.

Boris Stein looked out of the car window and was impressed by the mansions they was passing.

"This is it," said the taxi driver, pulling over.

Boris pulled on his raincoat, threw some money at the driver and raced up the drive to the steps of the house. He waited patiently for somebody to answer the doorbell.

He kept knocking until a man answered the door. "Yes?"

"I'm here for the dinner party," he shouted over the rain, as a crack of lightning lit up the sky above him.

"What dinner party?"

It wasn't the kind of neighbourhood people walked around casually asking for directions. Neither was it the kind of place where taxi drivers cruised by looking for fares. But it was the kind of place that a series of Mercedes and BMWs drove past, splashing water from the road surface all over Boris as he walked down roads anxiously looking for the Murphy house. The rain continued to pelt down on him. He cursed the taxi driver and tried ringing Chloe from his mobile again, but it just rang out.

". . .and until we start investing the same kind of money into cricket, tennis and show jumping that we do with football, then of course we aren't going to be getting the same kind of viewing figures on television," commented Reginald, standing at the fireplace.

"It's really a shame the other sports aren't having the

same draw they used to have," said Muriel, "but now it's all soccer, soccer, soccer."

"Maybe other sports just need to up their PR," said Chloe. "We should get on the case, Brendan."

"True for you," laughed Muriel. Everyone nodded their heads in agreement except for Rose who just sipped her sherry and only occasionally looked up from the floor. Chloe caught Rose staring at her a couple of times with an expression she couldn't figure out but could have been dislike or envy.

"I don't care what anyone says, you can't beat a good day at the races," said Muriel.

They only stopped talking when they noticed a tall broad man standing in the doorway of the parlour dripping wet.

"Have I missed dinner?" asked Boris. What confused everybody was that even though Boris was drenched, he was grinning from ear to ear.

"Your waist is bigger than mine so I'm not sure if I've anything to fit you," said Aran as he looked through his wardrobe. "You would probably have been better getting something from my father's clothes – more your type of thing."

Boris immediately detected hostile vibes from Aran.

"Some place you have here," said Boris stripping off his Armani suit. "You been seeing Chloe for long?"

Aran looked bored and ignored the question. He pulled out a suit and threw it at Boris. "This will do you. It was a gift from an ex–girlfriend – it was always too big for me. Don't be long. Dinner is late enough as it is." And Aran walked away.

"How is he?" asked Chloe with concern. They were all seated at the dinner table when Aran returned.

"Idiot. How could he not find the right house?" Aran sat down abruptly.

"It was obviously the taxi-man's fault." It was the first thing Rose had said all evening and everyone turned to look at her.

Boris had just stridden into the dining-room and gave Rose an appreciative look.

"You poor man," said Muriel. "Such a night to get lost in."

Lightning lit up the night sky followed by a quick crack of thunder.

"I brought the weather with me," Boris said, sitting into the vacant seat he assumed was for him.

"Now, Mr Stein, forget all about your unpleasant journey here. Relax, enjoy the food and the company and tell us all about your exciting life in New York." Muriel smiled warmly and filled his glass with red wine.

As delicious as the duckling and wine was, Boris found the whole evening a chore. The only thing of interest was watching the interaction between Chloe and Aran. There was no chemistry between them. Even couples who fought and argued a lot still had chemistry. But there was no spark between these two, Boris was sure of that. As dessert was being served, Boris excused himself and went out into the hall. He opened one of the back doors and slipped out onto the verandah where he lit up a cigar while watching the lightning and thunder.

After dessert, the party moved into the parlour and Chloe took the opportunity to go and find Boris. Seeing a back door ajar, she slipped a shawl around her shoulders and went out.

"I'd have thought you'd seen enough rain tonight," she said, disturbing his gazing into the sky.

He waved his cigar. "I didn't know what the smoking policy was in the house."

"Very thoughtful of you. You can smoke inside. Let's join the others."

"Nah! I think I need a break."

Alarm-bells rang for Chloe. She moved near, an expression of concern on her face. "You aren't enjoying the evening?"

"Well, I really appreciate the great rounds everyone went to for me. But that kind of company just bores me."

"What kind of company?"

"Well, you have Reg and Brendan, two obviously very rich and powerful men who never tire of letting the world know that fact. Then you have Muriel, quite happy to bask in her husband's reflected glory, and then you have poor old Rose who is totally unhappy to bask in her husband's. Then you have the lovely Aran who obviously wants to be here less than I do and can't resist getting his nasty comments in whenever he can."

"I hope this lack of . . . clicking isn't going to jeopardise our possible merger?"

Boris threw his cigar into the gardens and laughed. "Business before everything, huh? As long as the merger isn't jeopardised, that's the main thing, hey? I'll base my decision on a merger on what's right for Regency and not some stuck-up dinner party."

"Good." Chloe was relieved.

"So tell me. Who will you end up like in thirty years' time, Muriel or Rose? With this marriage you're contemplating."

"I never said anything about marriage," said Chloe.

"Oh, so no marriage?"

"In thirty years' time I hope I'm neither of them. I would hope to be myself, Chloe Gallagher."

Boris laughed loudly. "I don't doubt it for a minute. You'll be Chloe Gallagher all right . . . whoever she might be" He came nearer so his face was inches from hers and stared into her eyes. "Who are you?"

She felt herself go weak from the intensity of his eyes.

"We'd better go back in," he said and placed his hands on her shoulders. She shivered at his touch and, noticing her response, he looked at her curiously.

"They'll be wondering where we got to," she said, pulling quickly away.

"Goodbye and we hope everything is to your satisfaction with Boom so we can push ahead with the merger," Brendan said, shaking Boris's hand.

Boris then shook Rose's hand. To his surprise her grip was very strong and lasted longer than the norm. He smiled down at her and saw pain in her eyes as tears welled up. Boris's smile turned to concern, but suddenly Brendan and Rose were gone to their awaiting car.

"Mrs Murphy, the dinner was wonderful," said Boris.

"The pleasure was entirely ours," answered Muriel.

"And so pleasant to meet you." Boris said sarcastically to Aran. "I'll have the suit returned to you tomorrow."

"Don't bother, I don't need it any more." There was no tone of generosity in Aran's voice.

"I'll talk to you tomorrow," Boris said to Chloe before running down the steps to his taxi. Chloe stood at the doorway watching as the taxi turned and drove off.

CHAPTER 89

On the front page of *The Sun* the next morning, the headline read: "Top Model Is A Lap Dancer".

The article read: *"Ivanka Popova, top model with Spinner Agency, is exposed today as living a double life. By day she is a highly paid model who is the face of posh fashion-group House of Opera. By night she doubles by working in a sleazy Dublin lap-dancing club where she gyrates in front of customers for money."*

Chloe continued to read the article with complete satisfaction. The piece had been written exactly as she had instructed, mentioning Spinner as much as possible. Ben's visit to a lap-dancing club on a stag night, had paid an excellent dividend.

The first Audrey heard of the scandal was when Jackie Davenport rang her and started screaming down the phone.

"How dare you not vet your models properly! I've put my name and reputation on the line promoting your agency and your models. I've featured Ivanka numerous times in *Quest* and recommended her for the House of

Opera job. She's a bloody lap-dancer! It's in *The Sun*! Do you know what that does to my reputation?"

As Jackie continued with her diatribe, Audrey covered the phone and shouted to Mark to get a copy of *The Sun*. Mark promptly entered her office looking concerned and handed over the paper.

Still listening to Jackie screaming in her ear, Audrey began to digest the front page.

As Boris bought his cigars from the shop in the hotel, he did a double-take at the news-stand. Recognising Ivanka's photo, he picked up the paper and began to read.

His mobile phone rang. "Yeah?"

"Boris, Chloe here. Just wondering if you needed to see anything else at Boom?"

"No, I've seen everything I need to."

"I don't know if you've got today's papers, but there's a headline you might want to see," Chloe informed him.

"I've already seen it."

"We can sue them, the bastards – they can't make up lies like this." Peter's face was engulfed with anger.

Ivanka sat opposite him and Audrey, in tears.

"I'll call our solicitor now." He reached for the phone.

"Wait!" Audrey was studying Ivanka's tear-stained face. "They are lies, aren't they, Ivanka?"

Ivanka sighed deeply and shook her head. "No!"

Peter put down the phone and stared at her in disbelief. "We've already had House of Opera on cancelling your contract. Why, Ivanka?"

She wiped away her tears. "For the money, of course. Why else? I've a child to support back in Latvia."

"But you've been earning good money here modelling.

And it was only just beginning." Peter couldn't understand.

"The money from the modelling has only started coming in recently. You can't imagine how much I earn dancing. I couldn't bring myself to give up the cash. All I have is my body. I have to earn as much with it while I can."

"But –" Peter started.

"Please don't judge me. You have no right to judge me. You don't know where I'm from. I had nothing growing up, except my dreams. I tried to get a work visa to any country in western Europe or America. My daughter, I wanted her to have all the things I didn't. I always so wanted to be a model. Finally I got a visa to Ireland. I got a job in a bar while I tried to break into modelling and I was asked if I wanted to work in the lap-dancing club. I couldn't say no to the money."

"But Ivanka, you were earning a good wage here, why didn't you stop it?" Peter was exasperated.

"Sure, I was earning money with you guys. But the money as a dancer was so good, and I was saving it for my daughter's future.

After Ivanka left, Audrey and Peter sat staring at each other.

"I feel so depressed," said Audrey, "that she had to resort to lap-dancing."

"But she's wrecked her whole future, just out of greed for the money."

"Greed? Were you listening to her at all? Nobody does something like that unless they have to. We don't know what she's been through or what she's had to do. She's not Alison Flatley, doing modelling for her own ego, because she comes from a rich background. Ivanka had to rely on the way she looked to earn money, whether that was lap-dancing or modelling, and I just feel really disillusioned about our whole industry."

"What the hell are you talking about? There's no comparison between modelling and lap-dancing."

"Why? They both revolve around looks, don't they? Selling dreams to the young who will do anything to get there."

"Whatever about dreams, we've been left with one big nightmare. This is really bad PR that has tarnished our reputation. House of Opera are going mad. God knows what Stein thinks."

Lynn was juggling a very busy day at The Gallery with trying to organise that evening's dinner party. The caterers were at the apartment preparing the food.

Peter, of course, had been no help at all. She had phoned him to request he get fresh flowers, but he had made up some excuse about there being some crisis.

As usual, everything would be left to her. However, mindful of the importance of this merger, she didn't care and was putting her heart into it. She hadn't said anything to Peter, but as soon as the merger went through, Lynn would concentrate on kicking Audrey out of Spinner. A man of around sixty came into The Gallery and smiled over at her. It was a twinkly-eyed, flirtatious smile and he started to examine the works displayed.

"Can I help you?" she asked after five minutes, rising from her desk and approaching him.

"I'm looking for something by Rory Ryan," said the man. She felt his eyes sweep her up and down.

"I'm afraid I can't help. Rory is producing very little at the moment," said Lynn. Mainly because he's stoned out of his mind all the time, she thought.

"Pity. Maybe you could advise me on something similar. I'm looking for something for my office."

"Sure." She pondered for a second. "What kind of business is it?"

"A solicitor's office. I'm Larry Hennessy." He put out his hand and she shook it. His grip lasted a little too long and was a little too tight.

As Audrey waited for a taxi in her apartment that evening she was in foul form.

The day had gone from bad to worse. Contracts had been cancelled with clients concerned over the Ivanka scandal. The press had been on all day looking to further sensationalise the story. All she wanted to do was stay home and relax. To make matters worse, Aran had called and said he was delayed at the office and she should go ahead to Peter's alone and he would meet her there. But what she was dreading most was spending an evening in Lynn's company.

Lynn tasted the food bubbling away in the kitchen. The caterers had done a wonderful job and had now left. The setting of the table, the flowers, the whole ambiance was breathtaking. She lit up a cigarette.

"Unless he makes a point of the Ivanka thing, don't bring it up," Lynn advised as Peter came out from the bedroom fixing his tie.

"Of course, I won't. But what do you think the chances of him not knowing are?"

She sighed. "Try and look on the bright side, will you?"

The doorbell rang and Peter gulped back some wine before answering it.

"Hi!" Audrey stood in the doorway.

"No Aran?" asked Peter.

"He'll be over in a little while. He was held up at the office." She stepped inside and handed him her coat.

Lynn stood in the middle of the lounge, smoking, with a condescending look plastered across her face.

"Hi, Lynn," Audrey said, as she came down the steps.

"Audrey." Lynn nodded. "Wine?"

"Red, please."

Lynn handed her a glass and the three sat down in silence.

Aran rushed back to Howth, changed clothes and jumped into his car heading into town. He cursed Audrey for forcing him to go to something he disliked.

After the previous night's adventure, Boris made sure he was in plenty of time. The sun had been shining all day, drying up the previous torrential rain.

When Boris rang the doorbell, the three of them were delighted that the uncomfortable silence was broken.

Peter jumped up to answer the door.

"I hope you found the place all right," said Peter taking Boris's coat.

"No problem at all." He went and greeted Audrey with a kiss on the cheek.

"And this is my wife, Lynn," Peter introduced.

"What will you have to drink, Boris?" asked Lynn. Audrey noticed Lynn's personality had metamorphosed from sour to sweet.

"You got any vodka?"

"Absolutely." She fixed him his drink.

"My boyfriend will be along shortly," said Audrey.

"Something smells good," Boris commented. Noticing the cigarette in Lynn's hand, he was grateful there didn't seem to be a no-smoking policy here.

"It's a goulash," informed Lynn.

Twenty minutes later and Audrey's temper was rising. Lynn was completely dominating the conversation, and completely ignoring her.

"Are you in the business?" asked Boris.

"No, I'm an art dealer," said Lynn. "Are you interested in art at all?"

"I suppose the business I'm in revolves around photography. That's art, isn't it?"

The doorbell rang and Peter got up to answer it.

As Aran walked past Peter, he didn't bother trying to hide his disdain for him.

Peter remembered the confrontation when Aran accused him of wanting to bed Audrey. He had thought it ridiculous at the time. Little did he know how the situation would develop.

"You got held up?" Peter asked, as he took his coat.

"What's it to you?" Aran whispered menacingly before turning and stepping down into the lounge. "Sorry I'm late, everyone."

Audrey was delighted he had arrived. She was half expecting him to ring and say he couldn't make it.

"Hi, honey." Aran kissed her.

"Boris, this is my partner, Aran Murphy," introduced Audrey.

Boris stood up and turned around and the two men stared at each other.

"Have we met before?" asked Boris.

Aran couldn't answer for a while and then stuttered, "No, I don't think so."

"Aran has one of those faces. Common, I think the word for it is," Audrey teased, putting her arm around his waist.

Boris looked at the others to try and establish what was going on, but everyone seemed to be acting normally. Only Aran stood looking pale and nervous.

"If you all want to take your seats, I'll start to serve dinner," said Lynn.

As Lynn continued to dominate the conversation, Audrey looked at her in disgust. She was speaking as if Spinner was hers. "The potential in this country is amazing," said Lynn. "Every time I walk down Grafton Street I see girls who could make it as top models."

"Modelling is a lot more than just looking good. You have to be able to perform for the camera. The camera has to love you," said Boris.

"Oh, I know that," said Lynn, "but good looks help as well, don't they?"

"Not necessarily," interrupted Audrey. "One of the best models I ever worked with certainly would never stand out in a crowd. But once she got in front of a camera, something came alive in her."

Boris nodded his agreement, while Lynn gave Audrey a displeased look.

"Peter, be a love and refill the glasses, please," instructed Lynn. "Aran, I met somebody who works with you today. Larry Hennessy came into the Gallery."

Aran hadn't muttered a word all evening. He had been terrified that Boris was going to challenge him immediately about Chloe and Audrey, but discretion seemed to have stopped him. He prayed the evening would end quickly and he could get away from Boris Stein. How could he have not realised Chloe and Audrey were talking about the same man? But even so, Chloe had said her business associate was coming from New York, while Audrey said hers had flown from London. How was he to know? The question now was, what would Boris do?

Would he blow his cover?

"L–Larry?" stuttered Aran. "Yeah, he collects art."

Lynn turned and smiled at Boris, ready to resume her conversation.

"Still handling Rory Ryan?" Audrey asked, her eyes blazing with mischief.

Peter's mouth fell open in disbelief as Lynn blushed. Her eyes filled with embarrassment which then gave way to fury.

"No, he's taking a rest from painting," Lynn spat.

Satisfied, Audrey took another mouthful of food.

"I see you had some bad press today," said Boris.

"Yes," said Peter carefully. "I suppose these things happen."

"They shouldn't happen. For the fashion house she was working for, it's a disaster to be associated with a stripper."

"Are you trying to tell me that all of Regency's models are whiter than white?" asked Audrey.

"Of course they aren't. Anything but. But we do have a PR machine to protect them from these kinds of stories breaking. What the hell was she doing in a strip club anyway?"

"She has a young child to feed," said Audrey. "And OK she was making good money with us, but coming from where she did she couldn't resist more. Our models aren't earning millions like yours are . . . yet."

"Our top earners might be earning millions, but we've

a lot who aren't in that league and they don't go dancing around poles," said Boris.

Lynn placed her hands on the table and began to nod as she spoke. "Boris is right. It was a terrible lapse to allow that story to break."

Audrey looked at Peter, willing him to tell his wife to shut up, but he said nothing.

"Well, we all learn from our mistakes," said Audrey.

"No more nasty surprises then?" asked Boris, and he looked at Aran meaningfully.

"Absolutely none," said Peter.

Audrey began to gather up the plates and carried them into the kitchen.

Lynn got up and followed her in.

"Are you trying to be clever with that smart comment about Rory Ryan?" Lynn hissed.

"It managed to shut you up for a minute," returned Audrey.

"I want Peter to get this merger and I'm doing everything I can to achieve it."

"Why don't you just let Peter go at his own pace?"

"I do," Lynn objected.

"Peter is a talented and good man. Why can't you just respect him for who he is like everyone else does?"

"I don't care to discuss my marriage with you."

"I saw what you did to Peter when you left him. It was me who saw him every day in the office," said Audrey.

Lynn lit up a cigarette. "As I said, I don't wish to discuss any part of my life with you." She turned slowly and walked back into the lounge, fixing a smile on her face.

"So, Boris" said Lynn sitting beside him, "an ex-wife, but not children?"

"No, never happened for me."

"Children can be a blessing, but they are hard work. I've said to Peter that before we even contemplate having children I want a full-time nanny," said Lynn. Audrey raised her eyes to heaven, as she joined Aran on the sofa. "I strongly believe in the Edwardian role model for parentage. A whole generation was brought up being seen and not heard, and you know there was nothing wrong with those people – they all went through life happy."

"Except they were used as cannon-fodder in world wars," said Audrey, getting up abruptly and heading to the bathroom.

Peter waited a minute and then followed her. He tapped on the bathroom door and Audrey opened it a slit to see who it was.

"Come in," she sighed and he slipped into the bathroom.

"What's wrong? You don't seem in good form?"

"Your wife, Peter, she's appalling! How can you stick her? She talks such shite!"

"She's only trying to impress Stein."

"For God's sake, Peter, I know I'm talking out of turn but I can't help it. You aren't yourself around her . . . I don't know, you're frightened of losing her or something. Wake up and take a good look at your life!"

"I'm heading back." He was annoyed.

"Peter, you told me you never thought you were good enough for Lynn. Let me tell you something: you're too good for her."

"Well, I'd better be going." Boris, looked down at his Rolex watch and rose from the couch.

"We'd better make tracks as well," said Audrey, dreading being left with Lynn, without Boris acting as a buffer-zone.

They got their coats and went to the door.

"Hopefully we'll be seeing a lot more of you," said Lynn. "Maybe next time in New York."

Boris nodded and thanked her for the hospitality. "I'll talk to you two tomorrow," he said glancing at Peter and then Audrey, before turning to Aran, nodding and leaving.

CHAPTER 90

The headline in *The Mirror* newspaper the next day read: "Model In Cocaine Collapse".

The article read: "Tiffany Cooper was rushed to hospital a month ago, it has been revealed, after she collapsed at a top Dublin nightspot after a cocaine overdose. The information has only come to light now as an ex-employee at the Spinner agency which represents Tiffany has decided to reveal the cover-up. Tiffany, who stars in the new Backtalk video, has been battling a serious cocaine addiction since arriving in Dublin from her native Derry. This is the second scandal to have hit the troubled agency in a week."

"Tiffany's not answering her phone still," said Audrey.

"It was obviously Vanessa who broke the story," said Peter. "Did you know anything about this?"

"Of course, I didn't. You know how worried I've been about Tiffany lately. This is all too coincidental. Two stories breaking in the week Stein is over, and Vanessa going over to Boom. Chloe is behind all this."

Peter sat down at his desk and put his head into his hands. "What are we going to say to Stein?"

Audrey looked at the expression on Peter's face and realised how bad the situation was. She had worried all night about meeting him this morning after her outburst in the bathroom about Lynn. She had meant every word she had said, but she had to learn to keep quiet.

Chloe read the article with satisfaction. She was expecting Boris into Boom in an hour and placed the paper on her desk to make sure he saw it.

"Never mind the article, I'm more concerned about something else. It's like this, Peter – I don't enjoy being made a fool of." Boris was speaking to Peter from the phone in his hotel room. "I don't know what kind of game you are all playing but obviously the laugh is on me."

"What are you talking about?" Peter was confused

"This charade being played out at the two dinner parties."

"What charade?"

"The charming Aran Murphy. What is he – Rent-a-Date or something?"

"You've totally lost me."

"I go to a dinner party at the Murphy house one night and Aran is introduced as Chloe Gallagher's partner and the next night he is at your place very much with Audrey. What's going on?"

"What!" Peter tried to digest the information. "Aran used to date Chloe for a while but that's long over now."

Peter spent a further ten minutes trying to assure Boris there was no conspiracy with a hidden agenda. Afterwards, he sat at his desk with the reality of what had happened slowly dawning on him.

He steadied himself and went into Audrey's office and closed the door.

"I just had Stein on the phone."

"What did he say about Tiffany?" she asked, full of concern.

"Nothing. He was more disturbed about something else. Audrey, I don't know how to tell you this, or even if I should. But it seems Aran is seeing Chloe behind your back."

Audrey blinked a few times. "Peter, that isn't even funny."

He reached over and held her hand. "God, Audrey, I wish I was joking, but I'm not. And Stein is making so much noise about it you're going to hear it anyway. I guess I'd prefer you to hear it from me."

Audrey snapped back her hand. "Peter, you aren't making sense. What the hell has Stein got to do with anything?"

"Chloe had a dinner party the night before last and Aran was there, very much her partner according to Stein."

"This is because of what I said about Lynn, isn't it? I'm sorry if I hurt you or your wife's feelings, but this is a lousy way to get back at me. OK, you've managed to hurt me – now are you satisfied?"

"You know I'd never make this up or do anything to hurt you," said Peter.

"He wouldn't do that to me. It's a nasty lie!" She blinked a few times before abruptly standing up and marching out.

"Where are you going to, Audrey?"

Ignoring him, she raced down the stairs and out on to the street, Peter in quick pursuit.

She hailed a passing taxi, hopped in and gave the driver Boom's address.

Peter got in after her "Don't do anything stupid, Audrey. I'm telling you for your own good –"

She ignored him and stared out the window.

"Audrey, what are you going to do?" persisted Peter.

"Will you shut up!" she shouted, causing the taxi driver to swerve with fright.

A million thoughts raced through Chloe's mind but her face remained expressionless. Boris sat across from her in her office, having confronted her with the same line of questioning he had directed at Peter.

"There is obviously a logical explanation," said Chloe. "Aran was probably doing her a favour because she had nobody to go to dinner with. Aran's very kind like that and he has been friends with Audrey for years."

"They looked very much a couple from where I was standing."

"Well, I can assure you there is no conspiracy as you seem to be suggesting. I can understand your confusion and concern, but I hope this doesn't colour your judgement in relation to the merger." Boris raised an eyebrow. "I've just told you I met your boyfriend out with another woman and you are more interested in the merger?"

Through the glass walls of her office, Chloe saw Audrey storm through the agency, followed by Peter. She held her breath.

I am a strong and capable person. I can and will achieve this, she said quickly to herself.

"You are nothing but a bitch!" Audrey slammed through the office door.

Chloe rose from her seat and placed her hands on her desk, while Peter closed the door behind him, to keep the situation as private as possible.

"You couldn't let Aran go, could you? You just keep trying to get him back," Audrey shouted.

"I'm trying to have a meeting here," Chloe said calmly.

"Trying to steal our merger away." Audrey grabbed the newspaper from the desk with the Tiffany story on the front page and held it up. "With your dirty tricks. Organising all this bad press against us."

"I didn't need to organise anything. Your agency has discredited itself."

"Why can't you just get on with your own life and leave us alone? Leave our business alone and leave me and Aran alone," demanded Audrey.

"I believe it is you who are interfering in our lives. Aran went to this dinner party of yours as a favour because he felt sorry for you. You should accept the truth."

"What are you talking about? Aran is my partner. We love each other and are together all the time."

Chloe opened her drawer and took out a ring box which she opened. She took out the beautiful engagement ring and placed it on her finger.

"If that is so, why am I wearing Aran's engagement ring?" Chloe asked holding out her hand.

As Audrey looked at the sparkling diamond, she blinked back tears.

"I'm not my fiance's keeper," Chloe continued. "But I do know that you are kidding yourself if you ever thought Aran Murphy has treated you as anything other than a plaything, a distraction, something to amuse him – somebody to practise on."

Audrey ran from the office as Peter stared at Chloe and shook his head slowly before leaving too.

"Now, Mr Stein, if we could get back to discussing a more serious issue – the merger," Chloe said, sitting down again.

CHAPTER 91

Peter drove Audrey home. She sat dazed but refusing to cry.

"I'm so sorry this has happened," he said as she got out. She looked at him for a moment, then went into her apartment. It was only when she was safely inside that she allowed the tears to flow.

Aran had been living on his nerves all morning and, when Chloe finally came into his office, they finally broke. The sweat pumped out of him as she wordlessly approached his desk. As ever, he couldn't read her face.

"Boris Stein informs me you had an interesting dinner companion last night."

"I can explain –" he started.

She held up her hand. "I'm really not interested in hearing anything more on this issue."

He noticed she was wearing his engagement ring and became confused.

"I want her out of our lives, Aran. I want her out now. I won't expect to see you tonight, because you will be getting rid of her. And there's no point in keeping our engagement a secret any more. We are now officially engaged."

Aran was stunned by Chloe's reaction, stunned but grateful. He expected Audrey to turn up or phone him all day and start screaming at him. He went to ring her many times but couldn't bring himself to.

Now, as he stood at her apartment door sliding the key she had given him into the lock, his stomach churned.

She was sitting on the sofa staring into space.

"Audrey?" he asked nervously.

As she turned to look at him he could see she had cried bitter tears.

"Why?" she asked.

He shuffled from one foot to another. "I had to. I was going to lose everything to that bastard Galen."

"So you are marrying her out of convenience?"

"Yes. No. I don't know. She fits into my life, if that makes sense. She's what my parents want. She's what everyone expects from me for a wife." He sighed loudly. "She's what I expect to have as a wife."

"So I am just a plaything, then? A distraction?"

"No . . . I love you."

She put up her hand. "Don't! Don't even go there. The deceit you've shown me!"

"I'm sorry. I just tried to please everybody, but I couldn't lose you. I need you too much in my life."

"Oh, Aran! You haven't any strength in you, have you? But you are the worst kind of weak person, you're a selfish weak person. Did you expect this arrangement to go on forever? Chloe to get all the respectability and live up in the big house while I was your bit on the side?"

"Don't say that!" He wished she would scream or shout or throw something at him. Act the usual way she did when she was upset. He couldn't handle this calmness she was showing. "You mean so much to me," he pleaded.

"And you meant so much to me. I don't mean your wealth or your family's status. Oh, I admit at the start it was an attraction. But I've changed a lot and my feelings changed for you as well. If you had nothing I would have loved you all the more for it. Now I realise I didn't love you, because you were just a big lie. I can't love something that never existed. I suppose I could fight for you, Aran. Give her a run for her money. But you're not worth fighting for. Go home to your fiancée, Aran, and your family."

Peter sat with Boris in the bar at the Berkeley Court Hotel.

"It's hit her very hard. She had no idea," explained Peter.

"I'm sorry I was the one who brought it out in the open. Aran Murphy is quite a guy."

"A bastard is what he is. I'm sorry you were dragged into the situation."

"Couldn't be helped . . . I guess you want to know about the merger?"

Peter nodded, looking expectant and nervous.

"I can't go with it, Peter."

"Right." Peter was deflated.

"There is a lot of potential at Spinner. And I was very interested. But the press problems you've had this week, with Ivanka and Tiffany. Firstly you've lost your two stars, so to speak. You have other good models and your set-up is good. But it's glaringly obvious from what's happened this week that you haven't got your act together yet. My loyalty is obviously to Regency and I can't recommend a merger given your recent problems. Reputation in this business is everything and yours has just been badly tarnished."

"I see." Peter looked down at the ground.

"With the scandals that have emerged in the international modelling scene we have to make sure everything is whiter than white." Boris suddenly grinned. "I tell you one thing though – it sure has been entertaining!"

"That stupid idiot!" hollered Lynn. "Audrey and her stupid tangled love life. Of course, Stein wouldn't want to merge after that Aran Murphy debacle." Lynn was smoking after Peter had explained the whole situation to her that night.

"He didn't mention anything about Audrey and Aran. It was the bad press we got that made up his mind."

"So he said. I think it's all Audrey's fault. She's so unprofessional. Even apart from the whole Aran episode, she did nothing to try and butter Stein up the right way."

"She couldn't get a word in edgeways with you."

Lynn pointed her cigarette at him. "If everyone tried as hard as I did we might have a merger today. And what does Audrey have to say about Stein's decision?"

"She's not answering her phone."

"Typical, she's not even interested. It's time you got away from her, Peter."

"Spinner was Audrey's idea," said Peter firmly. "She pushed it along and she's half owner. I couldn't kick her out even if I wanted to. She's also been a good friend to me and I'm going to support her any way I can through this."

Lynn threw her arms into the air. "I despair of you! When you should be working ten times harder to keep Spinner on the straight and narrow you are concerned with some silly girl who only has herself to blame. She was

ANDREW O'CONNOR

deluding herself if she really thought Aran saw any kind
of a future with her. He wouldn't dream of ending up with
somebody like her."

"She's worth ten of him," Peter snapped suddenly,
surprising both of them with his reaction. "He's a bastard
who took a close friend of mine for a fool."

CHAPTER 92

Word reached Chloe very quickly through a contact that Stein had rejected Spinner. The next morning she looked through the legal documents she had drawn up for Boom's merger with Regency. She was expecting Boris in for an appointment at ten. She was feeling happy and satisfied, as everything in her life was falling into place. Aran had phoned her the previous night to inform her that he had dealt with Audrey. He hadn't offered any details and she hadn't wanted any. Aran, as instructed by Chloe, had then informed his parents he wanted to make their engagement public. Muriel had rung her that morning, suggesting an engagement party at their house. Glancing at the shimmering diamond ring sitting proudly on her finger she knew she had finally won. After being passed over as a nonentity as she grew up, she was finally the winner. Seeing Boris come into the agency, she rose to greet him.

"Good morning," she said brightly, as he came in.

"That ring is very becoming on you," he commented, taking a seat.

"Thank you." She started to shift through documentation.

"I guess it's all official now?"

"Our engagement? Yes, it is," she smiled.

"No concerns that he has been cheating on you with someone else?" Boris asked, half amused.

Chloe wished he would just drop the whole unfortunate incident, but picked her words carefully. "As far as I'm concerned, attending a dinner party is not an unfaithful act."

Putting his hands together Boris was lost in thought for a while. He finally spoke, musingly. "You're a class act, do you know that? I thought I had met all types . . . the vain, the chancers, the liars, the good, the bad and the gracious, but you . . . you're different. I don't know what you are . . . I don't know what makes you tick. You never give anything away. People need something from other people. They need compliments, or reassurances, they need to talk about themselves, even slightly. But you don't need any of that, do you? You have those huge walls built around you. Another woman would be distraught after what Aran did. But I doubt you even gave it much thought . . . it's almost like a psychological flaw."

"Fascinating as your thoughts on me are, if we could get this merger sorted. I've had our solicitors draft a preliminary contract –"

"That was a little premature," interrupted Boris.

"There's no point in wasting time."

"What makes you think I want this merger?"

"Because you put Spinner out of the picture," said Chloe.

"News sure does travel quick around this town. Yes, I'm not merging with Spinner, but unfortunately I'm not going to merge with Boom either."

Anger erupted inside Chloe. You won't break me, Mr

Stein, she thought, nobody has yet and you won't be the first.

"No?" she asked calmly.

"Your agency is very good. It does what it does very well. It's the leading Dublin agency which is well run. But it ain't what I'm looking for in a merger. You're not at the cutting edge enough for Regency. Your top girls are a little too long in the tooth to break onto the international scene. Sure, a girl like Alison Flatley we could do some work with but not enough to warrant a merger. I'm always looking for the next big thing. The next girl who has the special quality that will make her one of the leading faces over the next five years. And you just don't have anyone like that on your books. What's more, your agency isn't geared towards finding someone like that. Taking on that kind of a girl is a risk and the risk factor doesn't exist here."

"Thank you for your honesty," Chloe said.

"Well, talking of honesty, now that you have nothing to lose, tell me, were you behind all that bad press Spinner got?"

Chloe stood up. "I guess we've nothing left to talk about."

Boris stood up smiling. "I think going into business with you would be like taking a swim with a barracuda."

Chloe walked to the office door and opened it for him. "Have a safe journey home." She extended her hand.

"I'd like to get behind those walls one day and see who you really are." said Boris and he shook her hand. In spite of the anger she felt towards him she felt the same jolt of attraction.

CHAPTER 93

The phones rang all day at Spinner with the press looking for a statement about Tiffany or Ivanka. Mark handled the phones, informing journalists that nobody was available for comment. Peter holed himself up in his office trying to figure out the best thing to do. Tiffany's mobile was off all the time and he couldn't get in contact with her.

He wished Audrey was there, but she hadn't shown up for work and wasn't answering her phones either. If she had been there they could bounce ideas off each other as they normally did. Remembering how he used to dismiss her when they started off in business, he thought of what a shrewd operator she had turned out to be. Except when it came to her love life, he thought. And he remembered what someone had once said about her – a strong woman with a weak heart.

"I want nobody knowing about this," Chloe instructed Ben after she told him of Stein's rejection. "As far as I'm concerned it's Regency's loss."

"I won't say a thing," Ben said earnestly.

"The powers that be over at Macken still think this merger is going full steam ahead and they aren't going to find out until I've lined up a bigger and better merger with someone else. Compile me a list of all the major agencies in London, New York, Paris and Milan. I want contact names and numbers."

"I'll start on it immediately." Ben jumped up and left.

She was glad Ben was so eager to impress her; nothing was too much trouble.

There was no way Brendan was going to find out about this rejection. It would reflect too badly on her.

Lynn was in a bookstore glancing through the new titles on display. It was her lunch break and she could do with a good escapist read. Peter and his silly loyalty to undeserving causes, Lynn thought. She would simply have to put a stop to his continued partnership with Audrey – she was too much of a liability. As she flicked through a book she spotted a tall girl walking through the bookstore. She vaguely knew the girl. She had started working in an art gallery about the same time Lynn had started her career. They had done some slight transaction together and she couldn't even remember her name. She hadn't seen the girl for a few years but had seen her recently a few times around town. She had been struck with how differently dressed the girl was compared to before. She now seemed slightly scruffy and had lost the burgeoning chic she once possessed. Watching the girl continue to walk across the shop floor she realised from what she was wearing that she worked in the shop as an assistant. Lynn was surprised and wondered what had happened for her life to change so much. The girl had seemed destined to be a gifted art broker.

Lynn found herself suddenly overcome by a huge sense of insecurity. How fickle life could be! How a person's circumstances could change! And as she clutched the book tightly, she was gripped by a fear for her own future.

"Mrs Reynolds?" a strong voice interrupted her thoughts.

Turning around she saw Larry Hennessy. "Hello, how are you?"

"I'm very well. Has that painting I'm after arrived in the Gallery yet?"he asked

"I'm expecting it this week and I'll call you as soon as I get delivery."

"I'd appreciate that." He took the book out of her hand and read the cover. "You're a fan of this writer?"

"Not particularly. I'm just looking for some light entertainment."

"Aren't we all, Mrs Reynolds?"

"Call me Lynn, please."

"As well as that piece I've ordered, I'm looking for something special as a engagement present for good friends of mine. I wonder if you could advise me? "

"Of course I would," Lynn said.

Larry looked at his watch. "Have you time for a coffee?"

"I'd love to go for a coffee."

It was eight in the evening and Peter still hadn't heard from Audrey and so decided to drop by her apartment. It took a while for her to answer the doorbell.

When she did she was dressed in her nightgown.

"Come in," she muttered pulling her fingers through

her hair to try and make it look tidier. He spotted a half-drunk bottle of wine on the coffee table.

"Help yourself to whatever – tea, coffee, wine."

"No, I'm fine" he answered. She didn't look like herself at all and he was filled with concern.

Audrey stumbled back to the couch and sat down.

"We didn't get the merger," he said.

"There's a surprise." She took a gulp of wine.

"The press have been on looking for statements but I didn't want to say anything until we talked it through."

"Look, I really can't cope with the agency right now."

"Of course," he nodded.

"I just feel such a fool, Peter."

"You haven't done anything wrong. There's no reason for you to feel a fool."

"The whole of Dublin is laughing at me."

"Nobody knows. It's not in Aran or Chloe's interest to broadcast this."

"I bet Lynn is laughing," Audrey said.

"The important thing is for you to just get over this as quickly as possible."

"This isn't a PR job gone wrong that needs a bit of damage limitation. This is my life which has been turned upside down."

"I know . . . I'm sorry."

"When I started Spinner I wanted to change my life. To change me. I'd relied on the way I looked for so long and I wanted to be so much more than that. I wanted to be respected for my mind. To be this great business woman in control of her life."

"And you've achieved it."

"I've achieved nothing. Aran never considered me

good enough to be his partner. It's Chloe he's gone for."

As she started to cry softly, he sat down on the couch beside her, and pulled her close. Every so often he bent down and kissed her hair. They rested back against the cushions and didn't move for ages and then they drifted off to sleep.

CHAPTER 94

"Audrey called this morning and said she wouldn't be in today," Mark informed Peter as he came up the stairs.

"Did she ask to speak to me?"

"No. I've had *The Independent*, *The Times* and *The Sun* all looking for Comments."

He had woken at three in the morning, still holding a sleeping Audrey. He had quietly got up and put a blanket on her before heading home. Lynn had been anxious as he hadn't called and he had made up an excuse about meeting journalists to try and sort out their current problems.

Peter picked up the phone and dialled Tiffany's mother in Derry.

"I want this engagement party to be very exclusive. I want no rent-a-crowd here," Muriel explained to Chloe as they sat in the parlour of the Murphy house.

"I totally agree. Just close friends and relatives," nodded Chloe, thinking of all the work contacts she would be putting on the guest list.

"Such a pity your parents won't be home from the cruise."

ANDREW O'CONNOR

"I know," Chloe sighed. "But I couldn't ask them to jet back from the South Pacific."

"Such a shame. Missing their only child's engagement party."

"There will be plenty of other parties. And they are enjoying this cruise so much, I'd hate to interrupt it."

"Very thoughtful, my dear. Tell me, do you think Aran's been a bit on the quiet side this past couple of days?"

"I can't say I've noticed," Chloe continued to scribble down names for the invitation list.

Aran rocked back and forth in his office chair. He didn't know what to think any more. He felt mainly relieved that he hadn't been exposed to his family and friends. That would have destroyed him once and for all. Galen would have been delighted by his downfall. He had Chloe's cool handling of the situation to thank for that. Galen knew his future at Murphy Hennessy would now not be so glittering and rumour was he was looking for a new job. As Aran swivelled around he knew he should just be grateful for the way everything had worked out. But he missed Audrey so much and felt terrible not seeing her.

The worst thing ever to do in PR was to say nothing as people always assumed the worst and rumours would quickly grow into fact. Business at Spinner was already down to half, after the scandals and bad press. Some parents had even taken their daughters out of the agency.

Peter called a small press conference for a select group of journalists he knew he could trust and would give a fair deal to Spinner. He phoned Tiffany's parents and informed them of his intentions and told them what he planned to say. They were in a terrible state over Tiffany but gave their approval.

"I can confirm that Tiffany Cooper has developed a drug-addiction problem over past months. It is a fact she regrets immeasurably and she is now taking active measures to overcome her addiction. Her family and the Spinner management are fully behind Tiffany as she faces this difficult time. Until she has put her problems in the past she will be taking a break from modelling and we request she is given the space and respect she needs at this time."

Peter considered it to be a perfect statement which was fully supportive of Tiffany, but managed to distance Spinner from the scandal at the same time.

Kitty Mulcahy took the pencil which she was chewing out of her mouth. "Are you trying to tell us, Peter, that nobody here spotted Tiffany was on drugs?" Kitty asked disbelievingly.

"Unfortunately, we didn't. If we had, we would obviously have taken steps sooner to help her."

Kitty tossed her head to one side. "After all these scandals do you really think Spinner is a good agency for parents to entrust their daughters to?"

"Larry said none of the Murphys could stand Audrey," Lynn informed Peter over dinner. She played with the lasagne on her plate . "He said Aran's parents would have done anything to get rid of her out of Aran's life." Larry Hennessy had seemingly acquired the status of Lynn's new best friend, whom she quoted regularly. "Still no word from her, I suppose?"

"No, her mobile is still turned off," answered Peter.

"She's so selfish leaving you to deal with all this mess."

"Give her a break, Lynn." Peter was tired of the constant digs.

"She's the architect of her own destruction as far as I'm concerned."

"But I have Leslie booked for that date," Peter said down the phone.

"I'm sorry," said the irate advertising executive. "I've booked a model from somewhere else instead." The phone went dead.

Peter sighed. It had been the same story with a lot of bookings. People just didn't want to be associated with an agency tainted by the recent scandals. All that night at home he thought about how he could turn Spinner's fortunes around again. His thoughts drifted to Audrey.

The phone rang and he reached over to answer it.

"Hi, Peter," said Lynn. "It's me." He could hear lots of music and background noise.

"Listen, I'm just out with Larry and a few friends. This function we are at is going on longer than we thought so don't bother waiting up for me."

The phone went dead leaving Peter alone with his thoughts in the quietness.

CHAPTER 95

Audrey stared at herself in the mirror. She felt emotionally exhausted.

She had hidden away from the world in her apartment all day and now it was four in the morning and she still couldn't sleep. The overpowering need to run was overwhelming. Her suitcase lay open on her bed, a few outfits already thrown in. If she set off in the next half an hour, she could be safely home in the bosom of her family by breakfast. She would never have to see or hear about Aran Murphy or Chloe Gallagher or any of them ever again.

"You fool!" she said to herself in the mirror.

A fool not to have read the signs, to guess something was wrong. A fool to allow herself to think that she was the most important thing in Aran's life, when in reality she was nothing but a little bit of dressing on the side.

She sure as hell wasn't twenty any more – how could she have not seen past his bullshit. A fool to believe that Aran would sacrifice everything for her. She was obviously deluded, or stupid, or both. She rose up and started to fold her outfits into the suitcase. And now what was she doing? Running home for some tea and sympathy like she did the last time? You're a grown woman, she told herself. You might be a stupid grown woman but you're still an adult. An adult with responsibilities and lots of them.

She had a company to run, a company that was in trouble by the looks of it.

She had people whose livelihoods depended on her. She had a business partner who risked everything for Spinner to be a success. She couldn't just leave him in the lurch because her relationship fell apart. She emptied the suitcase out and hung back the outfits in the wardrobe. The she sat down and stared at herself again.

"You can stop feeling sorry for yourself, because nobody else does," she said out loud to herself. "You had it coming for being so self-obsessed you couldn't see what was in front of your eyes. And for you to think that you might one day have a happy and fulfilling relationship. You missed your chance of that years ago when you went off to pursue your ambitions. You might as well get used to the fact that happiness is never going to happen now, so you can avoid this kind of – humiliation – ever happening to you again."

Audrey marched up the stairs at Spinner and found Peter sitting at reception looking through the morning papers.

"Oh, hi," he said, his face full of concern. He noticed she was wearing very little make-up and her hair was pulled back into a severe bun. She was also wearing a sharp pin-striped business suit.

He thought she looked even more attractive than when made up. "I didn't expect you in today."

"And why not?" Her tone was cold and slightly aggressive.

"I just thought you might be taking some time off . . . after everything."

"Sorry if everyone thought I was going to go to pieces but I've a business to run. Well done on the handling of the Tiffany situation yesterday. It came across as good in today's papers."

"Er . . . thanks." Peter was taken aback by her.

"Now the merger has fallen through, I think we need a strategic meeting." She glanced at her watch. "Are you free at eleven?"

"Er, sure."

"Good, I'll see you in my office then." She turned and marched down the corridor.

CHAPTER 96

It was the day of the engagement party and Chloe was determined to be out of the office by five. She and Ben had been very busy all week contacting agencies in all the fashion capitals, pitching for a merger.

"Any word back from any of the agencies?" she asked Ben as she packed her briefcase ready to go.

"Nothing yet," he sighed.

"Contact Ford in New York again and see if they got our photos and information pack," she ordered.

"No problem. It's still only lunch-time there so I'll work late tonight again and contact all the agencies in the States and see if I can come up with anything."

"Good" she put on her coat. Brendan was still blissfully unaware of Boris Stein's rejection and was putting pressure on her to wrap up the merger with Regency.

What's more, he wasn't coming to the party that night and so she was being robbed of an opportunity to impress him.

As she made her way to the door she paused and contemplated telling Ben to drop by the party after he had finished work. She quickly dismissed the idea.

She raced home, packed an overnight bag and headed over to the Murphys.

Muriel had prepared a room for her to stay that night and she took her time getting ready there. She was wearing an off-the-shoulder sheer white gown that showed off her recently acquired sun-bed tan to perfection. Her hair had been highlighted during the week and the whole effect was good, she thought, as she looked in the full-length mirror on the wall.

As she made her way down the stairs, she saw Muriel busily organising the hired help for the night.

"If anyone asks for a drink not stocked in the bar, go into the kitchen and ask for it there and they should be able to find it for you –" She turned to see Chloe. "Ah, my dear, you look dazzling."

"Thank you."

Aran came out from the parlour dressed in a tuxedo, and kissed Chloe's cheek before heading out to make a call on the veranda.

By nine o'clock the driveway was full of BMWs, Mercedes and Audis.

Aran and Chloe mingled with the guests accepting congratulations.

Suddenly she came face to face with Larry Hennessy and froze. She hadn't seen him since the incident at his house.

"Aran, my boy, well done." Larry beamed and shook Aran's hand. "An excellent choice of bride. And, Chloe, welcome to the family." He leaned forward, kissed her cheek and whispered: "You look ravishing."

She felt sick from his touch and quickly brushed past him.

In the marble hallway Aran and Chloe twirled around

dancing with other couples as the band played Billy Joel's "Leave A Tender Moment Alone".

This is it, Chloe told herself. This is where she always wanted to be. She had everything she had ever wanted. She had arrived.

As the song came to an end, Aran and Chloe walked into the dining-room, hand in hand.

"Sorry, Ms Gallagher, a phone call for you," a member of staff informed her.

She walked over to the phone and picked up the receiver. "Hello . . . hello?" she called down the phone but couldn't hear a thing with the noise. "Stay on the line and I'll take the call upstairs." She put down the phone and quickly made her way up the stairs to her room.

Picking up the phone beside her bed she said again, "Hello?"

"Good evening, Chloe." She immediately recognised the voice as Larry's.

The bedroom door closed behind her and she looked around to see Larry standing with his back against the door, holding his mobile which he then turned off. She slowly put down the receiver.

Real fear gripped her at being trapped in the room with this man.

"I haven't seen you since you ran out on me that night," he said. "That was a clever little stunt you played on me when the doorbell rang. You told me you were into playing games, but I didn't realise you meant silly games."

"You mean the night you attacked me?"

"I didn't attack you. We were becoming mutually acquainted."

"You had me trapped in your house, like you are trying to trap me now."

606

"I just want to finish what I started." She didn't allow him to see any fear but said evenly and confidently. "Larry, this is my engagement party and I am now going to return to it." She confidently strode towards the door. But seeing he wasn't moving anywhere she stopped, fearing getting too close to him, in case he grabbed her like the last time.

"Larry, will you please get out of my way."

He turned the key in the lock behind him and began to walk towards her. She instinctively backed away.

"All I want to do is welcome you to the family properly," he smiled.

"I don't think you are going to try something with all those people downstairs."

"What will you do? Scream? I don't think so. These people have known me for years. I'm Larry Hennessy. You are just a girl who has got lucky by marrying into them. You can start shouting and then when they find us . . . imagine the scandal? The Murphys would be horrified and you'd be out on your ear. You're not going to risk that, are you?"

She refused to allow the fear that was sweeping over her show. That was what he wanted, she reasoned.

I am a strong and capable person, she thought. I can and will achieve this.

"What are you getting out of this, Larry? Some power thrill? How dare you behave like this to me. You may be Larry Hennessy, you may be a big and powerful lawyer and part of the establishment, but you are sadly mistaken if you think you are respected, Larry. People snigger and laugh about you behind your back. They know about the prostitutes you visit. Do you really think you are safe from what you did to Julianna and the others? I know that you attacked them. People know. It's said in whispers behind your back. You picked on Julianna and the others because you knew they wouldn't risk a scandal in exposing you. But they still tell people what a sick bastard you are.

"For your information, your reputation is shit. You consider yourself to be this great ladies' man, while in fact nobody would stay with you for long, once they realise what you are like. And that's why you are alone at nearly sixty. You were sick recently and you said yourself that nobody cared. Imagine yourself in another twenty years' time when you will be just a nuisance. You call the Murphys family because you have none of your own. You're a sad bad joke, Larry, and the joke is on you."

As she spoke she saw his expression turn from menacing to angry, then to sad. He stood staring at her as if every word she said was causing a wound.

"Now, I'm returning to my engagement party, so get out of my way." She walked past him, unlocked the door and walked out.

Only when she got to the top of the stairs, did she clutch her stomach. She felt physically sick.

She had felt so vulnerable in that room with him. But now she was safe, looking down on the crowd partying below. And despite the fact she was still shaking, she felt immensely proud of herself. She had stood up to that bastard and won.

"Where were you? We've been searching for you everywhere," said Aran as she rejoined the party. "Dad is about to make a speech."

"I'm sorry, I had to take a call," Chloe excused herself.

They took their positions beside Muriel and Reginald, halfway up the stairs.

"It's wonderful to see so many familiar old faces here tonight" Reginald said, beginning his speech.

"Less of the old," admonished Muriel, to the crowd's laughter.

"True for you, I'll correct myself and say it's wonderful to see so many friends here tonight. And it's a very special night as we are welcoming a most remarkable young woman into our family – Chloe Gallagher." There was applause from the guests. "We are delighted with our son's choice and hope the future shines brightly on them." He raised his glass. "To Aran and Chloe!"

The crowd raised their glasses and repeated: "To Aran and Chloe!"

Galen reached out his hand and Aran shook it.

"Congratulations, mate," Galen said, who seemed to have completely lost his usual smug expression.

"Thanks, cousin. I hear you're leaving the company," Aran smiled broadly.

"That's right. I've received an offer from another firm."

"You're better off going somewhere where you'll have a future."

"Fantastic night," said Muriel to Chloe as the guests began to depart.

"I really enjoyed it," answered Chloe.

Muriel sat down on a couch in the hall and patted the seat beside, indicating for Chloe to join her.

"And it should be fantastic with the amount of money it cost with the extra staff, and the band and the drink – people drink so much."

"Don't they!" Chloe tried to look disapproving.

"We couldn't really afford tonight's party. But it's our only son's engagement, so we had to push out the boat," said Muriel.

"Couldn't afford it?" Chloe raised an eyebrow.

"Since you are now one of us, I suppose I can confide in you. We put on a good show, aristocracy generally does, but we are on our uppers. Too many years of rich living and poor investments."

Chloe tried to take in the news. "But Murphy Hennessy is one of the biggest law firms in the country!"

"One of the biggest, but alas not one of the most successful. We've lost many cases recently. There's the land, of course, the shopping-centre land. That may stave off the debtors for a while. But even that won't make much of a dent in the mountain of debt we have. Still," Muriel patted Chloe's knee, "we have you now. I hear you have a brilliant business brain and that's sure to help us.

"That's why a girl like Audrey Driver would be so useless for Aran – she would just spend money we didn't have. But you, you can help us get back on our feet. That's why I thought you such an excellent bride for Aran."

CHAPTER 97

Peter tossed and turned in bed trying not to disturb Lynn sleeping beside him. He thought about Audrey and her businesslike approach to everything. It was almost as if she had cut herself off emotionally from what had happened. They had spent three hours in a meeting, during which she had come up with some brilliant ideas. He had wanted to ask her how she was but her manner didn't encourage any such sentiment.

As he turned in the bed for another time, he gave up and went to make himself some tea, his mind whirling in thought.

"What's wrong?" Lynn emerged into the sitting-room and sat opposite him.

"I can't get to sleep."

"You've been having this problem for a while, Peter – you should go to the doctor tomorrow and get some pills." Lynn didn't like to be disturbed at night.

He put down his mug of tea. "I know what's causing it."

All the guests had gone, the party was over, and Chloe was

pacing up and down her bedroom. She literally could not believe what Muriel had told her.

There had been absolutely no hint of the Murphys' true financial situation previously. Why hadn't Aran told her before things had reached this stage?

Now all she wanted to do was get away from all of them, as far and fast as possible. Not only were they poor but they were heavily in debt. And they were expecting her to work for the rest of her life trying to rescue their fortunes as they sat back on their aristocratic laurels.

Her dream had transformed into a nightmare. She simply could not let her life turn out like this. It wasn't an option. As she thought about Aran, she did feel guilty. But she then reminded herself of how he had cheated on her with Audrey right up to when he had been discovered. And if she had to be honest, and this was certainly a time to be honest, their marriage was always based on the fact that it suited both their needs. And it no longer provided for her needs. It would only be a matter of time until he was unfaithful again to her anyway, she reasoned. She sat down at the writing desk and began to pen a letter.

"So what's causing all these sleepless nights?" asked Lynn.

"Us."

"Us?" Lynn lit up a cigarette.

"I'm not happy, Lynn. This is really hard for me to say, but I'm not happy with our marriage."

Lynn's eyes widened in amazement. "Why aren't you happy?"

"We just don't have anything in common any more. We've drifted apart too far. You were right to leave when you did and we shouldn't have tried to give it another go . . . I'm sorry."

She focussed on the cigarette in her hand. "I don't consider myself to be a smoker any more, you know. I only ever have the occasional one. I have to be careful I don't slip back into the habit. Being a smoker is like being a Catholic – once you are one, you are always one. I thought we were getting on good, better than we ever did before."

"Only because I'm trying so hard to be what you want me to be. I'm not being myself. The real me doesn't make you happy, Lynn. When you left me I got used to being myself again and I just can't change back now."

"Don't you love me any more?" she asked.

He searched for an answer before slowly shaking his head. Rising up, he walked into the bedroom and closed the door firmly.

Chloe approached the situation as if it were a business transaction. She carefully worded the letter to Aran as if writing a press release and then folded the paper and placed it in an envelope. She changed out of her gown into a pale blue suit and packed her bag. It was almost three in the morning and there wasn't a sound in the house. Walking down the corridor, she paused outside Aran's room. Seeing there was no light escaping from under the door, she quickly slipped the envelope under it. Continuing down the corridor she reached the top of the stairs. Downstairs was in darkness and she carefully descended the steps and walked in the dark through the hallway. Suddenly light flooded the hallway, as the chandelier above her was ignited.

Muriel stood at the light switch in the doorway of the parlour.

"Are you going somewhere, Chloe?"

"I . . . er . . . I." For once in her life, Chloe was lost for words.

Muriel walked into the hallway. "Judging from your suitcase you seem to be leaving without saying goodbye."

Chloe stood silent.

Muriel's face changed from its usual pleasant, if aloof, expression to a hard cold look. "I never had you down as a coward, Chloe. If you decided to leave my son, I would have thought you would have had the decency to tell him to his face. You are leaving him, I take it?"

Chloe regained her composure. "I am leaving Aran, yes. I've explained everything in a letter to him and put it under his door."

Muriel's expression switched back to being pleasant.

"Aran's always had such bad judgement of character, especially when it came to girlfriends. I've always wanted the very best for him. That was why I was glad when you arrived on the scene. Now here was a strong, educated, successful young woman who could keep Aran on the straight and narrow, I thought. Of course, I knew your background, despite a wonderful show by yourself. But you weren't in our league. I can smell a person's background immediately. But what you lacked in your breeding, you more than made up in your talent. Aran is the heir to great wealth and so, of course, we have to be very careful of fortune-hunters. My son deserves somebody who will love him for himself. As I and Reginald love each other."

"You said you were heavily in debt," said Chloe.

"I had to ensure you loved Aran for himself. I had discussed the situation with Larry and he suggested this little test – to say we had no money, which thankfully isn't true. You failed the test."

Chloe quickly turned around and started to walk back towards the stairs.

"Don't bother. It's too late to try to correct the situation.

Or as you PRs would say, to try damage limitation. If you try to go back to your room, I'll ensure Aran reads your letter immediately and explain the whole situation to him."

Chloe turned and looked at Muriel. "Why do you control every aspect of Aran's life? Why can't you let him live his own life and let him make his own decisions?"

"A mother's love is a very special thing," said Muriel, as she crossed over to the front door which she unlatched and held open for Chloe. "Hopefully you'll know that yourself someday. But it won't be with my grandchildren."

Chloe walked out through the front door and down the steps to her car.

Audrey turned off her computer and looked at her watch. It was almost midnight. She had been working extremely hard trying to make herself feel tired so she could at last find some sleep. After she had left the office, she walked down the street to her car. She knew it was Chloe and Aran's engagement party, and driving home through the city despite herself the thought of the extravagant party being held at the Murphy house kept slipping through her mind. When she got to her apartment she took off her clothes and went straight to bed, falling quickly into a troubled sleep. When she was awakened at three in the morning by the sound of party revellers outside, she was surprised to discover her face was tear-stained.

CHAPTER 98

When Peter awoke he prepared himself for a long conversation with Lynn. He didn't care as he knew he had made the right decision no matter what. But as he walked around the apartment, he realised Lynn had already left.

Aran sat at the breakfast table holding the letter from Chloe in both hands.

Muriel and Reginald sat either side of him.

"I just can't understand why she went," said Aran. "She seemed so happy last night. She had everything she wanted."

"It's better you find out now rather than after you were married. I'll handle it, Aran. I'll put a good edge on the story that will bring you out in the best possible light," said Muriel.

"But why did she go?" repeated Aran.

"It wasn't meant to be," Muriel put a comforting hand on her son's arm. "Anyway, she was never good enough for you." Chloe had sat alone all that night looking out to the sea through the patio windows. She knew it was pointless to even try and do an analysis of the situation. In spite all her years of business savvy and shrewdness, she had been outplayed by Muriel Murphy and, of course, Larry Hennessy. Chloe guessed Larry had become aware that she was too dangerous an enemy, who would be getting too close and too powerful with her marriage to Aran. And so Larry had sown seeds of doubt in Muriel's mind and got her to lay a trap. A trap she had blindly walked into. She contemplated contacting Aran and explaining the situation. But she knew this would be a futile exercise. The main reason Aran had asked her to marry him was because she met with his parents' full approval. There was no way he would go against them, now that they had turned against her. She was at this moment very sadly and acutely aware that Aran had never loved her.

It wasn't in Chloe's nature to entertain regrets or maybes, but she couldn't stop re-running the night's sequence of events in her head over and over again, trying to figure out where she had gone wrong.

By eleven the next morning she was still deep in thought and hadn't even bothered phoning the office to explain her absence.

Her phone rang.

"Yeah?" she answered.

"Ms Gallagher, it's Mr Macken's PA here. We've been trying to contact you at Boom all morning."

"Er, yes, I'm sorry. It was my engagement party last night and so I had a couple of things to do this morning." Why was she bothering explaining herself to a secretary?

"Mr Macken would like you to be here for a meeting at two."

"I'll be there." She hung up.

Lynn sat at her desk in The Gallery.

She had returned home to her parents very early that morning. She didn't know what to do or where to turn. Peter's words had turned her life upside down. Despite everything that had ever happened to them, she had always been fully confident of Peter's love. And now he had told her he no longer cared for her. She knew she should be worrying about her future. About her finances and about the apartment. But all she could think about was that she no longer had Peter.

Peter felt an enormous weight lifted off his shoulders. He even surprised himself that he had no sadness that he had ended his marriage. He reasoned he had come to terms with its end when Lynn had walked out on him for Rory Ryan. When she had left that time he thought all he had wanted was to have her back. She had been such a central and important part of his life for so long. But slowly he realised he was far happier without her. He realised it especially when she came back. Now he could start living his life as he wanted to as opposed to as he thought Lynn expected him to. He could do what he wanted, when he wanted, without risking her judgement. He could make mistakes without her disapproval. He could live life at his own pace instead of this competition she was always forcing them to run. He could allow himself to be human again. He could see who he wanted when he wanted without Lynn voicing objections or asking were they any use to them. He was free to fall in love even, with whoever he wanted.

He tapped on Audrey's door and opened it to find her typing furiously at her computer.

"I'm just heading off to Galway now for that meeting with the advertising agency down there," he informed her.

"That's fine, I'll see you later." She didn't look up from her computer screen.

"You might not. As I'll be back late."

"OK then, see you tomorrow." She continued to type.

He paused for a moment and then came into the office and closed the door behind him.

"Are you all right?" he asked gently.

"Yeah, why wouldn't I be?"

"You can talk to me any time. I'm here for you."

"Peter, I'm perfectly fine. Now, you'd better hurry or you'll be late for your meeting." She began to type again.

He nodded and left her office. It was only after he had left that she stopped typing and started to massage her temples.

Chloe smiled brightly as she entered the boardroom at Macken Communications.

"Sorry I'm a little late. Somebody parked in my parking space," she said as she sat down, placing her folder in front of her. The folder contained accounts from Boom, which she had reworked to show an increase in profit. She hoped it would impress them.

She noticed both Brendan's and Vincent's expressions were more stern than usual.

"We have received some information that you have been deceiving us," Brendan announced immediately.

Chloe disguised her shock. "Deceiving you?"

"We understand the proposed merger between Boom and Regency fell through some time ago, while you have been assuring us the deal was about to close any day."

Chloe placed her two hands on the desk. "Unfortunately this merger has not come about. This had nothing to do with Boom or the way it has been run. It is strictly down to internal problems within the Regency organisation. Having said that, I am currently working on a new merger plan with a notable New York agency."

"Who?" asked Brendan.

"Ford," she answered.

"I understand there has been no interest whatsoever from the Ford people regarding a merger with Boom."

"That has not been confirmed," Chloe said, not liking this situation at all.

"I believe it has," Brendan spoke with certainty.

"If you don't mind me saying so, I think I should know what's going on in Boom. I'm running the place on a daily basis."

"Ben Egan has told us everything," said Brendan.

Ben!

Chloe paused before speaking. "I think you'll find a quiet revolution has occurred in Boom since I have taken over its running. Overheads are substantially down and profits up. I have personally overseen an overhaul of the company's image."

"Which does not change the facts that first you lumbered us with this company we overpaid due to your bad advice, secondly you have failed to off-load the fucking thing with a merger and thirdly you have lied to us, your bosses." Brendan's face was red.

Chloe was in shock at hearing Brendan swear and on seeing the anger in his face.

"I suggest the word 'lie' is too strong. We just haven't had a sufficiently long enough meeting recently for me to discuss the situation at Boom in any great detail." Chloe remained cool despite the hostility being shown towards her.

But she was aware her excuses were sounding long and drawn out, with no substance.

It was Vincent's turn, as he opened her personnel file. "You've been with Macken a long time."

"Ten years," said Chloe.

"And you were a driving force in the company in your heyday. That's why we made you a director."

Heyday, thought Chloe, how dare he!

"As discussed with you at a previous meeting some time back, you have made some very questionable decisions recently. That coupled with the fact you are hiding truths from us and covering up –"

"I am not covering things up!" Chloe snapped.

"We no longer feel we can trust you," continued Vincent.

"Trust? I have basically run this company for you for years and established it way beyond your expectations."

"That is why trust is so important, due the position you've held. We need to feel we can trust you," said Vincent.

"Having personally encouraged your rise and seen you excel over time, I find it personally upsetting, but necessary, to now ask you to hand your notice in," said Brendan.

His words were too great for her to comprehend. I will not let you destroy me, she thought.

Smiling, she stood up. "Consider my notice to be given." She reached forward and shook both their hands. "Good afternoon, gentlemen."

Turning, she walked out of the office. When she was outside in the corridor she wanted to sink to her knees and scream. But she found Brendan's PA waiting for her there with Dermot.

"You are to clear out your office immediately," the PA informed her coldly, "and you have one hour to leave the building."

"We are to remain with you at all times until you have left," said Dermot who to her surprise seemed sympathetic.

Chloe walked past them and up the stairs to her office as they followed.

"You are not to return to the Boom Agency. Your personal belongings and files there will be forwarded to your home by Ben Egan, who'll be taking over there as manager," said the PA.

How the whole picture fell into place! Quiet, unassuming, likable Ben whom she had never perceived as any kind of a threat. He had deceived and betrayed her – how wrong she had been!

As she looked around her office she wondered where she could start. Ten years of work was stored there. It would take her days to sort everything out. She would not rush around and grab stuff in an undignified manner, as these two looked on.

"You will only remove personal items. You are not allowed to take anything belonging to Macken Communications," the PA informed.

Chloe had copies of everything at home. She flicked on her computer and pressed in a command to delete all the information on it. She wouldn't allow them to go trawling through her files after she had left. Then, she took her handbag and coat and walked out. The PA and Dermot followed her right to the front entrance. She left the building without turning around or saying anything.

"So you're telling me you're deserting me?" Noel Flynn put down his fork and looked at Audrey with wide eyes. They were having lunch at The Unicorn.

"I'm afraid so."

"But you're my best hostess – what am I going to do without you?"

"You were in business long before I started working for

you, and you'll be in business long after I'm gone, I daresay."

Noel picked up his fork and started to play with his Caesar salad.

"I heard about Aran Murphy getting engaged to Chloe Gallagher."

Audrey shrugged and nodded.

"Has that anything to do with your resignation?"

"If I stay at The San Juan it will be only a matter of time before I run into them, and I don't ever want to see them again."

"I understand."

"Besides, I really needed to work in The San Juan when I came to work for you. But I suppose I've moved on since then. Now I want to concentrate on Spinner . . . our backs are against the wall at the moment, so it needs all my concentration."

"No more time for love?" Noel raised an eyebrow.

"Definitely not . . . I've taken care of the bill." She got up, leant forward and kissed his cheek. "Thanks for everything."

He watched her throw her handbag over her shoulder and stride out.

CHAPTER 99

Peter's meeting in Galway had lasted longer than he had expected and it was late into the evening when he got back to his car, parked just off Eyre Square.

The advertising company he had met were representing a new clothes label and seemed interested in using Spinner. But they had confirmed nothing.

He swerved the car out of the parking space and headed back to Dublin.

After an hour and a half he was getting tired and decided to watch out for a place to stop for a drink and a rest. Looking at his watch he saw it was 10.30. As he drove through a small town he saw a big pub lit up in neon and pulled over into the carpark.

He decided to try Audrey's mobile again, but as expected it went through to her voice mail: *"Hi, you've reached Audrey. Please leave a message and I'll be sure to call you back."*

"Hi there, Peter here. Just wondering how you are. That meeting in Galway today went fine . . . could have done with you there though. Call me . . . I'll see you tomorrow."

He rubbed his face as he walked into the bar. It seemed

a little run-down and he was surprised to see a large crowd inside all clapping. On the stage a young girl was singing.

He marched up to the bar and took a free seat. "A Coke please," he asked the barman and was served immediately.

The singer was drawing to the end of her song and the crowd cheered.

"Thanks, everybody," the girl called. "Good to see you all in such fine form tonight."

"Good to see you too," shouted a guy from the audience.

"Thanks . . . the next song I'm going to sing is . . . 'Just The Two of Us'."

The small band started to play and she started to sing.

Peter began to listen, half interested, but as she continued to sing he became more alert.

The girl was about five foot ten, with dark skin, long dark hair and a striking face. She had a great voice, but most of all she had presence. She had an aura that captivated everybody in the bar including himself.

"Just the two of us . . ." she continued to sing

"Who is she?" Peter asked the barman.

"Just a local girl who sings in here on Thursday nights. Her name's Shari."

When Chloe reached her home she closed the front door behind her and paced endlessly around the lounge trying to take everything in. Then she sank to her knees and started to sob.

Shari took a break from singing and went to join a group of friends at a table for a drink. Peter approached, feeling embarrassed. Audrey was far better at doing this side of the job than he was.

He bent down beside Shari and handed her his card.

"Could I have a word for a minute?" he asked.

She read his card and looked at Peter suspiciously. She shrugged her shoulders at her friends and followed him over to a quiet corner.

"My name is Peter Reynolds and I run the Spinner agency. I would like if you could come in and have an interview with us." If Audrey had been there she would have the girl eating out of her hand in seconds, Peter thought.

Studying Shari's features close up he observed her perfect bone structure, high cheekbones, and strong jawline. Looking at her dark colouring he wondered if she was a nationality other than Irish. But her eyes were the brightest blue. If her aura could translate to photos she would be amazing, he thought.

"I'm not so sure. I'm behind on a lot of college work." She was articulate and well spoken. "I'll check with my mother."

Chloe didn't feel she had just lost her job; she felt she had lost her identity as well. She ignored the phone when it rang. All she wanted was to be alone in her house. It was at Macken Communications that she had become who she was. She had begun to believe in herself there. It was that company that had allowed her to acquire such power. And now it had all vanished. Brendan had turned on her so cruelly. He had always given her a free hand and now he had turned against her because she had exercised that power.

But she knew business was business at the end of the day and Brendan was witnessing big money going into bad investments. She told herself they weren't bad investments. They had needed to eliminate Calder Media and Blast as competition and Boom was a good investment. She stood by her decisions.

Macken Communications had simply lost their nerve and it was convenient to blame her. And they had disregarded all she had done for the company. For them to have humiliated her by having her escorted from the building! How everyone must have revelled in her degradation! All this coupled with the ending of her engagement and her treatment at the hands of the Murphys.

She felt herself crumble but stopped herself. She was a strong and capable person, she reminded herself. She wasn't an insecure teenager any more. She knew her worth and any company would be honoured to have her. Any man would be honoured to marry her. She would rise way above Macken and the Murphys. But first she would make them pay.

She gathered her thoughts and dialled the number of the security firm she had used to bug office phones and carry out other little jobs she had required over the years.

Peter came into Audrey's office as she put down the phone.

"Another booking dropped," she sighed. "How did Galway go yesterday?"

"Nothing concrete, but very promising."

"Promising doesn't pay the bills," she said.

"On my way back I stopped off at this bar and there was this young girl singing there and she was amazing model material."

Audrey's face lit up as she knew Peter didn't make these judgements lightly.

"Was she as good as Tiffany or Ivanka?"

"She would certainly be their equal."

"Great. When are we meeting her?"

"Well, I gave her my card, so hopefully she'll ring."

"Hopefully?" Audrey was annoyed. "You got her number though?"

"No, but she seemed very interested."

"So you're telling me, we're facing bankruptcy and you met a potential find and you didn't get contact details?"

Peter felt uncomfortable. He was used to being the one telling Audrey off for her lack of business acumen. And now here she was, assertively and correctly pointing out his failings.

"Well, you know, Audrey. It's easier for you as a woman to push for those details than it is for a man."

"That sound like an excuse, Peter." She looked very angry.

He was going to say something smart to her but, considering her mood, he decided against it.

"Well, let's just hope she rings then, yeah?" he said.

"My name is Anne Delaney. You approached my daughter last night about representing her." The voice on the other end of the phone was husky.

Peter was delighted to get the call, though he had expected Shari to call personally and not her mother.

"Thanks for calling me, Mrs Delaney. I was very impressed with Shari and was hoping she could come into the office for a chat."

"Yes, she could, but she goes nowhere without me."

"Sure, you're more than welcome too. Could you make it up to Dublin soon?"

"Tomorrow?"

"Great, I'll give you directions to the office."

"I'm hopeless taking directions. Shall we say The Morrison Hotel at 4.30pm?"

Peter felt it was a command and not a question.

Shari was easily spotted in the Morrison bar. Her baby-pink suit contrasted with her dark colouring and she gave Peter and Audrey a friendly smile as she got up to greet them.

"Thanks for coming," he said. She was even more captivating in daylight.

"This is my mother," said Shari.

Peter was surprised to meet Anne. She was tall with black hair like Shari's

Their facial features were similar. Anne was casually dressed in trousers and a white oversized blouse. Audrey thought that she looked very well, but knew she was dressed cheaply.

"This is my business partner, Audrey Driver."

"So nice to meet you," Anne's voice was as husky as it had been on the phone.

A small girl accompanied them of about ten who was introduced as Shari's sister, Natasha, who shared her mother's and sister's looks.

"Have you eaten?" asked Audrey.

"Not since this morning," replied Anne.

"Let's have something in the restaurant then."

It was the start of a very interesting few hours for Peter and Audrey, as it quickly dawned on them that the Delaney family weren't ordinary. Anne was a hugely confident woman, who also seemed touched with bitterness as life had dealt her a mixed set of cards. Growing up she longed to be an actress and so at eighteen, armed with good looks and youthful self-belief, she set off for New York to be discovered. While she was studying acting by night she met a man ten years her senior who was studying engineering.

"He was the most beautiful man I had ever seen," Anne explained to Peter as she downed her fourth glass of chardonnay. "We met at friend's house party and started dating."

When Anne became pregnant, he didn't want to know. Her dreams in shreds, her faith in humanity destroyed, she returned home to her parents in Ireland where she gave birth to Shari. Audrey could only imagine the scandal this would have caused in the midlands in the eighties. Anne emerged a fighter and pursued Shari's father through every organisation available for child support and eventually managed a compromise where he would contribute to Shari's upbringing.

Meanwhile, Anne married Richard, and had four further children, one of them Natasha who Peter observed was causing some kind of mayhem in the hotel lobby to her mother's uninterest. Anne was far more interested telling her life story to her new and captivated audience. From what Peter gathered, the Delaney family seemed to live a life bordering on the hippy, while Anne projected all her unfulfilled ambitions onto her children, particularly Shari.

"From the moment Shari was born I knew she was destined to be a star," said Anne, proudly smiling at her eldest daughter who was tucking into a chicken salad. "I've tried to encourage my children to always believe in themselves and push themselves forward to achieve their dreams. I don't want to come across as a Mrs Worthington, but I fully encouraged Shari with singing and acting lessons and she is a magnificent writer, so very witty." Anne reached over and took Shari's hand and squeezed it.

"When she was fifteen I sent Shari to an audition for a movie. They offered her only a small part and I advised her against it. Shari is a star. If they don't want us, then we don't want them. That's always been our motto."

Shari began to demolish a huge slice of chocolate cake.

Peter would have liked to hear Shari speak to find out what she was like, but there was no chance with Anne.

" Myself and her daddy –"

"In Italy?"

"No, my husband, have put a lot of time and money into Shari. We sent her to the best schools, though we couldn't afford it, and now she's studying art at University. She needed to be equipped with this for her future." Peter realised Anne was a classic stage mother. Her unplanned pregnancy had finished her own dreams and now she was determined to live them through her daughter.

"What I would like to do is sign Shari to an exclusive contract with Spinner. With our management I believe she could have a very big future. We work with agencies in London and New York and I definitely would be trying to promote her internationally."

Anne Delaney's eyes lit up as she saw her dreams come true at once.

Audrey went over to the cash desk to pay the bill.

"Are you a nice man, Mr Reynolds?" Anne asked earnestly.

"It depends who you're listening to. But I can push Shari all the way."

"Our children are very precious to us. I'm just a little bit concerned about these scandals I've heard about Spinner."

Damn, thought Peter. "We can try to give our models as much guidance as possible, Anne, but at the end of the day, what they do is their own business. And what a couple of our models did has reflected badly on our business. But I do think if a girl like Shari comes from such a strong family unit as she obviously does, then she will be more inclined and equipped to resist the temptations fame may throw in her way," said Peter.

"When I met you first, I found you a little intimidating. The way you swaggered in all businesslike." Anne sipped her wine.

"I can't imagine you ever being intimidated," said Peter.

Anne raised her glass and smiled. "I think we'll do just fine together."

"Well, what do you think?" asked Peter as he and Audrey walked down the Quays after saying goodbye to the Delaneys.

"It's as you said, Shari has the makings of a supermodel about her."

"We need to sign her up immediately."

"And we have to get a watertight contract drawn up. There's no point in us discovering somebody like her and establishing her, only for her to run off when the hard work is done." She spoke with a determination which Peter admired. "Because it's obvious that Anne Delaney is not to be messed around and will be watching her daughter's career very closely."

Chloe's phone rang in the middle of the night.

She reached over and answered it. "Chloe Gallagher speaking."

"It's taken care of," a voice said down the line.

She hung up.

CHAPTER 100

"Police report a break-in at the office of Macken Communications last night," the anchor-woman said on breakfast-time news the next morning. *"It is not clear if anything was taken from the firm that represents some of the biggest names in Irish business. The thieves were disturbed and escaped."*

Shari was on her first photo shoot. Peter hired a stylist who was busy preparing her for the shots which would be for her portfolio.

Peter observed her as she giggled and joked with everyone and thought her to be quite immature for her eighteen years. He put it down to her having an overpowering mother.

"What the fuck is this?" Anne Delaney came storming into the photo studios waving a document in the air.

"It looks like the contract for Shari to sign for Spinner." Peter tried not to sound too sarcastic.

"But it's too strict. You'll practically own Shari for the next three years."

"If I'm putting all this time, money and work into her I

need reassurance that we won't be dumped as soon as Shari hits the big time. It's happened to us before and this time we want to protect ourselves."

"You can forget about it," said Anne.

"In that case our deal is off. I'm stopping this photo shoot immediately."

"Oh, Mummy, please, don't screw this up for me," pleaded Shari who looked on the verge of tears.

Anne took a long time thinking. "This is against my better judgement," she snapped as she scribbled her signature on the contract and passed it to Shari to do the same.

Shari was a natural in front of the camera as she posed and pouted. She seemed like a little kid, often bursting out laughing when the photographer said something to make her relax. At other times, she quickly lost her concentration and when he gave out to her, the hurt in her face gave an equally mesmerising look. Afterwards they shot a video of her talking, laughing, walking and posing.

"Let me see, let me see," squealed Shari. They played her back the video which caused her to roar with laughter.

At the end of the day both Anne and Peter felt very satisfied with the work completed and Anne winked over at Peter in appreciation.

After studying the photos and video footage of Shari, Audrey and Peter were in complete agreement what their next step would be.

Peter carefully put Shari's photos and a copy of the video into a padded envelope.

He then wrote a simple note:

Boris,
If you are interested, call me,
Peter Reynolds.

He slipped the note into the envelope, sealed it and addressed it to Boris Stein at the Regency office in Manhattan.

"So, Boris, you want the next big thing?" Peter said to Audrey as he wrote *Photos – Do Not Bend* across the package. "Well, you can have the next big thing."

"But on our terms," said Audrey. "What was it Chloe used to say? My way or no way."

Chloe switched on the television as the RTE nine o'clock news came on.

The newsreader was a man in his fifties.

"Good evening. A series of documents relating to payments made by the law firm Murphy Hennessy to Ronan Flatley were uncovered at a Dublin waste site today. The Corporation worker who discovered them passed them on to the RTE news room. Police believe the documents were taken during a break-in at the Macken Communications office earlier this week and were later dumped at the waste site. Macken Communications have been acting for the Murphy family in recent months as they tried to get commercial planning for a site. The land in the north side of Dublin received planning for an extensive shopping centre only last week. We now go over to our correspondent, Finola O'Brien, who is at the Dail."

The young reporter looked severely into the camera against the backdrop of the Parliament buildings.

"Rumours have been bounding about the Dail all day, as news spread about the payments to Ronan Flatley. Flatley who has been one of the most respected politicians in the country, was unable to be contacted all day, with phones in his constituency office and home going unanswered. Opposition parties have called for an immediate tribunal to investigate the alleged bribing scandal. I have here with me the Shadow Minister for Employment, Douglas Robinson. Mr. Robinson, what's your opinion concerning the setting up of a tribunal?"

"It's the only answer to find out what's been going on. A series of events has unfolded that has brought this scandal out into the open. And we see here exposed questions at the heart of Irish politics and business. If reports are to be believed these papers that were dumped after a robbery expose one of the most respected legal families in the country involved in a bribing scandal.

And this sordid business was overseen by a supposedly respectable PR firm. The Taoiseach has no option but to immediately set up a tribunal to investigate this fully."

The news programme then showed the front of the Macken Building as the voice-over said, *"Staff coming and going from Macken Communications today refused to comment on the scandal engulfing their company. There was no official statement from the PR firm."*

This was followed by a shot of Murphy Hennessy and Reginald coming out of the front entrance and being besieged by reporters.

"Mr Murphy, is it true you made payments to Ronan Flatley?" called a journalist loudly over the other din of questions.

"Excuse me please." Reginald slowly made his way through the crowd to his awaiting car.

"Mr Murphy, did you employ Macken Communications to act as a go-between to bribe Ronan Flatley?"

"I'm sorry, I'm trying to get to my car." He gently pushed through the crowd.

Muriel sat alone in their parlour transfixed by the image of her husband on the television being surrounded and hounded by the nation's media.

Boris Stein jogged through the New York streets to work. After having a shower in the en-suite off his office, he changed into a suit.

His secretary had left mail on his desk and he started to open it.

He opened the big brown envelope marked private and for his attention only and emptied the contents on his desk. The photos of Shari lay spread across his desk. Slowly he picked them up and studied them. He put the enclosed video in his machine as he read Peter's note.

As he continued to watch the video of Shari he looked up Peter's number and dialled it.

"Who is she?" Boris asked as soon as he got through.

Peter smiled on hearing Boris's unmistakeable accent. "You got my package, then?"

"I got it. Who is she?"

"I'm not saying."

"Why did you send me the fucking photos then?" demanded Boris.

"Just thought you might like to have a look." Peter spun around in his swivel-chair, enjoying the moment.

"Now I've had a look and I would like to know who the fuck she is!"

"Even if you found her, I have her so signed up with the tightest contract, even your lawyers couldn't find a hole in it."

"Enough with the games, Peter, what do you want?"

"She's going to be big, Boris. You know that by just looking at her and I have Ford and all the others hounding me wanting to work with her. But I thought I'd hold off because we know each other and I thought you should get first shot because of our friendship."

"I'm truly touched." Boris's voice dripped sarcasm. "So start talking."

CHAPTER 101

"I just feel so sorry for you with all the bad publicity you are getting," Lynn said to Larry Hennessy, speaking to him on the phone from her desk at the Gallery.

"It's been terrible," said Larry. "The press are phoning all the time."

"They have no right to intrude on your lives. At the end of the day, it was a private business transaction that was nobody else's business."

"The police want to investigate and there's all this talk about a tribunal being set up."

"The police won't be interviewing you, will they?" Lynn was alarmed.

"I sold my share of the land to Reginald and Muriel, so I'm not directly Involved."

"Thank God for that," said Lynn.

"But the firm is going to be left with a very bad image problem."

"Is there anything I can do, Larry? Just say it if there is."

"Thank you, Lynn. You're a true friend. . .What are you doing this evening?"

"I've nothing planned. Why?"

"Would you like to come over to my place for something to eat?"

"I'd love to, Larry."

"Peter won't mind?"

"Er, no . . . he's down the country on business, actually."

"See you around seven then."

Larry put down the phone and looked at his watch. He had to be over at the Murphy house in an hour for a crisis meeting with Brendan Macken. The whole situation was such a terrible mess. He had warned the Murphys not to proceed in handing money over to Flatley. Experience told him these things tended to backfire. But when they were determined for a quick-fix solution involving bribery, he had opted out and sold them his share. He shook his head. Despite all the Murphys' money, they couldn't resist a get-rich-quick scheme.

He sighed as he acknowledged that at least Chloe Gallagher was out of their lives.

He had totally misjudged her. Believing she was so hungry for power and success, he had thought she would be easy prey to manipulate to become his slave. But she had turned out to be a totally different type from what he thought she was. After he had exposed himself to her and she knew what he was really like, it was far too dangerous to allow her to marry Aran. She would be a bomb ready to explode in the bosom of the Murphy family. It had taken some fancy footwork to eliminate her. But he had achieved it by exploiting all of Muriel's fears for her son, her family and their wealth.

Thinking back to Chloe's harsh words the night of the engagement party, they had hurt him greatly. He was shocked and scared to find his personal secrets were in fact an open secret. Since her outburst he had become paranoid with nearly everybody he met. Did they know about the things he had done? How much did they know? Were they talking about him behind his back? He thought he had been so careful over the years. Occasionally, of course, some gold-digger would need to be paid off to be kept quiet. It had never been too much of a problem. But now he was frightened. With Murphy Hennessy on the news every night, it might encourage some woman from the past to come out of the woodwork and expose him.

He needed to restore his respectability and he needed to do it fast.

"How could this happen?" Muriel asked furiously as she sat in her parlour with Reginald, Larry, Aran and Brendan Macken.

"It was just a terrible chain of events which was set off after the break-in," explained Brendan.

"But why were our files stolen?"

"It wasn't just yours. Documents were taken from lots of other clients as well. I really don't know what the thieves were looking for. Money and computers were taken too. My guess is they just grabbed lots of stuff and dumped files they thought were worthless," said Brendan.

"Why did you keep copies of such serious transactions?" demanded Reginald.

"It's our policy to keep copies." Brendan felt very stressed and it was a feeling he was neither used to or comfortable with. He wished Chloe was still with them.

He wished she was there with him right now. Chloe had an amazing ability to take control of a situation and restore calm, he remembered.

"Has anyone managed to get through to Flatley?" asked Larry.

"Seemingly he is at his holiday home in the Cayman Islands," answered Brendan.

"I suppose there's no point in having offshore accounts if you can't enjoy the sun there as well," commented Reginald wryly.

"I can't begin to explain what this scandal has done to our family's reputation and the image of Murphy Hennessy," said Muriel. "The police are coming here tomorrow to interview us. The police! And I shudder to think of a tribunal."

"Our firm has suffered very badly too," defended Brendan.

"We don't care!" Muriel almost shouted, causing everyone to jump. "It's all your fault. With you keeping copies of intimate documents and having poor security. Our family name has never had a hint of scandal attached to it. We've hardly had our name appear in the papers . . . and now there's all this!"

Audrey sat in her apartment transfixed by the television as the Murphy scandal unfolded on the screen. And she was surprised that she just felt numb towards them all.

Boris Stein had been due to visit the Regency offices in London and he wasted no time making a detour over to Dublin. He knew a potential supermodel when saw one and this girl Peter Reynolds had signed up seemed to have all the right attributes. He knew if he didn't act quickly Peter would be on to Ford.

As Boris expected, Peter and Audrey wanted a full merger between Regency and Spinner as they had initially planned. But this time Peter had the ace up his sleeve and Boris agreed to his terms if Shari turned out to be as good in reality. Now, before Boris was due to sign the documents for the merger he was in the Spinner offices with Peter and Audrey, waiting to meet Shari and her mother.

"Anne Delaney is like a fine whiskey," Peter explained. "She should only be taken in small measures."

"We can cope with her, if that's the only problem," said Boris.

A knock on Peter's office door and Mark showed the two women in.

As soon as Boris saw Shari he knew that here was another Cindy Crawford or Naomi Campbell. Somebody who was going to the top and capable of changing people's perceptions.

After the introductions, Boris said, "I've seen your initial photo shoot and you looked great, really great," Boris spoke in the reassuring tone he always did when speaking to novices in the modelling world. "You certainly have the potential. We have the ability to polish that potential and direct you to the top. Do you enjoy modelling, Shari?"

"I love it," Shari smiled, revealing her perfect gleaming teeth.

"She should do, as she's been throwing herself in front of cameras since she could walk," said Anne.

As Anne continued to speak, Boris realised that Peter was right, Anne could be a problem. Studying Shari, as her mother continued to blather on, he noticed that unlike most teenagers Shari didn't seem to mind at all that her mother was grabbing the attention for herself. There seemed to be a genuine love between them, as they reached over and held hands frequently. Boris guessed this blatant display of affection hid a much more tempestuous relationship. Shari had a lot of growing up to do, Boris reckoned. Anne was obviously a very strong character, but he suspected that there was also strength in Shari that would emerge once she established herself.

"Peter tells me you're in college. How would this interfere with the modelling contract? Say, for example, we needed you over in New York for a long period of time?"

"I'm going to defer this year at college and see how modelling goes for me."

"Cool," said Boris. "Because I would like you to come to New York and do some work with our photographers. Don't worry, Mrs Delaney, we'll take good care of her," Boris nodded reassuringly.

"Oh, no." Anne shook her head and smiled. "She's not going anywhere without me. If Shari goes to New York, I go with her. I'm going to keep a close eye on her and her career."

Boris cursed to himself. The last thing he needed was this overpowering woman getting in the way, but for now he had no choice.

"Don't you have more children at home?" questioned Boris.

"Their daddy can look after them. I go where Shari goes . . . I think we understand each other."

"Well, we did it," said Peter. Boris and the Delaneys had left, everyone feeling satisfied with the situation. Audrey and Peter sat in the big front office, the signed contract for the merger on the table in front of them.

"It took some fancy footwork, though," said Audrey, getting up and reaching for her coat.

"Where are you going?" asked Peter.

"Home."

He got up and walked over to a cabinet, opened it and pulled out a bottle of champagne and two glasses.

"Thought we might have a celebratory drink."

"I don't think so, Peter."

"Oh, you're working at The San Juan tonight?"

"No . . . I've given that up."

Peter was surprised. "Why?"

"I just want to concentrate on my career here."

"Well, if you're aren't rushing for anything in particular, have a drink. We deserve it after all the work we've put in to get this merger."

She looked reluctant.

"Oh, come on, we used to have a quick drink after work in the office regularly." Audrey nodded and sat down again. Peter came to the table and popped the champagne open and filled the two glasses.

"Cheers!" he said, holding up his glass. She chinked his glass and took a sip while he sat down.

"Did you see Stein's face when he saw Shari – it was like he'd won the jackpot."

"He was quite impressed, all right." She looked into the bubbles sparkling up through her drink. He wasn't sure what to say. She seemed to be so uncommunicative. Not the Audrey he knew of old.

"I saw on the news the break-in at Macken and the scandal with the Murphys,"he said.

She shrugged.

"They sure do sound like a lovely bunch of people. Audrey . . . you used to be able to talk to me about things," he urged.

"What's there to talk about, Peter? I think we all know

what happened and how stupid I've been. I just want to get on with my life and be a success now. I don't want to rely on anybody for anything any more."

He looked at her and wanted to hold her and make her feel better.

"So this is the new Audrey Driver, is it? A tough no-nonsense businesswoman."

"That's about right," she nodded.

"You're not going to leave yourself open for hurt again."

"You've got it in one . . . . I've been a toy on the social scene for long enough. I was taking myself seriously, but nobody else was."

"That's not true."

"I was just a little bit of decoration. Well, no more. I've been so busy trying to have this model life, with the big house, and the perfect husband, and be a businesswoman and a socialite and most importantly to have love. I thought I could have it all. Well, you can't. You can't have everything. And I have to just realise that and get on with it. And then I'll never feel this disappointment again."

"You can't just close down like that."

"I will not allow myself to be a fool again. Life is all about choices and years ago I decided to put my career first when I walked out on a brilliant relationship. I can't suddenly expect to have a happy personal life now as well."

"Look, even if you had stayed with that guy, just because it was good when you were young doesn't mean it would have stayed that way. Just look at me and Lynn."

"You're fine together. You're an example –"

"We've finished."

Audrey looked at him intensely. "She left you again?"

"No, this time I asked her to leave."

"I see," Audrey felt shocked. "But you love her."

"Loved . . . I loved her. I realise I don't any more."

"And how does she feel about it?"

"I don't know and I don't care. I've spent too long wondering how Lynn feels and not enough time concerned about how I feel."

"I'm surprised . . . I never thought you'd leave her."

"Neither did I."

Audrey suddenly giggled.

"What's funny?" he asked, delighted to see her smile.

"I was just thinking about the future. The two of us can just run this place and get old and bitter together."

He reached over and took her hand. "I don't want to be bitter. I want to be happy."

Lynn waited until ten at night before going over to their apartment and letting herself in, hoping Peter would be home by then.

She called softly as she entered, "Peter!"

She unhappily realised he wasn't there.

Walking around their home she remembered all the happy times they had there. She wished he would walk in and she could ask for him to give their marriage another try. But as time went on she came to the conclusion he was out for the night. Going into their bedroom she took out a suitcase and began to pack her clothes. Opening his wardrobe she delicately ran her fingers over his clothes. She took out one of his suits and sat down on the side of the bed holding it close to her and breathing in his scent. Then she buried her face into the material.

Audrey pulled her lips away from Peter's. They could hear the traffic flying by in the city street below. The bottle of champagne was empty beside them.

"It's nearly midnight. I'm definitely going home," she stated.

"You've had two glasses which puts you over the limit." Her blouse was coming un-done, and his hand was caressing the small of her back.

"I'll grab a taxi then." She felt a little shiver, as he kissed her neck lightly.

"How do you feel?" he asked.

"Confused . . . I was beginning to feel quite content being bitter and twisted." She closed her eyes, and pretended to push him away.

"Yeah, and it kind of suited you as well!"

"Thanks for that! And I'm not comfortable being a rebound job." It was her turn to pull up his shirt and stroke his back.

"Nor am I!" he stated.

"And then there's the whole business side of things, and keeping emotions out of the workplace." He put his hands around the back of her neck and drew her close.

"That can be detrimental to a business, yes . . . oh, and also, I'm not a millionaire, and probably never will be at this rate."

"Yes, I'm slumming it really," she nodded, before resting her forehead against his. "And I'm used to dealing with such – classy – circles."

"And you know nothing about art or politics, horse-riding . . . anything that interests me really."

"In fact, we are totally unsuited to each other," she confirmed.

"As we've said before, we don't even like each other."

"True," she agreed.

"I've got another bottle of champagne in my office – will I get it?"

"Well, you know I never drink more than a glass, if ever, as a rule."

Peter nodded and looked serious. "I'll fetch it now then, will I?"

"I think you had better."

Chloe finished putting on her make-up. She was on her way to meet the head of a PR firm who was a friend of hers. She had delicately put the word out she was looking for a new position and interest had been strong. People were thinking she could do for their companies what she had achieved for Macken. Chloe had greatly enjoyed watching Macken Communications and the Murphy family fall. No reference to herself was in any of those stolen files relating to the Flatley bribe so there would never be any comeback for her. She and her reputation were safe and she had known it would be when she ordered the security firm to break into the Macken building. Now, most people assumed she had left Macken because she didn't want to be associated with the ensuing scandal.

The doorbell rang which surprised her as she wasn't expecting anybody.

"Yes?" she said into the intercom.

"Chloe, it's Boris Stein here. I was hoping to have a word with you."

What the hell was Stein doing back in Dublin? And what was he doing at her house? She was thrown into confusion as she opened the door.

"I hope you don't mind me dropping by," he said. "I went into Boom to meet you, but Ben told me you had left the company and gave me your address."

"Yes, Ben is very good at giving out information," she

said sarcastically as she closed the door behind him. "I can't talk for long. I have an appointment."

"Oh, I won't keep you long," Boris assured.

"So what has you in Dublin?"

"I've just come back to sign a merger deal with Spinner."

Has he come to rub my nose in it, she fumed. "Thanks, Boris, for coming out here to tell me that. But I'm really not interested."

"No, I didn't think you would be after leaving Macken and all. Where are you going to work now?"

"That's my business," Chloe said.

"And I hear your engagement with Aran is off. What a shame – he was a really nice guy." He beamed a big grin that made her want to go and slap him across the face. "Although if you don't mind me commenting –"

"I do –"

"I don't think that marriage was being built on very steady ground."

Chloe looked at her watch. "It's really been fun catching up with you again, but I have to dash."

"The reason I mention your broken engagement is because since you have no ties any more I'd like to make you a job offer . . . as PR Director at Regency."

She was stunned but intrigued.

"PR Director? What does that entail?" she asked.

"I'll have a job description emailed to you. It means what it says. You will be in charge of the PR for our company. Everything from corporate image to creating and protecting the image of models. I think you'll find our remuneration package more than satisfactory."

"I have received extremely good job offers from PR companies here in Dublin."

"I'm offering you a job that will bring you to New York.

Also spending time in London and the Continent and even back here in Ireland as well. You'll be working for an international company in a very high-profile and powerful role. You'll answer directly to me. This job will give you a platform to exercise your talents and abilities to the full."

"I'm not so sure I want to spend that much time away from Dublin."

"Yes, you do. Broken engagement behind you, it'll do you good to get away."

"You told me before you'd prefer to do business with a barracuda than me."

"That was with you as a partner in a subsidiary. With this job you'll be at my side. And I've seen the way you work and I want you to be at my side."

"I'll obviously have to give it some thought," Chloe said.

He walked over to her. "You take all the time you need." He placed his hands on her shoulders and she shivered from his touch. "I'd enjoy working with you, Chloe. I'd like to find out more about you. I'd like to find out what lies beyond those walls."

CHAPTER 102

3 Months Later

Audrey drove frantically back to Spinner having just dropped Shari and her mother off at Dublin Airport to catch their flight for New York. They had all worked tirelessly preparing Shari for her first photo shoots in the States. This was no easy feat, as Anne was proving more demanding and difficult by the day. But it was worth it, as Shari continued to blossom in front of them. Audrey cursed the heavy traffic she was caught up in, as she was late for a meeting. Business had been booming at Spinner since the merger, as anticipated. And as she and Peter became more and more frantically busy they were recruiting new staff.

Muriel Murphy braced herself as their car pulled up outside the tribunal building. She turned to Reginald and they gave each other a supportive smile and squeezed each other's hand. A crowd of press were awaiting their arrival.

It was lucky their marriage was so strong, thought Muriel, so they could withstand everything that had unfolded since the break-in at the Macken Building.

As both of them were the co-owners of the land, both of them were being called before the tribunal. Auditors had been given full access by the courts to investigate their finances, and intimate details of their lives and financial affairs were regularly reported in the press at length. For a family who had fought to protect their privacy, they were now instantly recognisable to the general public. And as reports of their lifestyle and financial deals became exaggerated, they had become the target of much resentment. Their driver pushed through the photographers and opened the back door of the car. Muriel, dressed in an immaculate navy suit, stepped out first and was then followed by Reginald. Their driver and two gardai helped them through the press. They both ignored the barrage of questions shot at them. Muriel looked haughtily and disdainfully at them all. They walked up the steps, and the doors were opened to allow them to enter. As they walked into the building, the cameras' flashbulbs continued to flash after them. They were due to start giving their evidence in thirty minutes.

Lynn drove her new car into the driveway of Larry Hennessy's house. She stepped out and took several shopping bags from the back seat, all of which bore the names of exclusive stores. She walked up the steps to the front door and let herself in. Throwing the bags on the couch, she fixed herself a brandy.

The phone rang and she answered it.

"Good afternoon," said the voice on the other end, "it's Cartiers here. I'm just calling to say the adjustment you wanted for your engagement ring is now complete."

"That's fine," said Lynn. "We'll be in London at the weekend and so we'll be in to collect it then." She hung up.

Resting back on the couch, she relaxed. She had cut down her hours at The Gallery and she only continued it as a hobby, but she had still had a hectic morning. She had felt so lost and distraught after Peter told her he no longer loved her. She and Larry had been supportive to each other at a bad time in both their lives. They had become closer and closer and she was surprised when their friendship turned to love. She had been delighted but cautious, as she was aware of how he went through girlfriends so quickly. She hadn't told him her marriage was over and suddenly he was putting pressure on her to leave Peter and move in with him. From what she understood, he had never reached this level of commitment with anyone previously. She was honoured when he started talking marriage. She met all his friends and got on great with all of them, including the Murphys. She and Muriel had quickly established a rapport, originating with a mutual love for art and antiques. They were now rushing through a divorce with Peter so they could be married as soon as possible. Peter had no objection.

She reached over again to answer the ringing phone.

"Hi, it's me," said Larry.

"Hello."

"The dinner party tonight at the embassy, what are you wearing for it?"

"I was thinking the lilac dress we bought last Saturday in Brown Thomas."

"No, that's too formal. Wear the white one you got instead."

"All right," she answered

"I won't be long at the office."

"I'm just going up to have my shower soon and get ready," said Lynn.

"We need to be at the embassy at seven, so go and get ready now. We need to leave the house at 6.30. See you then."

Larry hung up the phone. He couldn't believe himself he was engaged. But he knew when he wanted something he had to have it. And he wanted Lynn Reynolds. She was different from the others. Initially, with her being married, she had seemed unattainable compared to all his previous girlfriends, who all had marriage on their minds. They were presently working hard to get rid of her ex-husband. To quicken the process he had told Lynn not to claim any share of Peter's business. They didn't need it; he could look after all Lynn's needs. She was cultured in everything from art to literature to wine. Even Muriel and Reginald had been impressed by her. And unlike a lot of his exes, Lynn had a strong personality, which he liked. Larry had been thinking a lot about his life recently. First, there had been that time when he had been sick and there had been nobody around to care for him. Then there had been his run-in with Chloe. She had painted a nightmare vision of his future with no wife or family to care about him as he got older. And when she had revealed to him what his true reputation was like, he had conducted some investigation and found she was telling the truth. He hadn't been as discreet over the years as he thought he had, and it had caught up with him. His refined new trophy wife, Lynn, would restore and protect his reputation.

Lynn finished her brandy and went upstairs to their Clive-Christian-designed bedroom. She had the lifestyle she had always wanted with the type of man she had always needed. Larry took care of everything. She didn't have to worry about a thing. He was so successful and established, she didn't need to encourage him in the least. She took out the dress Larry had instructed her to wear and laid it across the bed. She wasn't particularly fond of it, but Larry had insisted she buy it. Taking out her jewellery box she went through all the beautiful necklaces and earrings Larry had bought for her. She chose one which would suit the outfit the best. She undressed and stepped into the shower and let the hot water cascade over her body. Afterwards she walked into the bedroom, drying herself with a huge white towel. She stopped and stared at herself in the full-length mirror. Numbly she ran a finger across the large bruise which ran across the top of her arm and chest. Then she got dressed, realising Larry had been right about the choice of outfit. The lilac dress wouldn't have covered the bruise.

Aran nursed his drink in The San Juan Club. It wasn't a busy night there. He had come with a group of friends earlier, but they had all drifted off, leaving him alone at the bar. He was under such huge pressure at work and at home with the tribunal going on, so perhaps he had one too many drinks that night to try and forget what was going on. He tried to figure out when everything had started going wrong for him. One minute he had two amazing women in his life and now he was alone. He had never heard from Chloe again. He knew she had moved on to new pastures after leaving Macken and had landed some high-powered new job. But it was Audrey he thought about the most. He came to The San Juan a lot, even though she no longer worked there. But it reminded him of her. Sometimes he rang her number, only to hang up after she had answered. Occasionally he drove out to her apartment block and looked up at her windows. He knew it was in the past but that didn't stop him having regrets.

Vanessa sat with a group of models from Boom in the members' lounge at The San Juan. She wasn't enjoying the evening. She wasn't enjoying the week. Her career had gone downhill big time. Since Chloe had left Boom, the new boss, Ben, hadn't bothered with her at all, and she wasn't getting any work. Then that week her small part had been axed on the soap. When she saw Spinner had joined up with Regency, she had rung Peter about going back. But he had got really angry and hung up on her. Eventually, she had taken the receptionist's job at Boom to supplement her income. She was trying to think of ways to relaunch her career when she saw Aran. She recognised him immediately from the time he had been dating Audrey. And, of course, like everyone else she had been following the controversy surrounding his family. He was on his own and looked fed up. She excused herself from her friends and walked over to him.

They were playing old music in the members' lounge and Dean Martin was singing "Little Old Wine-drinker, Me."

She flicked out her blonde hair and sat in the chair beside him.

"Can I buy you a drink?" she asked.

"I already have one." He cast an admiring eye over the glamorous blonde. "But maybe I can buy you one?"

"A Jack Daniels and Coke would be nice," she said, crossing her legs and leaning a little closer to him.

The next day Audrey looked up at the new sign over the front door: *Spinner – A Division of Regency International*. She raced up the stairs and saw the switchboard was ringing furiously and the receptionist was having trouble manning it.

A selection of girls sat in the reception waiting for interviews. Mark, who had been promoted to full-time booker, would be interviewing most of them. She went into her office and checked her messages. There was one from Shari to say they had landed safely and were in their hotel in Manhattan and would be heading over to the Regency office that afternoon.

Tiffany was due to come back to the agency that day. Audrey had visited her a lot in the clinic she had been in. It had been a tough journey for her, but she was now finally free of the drugs and ready to start modelling again.

Chloe sat at her desk in her new office at Regency in New York. She was speed-reading through information about some of the models on their books when her phone rang.

"Chloe, Shari and Anne Delaney are here to see you," informed the receptionist.

"Send them right in." She was looking forward to seeing this girl everybody was making such a fuss about. Boris was away for the day and so he had suggested that Chloe meet the Delaneys and show them around.

As they entered, Chloe stood up and smiled and shook both their hands.

"So nice to meet you, Shari. I've heard a lot about you."

"Thanks. This is my mother, Anne."

"Chloe, Mr Stein said you would look after us," said Anne, looking upset.

"I will certainly try to."

"I'm just a little concerned about the hotel we are staying in. It's lovely and everything, but I'd prefer something closer to Central Park. I don't mean to make a fuss or anything, but could we change hotels?"

"Of course, I'll get that sorted for you immediately." Chloe was smiling, but knew immediately Anne would be one irritating woman and full of demands.

"So, you must be very excited about this modelling contract," said Chloe to Shari.

"She's delighted," answered Anne. "A dream come true for her. But I do think it's very important that we all understand each other from the beginning, so no trouble can lead to any fall-out."

Which means your way or no way I presume, thought Chloe. And that would be the way it would have to be for now until she got a handle on the situation and put Anne in her place.

"I'm sure we are all going to be the best of friends," she assured them. Her phone rang. "Excuse me one moment, please. Yes, Chloe Gallagher. "

"Chloe, it's Barbara in Personnel. We have a problem. I've just received all the documentation from Shari Delaney from Ireland and there's a problem with her visa. It's only a holiday visa and not a work one. She can't do any work for us here until it's validated and changed."

Chloe swore to herself. "I'll check it out." She hung up. "I'm sorry, I just need to make a call. Could you wait outside for me in reception and then I'll give you a tour of the place?"

Shari and Anne left, Anne looking rather sour.

Chloe joined her hands together and savoured the moment before picking up the phone and dialling.

Anne and Shari sat side by side in the reception area.

"We'll continue to let them think they are in control for now," Anne whispered to her daughter. "But once you become famous, we'll show them who's boss. Incidentally, I called by your room last night around one, and there was no answer."

"I was probably fast asleep, Mummy," answered Shari.

"Really? Well, I got the porter to open your door, and you weren't there."

Shari cringed as she realised she had been found out.

"Now, you listen to me, young lady." Anne pointed her finger at her daughter. "You can leave your wild ways behind you. I've been waiting for this moment all my life, and you aren't going to blow it for me."

"Sure, that booking is fine for the fifth starting at ten in the morning," Peter confirmed and hung up his phone.

He read some papers on his desk concerning the upcoming divorce. They all seemed in order and he signed at the bottom. There was no point in dragging things on. He wanted his marriage officially over as much as Lynn. They were both getting on with their lives and luckily there was no animosity between them. He had been surprised to hear about her involvement with Larry Hennessy. Larry was so much older than her and had some reputation with all his past girlfriends. But obviously Lynn didn't have a problem with the man or the baggage. As long as the baggage was Gucci, he thought wryly. The more he thought about it, the more it made sense. Here, at last, was a man who could provide Lynn with the life she wanted. A man with enough money and status to allow her to be the trophy wife she was always meant to be. He felt slightly troubled about her though. He had seen a photo of Larry and her in a society magazine and at first glance thought she looked truly fulfilled. But as he had examined her expression the old saying came to mind: be careful what you wish for, it may come true. He was thinking of how unhappy he had been with Lynn, compared to how he now felt with Audrey when his his phone rang.

"Yeah?"

"Peter, it's Chloe Gallagher here."

Peter squinted his face in confusion and sat back in his chair.

"You're a blast from the past," he said, wondering what she wanted. Literally, he thought.

"Peter, we have a huge problem here with Shari Delaney. Her visa isn't valid to work in the States. She only has a holiday visa."

Peter was confused. "Sorry, Chloe, but what the fuck has this got to do with you?"

"Quite a lot actually, Peter. Since she is sitting outside my office and I will have to cancel the work that is lined up for her over the next two weeks."

"Outside your office?" He sounded incredulous.

"Yes, here in New York. Didn't Boris tell you? I'm the new PR director for Regency."

He was speechless.

"Peter, I was very surprised that you allowed such sloppy paperwork on your side. You should have checked the right visa was being organised. If we can't sort something out with the immigration people, we have a big problem on our hands."

"You are the new PR director for Regency?" Peter was in shock.

"Yes, Peter . . . I know we've worked together in the past so we understand how the other one operates."

"That's for sure!"

"So I hope we can make this work by both of us

behaving professionally. I don't want any changes in the day-to-day running of Spinner. I want you to continue working the way you always have, without any interference from me."

"Where have I heard this before? I'm going to have to talk to you later." Peter hung up the phone and stared into space.

Peter stormed into Audrey 's office, slamming the door against the wall.

"What's wrong with you?" Audrey was startled.

"Chloe Gallagher has just been on the phone to me. Stein made her PR Director for Regency."

"I don't believe it."

"Believe it. There's some fuck-up with Shari's work permit and she started lecturing me on the phone from New York."

"Lecturing you? Peter, you should have told her where to get off. We might be merged with Regency, but we are still the main shareholder here. She has no authority over us."

"I know that. But I was too stunned to speak. She's going to make life difficult for us whenever she can. Why the hell didn't Stein warn us? He knows the history we've had with her."

"He probably thought it was none of our business," said Audrey.

"Why are you defending him?" Peter's voice rose.

"I'm not. I'm the last person who ever wants to see or talk to that woman again. You should have asked when the merger was being negotiated that we be made aware of any personnel changes in their head office in advance so we can have some sort of say."

"We are a small subsidiary of a huge company – they wouldn't care what we had to say. Anyway, why didn't you pay more attention to the contract? Oh, I forgot, you were feeling sorry for yourself at the time!" he shouted.

"I was not feeling sorry for myself," she shouted back. "Don't blame me just because Chloe Gallagher has got the better of you again."

"And who organised Shari's visa in the first place?" Peter demanded.

"I did, actually." Audrey was defiant.

"Well, why the hell didn't you get her the right visa?"

"I made a mistake, Peter. It happens."

"A mistake that will cause a lot of trouble and make us look stupid."

"I'm too busy to listen to you any more." Audrey dismissed him.

"And I'm too busy to sort out your mistakes." He hit back.

"I don't want to talk to you any more. Just go," she demanded.

"I will." He slammed the door after him.

Audrey stared at the closed door in fury. She was furious with Stein for employing Chloe and furious with Peter because of his attitude.

She sat seething. As time went by and she thought about their argument, her anger eroded and she started to giggle to herself.

Peter sat at his desk consumed with anger. This was all he needed. Chloe back in his life on a permanent basis. Suddenly through the wall, he could hear Audrey laughing. He listened for a while as her mirth continued. Curious, he went into her office.

"What's wrong with you?" he asked, as he looked at her sitting there laughing loudly.

"I was just thinking," she said between laughs. "After all we've been through . . . we're still stuck with Chloe Gallagher . . . and we still end up in screaming matches."

As she tried to draw breath between giggles, he looked at her as if she were mad. But he found her laughter enchanting. And then he was laughing too.

THE END